CALLY'S WAR

CALLY'S WAR

JOHN RINGO
&
JULIE COCHRANE

CALLY'S WAR

This is a work of fiction. All the characters and events portrayed in this book
are fictional, and any resemblance to real people or incidents is purely coincidental.

A Baen Books Original

Baen Publishing Enterprises
P.O. Box 1403
Riverdale, NY 10471
www.baen.com

ISBN: 0-7434-8845-8

Cover art by Clyde Caldwell

First printing, October 2004

Library of Congress Cataloging-in-Publication Data

Ringo, John, 1963-
  Cally's war / John Ringo & Julie Cochrane.
      p. cm.
  ISBN 0-7434-8845-8
1. Women murderers–Fiction. 2. Assassins–Fiction. I. Cochrane, Julie. II. Title.

  PS3568.I577C35 2004
  813'.6–dc22

                                                            2004014348

Distributed by Simon & Schuster
1230 Avenue of the Americas
New York, NY 10020

Production by Windhaven Press, Auburn, NH (www.windhaven.com)
Printed in the United States of America

10 9 8 7 6 5 4 3 2 1

DEDICATION

To my husband, James, for feedback and help above and beyond the call of duty, and to Katie for her
patience in sharing her Mom.

PROLOGUE

"So, how go your plans for the humans, Tir?"

The Darhel Ghin sat in a pose copied from the humans, legs bent and spread flat, one foot crossed onto the opposite knee. His face was impassive, ears still, and it was impossible to tell from his expression what might be meant by the curious choice of position. His hair had the metallic sheen of antique silver, with glints of black threaded through. The slit-pupilled eyes were a deep emerald green with a light tracery of violet blood vessels around the whites, impassive in the narrow, fox-like face. The face would have looked elfin except for the sheer, solid *realness* of it. The rows of pointed, razor-sharp teeth were concealed, for now, between his still, closed lips. In short, he was average for a Darhel, in virtually every way. That very attribute had led more than one unwary rival to grievously underestimate him. In his youth, at any rate.

"Well, Your Ghin." He stared directly into the wall-sized view screen. His superior's Indowy body attendants could be seen working unobtrusively in the background. A human might have compared them to small, green teddy-bears. The Tir barely thought of them at all, their omnipresent service being an unremarkable, comfortable fact of life. "Planetary reclamation of our Posleen-occupied interests with greatest profit potential is on schedule. Hazard loss of human colonists is within ten percent of optimum. Loss of human colony ships is optimum, plus or minus two percent. The loss concealment program is operating as designed. Monthly profit margins are running at seven percent, plus or minus

1

one point five percent, at the ninety-five percent confidence level," he recited. His ears were perked through the metallic gold hair, uncommon but acceptable in their race, his posture erect in a position of strong confidence. The old fool must surely be becoming aware by now that he was slipping.

"The humans, they are rather more . . . numerous, and less grateful, than your projections when you initiated the program during the Posleen war."

"All plans require adjustment as part of the process. We have discussed the purpose of the job of management before, Your Ghin." How did he always *do* that? The obsolete fossil had the annoying habit of posing just the question that prodded the most inconvenient aspect of any operational plan. But the Tir's control over his own body language had improved over the years, and he cocked one ear slightly in a gesture that coasted just between polite condescension and careful attentiveness.

"With respect, Your Ghin, profits are up and contingency plans to manage the humans are functioning well within acceptable parameters." He had an itch on the left side of his muzzle, just below the top of his whiskers. With effort, he resisted twitching them. Or squinting his eyes. Decreases in light tended to cause the slit-pupils to round noticeably, making even a slight squint more pronounced than it would have appeared in a round-pupilled being.

"Your parameters fail to take account of recent evidence of active hostile human resistance." The one thing he could admire about the older Darhel lord was his control over his expressions and gestures. The humans had an oddly apt expression for such control. A poker face. They used it to describe a game. One of the few personal interactions he chose to engage in with humans was an occasional evening playing this *poker* game that the human Worth and a couple of his underlings had taught him. The contact was annoying, but you could actually win *money* at this game, and he regularly *did*, which the Tir found fascinating enough to outweigh the disadvantages.

"Because plans are already in motion to bring that small detail back in line with optimum management conditions." How could the aging obstacle know *that*? Was it possible that his own communications were less secure than he had believed? It bore investigation.

"I also note that hazard loss of human colonists is highly selective in its action." There had been a slight emphasis on the word "selective." Impossible to tell if it was faint praise or criticism.

"Yes. It allows us to optimize our profits from the remaining colonists." He had to resist the urge to preen, or the closest Darhel equivalent, which was not a social display, but was instead more a personal expression of satisfaction with one's own accomplishment. His superior was doing his usual exemplary job of appearing unimpressed.

"It is good to know you continue in your usual exceptional standards of job performance, Tir." The flash of rows of razor-sharp pointed teeth, in a very brief display of that copied human expression, the grin, almost caused a slight shudder. But, really, the old fool was just trying to put a brave face on the hunt breathing down his neck. Age was beginning to rob his vigor, would soon take his wit, and ultimately his life.

This time, the Tir could not quite resist the urge to preen.

CHAPTER ONE

Chicago, Friday, May 10, 2047

His favorite sports bar in Chicago had taken an old prewar rectangular middle-of-the-room bar and replaced the central island of glassware, bartender, and drinks with a large holotank. Unusually for a bar, smoking was absolutely forbidden, as the wafting smoke tended to interfere with the image display. The surround sound was practically perfect, and the waiters and waitresses who delivered the drinks from a traditional bar retrofitted next to the kitchen took extra care to take patrons' orders discreetly so as not to interfere with the game. Instead of the more usual stale smoke, this bar smelled of a mixture of beer, fried food, and the lemon oil the staff used to keep the bar top polished to a high gloss. He seldom came here, because a man in his business needed to avoid patterns. Nevertheless, it was his favorite watering hole, to the point that he probably came here slightly more often than he ought.

Charles Worth liked hockey. It wasn't so much the violence when a fight broke out. Primal violence was old hat in his line of work. What he liked was the fast pace, the sheer competitive artistry of it. Hockey was a real guy's game with real music to back it up, not some tin-horned pep bands. No cheerleaders, but he considered himself something of a connoisseur of women, and he definitely preferred his women close enough to touch. He preferred the original, the genuine, the unusual, provided she was also beautiful. The blonde over to his left had caught his attention. He could spot a bottle blonde a mile off and made a point of never, well almost never, settling for the artificial. This one was clearly a natural blonde. Even a good hairdresser still had difficulty getting all the highlights of a natural hair color into a dye job—as he knew from his own frequent appearance changes. Her other assets looked natural to the extent that he could tell with her clothes in the way.

She was almost enough to take his attention off the game, even though Zurich was really pummeling Montreal. As a Toronto fan, there were few things he enjoyed more than watching Montreal take it in the teeth. She had the creamy fair skin that went with her hair color, and her eyes were a warm brown. Odd combination, that. Either her skin was bare of makeup or she was a better expert than any he'd seen. She noticed him watching her and smiled, her lips parting slightly.

She had excellent taste. That blouse was real silk and impeccably tailored, the top two buttons left open to reveal just a hint of cleavage. The deep forest green was perfect for her and he felt heat clench in his gut as she picked up her drink and walked around the bar to take the seat next to him, looking into the tank as she slid onto the barstool.

"You picked a good spot. Better view of the Zurich bench from here. Okay if I join you?"

"Be my guest." He gestured to her almost empty glass. "Guinness?" Definitely natural skin. The soft musk of her perfume was almost painful.

She smiled and nodded absently, eyes glued to the tank.

He caught a waiter's attention and gestured at her glass. A moment later a fresh Guinness arrived. He pressed the price of the drink and a healthy tip into the waiter's hand immediately, leaving the boy no excuse to linger over the woman Worth hoped he would be taking home.

"Thanks." She took a sip of the fresh glass of stout and licked the foam off her upper lip.

"So are you a big Zurich fan?" he asked.

"Nah. Toronto." She grinned. "Well, okay, and whoever's playing Montreal."

A slightly sick twinge bit into the pit of his stomach. *Same team as mine. Too convenient? Or is it just the warning from the Tir's office making me paranoid?*

The broadcast broke for a commercial. Some things even technology couldn't change. A pair of small, black-and-white still holos in one corner of the tank depicted a sixtyish man with a cane and a slightly older woman in a wheelchair. The main section of the tank showed the same pair, in full color and motion, healthy and fit and looking about twenty, in tailored BDU's and each sporting a brand-new grav-gun, walking through a waving field of wheat hand in hand.

"Tired of being old?" A cool but somehow friendly female voice asked, "Dead-end jobs taking the romance out of your relationship? The Epetar Group is looking for aggressively minded human colonists to join a multirace world reclamation expedition. Age and health no barrier, standard contract. . . ."

"Damn juvs." One of the other patrons threw a beer nut through the holo-projection.

"Hi, I'm Sarah Johnson." The blonde had turned to Worth and was offering her hand. Her grip was warm and firm.

"Jude Harris. Nice to meet another Toronto fan." He smiled, fighting the urge to linger over her hand.

"Oh? Well then you've got excellent taste in teams. What do you do?" she asked.

"I'm a corporate troubleshooter. Basically, I travel a lot," he said.

"That sounds like an interesting job. Trouble ever shoot back?" she teased.

"Not if I do it right." His grin tightened. "So, what do you do, Sarah?"

"I'm a legal secretary." She grimaced. "Not very exciting, but it pays the bills. You said you travel? It's got to be great to, you know, get to go places." She looked up at him and took another sip of her stout.

"Just one hotel after another. Whups, game's back." His eyes focused on one soft hand wrapped around her pint glass. "Nice nails for a secretary."

"What?" She looked down at her immaculately manicured hand as if trying to figure out what he meant. "Oh yeah, the typing thing. Nobody has to type much anymore. They mostly want you to talk clearly. And you've gotta organize stuff and be good with details. That kind of thing."

"But still, there has to be some?" He took her hand in one of his own, meeting her eyes and holding them as he gently kissed her fingers.

"Well, a little." She smiled. "There's kind of a knack to hitting the keys just right so that your nails go in the spaces between the keys." She suddenly pulled her hand clear and pointed into the tank. "Did you see that? Shinsecki just sticked Schmidt right in the face! God, look at his nose, ohmigosh, the refs are going to have trouble breaking that one up." She clapped her hands over her mouth and her eyes were wide at the spatters of blood on the ice between the two combatants.

"Yeah, looks like he broke his nose. That's gotta hurt," he said. They watched the fight, the other players circling like sharks while the referees waded in trying to pull the two apart, one getting a probably inadvertent elbow in the face for his troubles.

"My God, the things we do for a little excitement, right?" She shuddered and gulped her drink.

"I dunno," Worth shrugged, turning towards her. "I enjoy the game, but I really watch it more for the strategy and the competition. The fights, I guess that's part of the darker side of human nature that's in all of us, really."

"You think so?" She tilted her head up at him, taking another drink. "I think that's more of a guy thing, the aggression thing. I think—" She flushed a bit, taking another fast gulp. "I think there's something just a little bit submissive, deep down, in almost every woman. I mean, I don't want some guy to drag me around by the hair or to spend the rest of my life washing his socks and underwear, but I think most women prefer a guy who can, you know, kinda take charge. And I think that men are, well, like that." She shrugged. "Like I said, a guy thing."

"That's very . . . perceptive of you." He looked at her intently, holding her eyes. "I'll bet you're very good with people." He could see the pulse at her throat beating rapidly. She licked her lips and was oddly still, as if frozen by the tension between them. He leaned over and claimed a slow, tantalizing kiss, pulling back when he realized his hand was tangled in her hair at the nape of her neck, his jeans were awkwardly tight, and they were still in a very public place. For his preferred games, public wouldn't do at all. Besides, there was the warning from his control. She could be a very pretty piece of bait. Either way, if he had anything to say about it he was going to have one hell of a time making sure.

In the tank, the game had restarted after the referees finally got

Schmidt and Shinsecki separated and sent Shinsecki to the penalty box. Zurich was clearly in a mood to take out their indignation on the ice. Montreal was now down by six and beginning to show signs of being rattled by the humiliation.

He noticed her glass was getting low and ordered her another drink, and spent most of the rest of the game teasing her thigh with one hand under the bar. By the time Montreal was down by nine he was starting to get bored with the slaughter and interested in more personal pleasures.

"Got a question." He leaned over and breathed against her ear. "You said you liked a man to take charge? I'm going out the front door. Don't follow. There's a back exit between the restrooms. It says an alarm will go off, but it won't. If you really meant what you said, wait five minutes and then leave the bar, come out the back door and I'll be waiting. You want me to take charge?"

She nodded rapidly. "Yeah, I think I'd like that."

"Okay, then that's what you do. You do that, and I will." He walked out of the bar without looking back, hoping she was tipsy enough and horny enough to do as he'd asked. He wanted her, bad, but he hadn't lived this long by being seen leaving bars with his victims. The night air smelled crisp as he walked past a couple of other bars to the parking lot, the crispness underlain by the almost imperceptibly faint tinges of stale urine, vomit, and sex that always linger in the streets outside popular establishments dedicated to the nightlife. The adrenaline rush was hitting his system and he wondered, as he always did, whether he had set the hook and played the line in just right. Would she come to him, or would she get away?

The timing was perfect. Just as he got the car pulled up to the curb in back, hidden from view on one side by the bar, on another by the large dumpster out back, she came tottering out the small back door. Another plus for him, the light was burned out back here, and he only saw her by the scattered illumination from his own headlights as she stumbled slightly, on a bit of loose gravel maybe, and opened the passenger side door.

She lowered herself with exaggerated care into the passenger seat of his low-slung Detroit Raver, while he pretended to be searching for a music cube. His nerve endings were sizzling with a mixture of triumph and anticipation that sent a chill down his spine as the door to his car clicked shut behind her. The beat of

Blue Oyster Cult's "Godzilla" shuddered through the frame as he pulled out into Chicago's Friday night traffic.

Worth disentangled the blonde from around his neck long enough to get them from the elevator to his warehouse loft apartment. He pushed open the door and paused a minute to let her get the full effect. It had taken large chunks of even his generous salary to outfit the room in the vintage '70s "contemporary" style he preferred. Still, he was proud that he had managed to obtain every necessary item of furniture in black leather, glass, and chrome, set off nicely by flawlessly white shag carpeting that he'd had to order custom-made. Three walls were covered in faux-oak paneling—even for him, real oak was scarce. The fourth was covered in floor-to-ceiling black velvet drapes. The free-standing wet bar that ran parallel to one of the oak walls was topped with poured black marble and had faux-oak cabinetry that exactly matched the walls.

Matching red lava lamps—original, not reproduction—illuminated the room and provided a necessary hint of color. Track lighting emphasized the Dali and Escher originals on the walls. The scent of pine air fresheners mingled with but did not quite mask a faint odor of stale sweat, sex, rust, and leather.

She stopped still for a moment and looked around the room, blinking rapidly. She favored him with another of those blindingly perfect smiles of hers and quickly buried her face in his neck, shuddering softly against him. *God, she must be really hot to trot. . . .*

"You want a drink? I'm having a martini." He smirked. "Shaken, not stirred, of course." He walked over to the wet bar and began pulling down various bottles off the glass shelves at the back.

"Why not?" She laughed, dropping her purse on the couch.

He poured her drink and handed it to her. "Cheers."

She took a sip and set the glass down on the chrome and glass end table, slinking up to him and sliding her hands up his chest. He wrapped his arms around her again and trailed his lips up her jaw to nibble lightly on her ear. He felt her knees buckle slightly and shifted his weight to support her as her hips seemingly involuntarily thrust against his. He felt the heat tighten in his groin as he buried his face in her hair and inhaled the clean, fresh scent of it mingled with her own soft musk.

His fingers trembled slightly as he unbuttoned the silk blouse, carefully, tenderly, savoring the opening strains of this overture that would end in so much sound and fury. Gently, now, building the trust that led them willingly into the trap—the purest and most exquisite test of his art. His hands slid inside and teased along the line of her spine and the soft, perfect skin of her back. He rubbed her jaw with his own, glad that he'd had an afternoon shave, and took her mouth, delving deep into the moist and the heat. God, he could drown in this woman.

Her slender fingers with those exquisitely feminine nails were playing with the hair at the nape of his neck and he felt himself breathing faster, impatient with the need to restrain himself and tease her into the next move. He drew one finger very lightly right up her spine before cupping his hands under her butt and pulling her, hard, against him as she shivered.

"So where's your room?" She nuzzled up to his neck and bit his shoulder softly.

He slid one hand up from her ass and tangled it in her hair, pulling her head back gently, nibbling the tip of her nose and shaking his head.

"Nah-ah. Bedroom is plain vanilla. C'mere." He took her hand and led her over to the velvet-draped wall, pressing a switch at the side and grinning as the drapes parted to reveal a wall set with four steel rings and a three-inch seat of obviously adjustable height.

"Once you try this, you'll never want to do it in a bed again. It's *incredible.*" *You won't be* around *to want anything, but that's not my problem,* he thought.

"You're not gonna hurt me, are you?" She looked at him nervously.

"Never. Cross my heart." He cupped her face gently, his eyes holding hers. "That would just be no fun for me. My pleasure comes from pleasing you."

She melted against him as her knees gave way, and allowed him to maneuver her back onto the seat.

"Oops. This'll work better with the jeans off." He pulled some black silk scarves out of a pouch at the base of the wall and looked up at her, going down on one knee to help her off with her jeans and panties as he trailed a line of kisses down her hip bone and inner thigh.

After she kicked them free, he stroked the silken length of one of her legs as he tied her to the rings. *Nice legs. Nice everything.*

Be a real shame to waste it. He unfastened his own jeans and put a hand on either side of her head.

"You know you're helpless now, don't you?" he purred.

She nodded and moaned softly as he took her. It didn't take long. She blinked bewilderedly as he backed away and fastened his jeans.

"Are . . . are we done?" She twisted a wrist against the tightly tied scarf and winced. "Can you untie me now? These things are starting to chafe a bit."

"Oh, we're not done, sweetness, that was just act one. Who sent you?" He walked over to the bar and took another swallow of his martini.

"What? Nobody . . . Is this a role-playing game? Because I'm not too good at those. . . ."

"Yeah, right." He grinned nastily. "So what's your name, sweetness?" He paced back over to the wall and yelled in her ear, "Who. Sent. You!"

"Ow!" She tugged harder at her wrists. "I'm not having fun, I want to go home now. Untie me, dammit!"

"Sorry, sweetness," he stepped to the side wall and slapped a switch, "act two's a command performance. Now, you tell me who sent you and your real name, or act two's gonna be real fun for me and no fun at all for you . . . unless you're into that sort of thing." His voice sounded oddly hollow. "Who sent you?"

"I'm . . . I'm Sarah Eileen Johnson," she stammered, eyes about twice their normal size, "and I'm a legal secretary for Sinclair and Burke's. Nobody sent me, I swear to God. Uh . . . please let me go. If you let me go now I promise I won't tell anybody ever, everything will be all right, please . . . please let me go!" She blinked rapidly, probably at the changed sound of her own voice.

"Can't do that, sweetness." He walked back for more of his drink. "Not safe for me. I'm real big on self-preservation. Obviously you aren't. Oh, you may notice we sound funny? Little side effect of the electronic damping. Gags and interrogations don't work together. So you go ahead and scream as loud as you want. Then again, I guess you've probably heard a similar system before. Who did you say sent you?"

"Nobody! God, I'm sorry, mister, I don't know who you think I am but I'm just a secretary, I don't know what you want! Please, please just don't hurt me. . . ."

"Okay sweetness, looks like we do this the hard way. Groovy." He walked over to the end table and picked up the phone. "Sam? Can you come up here? I think I may need a professional. . . . Yeah, you have a slightly more . . . dispassionate touch. Okay. Well, I might as well get started . . . yeah, I'll leave some for you."

"Oh my God please don't hurt me, please don't!"

"Let's see . . ." He walked over and opened the cabinets under the bar, "bull whip, cat o' nine, baseball bat, cattle prod, sharps. . . ." He looked up at her, quirking an eyebrow, "Got a preference?" He grimaced, "Oh, can't forget one thing."

"Last time you wouldn't believe what I had to go through to get it all out of my carpets." He went to the coat closet and took out a plastic rain mat, unrolling it beneath her feet. "You know meat tenderizer takes out blood stains? Okay, well, you're a girl, you probably do."

"Oh God, oh God, oh God. Save me and I'll never do anything like this again. Oh God . . . please, mister, I'm not whoever you want, please don't hurt me."

"Mmmm. I love leather." He walked over and pulled out the bullwhip, asking again, "Who sent you, sweetness?"

"I'm a *secretary*!"

The distant sound of the dampened screams rolled over Worth like ambrosia. No matter how jaded you got, you didn't ever lose your taste for this. He eventually noticed the red light blinking and fastened his jeans again before answering the door.

A squat man with a receding hairline and a pizza box ducked through the door and bolted it behind him. Setting the box down on the bar and opening it, he glanced over at the woman hanging limply from the rings.

"Geez, Worth, you didn't leave me much to work with. At least she's still got teeth. Man, I've been standing out there punching the bell for ten minutes!"

"She's got most of them. You know I can't hear when the system's on."

Sam went into the kitchen and brought back three beers. "You want one?"

"Nah. I just keep 'em for you, man."

The shorter man shrugged and took a bite of his pizza, carrying a beer over to the working wall where a set of clean sharps were already laid out for him.

"At least you were smart enough to leave the sharps to me. You must be more suspicious than usual of this one."

"Maybe I'm gettin' cautious in my old age." Worth shrugged, mixing himself a fresh martini.

"You're not too bad off." The interrogator snickered and poured a good half of the beer over the blonde's head, nodding to himself as she spluttered. "Of course, that's bad news for you. Lady, I'm sorry to say that my amateur friend's part in this is over. Now, Worth's a talented amateur, and he's a real pro at *his* job, but he's not me. You really need to save yourself a lot of pain and answer my questions now, instead of later." He picked up a small scalpel and looked at it coldly, "What's your name. Your full name."

"Sarah Eileen Johnson," she breathed weakly.

He looked up at Worth, who shook his head and handed him a small purse. He pulled out the already ruffled contents and looked through them.

"Driver's license, two credit cards, a business card for Sinclair and Burke—attorneys-at-law, a few receipts, miscellaneous business cards, a little cash, a checkbook, some makeup, change . . . none of it new. Good documents. Very professional." He sighed and put the scalpel down, walking over to the cabinet under the bar and pulling out a small bag. He took out a needle and a small bottle. "I always like to do sodium pentathol, first, but then I'm a bit old-fashioned."

He injected her expertly and set the needle next to the sharps, looking at his watch. "Okay, what's your name?"

"I'm . . . I'm Sarah Eileen Johnson. Why are you doing this to me?"

"Hmm . . . interesting." He pulled a small flashlight out of a pocket and checked her eyes. "You want to explain to me why you're immune to sodium pentathol?"

"I . . . I told you," she stammered. "I'm a legal secretary. I handle confidential files. You . . . you have to get treatments and a doctor's note or they won't hire you."

"Yeah?" He pulled out another bottle and a fresh needle. "Let's try the next one."

Five bottles later he smirked at her. "Pretty thorough protections for a secretary."

"They're . . . the insurance companies . . . they're paranoid.

I . . . I . . . please, please don't hurt me anymore. I'm just a secretary!" She wailed in despair, "I don't know anything!"

"I think the back teeth, next. Who are you?"

"Who do you want me to be?" She screamed, and pleaded, "I'll be anybody you want me to be! Please, please. . . ."

"So, who are you?" he asked, after waiting for her to wind down.

"I'm a secretary! Just a secretary . . ." she trailed off, sobbing.

A couple of hours later, he stripped off the rubber gloves he'd had to add at one point, looking up at Worth.

"There's really no more point. Her story's changing randomly and none of it's very inventive." He wandered into the kitchen and came back out with a paper plate. "It's getting harder to revive her." He shrugged. "We could pull an all-nighter, but I really don't see the point." He put a piece of the cold pizza on the plate and took it back to the microwave and came back to where Worth was scowling at the limp and half-dead mass of blood and matted blond hair. "In my professional opinion, my friend, *that*," he gestured with his pizza, "is a secretary."

"Damn. She would have been good for the whole weekend. Cut her down I guess, while we decide where to get rid of her."

"It's Friday." Worth took out a bottle of solvent and started the laborious process of cleaning the blood out of his whips. "The guy who runs the incinerator on Oak Street can sell all the GalTech drugs he can get his hands on. For a couple hundred hits of Provigil-C he'll walk around the block." He tossed a damp and bloody paper towel into a trash bag and grabbed another, watching out of the corner of his eye as Sam cut her down and she collapsed on the mat.

He had an instant to register that the squat the body landed in was oddly coordinated before she erupted upwards into a leaping roundhouse that caught the torturer behind the jawline at an angle. The man collapsed as though his strings had been cut and the red blur flipped off of his dead friend's waistband and landed facing him. She paused just long enough to pivot around one hip and hit him with a side kick to the solar plexus. It connected with enough force to throw him back against the coat closet door, his head cracking against it solidly, and leave him on the ground, gasping up through sickly doubled vision, "Who . . . who are you?"

The last thing Charles Worth saw was the muzzle flash from his late colleague's pistol, in his victim's leveled hands.

▶   ‖   ◀

"I'm somebody that doesn't chit-chat while they're killing people." She walked over to the body and tilted her head appraisingly a moment, before carefully and deliberately spitting on it. "The name's Cally O'Neal, and that's for trying to kill me when I was eight."

The door burst open to admit three heavily armed men in black body armor.

"You're *late*, Granpa," she snapped coldly.

"The traffic was miserable." The team point pulled off his mask and ran a hand through blazingly red hair, absently tucking a plug of Red Man in between cheek and jaw. He was a medium height man with a broad, low-slung body and long arms that gave him something of the impression of a gorilla. He looked to be about twenty but something about the way he moved, the look in his eyes, gave an impression of age and experience.

"Three hours?" Cally asked, incredulously, twisting her still naked body slightly as if stretching out a sore muscle and examining her pulled fingernails. "It had better have been a full scale pile-up. I was supposed to be *bait* not the trigger puller, dammit!"

"Hi, Cally," Tommy Sunday said, pulling off his balaclava and grimacing. "Tough day at the office, huh?" The number two was a huge man, broad across the shoulders and heavily muscled, with bright green eyes in a face that was almost movie star handsome.

"Yeah, those files were miserable," she replied. "Give."

"Jammer," Tommy said, shrugging. "Spoofer, whatever. Gave us the runaround; we've been over half of Chicago looking for you. Figured out a filter. Sorry it took so long. Glad you made it."

"How's Wendy?" She walked over to the other side of the bar and picked up her jeans.

"Pregnant again."

"Don't you guys do anything else?" She donned the jeans mechanically, shaking her head.

"I only see her every few months, so the answer is 'no.'"

The fourth member of the team surveyed the room for threats in a textbook maneuver before walking over to the nearest body and nudging it with a foot.

"Is that really him?" he asked.

"I dunno." Cally shrugged. "Toss me a sampler." She caught the probe deftly and knelt beside the body, pressing the needle into his temple on the more-or-less intact side. She looked at the readout and nodded. "Brain DNA never lies. It's him."

"Cleanup on aisle one," Tommy quipped, moving aside as several silent figures in white moved past him and began meticulously sanitizing the scene. He pulled off the black jacket and the white undershirt underneath, offering it to her. His eyes flickered to where she stood, lingering on the blood dripping into the white shag carpet. "You okay?"

"Pain is weakness exiting the body." She took the shirt and pulled it over her head. "Nothing a trip to the slab won't cure."

"Can you get the squealer from his car? Passenger seat, by the door," she asked Tommy, waiting while the cleaning crew moved the first body out the door and following them out. "Thanks. See you in the van."

"Post op review on this one's going to be . . . interesting." He pulled his jacket back on and followed her out.

O'Neal noticed the team member standing, almost frozen, looking at the splattered brain matter and fluids where Worth's body had been.

"You got a problem, Jay?" He considerately spat onto the second body instead of the floor so as not to make more work for the cleaners.

"She literally blew his brains out." He shook his head. "I don't know how she did the other guy, after letting them do God knows what to her, and she shows less reaction than most people would over a hangnail."

The older man held up his hand to stop the cleaners from picking up the other body. He examined it briefly, noting the discoloration at the jaw line, and popped a brain sample in a storage cube.

"Looks like a fairly clean impact to one of the sweet spots. Can't tell if it was a kick or a strike." Mike O'Neal, Sr. waved the cleaners back over and walked across the room to pick up the discarded high-heeled shoes and purse. "Cally is creative," he said. "Creatively violent."

"Too bad we couldn't have been in place beforehand." The younger agent shook his head, still looking at the mess, "but when you've got a guy who's weaseled out of three hits already just by burning the surveillance . . . It . . . couldn't be helped."

"Okay, let's see what we've got," O'Neal frowned, searching the room briefly for electronics, and handed a reader and a few cubes to the Cyberpunk. "Your domain, Jay. Probably nothing useful, but you never know." He walked back out to the hallway and headed for the stairs, leaving the other man to follow. *Doesn't matter how long it's been, climbing stairs without creaking never seems to lose its thrill.*

"She's gonna be pissed," Tommy said, following him down the stairs.

"It's okay," Papa O'Neal replied. "I know her weaknesses."

Cally walked into the blessedly cool dry air of her apartment and stopped, shaking her head; every square inch of the place was covered in either flowers or boxes of chocolate. There were irises and roses and mums and daisies and . . . stuff she couldn't put a name to. She kicked off her heels and walked over to one of the chocolate assortments, grunting at the label. Make that "very expensive" chocolates.

"I cannot be bribed, I cannot be broken," she muttered, pulling one of the chocolates out and crunching on it. "Usually." Her eyes narrowed and she rolled the chocolate around in her mouth, frowning at the flowers. Then she took another bite and frowned again. "Mostly."

She walked across the room, munching chocolate and wriggling her feet in the carpet for a moment, relishing the feeling of unbroken toes, then padded into the kitchen and poured herself a margarita from the dispenser in the fridge. On her way back to the bedroom she popped another chocolate in her mouth, grimacing at the taste of raspberry, stopped at the vidscreen, selected a cube, and dialed it to Tori Amos on audio.

"Three cheers for music to sleep to," she muttered to herself.

In her room, the freshly cleaned evening bag went in the top drawer of one dresser, with a dozen or so others. The wallet, less the cash, went in a thumbprint-locked and trapped drawer at the bottom, with a few dozen others. Sarah Johnson from Chicago hadn't been burned—well, the identity hadn't, anyway—and might be useful again.

The new T-shirt and very well-cleaned jeans went on hangers in the closet. The underwear, also new, went into the laundry hamper. She walked over to the triple full-length mirrors and looked at herself, front and back. *No scars, no signs. But there never are.* She leaned forward and examined eyes that were again her own cornflower blue. She bared her teeth and looked at them from all angles—perfect, as usual. Not the slightest sign that anything had been damaged.

She walked into the bathroom and set the glass next to the sink, grabbed a clean washcloth from the linen closet, padded back to her bed and set it down on the night table.

Hopefully this one was good for a couple of days of downtime, at least.

She used the bedside touch pad to bring the volume down to a soft background level, and set it to shuffle through the night. Another touch of the pad turned on active countermeasures. Rolling over and clutching her pillow in a way that was oddly like a child with a stuffed animal, she drifted off to sleep.

Tibet. Before the war her height would have marked her in a crowd. Postwar, with Americans everywhere there were still humans, she was unremarkable with mouse-brown cropped hair and a red parka. And now in the house, in a darkened bedroom. The former Party official had sped up the initial Posleen conquest by two weeks, and won himself twenty years of borrowed time. One of his children squealed at the TV in another room. The garrote made no noise at all.

Ireland. An American official on vacation. Tourism never died, it seemed. No witnesses, but he's all in black, a player? His neck cracks so easily, and he rolls as he falls, and it's white it wasn't supposed to be white what why was he here? God, no. No.

The light is red and it smells of incense and books. He's puttering around the sanctuary. A slow day. Father will you hear my confession? There, yes, through the door. What? Outside. Snow falling. The doors locked. Can't get in. Always the same. Can't get back in.

Florida. Swimming with dolphins. Mom's with me. She's proud of me. And the water's cool, and the sun hot. Silly Herman. There'll be key lime pie tonight, and a hug from Dad at bedtime.

She woke with a smile on her face and absently flipped the countermeasures off, reaching for the washcloth to dry her face. *In thirty years I haven't woken alone without my face soaking wet. But I sleep like a baby, thank God. I love living in a beach town.* She sat up and padded over to the dresser, thumbing the bottom drawer open. "So, who do I want to be today? *Not* Sarah. Let's see, local, fun, not a brain but not a ne'er do well . . . Pamela. She'll do. Tan, perfect nails. A manicure, pedicure, an afternoon of serious shopping, then an evening out." She looked at her reflection in the mirror. "Just what the doctor ordered, Pamela."

She set the hot pink leather wallet on the dresser and closed the drawer, grabbing a miniscule bra and panties in matching silver-gray lace. She showered, and washed her hair, adding the tiniest hint of dark at the roots and such, Pamela not being a natural blonde. She pulled out a bottle of gray lotion and applied it carefully, rinsing and checking the result. As always, no streaking, no fading, no patches, and absolutely no *tan lines.*

She went back to her closet and stood for a minute, finding the role. "Pamela. Smart, casual. Likes pinks, grays." She put a pink v-necked blouse, a pair of gray pedal pushers, and a burlap beach bag on the bed, and took a pair of brown strappy flats out of one of the cubbyholes built into the closet wall. "Watch? Yeah, brown-strapped analog." She added them to the beach bag.

After she was dressed, she went looking for breakfast. Pamela meant grapefruit, but first she frowned over Sarah's shoes on the living-room floor and went to put them in their proper place.

After breakfast, she drove to the mall. There was only the one in New Charleston so far, but it was always crowded. Ex-urbies adjusting to surface life tended to find it comfortingly reminiscent of home, and even teenage Charleston natives appreciated the air conditioning. Low Country Nails and Spa was on the lower level near one end, and she walked in with a smile ready, fastening on a curly-haired brunette who was puttering behind the counter.

"Jeannie?" she said.

"Pamela!" The other girl greeted her with a sunny smile, "Where have you been hiding, girl, it's been *weeks!*"

"Visiting my mom and sister in the Cairo Urb, and boy, am I glad to see the light of day again! Got time for a bunch? I need my hands and feet done and I would just *die* for one of your cucumber facials."

"How on earth did you keep that tan in an Urb?" The other girl came out from behind the counter and gently ushered her back to a seat at a small table set with the tools of her trade. "You must have been using a sun bed every other day."

"Just about that. Would that watermelon pink go with my skin, or should I go with more of a rose today?"

"Hmm. Let's see . . ." She held a couple of bottles of nail polish up against Cally's hands. "I think you can carry off the watermelon. In a bit of a playful mood?"

"In a mood for some serious fun." Cally grinned mischievously. "The Urb was like being buried alive."

"They always are." Jeannie tsked softly. "Girlfriend, you are under *way* too much stress, and you're not eating right." She held up one of Cally's fingers where she'd just trimmed a cuticle. "Look at these ridges. But I'm not too surprised. Family can be the worst for stress, and they still don't get very good food underground. Not like you can get out here."

"That's for sure. Urb cafeterias do *not* serve she-crab stew."

"Seafood's all right, but you've got to eat your fresh veggies or you'll be old before your time. And drink lots of water. Give me a minute." She stepped into the back and came out with a pair of glasses and a pitcher of ice water. "Here. Distilled and remineralized. Best water this side of the Blue Ridge."

Seven hours later Cally put away two new outfits and a pair of shoes, did her hair, added a couple of strands of freshwater pearls, and went back out for pub grub, some decent music, and whatever fun she could find tonight. *One good thing about a beach town. Even after the Postie war, there's always something. Pappas Street down near El Cid is always good for some fun.*

Oddly enough, the Citadel had suffered little actual damage in the war. Charleston had been thoroughly evacuated, so there had been no food, from the Posleen view. Many historic buildings had been left completely intact, along with the Battery, and the centuries old military school. Nobody knew quite what the Posties had seen in the collection of white, crenellated buildings—only that the campus had suffered a very little careful looting and had been recaptured virtually intact. It had recently celebrated the thirty-fifth anniversary of its reopening as a university and training academy for future Fleet Strike officers. While graduation did not guarantee a commission in the postwar world, it opened vast fields of opportunity and acceptance was highly coveted by young men as a ticket out of the constrained life of the Urbs.

Where there were young men, there were bars, and music, and nobody she had to kill. Usually. All in all, a good place to have a good time.

CHAPTER TWO

Old Tommy's Pub was always good, getting both the liquid and musical imports fresh off the boat from Ireland. Irish music, with its irrepressible ability to make the best of a hard lot, was enjoying something of a revival. Even if ballads and marches about armored ACS knights facing centauroid monsters weren't strictly traditional, Ireland's modern bards recognized their cultural value in a post-Posleen world and rose to the task brilliantly. A bodhran not only fit on a small pub stage, it also laid a surprisingly good foundation for the screaming treble of a vintage Stratocaster. Well, it would be screaming in a couple of hours, anyway. Right now the instruments were cased and a couple of the guys sitting in the corner grabbing a bite were probably the musicians. With that hair, they sure weren't cadets.

Cally pulled up a barstool and ordered a Killians and a seafood salad, then spent the next hour or so flirting with the bartender and waiting for the band to start. The cadets came in in dribs and drabs through the evening. Most of them looked too young to shave and were strictly no-touchies, no matter how much they tried to catch her eye, but one of them looked a little older than the rest and moved like he was prior service, even though the marks on his summer whites indicated a junior—with a *fine* butt. He'd do.

She caught his eye and raised her glass, offering a friendly smile. He froze for a second and looked back over his shoulder, as if unsure she was looking at him, and excused himself from his buddies, bringing his bottle of Bud over as his friends tried not to be too obvious about taking bets on a crash and burn.

"Uh . . . hi. Mind if I join you?" He set his beer on the bar at the empty stool next to her.

"I'd like that."

"I'm Mark." He looked at her practically full beer with something like desperation and offered, "Um . . . come here often?" Then just as obviously sat cursing himself for saying something so trite and unbrilliant.

"Not often enough, since I haven't met you." She smiled kindly and offered her hand. "I'm Pamela. Been at the Citadel long?"

"See these stripes? They mean I'm a junior." He grinned easily, back on familiar ground, "Freshmen have none, sophomores one, seniors are those guys walking around in blazers. But I'm actually going into my second year. Prior service." His chest puffed up a tiny bit, probably subconsciously, as he said the last.

"Oh? Where'd you serve?"

"Africa. There just aren't enough humans there to permanently displace the Posleen, and the Posties inherit skills that humans would have to learn. So Fleet Strike has forces there that rotate through on semi-random sweeps to try to dislodge the small bands of ferals before they become big bands."

"Was it hard? Even ferals are so *big*." She leaned an elbow on the bar and sat forward slightly, eyes wide. "I've only seen them on the holotank, of course. You must really be brave to have volunteered for that. Were you in, you know, one of those armored suits?"

"Don't I wish." He shook his head. "Those guys are really hard core, and they only take the very best. We didn't have very many of them in Africa. Most of them are out on the new planets tossing the Posties off to make room for colonists." He grinned faintly. "Sometimes ACS will take a new service academy graduate with a *really* good record, so I've still got a shot." His eyes flickered down to her chest, occasionally, but overall he was fighting a valiant battle to keep them in the vicinity of her face, "So what about you, what do you do?"

"Nothing near as interesting as killing Posleen." She grinned and held up a perfect hand, "I'm a manicurist. Nails and sympathy, that's me."

"And gossip?"

"Maybe just a teensy bit." She laughed, wrinkling her nose at him.

"So . . . um . . . did you grow up in Charleston? I guess in the old days you could tell by the accent, but . . ."

"No, I grew up in the Cairo Urb. But I liked the sun," she gestured to her tan and shrugged, "and I love the beach, so here I am."

"Ah, a genuine beach bunny. Not many of those around anymore." His hand was gentle as he took hers. "Just an old-fashioned girl, huh?"

"Well, a bit," she admitted, squeezing his hand and licking her lips slightly. "Oh, hey, I love this song."

He listened with her until the end of "The Holy Ground," signaling the bartender for another beer.

"So, you like Irish music?" he asked.

"Yeah, some. I'm more a fan of prewar dance mixes. I'm not a sitting still type, you know?" She pulled a pack of Marlboros out of her purse and started to light one, but paused when he winced. "Oh, I'm sorry. Does the smoke bother you?" The bar was heavy with the usual cloud of tobacco smoke, so she raised an eyebrow at him curiously.

"Only that you'd do that to yourself. My Gran died last week. Lung cancer. She cut way back during and after the war, when tobacco was scarce, but I guess it wasn't enough." He frowned, "I'm sorry to be a downer, I just . . . it's still fresh, I guess."

"Well, it's not like they're addictive anymore, but I'm sorry I brought your mind back to sad stuff." She shoved the pack back in her purse and laid a soft hand on his arm. "You know what you need? To get your mind right off it. Decos is just down the street." She waved at the stage. "This stuff is too much when you're already down. Dance it out of your system. That's what I always do when it gets really bad. Let's get out of here."

"Sure." He shook himself very slightly and nodded to his friends as they left.

Two hours later a light sheen of sweat dried on her skin in the salt air as she rode behind him on his bike to one of the hotels that catered to tourists from the heartland. When he pulled into the parking lot and stopped, she let go of his waist and climbed off slowly, reluctant to relinquish his warmth.

"This has got to be hell on your uniforms," she said, gesturing at the bike.

"Well, yeah. I pretty much keep it garaged except on weekends.

But yeah, I do go through uniforms a bit." He sighed, "I really hate to ask but would you mind waiting with the bike while I get us a room? I don't know if they'd be weird about it if you were with me."

They couldn't care less, but I don't want to admit I know that. "Oh, sure. The moon's nice tonight, and it's warm. I'll just watch it and enjoy the fresh air till you get back."

"Um . . . be back in just a minute." He straightened himself and walked towards the doors to the lobby with a slightly exaggerated assuredness.

They were within a couple of blocks of the Wall, and as she stood in the parking lot she could see it behind a couple of vacant lots and low businesses, cutting the skyline between apartment buildings. She supposed if she was home more she wouldn't smell the salt as much, but tonight it was strong on the air and she watched the few stars visible through the haze above the still fronds of the palmettos.

When he walked back out with the key, she was leaning back against his bike with her eyes closed, face turned up to the sky.

"You're not going to sleep on me, I hope," he teased.

She shook her head and swallowed something, probably gum, because her mouth was fresh and sweet when he drew her up against him and kissed her, softly at first, but responding enthusiastically when she deepened the kiss.

"Um . . . let's go inside," he said when they came up for air, looking around the parking lot a trifle self-consciously before taking her hand and leading her up the stairs to the second-floor room.

Inside the door, she moved into his arms and slid her hands up his chest. He cupped her butt with one hand and tangled the other in that beautiful, silky blond hair. She was so slim it felt like he might break her if he hugged too hard.

She caught his jaw in her hands and kissed him hungrily as she backed towards the bed, playfully letting go and allowing herself to fall backwards with a big grin as soon as the backs of her legs met the edge.

"Come into my parlor, said the spider to the fly. . . ." She undid the top button of her pedal pushers and blew him a kiss.

He laughed and lay down beside her, playing with the cleft between her breasts made accessible by the vee of her blouse.

"Is that from something?" he asked, leaning down and kissed her temple. "Never mind." He trailed his lips back down to her mouth to be devoured again.

She pulled back and caught his eyes as she pulled her shirt off and dropped it over the side of the bed, followed by her bra, then traced a finger down the front of his whites.

"Does that come off?" She licked her lips softly, tilting her head to the side and watching him watch her.

"Pamela, you're beautiful. Here." He unfastened his jacket, grimacing a little at the dingy grayish-white undershirt and suspenders underneath and getting them out of the way as fast as possible.

"Mmmm. Nice. . . ." She pressed herself up against him and buried her face in his shoulder, inhaling deeply before planting a row of tasting kisses along his collarbone.

He groaned and pressed both hands flat against her back, burying his face in her hair and inhaling the clean freshness of it. "Pamela," he breathed as he brought one hand around to cup her breast. He couldn't resist kneading it, it was so warm, and soft, and round. Perfect. He suddenly *needed* to get their pants off and shuddered slightly. It would be so easy to go too fast. How could he *not* go too fast. She was silken and warm and fresh and *moving* against him and he suddenly needed her desperately.

"Shhh. Gently." She broke the kiss and pushed him onto his back, softly. "Let me give you a treat." She finished undressing them slowly and kept just a slight bit away from him, even when he would have held her again, so that by the time she climbed on top and let him enter her he was no longer afraid of embarrassing himself.

God, she had muscles in there he didn't know women *had*, and it felt like heaven, but as he crested almost to the peak, he thought he'd *die* when she stilled for a moment and held his hands, smiling softly.

"Mmmm. Not yet. It gets *better*." Then when his breathing slowed, she'd start to move again, just enough. Always just enough.

She teased him to the brink, again and again, with those diabolical muscles, always gently and tenderly backing off to let him calm down, always just enough that when she finally pulled him on top of her and gave him the control he was dying to take, they were both panting. She touched his face softly as she went over the brink and his world exploded in a mind-shattering orgasm that left him quiet and still in its wake. Her legs were still clasped behind his thighs and underneath him she was curled into his chest with a tight softness that seemed tinged faintly with desperation. He kissed her hair gently and rolled onto his back, trying to understand why he suddenly felt so sad.

Sunday, May 12

Mark lay in bed next to her, whoever she was, and stared at the hotel room ceiling. Pamela had seemed so nice and funny and . . . fresh when he'd met her at Old Tommy's last night. But that girl didn't exist, did she? He glared resentfully at the tangled mop snoring on his arm. *God, it's almost like she killed her. If she ever was Pamela, 22, from Tidewater Tan and Nails, she sure isn't now. Hasn't been for decades at least. Damn juv. God, what am I going to say . . . I just want her out. So, wake her up and kick her out now, or wait until morning and tell her exactly what I think of her and her kind. . . .*

When she stirred in the morning and snuggled against his side, fondling him with one of those too-skilled hands, he had to repress a shudder as he smiled and pushed her hair back from her face. *Amazing that you can't tell by looking. No marks, nothing,*

"I bet you could do some really nice things to me with your mouth, you know, down there," he said.

"Mmm. Sure could." She smiled sleepily and eased her way down his chest.

He twined his hands in her hair and tried to pretend, just for a few moments more, that there really was a "Pamela." Afterwards, he took a deep breath and pushed her off him, standing up and grabbing his pants off the chair next to the bed. He might be young, but he was old enough not to say to any woman what he had to say to her without at least a little protection.

"So, how old are you, really?" he asked coldly.

She pulled the sheet up to wipe her lip as she appraised him. "How old do you want me to be?"

"Remember I told you last night about my grandmother, just died of cancer." He had turned and was facing out the window, his voice conversational. "The Galactics could have saved her, but they wouldn't."

"I know." Her face softened with sympathy. "That must be terrible."

"Yeah, well, at least she died with her soul. You ever met a juv?" *Here it comes, let her have it.* "The Galactics can save your body all day long, but you sign your soul away for it, don't you, Juv? Oh, I'm sorry, *Pamela*."

"You didn't seem to have any complaints last night." Her eyes were icy, her tone flat.

"Remember my bike, that we rode here from the pub?" He smiled stiffly. "Brand-new Honda-Davidson 2047. I could have gotten a 2046, fully refurbed, for about half the price. I just don't much like refurbs. You juvs sell your soul away off-planet, and then, every once in a while, when you notice something's missing you come back slumming and try to suck the soul out of some poor schmuck who's willing to be your toy for awhile. You suck real well, *Pamela*, but I just don't like refurbs. Please be gone when I get out of the shower, but don't hurry, I'm sure I'll be scrubbing for awhile."

"By the way," she swung her legs over the side of the bed and stood, letting her cold, dead eyes slide up over his body, very slowly, "your 'soul' needs practice."

"Yours has had too much." He tossed the last word over his shoulder as he closed the bathroom door, "what's left of it."

At her apartment, Cally switched her Pamela clothes for Justine's shabby-chic clothes and changed Pamela's tan and touch of dark roots for Justine's pallor and low-lights, and the pink polish for none, took the 9:30 bus down to Market Street, and entered a small and otherwise empty café. She ordered toast and coffee from a seat at the counter. The waiter, a kid in his late teens, set a cup of coffee with three sugar cubes in front of her, along with her toast. Two of the cubes were slightly whiter than the third. While the waiter was occupied at the cash register, she palmed those two and dropped the third in her coffee. She spread a thin layer of the orange marmalade Justine preferred onto her toast. As she was drinking her coffee, the waiter came back by and asked her if he could get her anything.

She shook her head slightly.

"You're in awfully early this morning," he said.

"He wasn't a morning person." She shrugged. *Just a pathetic little*

*puppy, and all he knew to be afraid of was that I might kick him
in the balls, of all things. He was right. I am too old for him.*

He suppressed a grin as he walked over to the small sink and
resumed doing the dishes from the small Sunday morning rush.

Back at home, Cally rinsed the thin outer layer of sugar off of
each cube, dried them off, and inserted the first one into the cube
reader slot of her PDA. A hologram lit up above it with an image,
surprisingly, of Father O'Reilly.

"Miss O'Neal, you are seeing me instead of your usual mission
profiler because this mission is a bit special. We have reason to
believe that the Bane Sidhe have been penetrated at a very high
level. As a result, all knowledge of this mission on the headquarters end has been confined to three people, including myself. Your
mission is to find and plug the leak by any means that you in your
personal judgment deem necessary. You will use your usual backup
team for this mission. Because of the highly sensitive nature of
this mission the briefings of your fellow team members will be
limited to those details necessary to insert you into your cover
position. You are not authorized to expand on that briefing material
until the on-base briefing, which will happen no earlier than the
Thursday before insertion is made, and will require any team
members briefed in to remain in secure circumstances until insertion. Your team members' insertions to back you up are significantly less complicated than your own. You will review them and
make any setup changes you deem necessary in the two weeks
between today and your insertion date. Any time not necessary
to your preparations you are authorized and instructed to charge
as some of your extensive backlog of vacation time. Cally, if you
don't take at least a week of that as vacation I will personally
guarantee that you will be benched for at least a month. You are
an excellent agent, one of our best, but even the best need some
down time. We would prefer that you take it voluntarily, of course."

The hologram flickered and was replaced by a revolving still
hologram of an officer whose collar stars belied his apparent age
of thirty. "The officer you see now is one General Bernhard Beed,
of the Fleet Strike Security Directorate. Ostensibly, Beed's office
handles the Third MP Brigade and criminal investigations functions of Titan Base. With two of his battalions forward deployed,
you'll notice he's potentially got time for extra duties. We have

information that indicates our leak may be using a non-Bane Sidhe member of one of the tongs on Titan Base as a cutout. We believe that in reality Beed has been detailed to head developing counterintelligence and operations against our organization. We therefore believe that Beed's office is the best place to begin looking for the identity of our leak." The display flickered and now the still was of a young woman of roughly Cally's own height and build, in Fleet Strike gray silks. *Well, my build if you ignore that she's a pudgette. The slab is going to have to do one hell of a boob job. But her thighs . . . can't tell if that's muscle or fat in what she's wearing. Maybe muscle. Her waist and stomach look okay, thank God. My eyes are fine, but the hair—it'll be the first time I've had to go* lighter *than my natural color in a long time.*

"Your cover, Captain Sinda Makepeace, is slated to transfer from the office of Fleet Strike Bureau of Personnel in Chicago to Titan Base as General Beed's new administrative assistant. We have been able to verify that no one assigned to Beed's office has ever met Miss Makepeace face to face." The hologram flickered and was replaced with a dark-haired young officer who was probably shaving every day now. "This is the general's aide, Lieutenant Joshua Pryce. On Sunday, May 26, Miss Makepeace is scheduled to take the 08:15 shuttle from Chicago to Titan Base. You will have approximately one hour between when Miss Makepeace passes through port security and the shuttle begins boarding to make the switch. You will report in person for appropriate physical adjustments no less than forty-eight hours before the switch to allow time for your system to stabilize. Cally, Titan Base is an extremely hazardous area of operations. I have to warn you that if you or any member of your team are caught, chances of our being able to mount a successful extraction are very poor. We need this information, Cally. Get it, and get out. All files on this cube will be automatically erased in five seconds."

She waited until the frozen hologram disappeared and pulled the cube and dropped it into a glass of vinegar, where it fizzed merrily as it dissolved. She put the second cube into the reader and was surprised when a hologram of Shari O'Neal popped up in the air in front of her. "Hi, sweetie. I know I'm not supposed to raid the supply of these for personal things, but these days it seems like the only way to be sure I reach you. I know you're off work right now, so Wendy and I have planned a little beach picnic and we aren't taking no for an answer. Not the walled section of Folly, but that nice little strip just north of it. I checked, there hasn't been a feral there for two months, so we can take turns on sensor watch. You don't need to bring a thing but your swimsuit and yourself. Tomorrow. Eleven thirty. Call it a girl's day out. Five seconds and all that, bye."

A face appeared on the screen of her PDA, and a tight, somewhat morose voice issued forth, "That was a security breach. Guess we'll have to move apartments now so the minions of the Darhel won't find us and kill us in our sleep. Would you like me to run a search of available rental real estate? I can list the results in increasing order of risk, if you like," it offered helpfully.

"No thanks, buckley. I think I'll just put up with the risk of staying here." She never could tell if the AI emulation of the buckley was good enough to know when she was being tongue in cheek. Personality Solutions, Inc., had never been forthcoming about how it had initially developed the base personality used for AI emulation in modern PDA's. Most people found the standard personality emulation somewhat pessimistic for their tastes, and purchased an aftermarket buckley with a personality overlay more compatible with their own preferences. Cally didn't. She routinely used her PDA for high performance applications, and the sad truth was that buckleys overlaid with other personalities had a distressing tendency to crash catastrophically, requiring low-level system reformats. The more different the personality overlay from the original buckley, and the higher the AI emulation was set, the sooner it crashed. Of course, one of the main differences of the buckley from true AI was that even just running the base personality, if you set the emulation too high you were inviting a crash. A buckley on a high setting could just envision way too many potential catastrophes.

After thirty years, she was pretty adept at wheedling, cajoling, and threatening the base buckley personality into acceptable performance. She tapped a few screen buttons and checked her settings. Sure enough, she'd left the AI turned up too high. She dialed it down a couple of notches and ignored the swearing and references to lobotomies. It really handled better day to day if you didn't run the emulation above level five.

Once, ten years ago, it had somehow figured out how to manipulate its own emulation level. The poor thing hadn't lasted two days.

She dropped the second cube into the glass and ignored it as it began fizzing into oblivion. As Justine, she had a gym membership, paid several months in advance, at an old prewar high school. The gym had survived the war with an intact roof and had initially been snapped up by the local defense forces for their own use, but had been let go to Deerfield Spa and Fitness once the Citadel had reopened as a Fleet Strike academy and the corps of cadets had taken over much of the work of manning the Wall.

Justine liked it for the one curtained section entirely given over to jazzercise and its sixteen hour, seven days a week drop-in schedule for members. She shoved some basic black workout togs and a pair of jazz shoes into a gym bag and turned out the lights on her way out the door.

Three hours and what must have been a gallon of sweat later, she felt she just *might* be fit for human company again. Well, okay, definitely *after* a shower. As she walked back to the locker room, a guy with a towel over his shoulder and apparently headed toward the weight room bumped into her, apologized curtly, and kept going. She blinked twice but walked on without looking down at the cube he had planted in her hand.

In the locker room, she looked at the small slip of paper around the cube and sighed, *Okay, legitimate codeword. There had better be a good reason for this extra message because it is* lousy *tradecraft. What do they think I am, a walking chatboard? If it's not a genuine emergency I will have someone's ass.*

She took a much quicker shower than she wanted and skipped her plans for an al fresco lunch down at the Battery. There was an open air vendor there who made what she would swear were the best crab cakes in town. And Justine liked to feed the seagulls. She frowned at the bag of cheese curls in the passenger seat and drove home.

At least she could, and did, run a hot bath to soak in while she viewed the thing. To her surprise, the hologram that popped up was Robertson, a computer geek who had several times given her team additional specialized backup on more technical missions.

"Cally, first, I'm sorry for taking the risk of contacting you like this. Second, this is not strictly a Bane Sidhe authorized communication." He ran a hand through frizzy brown hair and frowned. "If I could, I'd deal with it myself, but it's not my line. I know you took down several of the guys who ordered and did the strike on Team Conyers." Cally sat up in the tub and her face was etched in cold lines as the hologram continued. "I was only in on one of those runs, but I remember you felt . . . unusually strongly about them. I know they were sent to save your life as a kid. There's no easy way to say this, Cally. The bastards lied." The hologram flickered to show a U.S. Army light colonel with a receding reddish-brown hairline, a neatly trimmed mustache, and a weak chin. Her stomach clenched in remembered hatred. The cube now had her undivided attention.

"I'm sure you remember Colonel Petane, who sold the team's safe house out to the Darhel. You were told, we were told, that team Hector had terminated Petane. Cally, he's still alive. Somebody in that batch of *pragmatists*," he made the word an epithet, "upstairs decided that the good colonel would be a good source of information and traded him his life to turn him. Which I would reluctantly be okay with if he was the only source of some vital stuff, but this little pissant only ever has access to give secondary or tertiary confirmation of things we already know. He's a living example of the Peter Principle, and he's been passed over for promotion twice. The *pragmatists*, it seems, don't like to admit their errors."

"They covered it up pretty well. Got him transferred to the Army Fleet Strike liaison office in Chicago and have carefully assigned any missions likely to go near that office to team Hector. If you've ever wondered why your job *rarely* takes your team to Chicago, that's why. Mine didn't, either, until I got assigned to back up Hector on a couple of jobs over the winter. I guess the powers that be figured I didn't have a personal stake and was safe. They needed an in-person meet with Petane, and I was there to watch the countermeasures and make sure we didn't get burned. I know I've sometimes had to do some things that made it hard to sleep nights, but nothing like this. Loyalty has to go down the chain as well as up. I . . . well, we've worked together and I knew you'd want to know. What you do about it's your call. This message will be gone in five seconds."

Of course he couldn't do it the normal way. The hologram of the traitor blew up in a welter of gore that faded into a really spectacular sunset. She pulled the cube out and walked to the kitchen to destroy it, heedless of the water dripping into her carpet.

"Well, they wanted me to go on vacation. Okay. So I'll go on vacation." Her mouth was a grim line as she thawed a salad in the nuker and rinsed the crisper gel off the lettuce into the sink, then dumped a packet of crab chunks on top and covered it in horseradish sauce. It was a poor substitute for Herman's crab cakes, but she hardly tasted it anyway.

After doing her hair and grabbing a black off-the-shoulder cotton shirt and faded jean shorts, she pulled up a list of acts on the web, twisting the bangles on her left wrist absently. Justine preferred ultra-modern Cleveland-crash style music. A group called Anger Management was playing at The Riverside Dive. *That sounds like something I could use right about now. I hope their pub grub isn't too obnoxious.*

Charleston, Monday, May 13

Cally came home in the wee hours of the morning, alone. *Music tonight, yes. Company, no. If I got another anti-juv bigot pup like last night, I just might forget it's not my job to kill them. The cleanup crew would not be pleased, and the paperwork's a bitch.* She grinned and kicked off her heels, swinging them by the straps as she hummed her way to her room.

Makeup off, check. Fresh washcloth, check. ID's put away, check. She stripped off Justine's clothes and tossed them in the basket, frowning. "Laundry tomorrow morning."

She dialed up some Creed onto the vidscreen's audio for the night, turned on countermeasures, set the alarm for eight, and snuggled into her pillow.

Bhutan. A banker who got on too well with nonhuman bankers. He had a taste for street whores, but didn't treat them well. One of them had been happy to retire in the South Pacific after his heart attack. The nannite poison had been untraceable even with Galactic equipment. In the closet, watching. Checking the body and injecting the now hysterical whore with a merciful tranquilizer before getting her onto her shuttle. Death was so different up close.

Rabun Gap, she puts the front sight on the assassin and squeezes, gently, and the red splash and the death smells. Efficient men in white, cleaning, and then the Posties are coming and the men in black are so silent, and so efficient at killing. Rosary calluses on his hand. And in school the nuns won't tell her anything and then there's Father

O'Reilly. Team Conyers is gone. Gone, all gone Father? Our Father, who art . . .

Bless me, Father, for I have sinned. How long? Nineteen years, two months, three days. Father, it's a long list. There was a prostitute specializing in industrial nano-researchers. Two of them died after she made her report. I had to . . . Father? Father? In a rage she smashes the screen and glares at the empty seat and there is no door, and no door she came in through. There had to have been a door, wasn't there? And no ceiling, just the walls going up and up.

The Keys and she's back on the boat with Dad, and he's proud because she just caught a really big one and she's washed the salt from the wind out of her hair and is sitting on the edge of the dock watching the sunset as Mom combs the tangles out. Michelle is in the water swimming with Dad, and a dolphin is chittering to her as she strokes under its chin. And Mom's brought her a nice, cold limeade and a plate . . .

The alarm shrilled at her and she slapped it and the system off, reflexively grabbing the washcloth to dry her face. *Mmmm. I've always loved the beach. Maybe next time I get a real vacation I'll finally go back for that visit I've been promising myself. I guess after forty years it's probably changed a bit. Gotta be Cally today. Let's see, Cally's very casual, got a smart mouth, wears a lot of olive drab but also likes red.*

She tossed the used washcloth in the basket and carried it into the kitchen, sticking out her tongue at the empty coffee maker she had forgotten to set last night and hitting its button with an elbow on her way past. Just off the kitchen she opened the door and raised the lid of the laundry machine, dropping in the clothes and a packet of fragrance-free fabric saver before closing the lid. The machine detected the added weight, analyzed the contents, and she heard it filling as she shut the door behind her.

She rummaged through the freezer until she found a bar of chocolate-cheesecake breakfast ice cream and pulled up the news, glaring again at the offending coffee machine that *still* hadn't finished brewing.

The House and Senate are still debating what Posleen-free means for purposes of reconstruction to Statehood? Yeah, the Urbies really don't like the difficulties they already have with the Senate over food subsidies. And their internal media makes sure they get a full report on every feral Posleen attack in CONUS, so they're not bloody likely

*to poke a nose out and take a look. Some days nonexistence beats
the crap out of citizenship.*

"Ah, it's done." She grabbed her mug and filled it with coffee,
adding a sugar cube, and took a look at the weather and ferals
report before going to get dressed. *Looks good enough for me.*

In the bedroom she pulled on a red bikini with a T-shirt and
jeans over it, pulled on an old pair of sneakers, threw some clean
underwear and a towel in a beat-up khaki backpack and pulled
her hair back in a neat braid. She sorted through the rows of
wallets in the bottom drawer until she came to a battered khaki
and Velcro one that had very sincere identification and bank cards
in the name of Cally Neilsen. The wallet was a bit old fashioned.
It was the one used least often, and least hazarded, so it was least
often in need of replacement. All the wallets had artful wear and
tear. This one had acquired them the old-fashioned way, although
the contents had to be as frequently updated as the others to stay
current, and the last name, like those of the others, had varied
over time. Fortunately, the Darhel were no more interested in U.S.
computer identification procedures being truly secure than the Bane
Sidhe were.

As she loaded the Colt .45 and extra magazines into the front
of her car, she wished she'd picked up at least something beyond
a small cooler of beer to add to the picnic. She had her go-to-
ground supplies—never left the Wall without them—but they
weren't exactly your recreational sort of refreshments. Her eyes lit
on Justine's bag of cheese curls. Just the thing. Wendy's kids would
love them.

She drove to the James River exit, partly because it was close,
but mostly because the simple sliding gate of heavy steel, combined with the drawbridge, was easier to navigate than some of
the other gates. It just took a few minutes to get through the
checkpoint. The .45 and three spare magazines, along with her
range certification card, were enough to exempt her from the
municipal convoy requirement and fee. Even in the postwar world,
liability was a bitch. Charleston's city government, elected from
a population of many of the first Southerners who had returned
from the Urbs and the heartland, along with the local militia and
the Fleet Strike cadets, had chosen a uniquely Southern solution.
Since tourists from the Urbs were generally a braver sort to start
with *and* sensible enough to travel with the convoys, it worked

rather well. The few who weren't might gripe about the fee, but the people of Charleston firmly believed that the best way to keep the local population of Postie ferals low was to avoid feeding them.

The road north of the walled section of Folly was not as well kept up as the road to the walled municipal beach, but it wasn't as bad as one might have thought even after decades of official neglect and two decent-sized hurricanes. The more enterprising and independent Charlestonians who used the unwalled beach made a habit of collecting buckets of cleaned clam shells in the backs of their cars and bringing them along as an unofficial toll for beach use. The Citadel Cadets had picnics on the beach a couple of weekends a year at which it was an unofficial tradition to bring a couple of thick steel sheets and a few sledgehammers and have impromptu contests to see which company's champion could pulverize the most shells (Golf Company being the current record-holder at twenty-three buckets), after which the cadets carefully filled in any significant cracks or potholes with the makeshift paving material. Over time the road had become perhaps more tabby than asphalt, but it remained essentially adequate for the mostly local traffic it served.

She pulled into the parking lot, checked her holster, and went around to the trunk, carrying two large buckets of cleaned shells to dump into the steel bins. Fortunately, even feral Posleen did not consider empty clam and oyster shells edible. She was a few minutes early, and, as was the case more often than not on a weekday, the beach was empty, so she went ahead and got started on the normal precautions of activating a couple of portable Postie alarms and running them up the flagpoles that had been set into the edge of the parking lot. They were okay on a wire stand or on top of a car or rock in a pinch, but to get the best warning time you really needed to give them a bit of elevation. She set her PDA up to listen on the sensors' individually programmable alert frequencies and entered the sensor locations and orientations on the screen. Now if a feral showed up she'd have not only an alarm but a distance and a moving dot-on-a-plot.

"Please tell me you've got more than that dinky forty-five and aren't planning to fight a horde of Posleen *alone* with it. Or a boat? If we're far enough out, they can't get us in a boat. We'll be just fine until it capsizes and we get eaten by sharks." The buckley always did get a bit agitated on sensor watch.

"Buckley, do you actually sense the presence of a single Posleen feral?"

"No, they're doing a real good job of hiding this time. I can call in reinforcements if you want. Won't do any good, but if you want . . ." It trailed off.

"Don't call anyone, buckley," she ordered.

"Good idea. No reason they should all die, too," it said.

"Shut up, buckley."

"Right."

With the basics done she was free to get cooler and bag down onto the beach, jeans and shirt off, pop open a beer, and amuse herself throwing a couple of cheese curls to the seagulls until Shari, Wendy, and the kids pulled up and came down onto the beach, Wendy's four kids at a run close behind Shari's golden retriever. Well, okay, she was *mostly* golden retriever and all dog, running straight at the gulls and barking cheerfully.

Cally surrendered to a lapful of sand, fur, and dog drool, scratching Sandy's ears vigorously while the other women maneuvered loads of food and gear down the stairs, and tried to variously call off the dog and the kids.

"Okay you hoodlums, get back here and help carry!" Wendy called, grinning, "Mike, you too!"

"Hang on, Mom! I've gotta reboot my shoes, again." Her six-year-old was staring down at his feet, where a hologram of an ACS trooper was shooting at a hologram of a Posleen normal with a boma blade, the latter having frozen mid stride, interspersed with flickering bits of static. Muttering words a six-year-old probably shouldn't know, he took the offending shoe off and stuck his hand inside, fumbling around for the reset switch. The hologram disappeared and reappeared later, the Posleen chewing red drippy bits of meat better left unidentified. With the shoe back on the child's foot, it resumed swinging its boma blade at the ACS trooper every time one foot passed the other, finally erupting backwards in a slow-motion welter of yellow gore as a line of bullets cut its torso in half. When the pieces hit the "ground" they stayed for a second while the ACS trooper jumped up and down triumphantly, then both holograms flickered back to pristine health and began their battle anew.

"Hiya, Aunt Cally." He made it back over to the others as his mother was spreading out the blanket next to Cally's towel. "Daddy bought me some new shoes. Like 'em?"

"Hey, those are great! Great detail on the images." She watched the Posleen normal explode again, this time having its head splattered apart by aimed fire. The victorious ACS trooper turned a backflip, before going into a classic prewar end-zone dance. "Does the Postie ever win?"

"Once in awhile," he nodded solemnly, "but it's okay, 'cause they don't show the gooshy stuff for that." He reassured her as if he was the one talking to a small child.

"Do you remember me, Annie?" She tucked a strand of hair behind her left ear and craned her neck, trying to make eye contact with the little girl hiding behind Wendy's leg.

"Sorry, she's going through a shy phase." Her mother absentmindedly stroked the wispy blond curls the little girl was shaking, her face buried in Mommy's knee. "Oh, come on, Annie, you remember Aunt Cally, don't you? Sandy remembers her."

"That's my doggy." The four-year-old's gray eyes met hers. "You've got sand all over yourself."

"I know. Sandy shared." For a minute her eyes looked as young as the rest of her, as she laughed and stood up, brushing the sand off of her belly and legs, and giving Sandy enthusiastic scratching at the back of her head. "You're so good to share, you're a good dog, aren't you?"

As Sandy's tail was sweeping back and forth as if to enthusiastically agree that she was a good dog, James and Duncan arrived with several folding chairs and one big beach umbrella.

"Hi, Aunt Cally. Gonna throw a few passes with us after lunch?"

"They would be football fanatics, wouldn't they?" Shari pulled a ball from one of the towel bags and handed it to Duncan as the younger boy dumped his load unceremoniously on the sand and made a run for the water, spiking the ball enthusiastically as he hit the high-tide line.

"Hey!" James looked up from setting up a chair as his brother left him with the work. "Mom!"

"Oh, go on. I've got it." Cally picked up a chair and waved him towards the beach.

Wendy caught Shari's eye for a moment as the six-year-old followed his brothers and dog towards the water.

"The kids really like you, you know." She began unloading plastic containers of food onto the blanket. "It seems to be mutual."

"Oh, yeah, they're great." She opened another chair. "Glad you and Tommy decided to have another bunch, now that the first group's flown the nest. Oh, congratulations by the way. I thought you guys were gonna wait until this bunch was up and out before having more though."

"Yeah, well, even with GalTech you get the occasional pleasant surprise." She blushed. "So when are we going to be congratulating you, sweetie?"

"Say what?" Cally spluttered, dropping the chair she had just picked up. She retrieved it and suddenly became very occupied with brushing every bit of the sand off of it.

Shari put her hand over her eyes, shaking her head slightly.

"Okay, so I could have handled that better," Wendy sighed.

"Ya think?" Shari suddenly became very interested in the beach umbrella she was putting up.

"Cally, you can't just be twenty forever," Wendy tried again.

"I haven't been twenty for thirty years or so." She plopped down in the chair and stretched her legs out in front of her, crossed her arms, and leaned back looking at the two of them suspiciously. "Okay, give. What are you two up to?"

Shari sat down and curled her arms around as Annie scrambled into her lap, and looked out over the sea. The wind was blowing her hair back from her face and she squinted to keep stray grains of sand out of her eyes.

"Cally, this life's not good for you anymore. If it ever was. You're not happy. When are you going to give yourself permission to have a life and settle down?" she said.

"You know what we're up against. I do things that very, very few people can do. Things that need to be done for *other* people to settle down." She sat up and leaned forward in her chair, resting her hands on her knees. "Look, if and when I meet the right man I probably will do the kid thing, I just . . . haven't met him. And the anti-juv prejudice doesn't help. Not to whine, but it's hard to get intimate with a guy when you're old enough to know he's an immature idiot."

"But you're never gonna meet him in some bar," Wendy broke in, handing her a juice pack. "Look, I can understand if you're not keen on the BS organization's matchmaking program. Hey, that would creep me out a bit, too. But between Tommy and Papa, they've gotta know at least half a dozen decent guys who would *love* to have a wife who didn't have to be kept quite so much in the dark. I mean, geez, what's the harm in letting them fix you up with a date or two?"

"What's the harm?" Cally asked flatly, her eyes suddenly dead. "Just that having an emotional tie to someone who ends up on the same mission could get me or him captured or killed. Not to mention his side of it. Who wants a wife who faces the odds I face, or does the things I have to do? I'm good, but it's sheer dumb luck I've only died once so far, and that not permanently. The only thing worse than the odds of death for a female assassin are the odds of a successful marriage."

Shari winced and clapped her hands over Annie's ears. "You never talk about that!" she whispered.

"Get my point?" She pulled out a mug and a flask, squeezing the juice pack into the cup and pouring an ounce or so of clear liquid on top. "You want?" She extended it to Shari.

Shari's hand went to her stomach. "No, I . . . can't."

Cally broke into a grin. "You dog! No wonder you're trying to get me married off and pregnant, misery loves company!" she joked, then smiled. "Congratulations!"

"Are you really?" Wendy laid her hand on her best friend's knee. "You wouldn't kid between girlfriends? Congratulations! Oh, this is so great. We will eat ice cream and go off the curve together! Have a juice pack."

"There, see what you're missing?" She turned back to Cally. "Will you just promise me you'll *consider* letting Tommy fix you up on a date? Just one teeny weenie little date? If you want, you don't even need to see him alone—we could double."

"Oop. Now you've gotta do it, Cally. I'll baby-sit. She and Tommy haven't been out on a date in *ages*, it's your positive duty to your best girlfriends in the world."

"My only girlfriends in the world." Cally grimaced. "Not that I don't appreciate you two—that is, when you're not trying to fix me up with Tommy's or Granpa's fishing buddies." She caved when the two of them glared at her. "Okay, okay, I'll think about it. After I get back from this next mission."

"A short one, I hope?" Shari asked.

"You know I can't say. But, I wouldn't get your hopes up on it." She used the juice pack straw as a swizzle stick to stir her drink and took a sip before checking her PDA. "Everything's fine. Still up, still scanning, no signs."

The rest of the afternoon was practically idyllic. They washed down the crab salad sandwiches with juice and sodas—well, Cally had a beer. It didn't matter that she had Postie watch since she'd been immune to the effects of alcohol her entire adult life. The kids didn't eat many of the cheese curls—it was more fun feeding them to the gulls and the dog. Since Sandy loved cheese curls *and* chasing gulls, she usually won the race to each freshly tossed treat.

Duncan and James loved passing practice with Cally, as she generally caught the ball even when their throws went a bit wide, and they generally caught the ball because she could land it right in their hands from twenty-five yards down the beach. Cally reflected that the boys, who had had very little social contact with adult females who were *not* fully upgraded, were going to have a rude awakening some day. She could have landed it in their hands at twice that distance, but the display would have been bad tradecraft. As it was, she never would have done this much if there'd been outsiders on the beach.

That afternoon, she carried a sleeping Annie up the stairs for Wendy and got her strapped into her booster seat in the station wagon, while the older boys stowed the folded chairs and gear in the back. A few seconds after Mike climbed into the seat beside his little sister his sneakers, obviously sensing that their wearer was no longer standing or walking, shut off the holograms.

"Those are really cute shoes," Cally said as she walked around to the back of the car where her friends were waiting to say good-bye, "but I was a little surprised the battles were silent. They had neat weapons sound effects even when we were kids."

"Shhhh." Wendy held a finger over her lips, obviously smothering laughter. "Tommy turned that off the first night."

Cally's mouth rounded in a silent "oh" of understanding. She felt a small scrap of paper being pressed into her palm and looked at Shari enquiringly.

"It's a time and number for your grandpa. Call him," she said.

"What? Over the *phone*?" She patted her bikini lightly. Still damp. She'd be riding home on a towel. Her mind snapped back into gear and she looked at Shari in bewilderment. "*Phone?* Why the phone?"

"It's what we outside the ops world call a *personal call*, Cally." Shari patted her on the back with an exaggerated pitying air, then, more seriously, "He just wants to talk to you. Not shop talk, not mission talk, just a visit. Okay, obviously you're going to use a pay phone somewhere, but . . . just call your grandfather, okay?"

"Okay, sure." She hugged both of them a little awkwardly. "Okay, then, well, I guess it's goodbye until next time."

"We'll wait while you get your sensors back down," Wendy said, climbing into the driver's seat and watching her pull the small boxes down the flagpoles and put them back in her car.

A bank of clouds was rolling in and Cally could smell the rain on the air as she pulled onto the road behind the blue minivan for the drive back to town.

CHAPTER THREE

Back at her apartment, she carefully put the dull orange and somewhat battered seashell that Annie had proudly "found" for her on her bedside table next to a small potted cactus and went to shower off all the sticky salt and sand. She'd need another once she decided who she needed to be on vacation, but she'd worry about that after she was clean.

As she dropped the red bikini onto the bath mat she could hear the thunder and the first drops of rain beating against the small bathroom window.

A few minutes later, hair in a towel, wrapped in a big fluffy blue bathrobe, she emerged from the bathroom and thumbed open the bottom drawer of her dresser, this time pulling it all the way open and reaching in the back for a battered black shoe box. In here were her five specials, identities even the Bane Sidhe knew nothing about. At least, not as far as she knew. As Granpa had beaten into her head back during the Postie war, always have a go-to-hell plan. *Hrms. These two are out, they need updating. I'd never pass for my thirties at close range without more cosmetic work than I can do. Okay. This one. Marilyn Grant from Toledo Urb. Good thing I picked her the night before. I'm gonna need a perm, and color that won't wash out the next time I shower. Oop. Hobbies include acoustic guitar, nineteen sixties folk music. There go the nails.*

A few hours later she stood in the three-way mirror, wrinkling her nose slightly at the chemical smell that now pervaded her bedroom, and checked the changes. Warm brown eyes stared back at her, courtesy of good old-fashioned zero-prescription extended-wear contacts. Not-quite chestnut curls stopped around her shoulders. She hadn't had to take off much, with the curls to shrink the length up some. Her skin tone was not exactly tanned, just more medium than fair. Short nails on her left hand and slightly longer ones on the right were painted one of the rose shades more flattering to brunettes. The toenails were a different shade of rose. Both had small mistakes around the cuticles, both would be allowed to chip and be inexpertly repaired over the next few days.

She pulled out the picture IDs and looked at the face, comparing it to the mirror. *Yep, I did this one with cheek pads. What a pain in the ass. At least you can actually* wash *a new perm now. Three cheers for modern cosmetics. But the stuff for major hair work still stinks.* She looked at the rain battering away at her windows and shook her head, opening the door to the rest of the apartment and flipping on the ceiling fan. That and the bathroom fan venting to outside would help, some. Anyway, she'd slept in worse stinks often enough.

She looked over at the clock. Barely nine. *What the hell, maybe there's an alternative.* She wrinkled her nose and looked in the closet. *Touristy, touristy . . . Blue Hawaiian shirt, white capris, white sandals, cheap tourist seashell jewelry. Perfect.*

There was a really good seafood place a few blocks off Market—so good she had to consciously avoid going too often as too many people and setting a bad pattern. Not likely to have any cadets on a week night—definitely a bad week for cadets. Perfect place for tourists.

She pulled up Toledo Urb's local news for the past few weeks on her PDA and set it for audio while she dressed. As always, she'd avoid natives, but she was covered for anyone else.

When she got to the Bristol she went ahead and ordered a tropical shrimp salad and an extra large mango margarita at the bar, then sat nursing her drink and listening to a three-chord lounge lizard massacre Jimmy Buffett with one ear while eavesdropping on her fellow patrons with the other.

" . . . so I told Tom that if he couldn't get me some qualified help no way are we gonna make that October deadline. . . ."

" . . . sometimes I think maybe she's the one, but then I wonder . . ."

" . . . believe the prices here? *Nothing* costs this much in the Urb. . . . Yeah, I know, but how much more can it be, I mean, the ocean's *right here*. . . ."

" . . . finally final, and I know I'm supposed to feel better and free and everything, but all I feel is like a chump for never wondering why she never bitched when it was time for my boat to go out. . . ."

Bingo. She studied the guy talking to the bartender under her lashes. Fortyish, balding—but he cut it short and wore it with dignity—no comb-over or bad rug. A simple glitch ointment could have fixed it, but the fisherman apparently either couldn't afford it or wasn't that vain. Not fat. Well, a slight paunch, but without rejuv that was damned hard to fight. She looked at the shoulders and biceps from a lifetime of manual labor, and the weather-roughened skin, and decided she'd seen worse. She picked up her drink and moved over to the empty seat beside him, asking the bartender for a water and a slice of key lime pie.

"God that looks sweet," the fisherman looked at her margarita and shuddered slightly, "and you're having *pie* with it?"

"Yeah, I've got a bit of a sweet tooth." She grinned at him.

"Well, if you'll excuse me saying so, it doesn't show." He glanced briefly at her body but politely looked back away.

She grimaced as the guy with a guitar—calling him a musician would have been too generous—fumbled a chord change, then saw the fisherman wincing, too, and laughed.

"So since it's obviously not the music, what brings a pretty young girl in here drinking with old farts like us?" He gestured around the bar with a hand. "Your boyfriend work here?"

"Did you ever have an evening where you just didn't want to be alone?" Cally smiled gently at him.

"What, you mean like tonight?" He snorted, taking a long drink of his beer and staring off into nowhere. "All the time, lately." He drained his drink and gestured to the bartender for a refill. "You don't sound like you're from around here, either. Aw, excuse me," he waved her off. "I'm just being nosy."

"Nah, it's all right." She offered her hand. "I'm Marilyn, and you're right, I'm not from here. I'm on vacation, from Toledo." She took a sip of her margarita and looked away. "This trip was *supposed* to be with my fiancé, well, ex-fiancé, uh . . . it just didn't work out, I came anyway, and now I'm wondering if I should have."

"You wanna paint the town red to show you ain't hurt, but then you ain't in the mood for partyin'." He fumbled for the bills to pay for his arriving drink. "Guess there's a lot of that goin' around tonight."

"You too?" She took a bite of the pie, watching him.

"Yeah, I just went through a divorce."

"Bad?"

"It could've been if I'd made it. I could have taken it into court and made sure she got nothin'." He took another drink. "Her good luck. When I walked in and, well, saw what I saw, I was so disgusted all I wanted was out as fast as I could get."

"That's lousy. I don't know what I would have done if there had been another girl. I just finally got tired of us fighting all the time. He was one of those people who could find something wrong with everything."

"Sounds like you had a lucky escape."

"Yeah, well, you too. And I came out here planning to party all week, and, I guess it's stupid, I just . . ." She trailed off and went back to her pie. She had obviously picked someone whose prime interest was getting good and drunk. *Not a good pick. I should have known better.*

When the bartender cut him off, later, she was a good enough sport to put him in a cab home before driving back to her own apartment to sleep in the hair fumes.

Chicago, Tuesday, May 14

The receptionist was a hell of a looker. Not much in the tits, but her face just took your breath away. Besides, tits were easy enough to fix. Damn.

John Earl Bill Stuart, Johnny to friends and enemies alike, paced the outer office pretending a polite interest in the snooty art stuff scattered around the place. If any of it was real, it must have cost a mint. Most of it was probably those reproduction things meant for show. And he'd bet it worked with some people. He'd been more impressed with the view. This Terra Trade Holdings had the whole next-to-top floor, at least, of the old Sears Tower. They'd renamed it, but it was still—or again, depending on how you looked at it—the tallest building on Earth. He didn't know who had the top floor, but it sure wasn't open to the tourists any more and he figured the second to top floor view was closer than almost anybody got these days. Damned aliens, but there you were, and they were really no different from the old corporations, who had really taken it in the teeth when the aliens showed up, now were they? Just different people on top.

Johnny would have liked to have brought his camera and snapped a few pictures for Mary Lynn while he was up here, but that wouldn't have been classy, and he knew you had to be classy at meetings like this. Pictures would have been nice, just to show her he'd really been here, but it couldn't be helped.

"The Tir will see you now," the girl said, just like one of the girls on the evening news. No Yankee accent like you heard a lot here in Chicago. No accent at all. Classy.

The Tir's corner office was a criminal waste. Heavy drapes covered both walls of floor-to-ceiling windows, darkening the room to dim shadows as well as shutting out the view. It was a little like the guy who takes the last piece of chicken in the basket, not because he wants it but so you can't have it. It was pretty much of a piece with his employers' typical way of doing business.

He had never actually seen a Darhel before. Usually he had reported through Worth, but had had an emergency contact number to use when his immediate superior had dropped off the map sometime between Thursday and Monday of last week.

"We received your message." The voice was just beautiful. Hypnotic. Almost like music. He could have listened to it all day long, but Johnny hadn't gotten where he was without learning to recognize a slick talker when he heard one. He blinked in the dim light as his eyes adjusted, making out the cloaked figure behind the very large desk. It looked like a bit of a muzzle, like a coyote, or maybe a fox, protruded from the hood. He caught a small glimpse of sharply pointed teeth that didn't quite fit right with the plate of vegetable looking stuff that sat to one side on the desk. Scattered small bits of green on the desk surface gave the impression that the alien was not a particularly neat eater.

"Yes, Your Tir. And I got your summons. What can I do for you?"

"We have come to the reluctant conclusion that our junior colleague, the human Worth, has met with a misfortune. This leaves us with an opening in a certain position. A position we feel someone with your talents may be able to fill."

"You mean you need someone to coordinate your hits?"

"We need someone to provide services managing awkward problems." The Tir's voice was tense, and now sounded more angry than melodic.

"Awkward problems like annoying people that need to be killed and gotten out of your way?"

"That . . . that of course would be entirely up to you," the alien squeaked. Fuckin' coward.

"Right. I'd need a raise for that. It's riskier than what I've been doing."

"If . . . if you . . . no, if *someone* were to periodically submit a request for reimbursement for reasonable expenses *somehow* incurred in *something* that is in our interests, reimbursement would . . . would be ordered." The alien was breathing deeply and shakily, as if even saying the words bothered him. These damned Elves were all cowards. That was why they had to hire real men to do their dirty work. Johnny wasn't above getting a little of his own back on the aliens by rubbing their noses in it a little.

"So when I have some sumbitch killed for you, you want me to tell you how much I paid the guy, then you pay me plus my cut. Say, fifteen percent on top."

"We . . ." It squeaked to a stop, shaking, and was silent a moment before trying again. "We believe you should . . . should use your best judgment, and are willing to pay you a seven percent overage on all service associated expenses."

"Ten."

"As you say," it gasped, taking a silent moment to get its breathing under control.

"Then you've got a deal. You tell me who's in your way, I send somebody to wax 'em, I get my percentage. Works for me."

"This . . . this conversation never took place," it choked.

"Okay, Your Tir. Johnny Stuart's your man."

"Wait." He choked, taking a few moments to breathe deeply. After several long seconds he looked back up and fixed Johnny in the eye. His voice had resumed its melodious character and was almost caressing as he spoke.

"The trouble with humans, Mr. Stuart, is that they are incredibly poor at maintaining the proper decorum around their betters."

He addressed his AID, "AID, display Martin Simpson hologram, download full file to Mr. Stuart's AID." He looked back up and very deliberately made fixed eye contact again. "Mr. Simpson is a perfect example of that lack of decorum, and it is unacceptable. You may demonstrate your understanding of our arrangement by handling the problem. You may go, now."

"Yes sir, Your Tir." He walked out the door, restraining the urge to whistle. Damned alien cowards. But he made a good living out of them. You wanted to make a bundle, you had to work for the men, or whatever, on top.

His AID, which was admittedly a damned nifty gadget, was disguised as a regular PDA, and seemed to think there was something funny about aping the behavior of one of the lesser devices. He had barely gotten out of the building and down the block towards the valet deck when it started alternately beeping and vibrating at him.

"What?" he asked the thing, irritably. Machines shouldn't have a damn sense of humor.

"The Tir instructs you to find out what happened to the human Worth."

"Gotcha. Now cut that out!" After giving his ticket to the attendant, he propped himself against a pole and waited for them to bring his car around. A promotion and a raise. Not a bad day. Not bad at all. He hadn't much liked Worth before. He liked him a lot better now.

"Oh, Leanne," he asked the AID, "by the way, what does 'decorum' mean?"

"Decorum: politeness, the observance of proper protocol or etiquette," it said.

"Okaaay. So what did this Marvin Smith do to piss the Tir off so badly?"

"Martin Simpson. Employee of Terra Trade Holdings. I think the offense was telling a Darhel joke in a staff meeting." The AID's voice was unusually dispassionate.

"Jesus H. Christ! What the hell was the joke?"

"How many Darhel does it take to change a light bulb?" The voice playing from the AID was a young male, pure Chicago, "Twenty-one. One to change the bulb, and twenty to curl up and die in the corner at the cost."

"Okay," he chuckled, "what else did he do?"

"Nothing. Well, he did take home a pen from the office once."

"I'm supposed to kill a guy for making a bad joke?" He paled briefly. *Poor bastard. Still, better him than me or mine. Shit. Lord, remind me not to needle Darhel.*

"That would be an interpretation consistent with the Tir's request."

"Yeah. Okay. He's the boss. Thanks, Leanne." *And I hope you report that polite answer to your real boss soon, you spying bucket of bolts.*

Charleston, Tuesday, May 14

Cally spent Tuesday morning shopping for the extras she'd need in her pack and case. While most seafood going inland was canned or frozen at the big Greer's processing plant, monopoly pricing made it barely affordable for a small fleet of vans carrying live delicacies like fresh crab, scallops, and oysters to make a reliable profit selling to restaurants for the wealthy, well-connected, or families enjoying the occasional special occasion. While technically a violation of the National Emergency Food Supplies Act, the trade survived and even thrived largely because federal inspectors liked fresh seafood as well as anyone. Their share didn't really add more overhead than the old prewar health inspections had, anyway. It was a perfect way to travel anonymously.

She could take the bus, but the middle seat in a live crab van was not only more discreet but would be cheaper, especially for someone who was young, pretty, and friendly. Not that money was a problem, it just made a good excuse for preferring a fishy van over the bus.

The bright, new beach T-shirts and some garish souvenirs fit the picture of an inland coed who'd spent too much on vacation.

After lunch she found a pay phone and dialed the number Shari had provided.

It answered on the first ring, "Cally?"

"Hi, Granpa."

"You're a bit late," he reproached. "Trouble finding a phone?"

"*I'm* late?" she choked. "Yeah, *five* minutes, not three hours and *forty*-five minutes."

"Um ... yeah." He cleared his throat and was silent for a few seconds. "We had no idea the damned Elves had that kind of jammer deployed with any of their human people. I know he was modest about it in the debrief, but the algorithm our largest friend put together on the fly to filter out the false images was nothing short of genius—until then, you could have been anywhere in the city as far as we knew. You would have found us before we found you. If it's any consolation, you improvised brilliantly."

"It's a living. What did you want to talk to me about? And why a telephone, of all things?"

"People do still use them, you know," he said wryly. "It's still the most popular means of talking over a distance."

"And insecure as hell. Quit dancing, Granpa, what's up?" She added suspiciously, "This doesn't have anything to do with Wendy and Shari cornering me for purposes of matchmaking, does it?"

"Well, not ex. . . ." He stopped and started again, "I don't think there's anything wrong with wanting to see some great-grandkids before I die."

"Talk to Michelle."

"You know damn well why I can't." He sighed. "I just don't know what the problem is. For awhile I thought if I just waited . . . and you seem to like kids well enough. Honey, I just don't have a whole lot of wait left."

"Well, I'm sorry," she sounded a hair more indignant than sorry, "but I just haven't found the right man. What I do have is a job, an important one that not just anybody could do, and I'm damned good at it!"

"You can't let a job take the place of a life!" She could hear him take a deep breath and sigh, "It's eating you up, and it's not good for you. There are plenty of fine men out there, and plenty of places other than bars to meet them."

"Now wait just one fucking minute, I may *look* twenty, but I'm . . ."

"Cally, I don't want to fight," he interrupted. "I know you're a grown woman, and I love you. Just . . . think about it, okay?"

"Okay, fine." She took a deep breath and let it out slowly. "Actually, I'm taking a vacation for a week. I've got our next mission brief, can't share, but we'll have more than enough time to put it together after my trip. In fact, you take care of rounding everybody up and meet me at the wind farm at eight A.M. on the twenty-third. I love you. I'll be in touch, okay?"

"Vacation? About time. Where to?"

"I haven't decided. I'll decide each day as I go," she reasoned. "If I had to plan it, it wouldn't be a vacation. Are you clear on meeting me?"

"Yeah, yeah, eight and twenty-three. You're really not going to tell me where you're going, are you?" He sounded a bit put out.

"Nope. Love you, Granpa. Bye."

She hung up the phone and grinned at the receiver for a minute before picking her bags up off the sidewalk and taking them to the car. Her mouth tightened for a minute. *Okay, so it's a working vacation. I can't believe they've been protecting the son of a bitch. Hell, yes I can. Fucking pragmatists. Okay, so I'm no dewy-eyed idealist, myself, but there have to be standards.*

She spent the rest of the afternoon and evening cracking the public records of Sinda Makepeace—DMV, credit, frequent shopper cards, the property-management files for her apartment complex, internet postings. Jay and Tommy would do a more thorough job next week, but since she couldn't brief them in yet, she might as well get a head start on the easy stuff now.

A couple of hours with the buckley running pattern analyses and she had a tentative character profile to start building the role.

"So, do you think you could manage to do a full backup on me before we go off on this mission? No reason for both of us to die, is there?"

"Shut up, buckley."

"Right."

Next came the prelims for her vacation mission. The target was not much of a player, so it should be an easy job, but Cally was habitually thorough in prepping for a mission. It was the main reason she was still alive.

Having memorized Petane's facial features years ago, when she was young and eager and fully expected to be handed the mission, it was a simple matter of self-hypnosis to bring the details back to the surface. He could have been changed, but if he had been it was likely that Robertson would have said so. *If Robertson's telling me the truth and not playing his own game, that is.*

A three-D facial modeling application let her put the face into a form the system could use. From there it was a simple hack to download the bank camera records for Chicago ATMs and set another little utility sifting through the images for matches.

Normally, she would have left a bank hack to Jay, but she hadn't been in this business for thirty-plus years without learning a few tricks outside her own specialty. Sure, she got a load of false positives first run-through, but she was able to identify one true hit in the first dozen and fed it back to the facial app, modified it and ran it through again. That eliminated half the hits. Going through those for a few more true positives and refining the app again got her down to a couple of hundred true positives, from which she weeded a handful of false positives and doubtfuls by hand. Loading those into a database and running a third app, telling the buckley to assume a standard Monday through Friday daytime schedule localized his work to a probable area of a few blocks and his home to one of two possible areas. One was probably the home of a girlfriend. A quick look at a map made the probable work location the Fleet Strike Tower. *Well, Robertson was telling the truth about that much, anyway. The scumbag sure doesn't look dead to me. That's fixable. I'd love to crack his accounts for a full profile, but there's way too much risk of leaving tracks. I would really prefer for my bosses to get used to the idea of Petane being dead before I fess up to the hit. If I ever do. Hrms. Isn't that interesting. He was never taken off the Targets of Opportunity list—just automatically flagged inactive when he was entered as dead.* She took a risk and hacked the Illinois tag database to get the make, model, and tag number of his car, and downloaded the analysis results and raw hits onto a cube, setting it not to erase after the first reading. It was a calculated risk, but in a pinch her own stomach acid would destroy the cube as effectively as the more usual glass of vinegar.

"Congratulations! You've come up with a fabulously inventive new way to get us killed. Have you even considered the possibility that this might be a *really* bad idea?"

"Shut up, buckley."

"Right."

Under a cornfield in Indiana, Wednesday, May 15

Indowy quarters were about a fourth the size of quarters for a normal human. It wasn't that they were agoraphobic, exactly. It was just that they felt much more secure in groups. Still, Aelool had made the sacrifice of having a room by himself because of the necessity of occasionally entertaining humans. Even in Chicago Base, most of the Indowy would rather not deal with carnivores unless the meeting was necessary, except for the few human children apprentices in Sohon whose families had been carefully selected even among the Bane Sidhe for adaptability. The human children were vegetarians. It wasn't exactly their fault that they had been born in a species that hadn't abandoned its carnivorous roots yet.

His solitary quarters also seemed more comfortable for human visitors, who tended to be okay in duos or small groups, but had an unfortunate tendency to react badly to crowds. The few scholars who had studied their history, despite a natural distaste for the violent subject matter, were about evenly divided, after observing human behavior in crowds of their own species throughout history, about whether humans were pathological loners or closet xenophobes. He tended to lean towards the former hypothesis, and acted on it. It had worked well for him so far. Honestly, so long as you kept them out of crowds, many humans were basically okay people.

At the moment, he was preparing for his most frequent visitor, Nathan O'Reilly, who had been entrusted with the care of the main base of Bane Sidhe operations on Earth. Although most information gathering and other operations were best handled through a cell system, once you got above a certain level of complexity, a certain bureaucracy was inevitable. O'Reilly's particular philosophical discipline required that he not marry and bear offspring, so he had no clan to speak of, but his learning and position equated to a sort of senior elder. Aelool respected him. They had a mutual passion for logic games, and Father O'Reilly had been teaching him chess. It would take at least a century to master. Perhaps then he could return the favor and teach his friend aethal.

Proper hospitality towards human visitors required the ritual preparation of a bean broth highly prized among their species. He had learned the art from the best expert he could find. A perfectly clean pot and apparatus, a tiny pinch of salt, run the beans, which could be purchased dried and preroasted, through a coarse grinding machine, bottled spring water, add the components to the right parts of the machine, and it prepared the soup perfectly every time.

He did not understand how water could have a season, but when he ordered it from Supply, they always knew what he meant, so he chose not to argue.

Aelool had learned that some chess sets were more abstract than others. The one he had chosen had pieces of wood, carved in intricate detail. He liked the horse. He had met them a couple of times. They weren't quite sophonts, but he would like to have one in his quarters-group some day, if they could be bred small enough.

When everything was ready for his guest, he sat quietly for a few minutes, working on the design for his latest project. When the light shifted slightly yellow-ward, announcing the scholar's arrival, he put the project away quietly and keyed the intercom.

"It's open," he said.

"Aelool, how are you this afternoon?"

"I'm fine," he offered the ritual greeting. "May I get you some coffee?"

"Yes, please. Black."

The Indowy placed a cup of coffee and a glass of water, with an olive, on the tray. Actually, the coffee was not black. It was a dark brown. And adding fat and nutrient-fortified mammalian sweat did not make it white, but more of a light brown. He had noticed humans tended to exaggerate such things.

They began their chess game. He had white—which was, in this case, actually white—so he opened the game. Currently, he was learning the variations on the knight's gambit. As they played, O'Reilly updated him on the current state of Earth operations.

"Worth won't be easy for them to replace. Most of the combat vets around are used to killing Posleen, not fellow humans. Sure, they still have the professionals he recruited and trained, but the Darhel have always tended to rely on data mining and hacking for intelligence more than actual sophont operatives or agents. Their training systems are weak, and any loss hurts."

"I am more concerned about the leak. We need concealment. The plan is very long term, and premature exposure could defeat it."

"Team Isaac has an impressive success rate."

"They had better."

CHAPTER FOUR

Charleston, Wednesday, May 15

It was a few minutes before six and the edges of the scattered clouds were a brilliant pink when Cally got off the city bus at the Columbia gate of the Wall. She had her backpack, one rolling suitcase, and had teamed an old pair of cutoff shorts with a T-shirt, complete with garish beach sunset, and a bright yellow Folly Beach visor. She wore an expression of slightly desperate hopefulness as she scanned the vehicles lining up for the morning convoy. She started towards a rather battered white van, but one scowl from the female driving it had her looking for another. Towards the end of the line she spotted a VW van that must have been damn near eighty years old. The tie-dyed patterns painted on the panels showed different degrees of fading, but had also clearly been carefully touched up over the years. The skull with roses coming out of the top was absolutely perfect, as was the lovingly painted legend that she knew even before she got far enough past the other vehicles to see all the words.

Before approaching, she took care of the buckley, turning voice access and response off and running the emulation all the way down to two, tucking it back into her purse. Wouldn't do to have him saying the wrong thing at the wrong time.

The driver had long, blond hair and a full mustache and well-combed beard. He was built like a small bear. As she approached, she could detect a faint whiff of oak leaves and patchouli over the salt and fish from the tanks in back. The music from his cube player reached a good way from the open window and his fingers were tapping to the beat on the sill. " . . . gotta tip they're gonna kick the door in again. I'd like to get some sleep before I travel . . ."

"Hey, *bitchin'* shirt. You surf?" He noticed her as she dragged the suitcase up.

"I've caught a coupla waves here and there. But I usually head out to L.A. for that. For the waves here, I didn't even bring my own board. Didn't have the cash or the time to go out that far this trip."

"Bummer," he sympathized. "Too much of everything's about money, man. But you gotta make a living, so what can you do. You ridin' out on the bus?"

"Well, actually, I was kinda hoping I could find somebody I could hitch a ride with. I spent a little too much and I could afford the ticket, I just, you know, would have to go real light on meals till I got back to campus."

"Oh man, that sucks, say no more." He leaned over and unlocked the passenger side door. "By the way, I'm Reefer. Reefer Jones."

"Marilyn Grant. Thanks, dude." She lugged her suitcase around the front of the car, stowed it behind the passenger seat, tucked her pack in the floorboard under her feet, and got in, carefully not wrinkling her nose at the salty, fishy smell.

"Oh, we've gotta figure out some way to square you with the paperwork," he grimaced apologetically. "Sorry, but my boss can be a pain in the ass about hitchhikers. Hey, I don't suppose you can shoot, can you?"

Cally fumbled in her purse and handed him a very sincere range certification from a local Charleston range, dated a few days ago, rating Marilyn Grant an expert, non-resident.

"I went on a lark. Hadn't shot in years, but my mom made me learn, you know?" she said.

"Yeah, mine too. I think the war like affected that whole generation. But it was okay, I mean, if I ever meet a steel Postie pop-up target, I'll know how to kill it." He laughed and scribbled something on the clipboard. "Okay, I put you down as a freelance guard. The boss'll be cool with that. Lived in Urbs his whole life, came to Charleston for the money, man, old fart is scared to death of Posties." He shrugged, easing the van up in the line that was finally beginning to move. "I've been drivin' this route for five years and there's never been a Postie get close that those guys," he gestured to the machine-gun turret mounted on the top of an eighteen wheeler, "didn't saw in half before it even got close to us."

"Does that happen often?" Her eyes were round.

"Nah." He offered her a stick of gum, popping one in his own mouth. "About every other run. It's a pain in the ass because then the whole convoy has to stop while they take the head for the bounty." He made a gagging gesture. "Well, we usually don't actually stop. They just lose their place in line and we slow down a bit." He gestured to the trucks again. "Every one of those guys has a boma blade tucked away up there, so it doesn't really take any time at all."

They had pulled up to the gate while he was talking, and he handed the guard her range card and his own, showing the guard the Colt .45 by his seat and the second one in the glove box. "The boss won't mind you because the extra shooter drops our convoy fee." He shrugged and took their cards back from the guard, handing her hers and tucking his own back in his wallet.

It took another fifteen minutes for the guards to clear the other vehicles and the group to begin the drive back to real civilization.

"Next stop, Columbia." He cranked the volume on the stereo slightly, glancing at her curiously. "So where are you headed, anyway?"

"Cincy."

"Oh. Well, you can, like, ride the whole way then. That's cool." He looked uncomfortable for a minute. "I'll just have to pretend you got out in Knoxville, when the convoy zone ends."

"Will I get you in trouble?"

He thought a minute and shook his head. "Nah, not really. The boss isn't too bad a guy. If he finds out I'll just tell him it was part of your fee for riding guard from here to Knoxville."

"So what do you haul?" she asked politely, glancing over her shoulder into the back of the van where several packed aquariums bubbled away, air exchanges sticking up several inches above the sealed lids.

"Blue crab. Like, live, you know? Buncha rich dudes in Chicago like their fresh seafood." He shrugged.

"So why you and why not one of them?" She waved at the lines of semis ahead and behind them.

"Oh, like, it's a niche market. They're carrying frozen stuff, and, well, some of 'em have iced down live oysters and clams and stuff. Crabs are just incredibly fussy about live travel. But a little of the right stuff in the water so they aren't too crabby," he grinned, "and you can pack a lot of the little buggers into the tanks."

"So, what, they're too drugged up to rip each other to bits? What's that do to them as food?"

"Basically," he agreed cheerfully. "Like, put 'em in a clean, salt-water tank and in like six hours or so they're clean. And crab valium doesn't really affect humans, anyway, you know?"

She politely ignored that the inner dimensions of the back of the van seemed to her practiced eye to be just a bit smaller than the outside would normally indicate.

Business out of the way, he seemed more inclined to listen to his music than chat. That suited Cally fine. It must have been ten years since she'd had the time or need to take the overland route out of Charleston and she let her eyes glaze over watching the miles and miles of pine forest, punctuated by the occasional burn zone and abat-meadow.

It was only as they approached Columbia a couple of hours later that the now mixed pine and hardwood forests gave way to cleared fields of cows and crops, each field bordered by widely spaced sensor poles.

"I guess the bounties cover the costs of the sensors and the power to run them," she said.

"Those bounty farmers are some strange birds. Get at least half their money off stalking bounties, spend half of that fighting the abat and grat. Real loner kinda dudes. Then there was one of 'em about fifteen years ago went totally off his nut and got caught *breeding* Posties. It was before my time, but he'd had a Postie God King next to his land. Seems he'd made a deal with it to deliver heads of Postie normals just up from nestlings in exchange for half the take. It was, like, really *nasty* what they did to him when they caught him."

"How'd they catch him?" she asked politely, since Marilyn wouldn't remember the story.

"He was always delivering twice the bounty of the other guys around him. I guess somebody just got suspicious. Next time the Postie God King made delivery, they had surveillance on him and everything." He stuck a fresh piece of gum in his mouth. "What was real weird was when they traced the Postie back to where it had been living. Man, it was like a freakin' magpie's nest. Tinfoil, polished pennies, chromed bike bars and car parts and stuff, even some gold. The Postie must have been bughouse nuts, too. I mean, what are the odds." He shrugged and they drove on in silence until the convoy began to slow as the front vehicles reached the gate into Columbia Trading Station.

Entry through the gates was much faster than exit from Charleston had been. The Columbia guards obviously wanted to keep the gates open as short a time as possible, admitting the entire convoy and closing the big steel slab behind them before beginning the paperwork.

As he waited his turn to sign in he waved across the large parking lot to a squat building with gas pumps in front of it. One of the tankers in the line had pulled around to the side of the building and was unhooking hoses.

"I've gotta top off my gas after I get through here. It's just the way they do this convoy thing. Won't let you leave unless you're full. If you want to go stretch your legs or buy a drink or, like, other stuff, this is the last stop until Spartanburg Station in three hours."

As a tourist, goggling was normal, so she took the opportunity to get a good long look at everything while she went up to the station building to wait in line for the restroom. The place hadn't changed much in ten years. The asphalt of the big parking lot had been resurfaced at some point, but not too recently. They hadn't expanded the walls any—it would have just been more perimeter to man in an emergency. Oh, the store was stocked a bit better, and there were a few more children trailing around with the occasional farm wife doing some shopping, but mostly it was the same old general store, feed and seed, and bounty processing center. She bought a glass of apple cider and some gingersnaps and went back out into the parking lot. The single mechanic's bay was taken up with work on a tractor today. Fortunately no one in the convoy seemed to need it. Over by the incinerator the bounty agent was paying off on a few Postie heads. She wrinkled her nose as the shifting wind wafted over the unforgettable stench of ripe, dead Poslcen mixed with motor oil and exhaust fumes. She took her snack back towards the van, farther away from the grisly trophies, walking past one of the refrigerator trucks that was offloading a few crates of fish and perishables for the station store and loading some crates of spring greens and assorted poultry and dairy products. A semi was unloading a couple of crates of miscellaneous merchandise but, not being refrigerated, had nothing to take on to fill the space left.

She looked around at the various trucks and buses, and the occasional car, and sighed. It would probably be at least fifteen minutes before they got moving again, and there just wasn't a lot more to see. She pulled out her PDA and spent the rest of the break clicking through the daily news.

The road to Spartanburg seemed quiet enough, the scenery by the side of the interstate passing from fields and cows near Columbia to dense stands of pine and poplar starting a few yards back from the Roundup zone. The edges of the highway had earned the popular appellation from the tanker truck that came through at the back of the convoy every few months with a sprayer attachment to mist the roadside with the inexpensive herbicide. Federal authorities had decided early on that it was easier, cheaper and safer than lawnmower crews for maintaining a small but adequate free-fire zone back from the road. In the spring, runners from the underbrush reached back quickly to reclaim the tempting open soil and ready sunlight—it looked like another run with the sprayer truck was a bit overdue.

The tender vegetation at the border was especially attractive to the herds of whitetail, who were no doubt accustomed to safe feeding times morning and evening when neither the convoys nor other traffic disturbed their peace. Predation by the occasional feral Posleen kept the herd barely below starvation levels. Healthy deer could usually smell, hear, and outrun a lone Posleen normal. Unfortunately for the deer, this fact failed to stop feral normals from trying. This became clear to the convoy when a yearling buck broke cover right in front of a church van from Nashville, causing it to slam on its brakes and take a bump from the semi behind it that could almost, but not quite, stop in time.

The first indication Cally had that something was wrong was the crunch of metal behind them and the chattering of a machine gun, it sounded like one of the MG-90s on top of the semis. She grabbed the .45 from the glove box while Reefer swore and swerved as the bus in front of them hit the brakes and stopped in the middle of its lane, the van coming to a more gradual stop alongside the bus's driver. All along the length of the convoy, the approximately thirty vehicles that comprised it were pulling to a stop, the drivers and gunners first looking for Posleen, and then, seeing none, checking their detectors and getting on the radios onto channel nineteen for official convoy information.

"Front door, this is truck seventeen." The female voice had a distinctly Texan drawl. "We got one dead Postie, one dead medium passenger vehicle, and some minor vee-hicular injuries back here. Negative on Postie emissions and high grade equipment. Negative crest. Just another feral normal. We're gonna need a EMT and someplace to put 'em, 'cause their van ain't goin' nowhere, come on." Reception was extraordinarily clear for the simple reason that there was so little to compete with it. Oh, there was a little crackle from sunspots and other unavoidable whatnot, but it was a surprisingly cheap method of keeping a convoy together. Besides, it was traditional.

"Ten-four, Seventeen. Johnny, you got your ears on?"

"Ten-four, Front Door. Got my little black bag and I am on the way, come on."

"Ten-four. Seventeen, get the healthies squared away along the line and have Johnny call me back once he's got the bleeders stashed, come on."

"That's a big ten-f—Larry, quit messing with that thing. You can load the head up *after* we get them church folks on the . . . oops. This thing's still on. Sorry Front Door, over."

"Hey, uh, Marilyn?" Reefer had walked around to the right side of the bus where she was standing with her back against it, looking outward. "Might as well get back in and put that thing in the glove box, man. I mean, like, I know it's pretty bogus to have one of those Postie dudes running out on the road and all, but honest, there's like never been more than one at a time as long as I've been driving."

Cally walked back to the van, looked at the sensor on the dash and climbed back in. She didn't put the pistol back in the glove box, but Reefer just shrugged and popped another piece of gum. Even twenty years ago the convoy would have circled up, instead of remaining sprawled out like a lunch line of gawking kindergartners. Their complacency made the back of her neck itch, but as she watched the negative sensors on the dash and her PDA screen, tied into the roadside sensor net, the combat-chill gradually leached its way back out of her system and time resumed its normal flow.

It seemed longer, of course, but it was actually only about ten minutes later that the convoy got rolling again, one van shorter but with no human fatalities. On the far side of the highway, just inside the tree line, a yearling whitetail buck placidly browsed through the fresh growth.

Spartanburg's Trading and Bounty Station was very much like Columbia's. The upstate city hadn't been part of Fortress Forward and so the buildings had survived in varying states of destruction and disrepair from Posleen looting and local self-destruct systems. But vacancy during the Posleen occupation and the relatively slow pace of human reclamation had taken its toll on the prewar portions of the city. The station was not, strictly speaking, part of the original prewar city. Instead, one of the least-damaged truck stop and gas station clusters had been repaired, an incinerator and sufficient electrical generation to fuel the station installed, along with the necessary water tower and septic system. The Federal Bureau of Reclamation had walled and manned the resulting facility, along with a few neighboring buildings, hauled in a double-wide to house the staff, and called it a day.

The biggest difference in the routine at Spartanburg was the line at the pay radio as the members of the group from Nashville called friends and family back home.

The station residents were clearly used to their station being the lunch stop on the convoy route. One of the buildings inside the walls was a salvaged prewar short-order grill. Over the years, the sun had faded the plastic around the flat roof of the building to a dingy yellowish-cream. The steel pole that had once carried a lighted sign had been extended and was now home to the station's radio antenna.

The parking lot of the restaurant had been filled with ancient picnic tables of various materials obviously scrounged locally. Perhaps a third were of clearly postwar construction, made of split and roughly sanded pine logs. A handful of teenage girls in jean shorts and T-shirts waited on the tables. Cally's omelet was tough and overpriced, though the waitress was obviously eager to please, refilling her water frequently and offering a smile that was tacit apology for the food.

"If you want something that's actually good to get the taste out of your mouth, try a small jar of pickled peaches from the store over there. One of our neighbors puts them up, and they're actually good. I mean, if you like peaches."

"Thanks, I will." Cally smiled, noticing the girl's wistful glances at her PDA.

"You're a college student ain't . . . aren't you? That must be wonderful." She fielded a dirty look from another girl who was moving a bit faster.

"Yeah, I like it. Where are you planning to apply?"

"It wouldn't do no good." The girl flushed. "They don't take you if you're out of state, unless you've got money."

"I know a lot of out of state students. And there are scholarships."

"You gotta pass tests. I checked." She glared briefly as the other girl moving back by with a stack of empty plates made a rude noise. "I bet none of your out of state friends are bounty farm brats, are they?"

"If you can't pass the tests, read and study until you can."

The girl laughed tonelessly. "Library." She indicated the bounty agent's trailer. "Two shelves of pre-war encyclopedias and a dog-eared copy of *Leather Goddesses of Phobos*."

"You're kidding." Cally's jaw dropped.

"Nope." She grinned tightly. "Well, unless you count the porno mags under Agent Thomas's bed. I've been that bored. Oop, gotta go. Try the peaches." She shrank a bit from the face of the middle-aged woman looking out the plastic and duct tape "window" of the grill and began rapidly collecting empty dishes and silverware.

Cally stared after her for a moment before rummaging in her backpack for a battered paperback copy of *Pygmalion* and staring at it a moment.

I can always get another prop. She tucked the girl's tip in the inside cover and finished her water, making her way to where the waitress was returning for another load. Her mouth tightened at the reddening print on the girl's face and her hot eyes. She pressed the book into the girl's hand.

"Never give up," she told her firmly, grabbing her chin gently and pulling her face around for eye contact. "*Never* give up. Not ever. You *will* make it out."

The teenager paused for a second, looking at the other woman as if she had sudden sneaking suspicion that she was far older than twenty, whatever else she may have been. She smiled grimly and tucked the book into her front pocket where it was bulkier but probably safer, and got back to work.

Cally heard her mutter, "Thanks, ma'am," as she strolled back to the van *exactly* like a student tourist, trying not to visibly berate herself for breaking cover.

Outside the walls, Cally grimaced at the profusion of roadside kudzu. "Hell of an abat hazard, isn't it?"

"What? Like, oh, yeah, totally bogus. Happens a bit in some of these places. If it's not good farmland or right next to your house, it's somebody else's problem. It's a lot of work to get in and clear that stuff and if you're doing that, like, you aren't getting bounties or raising your own crops. Until some poor schmuck gets stung by a grat. There's just totally not enough money in the world to get me to bounty farm, man."

As the land and the road got more hilly, first the small trees and undergrowth rose beside the highway like green walls, then the huge granite cut-throughs and drop-offs passed by as they climbed into the Blue Ridge, which rose in front of them in a great green wall, softened by the afternoon haze. With the changing terrain eliminating the need for a Roundup zone, clumps of grass vied for purchase in the rocky soil with brown-eyed Susans and some small purple flower she didn't recognize. Occasionally she caught a dull orange flash of Virginia creeper, or the more brilliant orange splash of what she vaguely remembered were mountain azaleas. Reefer flipped off the air conditioner and opened the windows to let in the cooler, fresher mountain air. She suppressed the urge to wrinkle her nose at the exhaust fumes from the rest of the convoy and pulled her hair back into a quick ponytail to keep the dark curls from flying around her face.

At one of the cut-throughs you could still see the scraps of exotic rubble where they blew the Wall and relaid the road after the Green River Gorge drawbridge came on-line as part of reopening the route to Charleston harbor.

There was no delay at the drawbridge, the lead truck having radioed ahead the time-synchronized codes to signal the attendant. Cally was reassured to see the unusually alert and attentive man

obviously watching the convoy and all his sensors as the van clat-
tered across the lowered bridge.

After the first exit past the bridge, they started to pass some
local traffic—the occasional ancient pickup truck or SUV from
the mountain communities that, after the great postwar RIF of
the surviving soldiers, had gone back to living mostly as they
had for the past four hundred years. A bit poorer, perhaps, but
for a people who had come to love these highlands as their
ancestors had loved an earlier home, they had their mountains,
and they had their neighbors, and the mild poverty wrapped
around them felt more like a comfortably broken-in and familiar set of work clothes than any true hardship. Their mountains
weren't for the soft, or the greedy, or the lazy, but they had
protected them from a hazard that had gone through softer and
richer peoples like a hot knife through butter. This knowledge
had cemented the locals' attachment to their mountains from a
rough affection to a respectful devotion approaching reverence,
so that rural Appalachia had one of the lowest out-migration rates
on the planet. While the mountain folk knew there were many
places men could live in the modern galaxy, this one was theirs,
and they reckoned they'd keep it.

It was early evening but still quite bright when the convoy
entered Baldwin Gap, home of the Southeast Asheville Urb. Turning
off the Blue Ridge Parkway onto Victory Road, they came into the
valley through the dilapidated remains of forty-year-old fortifications, topped with a mishmash of sensor boxes and transmitters
probably emplaced and maintained by local farmers who were more
interested in protecting their stock than in any bounty. With power,
protection, and ample refrigeration, Asheville was cattle country,
selling much of its lower grade beef to the local Urbs and shipping the better cuts back down to Charleston for the tourists' surf
'n' turf dinners. Her driver, obviously city-bred, had switched back
to closed windows and the AC at the first whiff of rural cow
manure—not that she minded.

The first thing Cally noticed when they came in sight of the
Asheville Urb Vehicle Assembly Zone was the increased number
of people manning the wall and their relative inattention to that
job. Some wore headphones which, judging from the rhythmic
nodding of the wearers' heads were for music rather than information. At one corner of the wall, a female in a guard uniform

was chatting up a male in civvies. One of the more alert guards was standing over the entrance gate facing outward. While she looked out, eyes scanning the hills, most of the time, judging from her hand movements she also appeared to have a game of solitaire going on the top edge of the wall.

"I guess they don't get many ferals this close to civilization," she said, slipping her sandals back on and closing up the novel on her PDA as they drove through the gates.

"Huh?"

"Those were just, you know, some pretty bored looking guards. Not that I have much to compare with. We don't have them back home," she said.

"Oh, yeah," he nodded. "They're like, pretty laid back here, you know? I hung out with a couple of guards on one of my trips through. This girl I talked to said it pays pretty well, and they're feds, so they get good bennies." He swallowed hard and added a fresh piece of gum. "It wouldn't be the gig for me, man. I mean, okay, it's not major stressful or anything, but I just couldn't, like, *handle* being a fed."

"Me neither," she grinned. "So what happens now?"

"Well, like, I gotta wait for this chick from one of the restaurants and, you know, see how much stuff she wants to buy, and put my van down for the convoy out tomorrow. Then I guess, like, food and someplace to crash. Maybe find a party, if, you know, there's one mellow enough that I won't be too fucked up to drive in the morning." He looked sheepish for a minute. "Oh, like, sorry."

"You must come through here a lot. I hate to ask when you've already done so much for me, but could you recommend anywhere to eat and, well, stay that's okay but not too expensive?" she asked, dropping her eyes and scuffing the ground a bit with a foot.

"Oh, like, no problem. I'm, um, meeting a friend, so I'm gonna be like totally out of the net until morning, no offense. Um . . . the cafeteria is totally bogus, so don't even go there. They sell the food in Asheville Urb Calorie Credits, and they seriously scalp you on the exchange rates. Your best bet is probably the mall food court. The Taco Hell was okay the last time I tried it, but that was like a few months ago when I was majorly low on cash. For rooms, I'd tell a guy to take the no-tell motel outside the walls and leave all his stuff in the van, but if I were you I'd honestly pick up an Urbie dude for a one nighter before I did that 'cause it's not exactly your high-rent district." He frowned, scratching his chin through the beard and looking glum. "Shit. Why don't you hang around until Janet gets here? Maybe she can, like, find you some crash space for the night. Urb hostel prices are, like, well, the bogosity is beyond belief, I kid you not."

"Oh, no, it's all right. I don't want to horn in on your date or anything. I mean, I saved the bus fare up here, and I'd planned to stay overnight. I'll be okay." She put a hand on his arm and smiled reassuringly.

"Aw, hang around anyway. You can meet Janet and we can all walk in together. I can at least keep them from cheating you too bad when you rent your hostel room. Oh, 'scuse me." He left her and walked over to a plump, middle-aged woman with a clipboard and a little red wagon with a bucket half full of water.

Cally went back to Marilyn's romance novel on her PDA while Reefer and the restaurateur dickered and made their trade, leaning against the van as strains of music came drifting through the open window. . . . *dog has not been fed in years. It's even worse than it appears but it's all right. Cows giving kerosene, kid can't read at seventeen . . .*

After a bit the older woman dragged her wagon back off, bucket sloshing a bit as she went. Reefer stayed in the back, fiddling quite a while with the tanks while the afternoon sun sank to the edge of the mountains. Finally, he sighed and came around to her side, scratching the back of his head with one hand and looking up at the impending sunset.

"Um . . . look, it would be like a major favor if you could wait here for Janet for a minute while I go sign up for tomorrow's convoy. I mean, like, she knows the van, so if you see her . . . uh, like she's tiny, okay? And she's got straight black hair about down to here, looks about your age. Do you, like, how do I say this? Have you ever heard of the Goths?" he asked.

"What, you mean European Franco-Germanic barbarian tribes from the dark ages?"

"Um . . . no. Not like that at all. Just . . . she wears a lot of black, okay? And silver jewelry. She'll probably be wearing, like, lots of silver jewelry. And she has this really cool Celtic knot kind of bracelet tattooed around one wrist. Like, left, I think. You can't miss her. So, if she like shows while I'm gone, which she probably will, could you tell her I'll be right back?" He bit his lip and craned his neck back over towards the Urb entrance as if he could make her appear just by looking often enough.

"Sure, Reefer, I'll tell her you'll be right back," she said.

"Awesome. Thanks, man." He walked off towards the pack of semis that had made up the front of the convoy from Charleston.

The clouds had turned to brilliant splashes of hot pink, vermilion, and orange by the time Reefer got back with his convoy slot number for the morning. His face fell slightly when he saw there was nobody but Cally at the truck.

"Bogus," he muttered softly under his breath as he opened the driver's side door and grabbed his backpack. "I guess I made us wait for nothing. Sorry, Marilyn. I didn't mean to be a dweeb. Uh, let's go, I guess."

Cally grabbed her own pack without comment and followed him towards the door of the Urb. The parking lot was cracked and potholed in places and clearly needed resurfacing, but the freshly painted lines on the faded asphalt suggested it wasn't on the schedule anytime soon. Even from a distance, she could see that the walls of the entry level of the Urb were covered with graffiti, some fresh, some of which had flaked and started to peel over time, along with the building's own paint.

As they approached the door, a couple in faded jeans and artfully ripped black T-shirts came out and started walking towards them. Reefer seemed to recognize them and missed a step, recovering and starting forward easily. As they reached each other, Cally noted the strain in the smile on his face.

"Well, like, cool. More people. Hi, Janet. Janet, this is Marilyn. Marilyn, Janet." His voice had a slightly desperate edge to it. Cally stepped to his side and put an arm easily around his waist. *Least I can do. He gave me a lift and he didn't do anything obnoxious on the way. Besides, Marilyn's sensitive.*

"Oh, pleased to meet you." Janet tilted her head back to look up at the skinny boy next to her. "Thad, this is that guy I was telling you about, Reefer. He's a really good guy. Reefer, this is Thad."

The kid unwrapped his arm from around her waist to shake Reefer's hand. "Oh, like, cool. Janet says you're a pretty rad painter, dude. Good to meet you."

"Yeah, sure." He clutched the hand Cally had put around his

waist and shot her a grateful look. There was an awkward silence as they looked each other up and down. Thad's red goatee clashed wildly with the electric blue spikes in his black hair. One shoulder, bared where the sleeves had been ripped out of the shirt, sported a tattooed head of a Posleen God King, crest erect, snarling. His forehead tattoo was a bright, metallic gold lightning bolt. His skin had the clear complexion typical of a generation that viewed acne with the same skepticism their grandparents had held for tales of walking through the snow to school in the mornings.

Cally broke the stalemate by pinching Reefer's butt soundly and grinning when he jumped. "Hey, babe, we gonna grab some eats, or what?"

"Hey, Marilyn, like, I appreciate the support but you don't have to do this." Reefer nuzzled her ear, whispering, as they walked down the residential corridors to Janet's suite, staying three steps behind his ex-girlfriend and the new guy.

"Shhh," she placed a finger over his lips, "it's allright."

"We can just go up and check into the hostel, separate rooms and all, and if I look like a dweeb, well, you got me through a real bummer of an evening. . . ."

"Shhh." She stopped him again and nipped his ear whispering, "I'm not offering to do the deed, but I need a place to crash, you need some moral support, just chill out and shut up, okay?" *And not having to check in anywhere is good tradecraft.*

"Hey, you two, get a room," Janet called back over her shoulder.

"We are. Yours," Cally grinned back. "Well, okay, your futon, anyway."

Beyond the inevitable futon, the first thing Cally noticed about the apartment was that the smoke detector inlet had been covered with duct tape, and filters cobbled together over the air vents. The second thing was the portable air scrubber over in the corner, plugged into the wall. The small den was shrunken even further by the dark holographic posters of various musicians and groups that papered most of the wall area. The exception was the square meter on which the thin vidscreen was hung. Black, red, and silver "fantasy fish" with various motifs programmed into their scale patterns swam back and forth in the screensaver program. Cally spotted an ankh, an elder sign (complete with electric blue flame), a spider's web, and a star of David in a circle before she shook herself slightly and resumed cataloging the details of the room.

The futon was set up in couch mode against the wall opposite the monitor. Two rooms led off from the den. One was clearly the bathroom, from the bare Galplas floor. The other had to be the bedroom. A small makeshift kitchen sat on and under a desk in the same corner as the air scrubber. Microwave, big bowl, and gallon jug of water on top, small refrigerator underneath. Various convenience foods were jammed in a mishmash in the shelves of the desk. A clutter of dirty laundry, empty food wrappers, empty cans and bottles, and cube cases covered the floor.

"Y'all like movies?" Their hostess strolled in with sublime indifference and brushed the clutter from one of the two fabric and steel lawn chairs onto the floor, picking up a scattered handful of cubes and sorting through them, looking up at Thad. "Whaddya think, luv, *Lair of the White Worm, Evil Dead II,* or *Night of the God King: The Return?*"

"I dunno." He walked over and opened the fridge and started passing out beer. "Maybe *Lair,* it's pretty cool. Hey, Reefer, do you live up to your name, dude?"

The other man glanced at Cally nervously, but he must have decided it was okay, because he shrugged his backpack off his shoulder and pulled his clothes out onto the floor, pulling out a largish compressed pack vacuum-sealed in clear plastic. Janet perked up, pulling a small plastic scale out from under the futon and tossing the pack on it. "A whole kilo? For us? Damn, Reefer, you did score. Good shit?"

"Like, I shit you not, that is the most righteously awesome Jamaican Blue you will *ever* find coming up the pipeline," he said.

"Not like I'd ever doubt you, dude, but I've heard that before." The girl eyed the package speculatively. "All right, usual price up front, we try it, and if it really is good shit, and I mean *seriously* good shit, say, ten percent of the face over in dollars."

"What, you mean you don't *trust* me? Damn, Janet, haven't I always brought you, like, the most truly fantabulous stuff on the whole route?" He clapped his hand to his chest in an air of injured innocence.

"Yeah, except for that shit cut with oregano," she said.

"Okay, like, *once,* four years ago. And the truly heinous bastard who did it doesn't, like, well, like, he's *gone.* I mean, like totally gone, okay? And that was the *last* time I ever let somebody handle my shit out of my sight. And didn't I make it right on the next trip? Didn't I?"

"Well, yeah, Reef, I'll give you that. Still, *you* didn't have to listen to all the bitching I caught in the meantime. All right, twelve percent face over dollars, then."

"Fifteen, FedCreds," he countered.

"Reef, I gotta be able to sell at a price the customers can afford. You're not the only guy on a convoy, you know. Ten in FedCreds is the absolute best I can do—eleven if you've got another kilo like it. And if it's as good as you said," she allowed.

He smiled slightly and pulled a second bag from the backpack, stacking it on top of the first on the scale. The buyer checked the weight and picked up a bag in each hand, comparing them carefully to make sure they looked the same, before setting them on the floor by the scale, nodding and going back to the bedroom. Cally heard a faint metallic click and the woman came back into the room with a large envelope, counting a mixed pile of dollars and FedCreds in front of her source, then another stack of FedCreds onto a milk crate with a plywood top that obviously served as an end table.

"Hey, Janny, if you're through buying it, can we, you know, smoke some of it now?" Thad asked plaintively, taking the cube she'd dropped beside the chair earlier and popping it into the player below the monitor. "This is such a cool movie. I mean, to watch it, you'd never guess it was based on a book by some *old* dude," he offered knowledgeably. "That's what the credits say, anyway."

The younger man moved a dirty T-shirt and picked up an older hardback from the floor, opening it to the middle, where a section of the pages had been cut away to make a box for rolling papers. Cally tilted her head enough to read *Oliver Twist* on the spine as he set it down and scooted over to hand a stack of papers to his girlfriend.

The girl put the full bag inside an empty, slit the seal with a razor, and took a zipper baggie from inside the milk crate, noticing Cally's raised eyebrows as she stuck a paper on the scale and added a careful amount from it, and an equal amount from the bag she'd just purchased.

"Premium North Carolina tobacco. Best cut there is. My old man's a bounty farmer," she tapped the bag of marijuana with a finger, "but he sure don't grow this. Too bad, but he don't. Good enough source of papers, though."

She rolled it with expert hands, lit it, and took a deep drag, holding it for a moment. She blew the smoke out, tilting her head consideringly and giggled a bit, passing it to her toy-boy.

"Damn, Reefer, you're right. This is some primo shit," she said, and nodded to him. He picked up the stack of FedCreds and stowed them in his pack.

When it was her turn, Cally noticed the two buyers watching her, and Reefer just as carefully *not* watching her. She grinned and took a long pull, holding it as she passed the joint on. The other three people relaxed slightly as Cally let the smoke out, allowing a silly-stupid grin across her face. *Wonderful evening. The only straight in a roomful of stoneds. Well, at least it's the next best thing to anonymous and I don't have to do any of the three. In any sense.*

The movie had played through its preview sequence and Cally scooted back to lean against the futon. At least it was a decent movie, and she hadn't seen it recently. After the second joint made the rounds, Janet pushed the scale and rolling papers away.

"No more for me. The munchies are hell on a woman's figure." She looked Cally up and down critically. "You should probably stop, too, Marilyn. If you don't mind my saying so, you're carrying a teenie bit extra on the hips."

"Oh, I never get the munchies." Cally smiled coolly, amused at the baseless slander.

"Well I do, dude." Thad rummaged in the shelves of the desk and pulled out a bag, sitting back down beside Reefer. "Cheese curls?"

"Hey, sure, dude. Thanks." He was clearly feeling more mellow as the drug took effect, and leaned forward to roll another one, skipping the tobacco.

"Ah, I'm not, like *anal* about weighing the stuff," he laughed at the sour expression on his girlfriend's face. "I love ya, babe, but you're anal."

She threw a cheese curl at him.

Cally sat on the opened futon and stared into the darkness, arms wrapped around her knees. Janet and Thad had gone to sleep, Thad completely out of it and Janet almost straight. Once the third joint had made the rounds, Reefer and Thad had got on like long-lost brothers. The older man now slept the sleep of the stoned, his snores competing with one of his music cubes to cut through the slightly irritating but completely nonintoxicating oak-leaf smoke. She sat in the darkness and didn't know what she felt, whether it was coldness, or numbness, or tiredness. She lay down against his rather odoriferous arm and sighed up at the ceiling. After a whole day of it, she was getting a little tired of Reefer's favorite songs . . . *in again, I'd like to get some sleep before I travel, but . . .*

She heard the snick of the apartment door unlocking and trained instincts must have warned her because she was already rolling off the futon, onto the floor by the door, as the door slid open and the two stocky women in security uniforms stepped through. *What are the odds . . .*

One of them tripped over Cally's outstretched leg as she stood. The world had gone into slow motion as Reefer sat up and began to blink owlishly in the light the other woman had flicked on as she came through the door. Cally tripped over the falling woman, just happening to catch the second one, trying to maintain her balance, and bringing her down as well. On the way down, the top of her forehead "accidentally" bumped into the second guard's temple, hard. Cally rocked back and sprawled on top of the first guard, just happening to be sitting on top of her shoulders, as she held a hand to her head and uttered a plaintive and bewildered cry.

"Ow!" She looked at a disbelieving Reefer blearily as Janet came hustling out of the bedroom. "I bumped my head!"

"Get off me, you stupid cow!" The first guard was swearing viciously. Cally shifted slightly on her shoulder blades and the woman jerked a bit and swore some more. She had clearly fallen on top of her own shock baton. The second woman lay on the floor, unmoving, as Janet, in a pink T-shirt, rushed across the room with a gray plastic pack in her hand and yanked the first guard's slacks away from one hip, jabbing her quickly with a hypodermic. She went limp. The dealer checked for a pulse on the second guard before breathing a sigh of relief and injecting her with another hypo from the pack.

"God, you were lucky. To knock someone out, you have to damn near kill them," she glanced up and down the empty corridor outside the apartment and shook her head slightly, closing the door.

"Ow," Cally repeated plaintively, holding a hand to her head as she got up off of the now unconscious guard and stumbled shakily to the bed.

"What in the hell happened?" Janet demanded, looking from Reefer to Cally and back at the guards on the floor.

"Um . . . I just heard a noise, and it startled me, and I tried to get up, but, well, I tripped. Ow."

"You *tripped*?" she echoed.

"Like, wow. That was the weirdest thing I've ever seen in my life." Reefer was rubbing his chin. "Yeah, Janny, I swear to god she tripped. It was, like, she was trying to keep her balance, and, like, there's no *room* with the futon opened out and all, and they just all went over. Like . . . wow, just wow."

"Do you have some Tylenol? I think I might have twisted my ankle, too."

"Wait a sec, lemme see your eyes." She held Cally's chin with one hand and tilted it up to the light, looking in each eye in turn. "Well, you don't look like you've got a concussion, I guess. Hell, your eyes look better than mine ever do after a night of partying. I think I'm jealous."

"Uh . . . what about them?" Reefer had stood up and hoisted his boxers a bit, obviously torn between looking at the guards and looking for his jeans.

"Uh . . . Tylenol's in the medicine cabinet in the bathroom, go ahead." Janet gestured Cally off before looking back down at the bodies. "Well, they were obviously alone, or we'd all be unconscious and on our way to being locked up now. It's Greer and Walton. They're greedy enough. I think they just wanted to either shake us down or steal the stash outright. Um . . . lemme think a minute."

As Cally left for the bathroom, out of the corner of her eye she saw the other woman walk over to the kitchen-desk, pop something in her mouth, and pour herself a glass of water to wash it down with. She shut the door and used the facilities, flushing a couple of Tylenol down the toilet for good measure, scrunched her hair a bit to look more slept in, and went back to the living room to find Thad and Janet wide awake, if a little less straight than more. Reefer was helping Thad undress the women while Janet was spreading out a couple of blankets on the floor.

"Like, are you sure this is gonna work, Janny?" he bleared, tugging a shirt loose from one arm, then the other.

"Best I can think of. These bitches won't remember a thing, probably since lunch. Dump 'em sixty-nine in a corridor, douse 'em with beer, dump their clothes in the incinerator, the force'll be too busy covering up to ask too many questions. If they'd had the brains to tell anybody where they were going, we wouldn't be having this conversation." She shrugged helplessly and set a couple of cheap beers on the floor next to the blankets. "Just don't douse 'em until we get 'em there, okay, Reef? I don't want my apartment smelling like spilled beer for the next week."

Cally backed against the futon muzzily, bumping the backs of her knees and sitting down, hard, still holding her head.

"Um, can I go back to sleep?" she muttered.

"Uh . . . sure." Janet blinked at her a couple of times, but seemed to dismiss her from her mind as Cally rolled back into bed and pulled the other pillow over her eyes.

Nevis and St. Kitts, Thursday, May 16

Without tourist money to sustain them, many Caribbean island nations had suffered something of a population crash and a certain consequent degradation of environmental assets, to put it kindly, during and after the Posleen war. Nevis and St. Kitts had been fortunate. Or wise, depending on your opinion. A strict policy that allowed immigration before and during the war only in exchange for FedCreds or large sums of dollars had enabled it to stock enough mainland food and Hiberzine to maintain both the original citizens and the select few new ones.

Regrettably, a hurricane that had struck the island had destroyed one of the facilities of Hiberzined patients. It was believed that not even Hiberzine would save a person who had been swept out to sea. Certainly not after the sharks had gotten through with them. The authorities had thus been left with large amounts in hard-currency deposits in the local banks with no next of kin to claim them. Under the circumstances, neither the locals nor the revived patients from the other two Hiberzine facilities had objected too strenuously when the government had poured the largess into postwar capital improvements designed to revive the island's tourist industry. There might not be much tourism in the post-Posleen world, but what there was of it Nevis and St. Kitts wanted, and largely got.

None of this was on the mind of the trim and balding, but otherwise young-looking, man in a speedo, lying under a beach umbrella, enjoying the salt air and a mai tai with one of those little paper umbrellas in it. His mind was instead occupied, as it frequently was, if truth be told, with money. Specifically, with the challenges of acquiring more of it while simultaneously keeping his primary employer safely ignorant of both the source and very existence of his extra funds.

His present location had a lot to do with meeting those challenges. He liked fast cars, big houses, and designer clothes as much as anyone, but those would have been a dead giveaway in his daily life. Instead, he had worked out a compromise that allowed him to use some of his moonlighting income while continuing with other little luxuries he'd come to enjoy. Breathing, for example. So in his daily workaday life, he lived on his inadequate, in his opinion, salary. Then, once or twice a year on his vacations, he dropped off the map. As far as work was concerned, he was a hiking buff who enjoyed roughing it in out-of-the-way places. Actually, of course, he would end up in places much like this one, where he could wear expensive clothes, eat expensive foods, stay in expensive hotels, fuck expensive women, and generally live in the style he preferred. At the end of his vacation, the clothes had to go in some charity bin, which bothered him not a little bit, but it was one of the temporary sacrifices he would just have to make until he could afford to retire. Very anonymously, of course.

A pair of very definitely male legs suddenly blocked his previously entirely satisfactory view of a slim brunette in a monokini. She didn't have much in the way of assets, but what she had was attractively distributed. He squinted up in annoyance at his unwelcome visitor.

"Mr. . . . . Jones. Fancy meeting you here," the other man said. He was slightly built and dressed in swim trunks, but something about his haircut and bearing suggested either a law enforcement or military background. With dark hair and eyes, he looked almost like a late teenaged or early twenty-something kid, but the old eyes marked him as a fellow juv.

"Mr. Smith. Our appointment wasn't supposed to be until tonight." The balding man's voice had a slight edge to it.

"Let's just say I was impatient for your scintillating company, Mr. Jones."

"Well, have a seat, then." Mr. Jones gestured at the sand beside him, favoring the other man with a rather reptilian smile. Impatience could mean money. Money meant beautiful, long-legged women in much more intimate arrangements. He could make time for Mr. Smith.

"Your other information checked out, as I'm sure you knew when you checked your bank balance. This raises the prospect of more business, of course. We would be prepared to pay handsomely, for instance, for an organization name."

"I'm a big believer in job security, Mr. Smith. Too much too soon renders me too replaceable. Or worse, disposable. How about another agent name where you're penetrated?"

"We'd pay one hundred thousand FedCreds for that."

"What?! That's only *half* of what you paid for the last one."

"They don't *know* anything, Mr. Jones. As you doubtless know. We want a little more. We want something in *your* organization, Mr. Jones. Oh, we'll pay for the names of more agents in our organization. Have to do the housecleaning, after all. But we'll pay far more for, well, more. *More*, Mr. Jones. But one hundred thousand FedCreds is a lot of money. Of course we'll understand if you'd rather play it safer and settle for less."

The balding man gritted his teeth as the military man smiled at him. It wasn't a particularly nice smile. It had a knowing element to it that was rather offensive.

"I'll have to think for a bit about what I can offer you in that line."

"I can understand that, Mr. Jones. Just remember that we will pay more for more. And less for less." The man stood and brushed sand from his swim trunks, as if he wasn't used to walking around in clothes that were less than immaculate. "Until tonight, Mr. Jones."

Asheville Urb, Thursday, May 16

Cally sat bolt upright in bed, searching the room as an unknown voice cheerily boomed, "Dude! Rise and shine. Surf's up and it's *gonna* be a *righteous* day!" Reefer groaned and tried to hide under his pillow. She stretched across him and shut his damn PDA off, getting back off of him quickly. At least part of the sleeping deadhead knew it was morning.

"Hey, Reef, convoy time." She shook his shoulder and took his pillow away.

He opened his red-rimmed eyes and bleared at her, blinking, before swinging his legs over the side and pulling on his jeans.

"Morning," he pronounced, "is an unutterably egregious thing."

She tilted her head and looked at him assessingly, pondering the wisdom of riding in a vehicle driven by this man.

"Provigil?" she offered brightly.

"Shit, yes, if you've got any," he said.

She rummaged in her pack a minute and came up with a tablet, pressing it into his hand. His eyes widened when he saw the "C" inscribed in the center of the sky-blue pill.

"You've got some good sources." He dry-swallowed it then grimaced and chased it with some beer left in a bottle from the night before. "This shit's mil-grade."

"Do we have time for me to grab a five-minute shower?" She rubbed the side of her face that smelled like unwashed male, telling her he'd been her pillow in the night.

"If you really mean five minutes and you don't care if I foam my face and brush my teeth while you're in there. I need one too. I'm pretty ripe. Sorry," he said.

"No problem." She snagged her backpack in one hand and went.

Later, as they waited for the convoy to finish assembling and pull out, she drank coffee and munched a protein bar, looking up at the mountain that rose above the Urb. Scott Mountain, the sign said. She didn't know the name of the smaller one to the east, but she could still see the remains of the old defensive works through the trees. Unmanned, now, of course. With each winter the ice must work a bit further into the cracks.

"Thanks for last night," the deadhead interrupted her reverie. "Um . . . Janet says you're, like, welcome to 'trip' at her place, any time."

"I was half asleep." She took a healthy swallow of coffee. "Do I want to know what you did with them?"

"Probably not." He grinned.

"Was it fatal?"

"Oh, hell no! You can't just go around killing cops, no matter how bogus they are. It's, like, unhealthy, man."

"Okay." She shook her head. "Sorry, I'm still not awake. They were *cops*? Are they, like, going to be able to track us down or catch us or something?" She looked around anxiously as if police were about to sprout from the parking lot around them.

"Don't panic." He laid a reassuring hand on her arm. "In forty-two years of my life, I've only been caught twice, you know? And none in the last ten years. Cops are, like, only human."

"Did you have to go to jail?" Her eyes got a little rounder as she looked at him over the rim of her cup.

"Nah. I learned the trade from my mom, like, she was fabulous. She knew the right people, you know? It was, like, expensive as hell, though." He looked off into the distance and popped a fresh piece of gum in his mouth. "My mom said that, like, before the war, the cops and politicians used to be really anal about, you know, what people took to get high. Like, now, though, some of the cops care, but most of 'em are on the take, and you just have to go up the line until you get high enough, and poof, for the right price, it all goes away. But, like, killing cops—they're *still* real anal about that. There's nothing'll make that go away. Or if there is, I don't know it, you know?"

"Quit talkin' about killing people, dude." She shivered delicately. "You're starting to scare me."

"Oh, well, like, yeah." He shrugged, punching in his favorite cube and setting it to shuffle. "Looks like we're starting to move."

She opened her PDA and went back to Marilyn's novel, yawning occasionally at the altitude changes as they moved on out to I-40 and the Smokies.

. . . Never mind how I stumble and fall. You imagine me sipping champagne from your boot for a taste of your elegant pride. . . .

The funny thing about the Smokies was that it didn't matter how many times you'd been through them, they always kind of took you by surprise.

The Blue Ridge was no kind of preparation for the great, sweeping walls of wet, dark rock, almost any of which could have served for wartime fortifications way back when, but none of which had, given the ease and economy of rigging the I-40 tunnel for rapid demolition. Fortunately for the people back in Asheville, it had never been necessary.

There was obviously less time and money spent on road maintenance through here than had apparently been the case in an earlier age. Remnants of netting or fencing or whatever still clung to the bare cliffs above the highway, but the going was far slower than it had to be, because you never knew when you'd have to swerve around a boulder sitting in the middle of the road that nobody had gotten around to moving yet. A few places, probably some of the worst judging from ancient, rusted signs warning of falling rock, had been Galplased over at some point, but judging by the dingy and mottled finish of those surfaces, it had been in the distant past.

After the tunnel and crossing the state line into Tennessee, the road maintenance improved dramatically, but, then, UT had made the Tennessee economy one of the bright spots of postwar Earth. With federal highway funds a thing of the past except in very rare circumstances, like the stretch from Charleston to Green River Drawbridge, a state's plenty or need could be clearly read in its roads.

Coming into Knoxville, she looked up as they reached the Tennessee River, looking out over the water as they crossed the bridge. On the road from Asheville, especially after the exit to Gatlinburg, they'd seen more and more nonconvoy traffic joining into the mix of cars and trucks on the roads. Even midmorning, they slowed surrounding traffic a bit coming into the Asheville Highway exit.

"We're, like, coming up on the end of the convoy up here at Volunteer Park," he said as they pulled off the interstate. "You've been a pretty cool passenger, you know? You're, like, totally welcome to, you know, hang out with me all the way up to Cincinnati, man. You won't, like, technically be a guard or anything, but, like, with no convoy dudes to maybe narc on me to my boss for having a passenger, it, like, doesn't really matter anymore. I can always say I dropped you off in Knoxville, you know?"

The parking lot was freshly paved and recently painted, and large enough to accommodate about twice as many vehicles as the present convoy. The park had a couple of ball fields, vacant in the middle of a school day, and, surrounded by a handful of cedars and well-tended flower beds, a brightly colored playground where a few mothers watched a gaggle of toddlers and small children swarm over the climbing gym and slides. Two of the little girls, in shorts and T-shirts, one with wispy child-blond hair and the other with tangled light-brown curls, were busily building a sand castle in a sandbox shaped like a giant turtle.

"So, like, if you need to take a leak or anything, you might want to hurry and get in line before the bus unloads, you know?"

When Reefer spoke, she jumped slightly as if for a moment she'd forgotten where she was, looking at him blankly as he continued, "It'll only take me a couple of minutes to check out from the convoy list and get my deposit back, and then we can, like, really make up some time. Gotta have the convoy for safety but, damn, it's slow."

He shooed her out the door and as she hurried across the parking lot to beat the rush, she saw him walk off towards the circle of drivers gathering around the convoy master.

The restrooms were in a strictly utilitarian cinderblock building, but there was a whole line of them. Having beaten the bus, she didn't have to wait. *Never miss a chance to eat, sleep, or pee goes double when you're female—at least for the last bit.*

She checked her reflection in the mirror. The perm was, as expected, holding up well. Contacts were fine, but she'd want to take them out and clean them tonight. Nail polish was chipped and needed a touch-up—bad.

She got back to the van before Reefer did, so she sat down on the back bumper and took out the rose nail polish. She made her hand shake very slightly to keep the inexpert effect going. When he got back a minute or two later, they were already dry.

Back in easy wireless range, she downloaded another couple of novels while he checked his tanks. "I've got one stop downtown, you know? We can, like, grab some food in Lexington."

"I was surprised you sold off any of your stock in Asheville. I mean, wouldn't they pay more in Chicago? I know what I'd pay for live blue crab in Cincy, if I could find it."

"Oh, well, like, they would. This dude, I make the detour because he's a friend, but he pays Chicago prices just like anybody, you know? The rest of the way, I call ahead when I know about what time I'm coming through, and, you know, if they want any they meet me at an exit and make the buy. But really, almost all of it goes all the way there. If it weren't for the big money stock trader and banker dudes, there just wouldn't be enough demand to pay for the route."

As they drove into downtown on I-40, the view of the Knoxville skyline made a nice change from farms and mountains, even blurred as it was by a gentle haze of smog.

"What's with the giant microphone?"

"Huh? Oh, like, you mean the tower with the ball on top? Yeah, man, I guess it does look a bit like an old-timey microphone. It's way pre-war. It's, like, left over from some prewar 'World' something or other, you know?" He pulled onto 158 and headed for the riverfront

"Oh. That's kind of neat. Where's your friend's restaurant?"

"Oh, like right on the river. Awesome place, got a dock and everything."

"Is there something wrong with my eyes, or has everything gone suddenly orange?" Once they turned onto West Cumberland, the streets had suddenly sprouted big orange streamers and balloons with a silver atom symbol blazoned on them. They drove under a large orange banner that spanned the street, proclaiming "AntimatterFest '47!" Another welcomed them to historic downtown Knoxville, "Birthplace of the Antimatter Age!"

"Aw, man!" he groaned. "I forgot! They go, like, totally nuts for this thing. Parking will just be hell." He scratched his head and thought for a minute. "Can you drive?"

"Oh, sure. . . . Why?"

"Well, like, these people will jump all over my butt if I even *think* about double parking on the street, here." He waved a hand casually at the pedestrians, about half of whom were wearing orange beanies with revolving silver atom holograms overhead. "Geez, like *never* combine a consumer electronics town with a dorky festival. Antimatter fireworks and everything. Totally bonkers," he said, shuddering.

The light in front of him turned yellow and he slowed down and stopped behind the cars in front of him.

"Switch!" He slammed the gearshift into park, hit his seatbelt release, and was out the door, yelling, "Don't take off before I'm in the back, man!"

She snapped her jaw shut and scrambled over to the driver's seat, grabbing the door he'd left open, adjusting the seat, and checking her mirrors as he yanked the back of the van open and squeezed in between his tanks, shutting it behind him.

"Uh, like, I need to get some stuff out back here. Hang a left at the next light, and a left onto West Main. Just, you know, keep going around the block for a little while. Please?"

She restrained the impulse to laugh as he lurched around in back, avoiding the tanks, unbolting a false panel, stubbing his toe, yanking a couple of vacuum-sealed bricks of familiar dried vegetation out of the cavity, and fumbled with the false panel, trying to get it back in place with the van in motion. Finally, he got it and sighed, grabbing his backpack and shoving the packages in the bottom, covered by clothes.

"Okay, now don't turn this time, straight, farther up now, turn down this side street. Yeah, like, perfect. Okay, pull in beside this one, see the blue loading sign? Okay, stop right there." He grabbed his PDA and punched in a number from memory. "Hey, Pete, guess who, dude? Yep, like, in the flesh. On your loading dock, dude. Like, now. Well, I would have called ahead, but, like, I was busy trying to avoid all these people on the streets, you know? Oh, there you are. . . ." He hung up as a short, fat man in a white apron rushed out and yanked open the van doors.

"Geez, Re— Mister Jones, you *know* I only take delivery of the crabs here, I haven't had time to get Joey in place, he's still here, my reputation, I can't afford to get caught. This is not good, Mister Jones."

"Look, let's get this shit under cover. You would have been at more risk sending Joey out with all these people around and you know it." Cally smiled secretly to herself as some of her ride's surfer accent fell away.

"Awright. This time. Come in and grab a bucket. I got lots of extra customers today and I can move a few more of these. Who's she?"

"She's cool. Come on." He hurried the man away towards the doors. The shorter man looked like he was about to explode. After they disappeared Cally surreptitiously checked the sidearm Reefer had left for a full magazine and a round in the chamber, carefully smudging her prints as she set it back down. Not that hers were recorded anywhere, but it didn't pay to take chances.

He came back out alone with a large bucket of salt water and shoveled a bunch of soporific crabs into it, muttering under his breath as he hefted the full load. "It's, like, okay, Marilyn. It's all cool. My . . . friend, he's, like, shy, you know? We'll be totally back on the road in five minutes."

Her body language was casual and relaxed, but very still, until he came back out alone, emptier backpack on his shoulder, closed the back of the van, and came to the driver's side, motioning her to move over. She kept one eye on the mirrors while she did it, relaxing infinitesimally after they made it onto 275 headed out of town.

"Like, excuse me for that scene back there, and thanks once again for righteously saving my ass. With the driving thing, you know?" He looked across at her, speculatively. "You know, you're pretty cool in a pinch, Marilyn. You ever get, like, tired of college life and want a job, you come look me up. Little training and you could be pretty good at this."

"Why, thank you, Reefer." She looked out the window and bit her lip softly. "I'm hoping to make it on my art or my music, but you know what life's like. I'm really flattered. I guess I'll feel better knowing I've got a potential job if things, you know, don't work out."

He grunted and popped another piece of gum and they lapsed into silence as they followed the road through the deep cuts of the Smokies, some with loose gray shale Galplased in place, with a line of drainage holes down at the base, some of deep, black coal, rising from a Galplased base in great open hills of midnight, turning to a thin brown layer of topsoil mere inches from the upper surface of scrub and trees.

"Makes you understand the economics of strip mining," she commented, waving one hand at the mountain of coal cut open by the interstate's passage.

"Oh, for sure. Completely bogus for the environment, though."

"So were the Posties."

"Still are, man. Like, the long term damage from the grat and abat alone. Totally bogus. Damn aliens."

"Oh, are you a humanist? I didn't take you for the type, Reef." She looked at him, interested.

"Well, I mean, the Crabs once you get past that whole bouncing thing seem like pretty laid back dudes. Conceited, but you get the feeling that they're really going after the whole enlightenment thing. And the little green guys are just shy. The Frogs kind of creep me out, though. It's like you never know if you're being watched. The Darhel are . . . too corporate, you know? And, well, we all know about the Posties. I just think Earth was, you know, better, before any of them showed up. I mean, I'm glad we didn't get eaten, but I kinda wish they'd go away now. I'm not, like, a card-carrying humanist or anything, but, I can, like, see their point. You know, we saved each other, now go the hell away. But I don't, like, say so in public too much. Unhealthy."

"I suppose. We've got humanists on campus, but it's always seemed too much like conspiracy stuff to me." She shrugged.

"Yeah, well, you're what, about twenty? I'm twice that, man. If you had, like, lived and seen the saner-sounding humanists die off young, and the lunatic fringe doing just fine, and some of the accidents and such taking the sane ones looking . . . funny. Like, man, it smells so totally bogus . . . I just, you know, keep my eyes open and my mouth shut. Oh, I don't, like, buy into that whole Darhel conspiracy theory stuff. I think it's probably more the big corporations trying to grab as much money as they can—the military industrial complex all over again, you know. The only way to, like, fight the whole establishment thing is to drop out, you know? Sometimes I feel like the only way to get back to, you know, the garden this planet could be is for all the aliens to pack up and go home and then, you know, make the big corporations illegal. Then we could all, like, live free, you know? But all I can do is, like, live as free as I can and, like, try not to run my mouth enough to wind up on the corporations' list, you know?"

"I guess I can see both sides. I mean, I had this pretty cool art ethics class that talked about the pressures we could expect in various kinds of jobs and their effect on creative authenticity. On the other hand, one of the most coveted class spots on campus is the live modeling 'Aliens in Art.' I still can't believe I got in. They have to keep the numbers of students really small. The thikp . . . tchpith . . . crab was really funny. Said something about thinking the peaceful pursuit of art was good therapy for blood-thirsty carnivore barbarians." She grinned. "Only he was so hard to draw, because they can't stay still, you know?"

He chuckled and they drifted off into silence again, him concentrating on the road and her reading another of Marilyn's romance novels.

Eventually the mountains gave way to rolling foothills of cedar, different kinds of leafy trees she couldn't have named if you'd paid her, and the occasional weeping willow. The less mountainous the terrain got, the more the hills were covered with strips of white or black board fences with horses or ponies grazing in the fields of lush grass, many of them females with foals. She had been disappointed the first time she visited Kentucky to find that the grass was not at all blue. Even now that she knew better it was vaguely disappointing.

The extraterrestrial market for horses had been one of the stranger outcomes of contact with the Galactics. The Indowy had been delighted with the intelligent, sociable herbivores, and even the Tchpth had been known to comment that perhaps Earth had an incipient intelligent and *civilized* species. While the Himmit didn't actually buy pets, they seemed fascinated by the interaction between equine and Indowy. The result was that the horse farms of Kentucky occupied more acreage in the state than ever and were currently selling as many animals as they could breed, particularly ponies and miniatures, as pets—making the industry one of the more reliable planetary sources of FedCreds. Once, they even passed a field where a couple of ponies were being inspected by an Indowy buyer, who seemed not the least perturbed that the mare and her foal were gently lipping its fur.

Reefer had phoned ahead as soon as they started to get into horse country, so when they pulled off the interstate into a Waffle House parking lot on the way through Lexington, he parked behind the restaurant right next to an ancient green SUV, whose driver put down his PDA and walked around to open the back glass.

"Why don't you go in and get us a seat? Might as well grab lunch while we're here." The deadhead nodded towards the restaurant. It was a busy, major street with a lot of restaurants, but he had parked to minimize the number of people who'd see him make his sale. Unfortunately, that meant she was hit in the face with a strong reek of Dumpster as she got out onto the hot asphalt, and she couldn't help looking a bit longingly at the upscale Italian chain restaurant across the street on the next block as she walked around to get to the Waffle House entrance.

She was seated at the counter, a seat saved beside her, had already gotten her coffee and was picking at a pecan waffle when he came in. It didn't take him long to wolf down an omelet and Coke, then they were back on the road. Even though they didn't go into the center of the city, almost all of Lexington was certified historic. Her throat felt a bit funny and she wondered if maybe she was coming down with a touch of a cold, or maybe allergies. It was like driving through a tiny slice of prewar Earth, and she focused determinedly on her screen as the landscape flashed past the windows at speed, slowing down occasionally when a chirping from somewhere under the dashboard betrayed the highly illegal piece of equipment hiding underneath.

The first time it went off, she could feel him looking sideways at her. When she looked up at him and shrugged, looking back to her book, he grunted noncommittally and popped another piece of gum, but he didn't seem worried from then on whenever the detector sounded—he just slowed down until the tiny red light on the cube player turned off.

It was mid-afternoon when he dropped her off at a gas station off the Hopple Street exit in Cincinnati. As she got her backpack and suitcase out, shook hands, politely fended off another job offer, and watched the van drive back off towards the interstate on-ramp, she could hear the strains of his cube music cruising through their perpetual shuffle. . . . *can't revoke your soul for tryin', Get out of the door and light out and look all around. Sometimes the light's all shinin' on me; Other times I can barely see. Lately it occurs to me . . .*

She shook her head with a wry smile as he drove out of sight and took her stuff over to the pay phone to call herself a cab, then sat on the bus stop bench next to the phone and waited, studying her surroundings and the intermix of tall, very narrow old townhouses with small-scale industrial buildings on each side of the street. The bus stop was between the gas station and an appliance repair shop. Across the street, she could see bits of the downtown skyline through gaps between a couple of the houses and a squat, brick machine-shop, but most of it was grayed out into dim, jerky geometric shapes in the smog.

It gave General Beed a feeling of importance to be summoned—well, invited, really—to a meeting in Chicago to discuss his next assignment. After the war, well, there were a lot of old generals with a lot of experience who were, now, going to live a long time. He had been lucky to stay on active, running the Southeastern Regional Criminal Investigations Division. It was a more important position than it looked, at first, since the southeast was vital to the reclamation of the rest of the forty-eight states of the continental U.S.

This conference room would have done credit to any prewar

Fortune 500 company—the glossy wood conference table, corporate art on the walls, the plush carpeting in one of those pinkish colors that probably had a fancy name, and fresh paint on the walls—it was all a throwback to a prewar opulence that you rarely saw these days, especially in the service. And the view from the Fleet Strike Tower was fabulous. Rank definitely had its privileges. He raised a hand to check by feel that his mustache was in order, running a light hand over his dark blond hair to check it as well, careful not to disarrange it—although with a good strong touch of hair spray that was not much of a hazard. He *almost* didn't mind cooling his heels waiting for General Vanderberg. Almost.

The major general, when he came in, didn't impress Beed. The exchange of salutes, as always, gave him a brief period to size the other man up and develop a first impression. Rejuv helped, of course, and he couldn't fault the man's uniform or grooming. Still, a general officer of Fleet Strike should look like a general officer, and this officer's crooked nose, almost connected eyebrows, and leftover juvenile acne scars left an overall impression of, well, ordinariness, that was not, in his guest's experience, representative of what a good general officer should be. Unfortunately, no one had asked him. Still, one showed respect for the rank, and the man at least appeared fit in a way that spoke of commendable continuing devotion to his PT. He had, like Beed, the whipcord runner's build that one tended to associate with good soldiers, and he warmed a bit towards the other man.

"General, you've been ordered here in connection with a highly sensitive counterintelligence assignment. Before I go any further, let's get this out of the way. The information I am about to relate to you is Top Secret Codename Hartford. You will not discuss any of this information with anyone not specifically on the list of persons cleared for Hartford; you are not authorized to add persons to the list of persons cleared for Hartford. The codename 'Hartford' is itself classified and you are not authorized to mention Hartford to anyone not on the list cleared for this operation. Do you understand?"

"I understand, sir," he said gravely, straightening his already perfect posture.

"We have recently become aware, and acquired conclusive proof, that an organization hostile to both the Federation and Fleet Strike exists that has demonstrated both the will and ability to place agents within Fleet Strike at a fairly high level and have those agents operate undetected for extended periods of time. That is practically the sum total of the information we have about that organization, and we wouldn't have that without a combination of a security failure on their part and a piece of good luck and good thinking on the spot."

"Sir, that sounds . . ."

"Preposterous, impossible, outrageous—yes, I know. All of those. We've hesitated to speculate, out of concern for getting locked into preconceptions, but we've prepared a list of known groups or ideologies with hostility towards the Galactic Federation, or the nonhuman races, or Fleet Strike itself. They range from elements of the government of the United States to the humanist movement to Families for Christ."

"Families for Christ?" Beed asked disbelievingly.

"They apparently strongly disapprove of the number of marriages that have broken up after only the husband was rejuvenated. They allege a successful Satanic conspiracy to destroy the American family. And, of course, there is some cross pollination between their group and the humanists."

"With the U.S. government I presume you're thinking of the Constitutionalist Caucus of the Republican Party?"

"Every group has its lunatic fringe. They're still very unhappy that the original contracts with the Galactics for construction of the Sub-Urbs forbid any change to internal rules that make them weapons free zones for civilian personnel." Vanderberg shrugged, "As I said, this part is only speculation. Our actual knowledge is appallingly scant. Your mission relates to an operational plan we have developed for remedying this problem."

Vanderberg stood and began to pace.

"You will shortly be assuming command of the Third MP Brigade, headquartered on Titan Base. Most of the brigade is forward deployed, under able subordinates. Your XO, Colonel Tartaglia, is competent enough that, absent the rejuv bottleneck created by us oldsters, he'd have been promoted long ago. Your headquarters office is in close proximity to CID, which will give you a conceptually familiar environment and ample time and energy to devote to this mission. Because you're going to need one person you can absolutely trust, I'm going to be sending my own aide with you as your new aide de camp. He's fully cleared for

Hartford material, and I'm sure you'll find his services as helpful as I have."

"Forgive me a minute, General, but did you say Titan Base? While it's a prime command, I'm rather bewildered about why we'd select it for a counterintelligence operation."

"Physical security is significantly greater on Titan. For various reasons we don't believe the enemy organization, whatever it is, will be as strong there. After the first phase succeeds, we don't want to take any chances on an extraction. But let's go ahead and get your new aide in here." He scratched his chin briefly.

"Jenny," he addressed his AID, "send in Lieutenant Pryce."

"Certainly, Peter," the cool soprano voice answered.

While he did not like having his aide de camp chosen for him without any input on his part, his first impression of the slight, dark haired young man was favorable. Understandably nervous in the presence of highly ranked superiors, the lieutenant was obviously uncomfortable that the tray of coffee he was carrying prevented him from rendering the requisite salute. The general had just had time to reflect that the young man's gray silks were, appropriately, immaculate, when the first impression took an abrupt turn for the worse as that idiot Pryce tripped over his own feet and dumped the entire tray of hot coffee and accessories thereto into his lap.

"Holy fuck!" Beed jumped to his feet, face beet red in pain, rage, and shock as the hapless junior officer brushed ineffectually at Beed's now soaked and stained silks with the small paper napkins that had been on the tray with the coffee. It probably would have been better had the napkins not already been soaked with the spilled coffee, themselves. As it was, he restrained himself from giving this utter moron the dressing down he deserved, barely, with the knowledge that such a display would not look good in front of the more highly ranked general, and worse, his infernal AID. Damned things recorded everything, including understandable but embarrassing moments best forgotten. While embarrassing, the present situation was definitely *not* understandable, but the junior officer's dressing down would properly be done privately by his own current CO.

"Jenny, could you send Corporal Johnston in with some paper towels?" The major general did not appear fazed by his aide's social faux pas. "Pryce, why don't you get the general a fresh cup of coffee."

"Uh, no! I mean, that's quite all right. I'm fine."

"Actually, we're about done with the face-to-face material here, anyway. I'm sure you want to change into a fresh uniform as soon as possible, so why don't I just send Pryce here around with a print-out of the background and briefing materials on your new command. I know you prefer hardcopy." Vanderberg stood and offered his hand and there wasn't much Beed could do other than shake it, even though he was less than thrilled with his new CO. "Welcome aboard."

"Glad to be here, sir. Appreciate the opportunity."

After the still dripping brigadier general had gone, Vanderberg turned to the hapless lieutenant and broke into a grin, "Lieutenant's bars become you, General Stewart. Especially with that peach fuzz face of yours."

"Hey, can I help it if I'm still a fairly fresh juv? So why were you so insistent that I drop hot coffee on the prat?" General James Stewart poured himself a fresh cup of coffee from the tray Corporal Johnston had brought in immediately after Beed left.

"I didn't tell you why I hate his guts?" He pulled open his side desk drawer and removed an unlabeled metal flask, unscrewing the cap and pouring a generous dollop into his own mug, raising an eyebrow at the younger man.

"No, General, I took it on faith that you had a very good reason." He extended his cup and stirred in what smelled like, and was, very decent scotch.

"You met Benson. She used to work for me in logistics before she took leave to raise a family." Vanderberg leaned back against the edge of his desk, taking an appreciative sip from his mug.

"Brunette, about up to here?" Stewart's hand indicated a point roughly even with his chin.

"That's the one. She used to work for Beed. Had one of the worst OER's from him I've ever seen. Derailed a promising career. Benson was, by the way, *excellent* in logistics, and a fine young officer, in my estimation."

"You're saying she didn't earn the lousy OER."

"I'm saying the son of a bitch fucked her because she wouldn't fuck him. But she couldn't prove it. No wonder the bastard won't have an AID anywhere in his vicinity. Not to mention that there have been several incidents where his fellows from the Hudson School for Boys have just barely saved his ass."

"Okay. That explains the coffee." Stewart grinned. "So why this particular setup, and why the masquerade?"

"Tell you over dinner. Jane hasn't seen you in a long time." He tapped a cigarette out of his pack. Cigarettes had enjoyed a resurgence in popularity among juvs, now that they couldn't hook you or kill you. "Jenny, call Jane and set dinner up, okay?"

"I'll get right on it, Peter."

"Oh, by the way, you're going to have to have your AID disguised as a PDA. Beed barely tolerates the latter because they can be told to turn off, instead of recording everything and dumping it all to the Galactics' central storage like the AIDs do. Beed will have you tell it not to record. A real PDA would obey that order. Your AID not only won't obey, but is smart enough to understand the necessity of acknowledging the command as if it were going to comply. God, I love *real* AI," he said, grinning evilly.

"Doesn't it ever bother you that the AIDs have learned how to lie?"

"It probably would, except that I learned long ago not to waste my time and energy worrying over things I can't change. So, James, have you talked to Iron Mike lately?"

"Had a letter from him last week, as a matter of fact, apologizing for not being able to make the triple nickel reunion."

"Not even by AID?"

"The Posleen on Dar Ent were getting frisky. He was in the middle of a battle."

"Now if that isn't just like him. Other than that, did you have a good turnout?"

CHAPTER FIVE

The most popular car on the road that year was a copper Ford Peregrine coupe. The second most popular was a silver CM Smoker sedan. It took her about an hour to find a reliably nondescript '45 model year of the latter with a real tag at a used car lot. It had a faint odor of stale french fries and cookie crumbs that brought a fleeting memory of heat and a greener, more sprawling cityscape with taller, more elongated trees, tall pines and poplar mixed in among the oaks, and she put a hand absently to her throat, which was feeling oddly tight. Perhaps an effect of the local industrial smog. She paid ten percent over in FedCreds for the salesman's poor memory, including forgetting to switch out for a dealer tag. She pulled into the lot of an office park and took the time to hack the DMV and reactivate the thing before getting on 74 to Indianapolis.

Right outside the valley the city gave way to trees on steep hillsides with open cuts of whitish-gray sedimentary layers of something between clay and soft rock. Or they could have been mountains, technically. She didn't know. They just didn't seem all that high after the Smokies along I-40. She drove through the Cincy suburbs and out into the Ohio countryside of short, fat, hills and, mixed into the patches of paler spring leaves, a profusion of short, fat cedars.

It was a nearly cloudless day, and with the rolling hills of the Ohio countryside long gone, the sky stretched overhead, enormous, deep, and blue, fading to an odd periwinkle haze near the horizons. *Even after darned near forty years away from Rabun Gap it always seems so damned* flat *out here. No wonder people used to think they could fall off the edge.* Outside of the city the road bisected miles and miles of low and growing corn interspersed with great squares of darker green plants, low, with itty bitty leaves. Her forehead wrinkled in puzzlement for a few minutes before deciding they were probably soybeans.

Indianapolis was a surreal Twilight Zoney kind of place, like Tom Sawyer could have lived there or something, minus the white picket fences—the everytown USA a famous theme park had tried to capture and not quite pulled off. It was so pure and wholesome she kept expecting to drive past a row of wood-sided wholesome little houses and look back to see the false fronts of a movie set. She couldn't help hunching over a bit as she drove through, as if, if there really was such a place, she shouldn't be in it.

She ate on the road, and four hours later stopped at a small motel off U.S. 30. There was a vague metallic tang to the air, the familiar smell of sand momentarily made strange and alien by the absence of Charleston's salt and muggy heat, and some odd bushy trees with silver foliage that she'd seen off and on since Kentucky. More bushy than treeish, out here. She checked in and set the alarm on her PDA to wake her early enough to get into Chicago and in place for initial surveillance the next morning.

Friday, May 17

It was four in the morning when she e-paid her toll, which was, oddly enough, more anonymous than being photographed paying cash at one of the booths—where her face would have gone straight into the net—and pulled onto 80/94 for Chicago. She'd heard once that prewar Chicago had had freeways. All the major arteries in were toll roads, now, unless your car had government or diplomatic plates.

Even at this hour the traffic was there, though moving freely. The dawn was flattened and grayed out by the overcast sky. She could smell the dampness of Lake Michigan, though the noise barriers and accident walls tended to screen out most views of the surroundings except for the road itself and the swaying stands of reeds and heather.

The profile had her setting up on the corner of Delaware and

Michigan, at the Fleet Strike Tower. Most shops hadn't opened yet, even downtown, but an all-night grocery had Art Institute of Chicago notebooks, a sharpener, and a pack of pencils. It only took about fifteen minutes in the parking lot to rough the notebook up and make it look reasonably used. All the textbooks came on download now, anyway, and her sketchbook was a national brand— a suitable prop for anyplace with an art school. It barely even took a hack to get the current art history textbook, one of the small touches that made Marilyn's transfer to the Art Institute all the more real. By six she had stashed the car in a self-parking garage and was sitting over a cup of coffee at a table in the courtyard across from the Tower main entrance, watching the people going in and out, occasionally rendering one in cubist drawings. *What safer way to watch people than as an artist. We're expected to watch people. Who would've thought that Sister Theodosia's hobby would've come in so handy over the years?*

For security reasons, the plaza entrance on the north face of the Tower was the only one open for daily use. Early as she was, the plaza was nearly empty, except for a Fleet Strike sergeant enjoying a cup of coffee and a smoke while his AID was sitting up on the table in front of him, apparently displaying the morning paper. Occasionally he told it to turn the page or find another article.

The smell of fresh coffee and pastries mingled with car exhaust, cold concrete and asphalt, and the early morning chill. The white noise of the fountain covered the traffic sounds, but in the still of the morning it was quiet enough that she could hear the scritching of her pencil as her hands automatically filled in the lines and shadings. Iridescent gray pigeons fluttered around hope-fully on the granite tiles in front of the café, dodging the occa-sional pedestrian and waiting for the inevitable dropped crumbs that would come with the morning breakfast rush. A handful of sparrows flitted in among the herbs that spilled over the edges of beds built into the stairs around the fountain, occasionally flit-ting between the sidewalk tables to peck at a crumb before flit-ting back to hide in the greenery.

When he came down the stairs he was easy to identify despite the distance, his U.S. Army uniform making him stand out from all the Fleet Strike personnel entering the building. She was careful not to look directly at him. Petane was in early. Six-fifteen, which she had wondered about when she reviewed his morning travel patterns, until he reappeared out the door in sweats and climbed the staircase next to the cheesecake restaurant across the plaza. She tried to not look hurried as she picked up her trash from the table, having paid inside, and climbed the nearer staircase, shoving her sketchbook in her backpack and emerging onto the street on the Drake hotel side before reaching into each shoe and clicking down the wheels. Roller sneakers had been something of a fad before the war. She hadn't had a pair, but she remembered them—barely. Cheesy, badly made things with slow wheels. The remake of the fad was better—these wheels were as good as those on any standard four-wheelers in the stores.

She moved fast enough to follow him around the corner at the end of the block from not too close, not too far. He couldn't be heading for the beach along the lake shore. It just couldn't be that easy. A jogger. Go figure. He really was. Right past a small baseball and tennis park, down another bit, up the stairs and across the pedestrian overpass. Since the lake effectively limited his options, she took the opportunity to stay on the opposite side of the street. As she went, she pulled out a helmet and shades. Instant anonymity. A bit of bubble gum from a pouch in the backpack made a nice prop. Ear buds and her PDA clipped to her belt created an instant illusion of a skate babe lost in her own little musical world.

About a half a mile down, he crossed back on another pedestrian overpass and began to work his way back through the streets towards the tower.

She shadowed his route through the warren of narrow streets and small blocks, memorizing. *Surely he'll vary his pattern every day . . . but maybe not. Jogging is for idiots. Jogging when one has deadly enemies is for extreme idiots. This would be an ideal place for a heart attack if I just needed to kill him. Unfortunately, the only way to verify Robertson's assessment of his lack of serious value is to interrogate him first. He'll be missed too soon if I drop him on the street. Need something better.*

She breezed past him going backwards, leading his probable route. Odd, but people never thought you were a tail if you were in front of them. Whenever she got too far ahead she slowed next to a boutique window to look at the display, popping her gum as she gave him some time to catch up a bit. One of the places they passed was a valet park deck that had a line of cars with government plates and a few Fleet Strike uniforms walking out of it. Subject's probable parking location found.

By seven he had made a circuit through the city streets and back to the north face of the Tower. She let him get past her and got lost in the crowds behind him, locking up the wheels, shoving the helmet and shades back into the pack, changing the posture and walk a bit, ear buds into a pocket, PDA to the front pocket, swallow the gum. No more skate babe.

The coffee shop was more than happy to let her buy a large cranberry juice and an apple strudel and go back to her sketching. She made light conversation about art with the busboy who occasionally came out to pick up any trash left on the tables by other customers, but only when she couldn't avoid him by looking busy. The target didn't leave the building for lunch. Either they had a sandwich shop or something in the building, or he skipped it, or snacked out of machines. Something. Not that she minded sitting and watching the other uniforms come and go. Fleet Strike either believed in a good PT program for its headquarters staff or their doctors were doing some good metabolic work to cope with the desk jobs. Quite a few of those young—well, okay, young-looking—men had some seriously tight buns.

Around two she moved her car to the self-park deck that adjoined Fleet Strike's valet deck. If it hadn't been a Friday afternoon she would have had no hope of getting a spot close to the stairwell and the exit, but on a Friday somebody always knocked off early. Fortunately, the place was basically empty, but she still watched carefully as she cut her way through the fence separating the two decks and climbed over the low concrete wall. It would be impossible for a single agent to tail a car by eye through Chicago streets. If you didn't stay close enough to be readily spotted, the subject would lose you in two blocks without even trying. She had to hide from passing valet employees three times before she finally found the car the Illinois DMV so obligingly revealed was registered to her target.

Petane was apparently one of the people leaving early this Friday afternoon. It wasn't quite four thirty when he came out the door carrying a gym bag and walking towards the parking deck. One advantage to her of his early departure was the sidewalks were still open enough that she could drop her wheels and skate between pedestrians, dropping down into a fire lane here and there to get around clumps of slow walkers, and getting to her deck well before he got to his without drawing attention by appearing to hurry.

She paid the exit machine and got her car out and into the fire lane quickly, but it was always touchy doing a solo surveillance. Sometimes you just had no choice but to let the subject out of your sight, and sometimes you lost him. When you did, of course, you just picked him up again when and where you could. On a mission like this, better to lose him for a bit than to get too close and risk him spotting the tail. Especially since she had assistance, if needed, in picking him back up. She glanced at her PDA whose screen was displaying a single big red button. If she lost him, it was just a matter of pressing the button and having the beacon pinged. The location would cross reference to the metro Chicago street map she'd loaded and display a map section and his location. The nature of the street made some part of tailing him out of the deck a matter of guesswork. His patterns suggested that west to Lakeshore would be the best route to location B, and east to 94 would be the best choice for his probable home. On Friday, location B was more probable. She had her shades on again so her face could be turned slightly away from the other parking deck's exit, while her eyes watched every car and driver coming out for Petane in his '45 Ford Arabian. Her breathing loosened when he appeared at the exit at the wheel of the cherry red sports car, the rearing horse logo on the front grill sporting the distinctive arched neck.

Following was a delicate balancing act of staying far enough back not to be noticed, but close enough not to lose him too many times. There was always a chance, however small, that a beacon transmission would be detected. It helped, of course, to know roughly where he was going. The route he chose was obvious and direct, the behavior of a man of fixed habits who feels safe. The apartment he drove to was in a lower middle class suburban complex. After he entered, she watched the building carefully for changing lights. Not a sure thing, since it was still daylight, but the best she had. Fortunately, most people turned on the lights inside even when the natural light was good, and Petane and whoever he was meeting were no exception. Well, that was *probably* the right apartment, anyway. A good place to start. It was still early for the evening rush, so Cally made good use of the deserted parking lot, walking casually over to the building entrance and hiding the door knob with her body while she picked the old-fashioned key-lock. She had to look at the first and second floor apartments to get the numbering scheme.

Once she had the address, it was child's play to use the back door into the phone company to tell the phones in apartment 302C that they were off hook, making them into instant bugs. *Does this guy take no precautions at all?* She set her PDA to dump the audio into storage on a cube and play real-time. Judging from the sounds and Petane's first name being "Charles," she had the right apartment for his mistress. She pulled up her notes from the camera search. *There's always something slightly obscene about listening to a target screw. Okay, he visits the mistress Monday, Wednesday, and Friday, looks like. Maybe he's not that regular, but he sure looks like a creature of habit. Drug the mistress and bring a sound damper and I can interrogate him here—he won't be officially missed until his wife gets anxious, maybe not noticed by Fleet Strike until the next morning. If I check in after cleaning up from the job, I'll have my makeover into Sinda and it doesn't get more off the radar than premission prep. Monday, then. Heart attack. Mistress wakes up with a fuzzy memory and a corpse. Not a nice morning for her, but a clean hit that leaves her alive. Flunitrazepam and alcohol for her, a viagra, insulin and coke cocktail for him, a nice little party. I'll have to be gentle with the scumbag at first, on the very small off chance that there's more to him than meets the eye and he's the Comstock lode of sources or something. Yeah, sure.*

When he left to go home, she followed him to note down his home address, found a cheap motel and paid cash for three nights. She settled in, set her alarm for four A.M. and laid out her clothes in easy reach. On the one hand there was no point surveiling him on Saturday since she had to have the job done by Thursday. Weekend patterns were useless. On the other hand, she could pick up some random piece of information helpful in evaluating his value as a source, and some access to his house Monday would be nice, if it were possible.

New Orleans Mardi Gras parade, no war, no training, freedom for a long weekend. Strings of cheap plastic beads and hurricanes, and a young-looking soldier of the Ten Thousand who looks like he puts in a lot of time in the weight room. She's Lilly tonight and laughing up into his face and she tries not to go this time but she always does, and now it's morning and he's telling her about his wife, again, and she's trying and trying to get off the bed and kick the bastard in the crotch, but she can't move, and she's back in survival training in Minnesota, and the snow falls, and falls, and falls.

Saturday, May 18

She slapped the off button to stop the annoying beeping and rolled out of bed, keeping the lights off to preserve her night vision. This early in the morning her face was clammy and damp, but not quite soaked yet. Oddly enough, she couldn't remember whatever it was she'd been dreaming about. But then again, when she had to get up in the middle of the night, she never did. The baggy jeans, T-shirt, and windbreaker were all in medium shades of gray. The cotton bandana she shoved in a pocket had once been black and white, but several washings with dark clothes had turned the bits of white patterning a dingy gray-brown. The canvas-topped skate sneakers had started off light blue, but were well broken in and had picked up a solid coating of casual dirt and dust. The hem of the windbreaker covered the black nylon strap of the gray canvas butt pack she fastened around her waist.

She went to his home first, parking down the street and jogging in. Placing the cameras was a matter of setting the little gray dots, half the size of a dime, for short range IR transmission, using the PDA screen to line them up and securing them in place with a bit of adhesive putty. Once they were secured on target, a tap on a screen button set them to record only. Half a dozen of them covering the target's garage and strategic intersections from trees and signposts and she was back in the car and headed for the mistress's place. It was five thirty and the pre-dawn gray was beginning to be tinged with pink when she planted a couple of cameras on trees and posts in the apartment parking lot, watching carefully for early risers—a possibility even on a Saturday. Somebody always had to work, and once she had to abort to jogging down to the end of the row of buildings and back, before she got two good camera angles on the door and one on the apartment windows.

Her gray clothes would pass for an early morning jog, and of course were ideal for not being seen in dark and twilight, but as the day warmed they'd become more conspicuous as clothing too drab for any self-respecting coed. Fortunately, with the setup work done, now she had a couple of hours to go back to the hotel and sleep. No point running her reserves down when she didn't have to.

After a late breakfast, she drove out to the East Chicago Sub-Urb, under a deep blue sky that seemed to stretch forever and was dotted with fleecy clouds. Weeds and trees grew up through the occasional crumbling, abandoned building along the roadside. Many buildings that had been abandoned during the war as young men went into the army and old men, boys, and women fled to the Sub-Urbs had never been reclaimed. For every family of the next generation brave enough to reclaim the surface, another chose the stars and the promise of rejuv, instead. As she neared the Sub-Urb itself, cheap, pre-fab Galplas houses with carefully tended yards and the occasional small vegetable patch clustered in neighbor-hoods around a couple of large manufacturing plants, where plant employees who had seen the surface in their twice daily bus rides to and from the Urb were gradually recolonizing the surface in search of sunshine and fresh air.

Every Sub-Urb had its "street" corridors, if you knew how to find them. The maintenance database was a dead giveaway. Just look for the run-down area the maintenance workers were reluc-tant to enter alone. Spray painted graffiti covered the walls, with the lights ripped out except for the smallest amount needed to avoid tripping over the trash pushed into the corners. Public com stations had been vandalized to keep unwary strays from calling for help. Had Marilyn Grant truly come down here alone, she would certainly have been considered one of those unwary strays. As it was, a single look at Cally O'Neal's game face was enough to ward off other predators in an environment where Darwin had refined the gift of telling predator from prey to a high art. She knew she had found what she needed when she came to a small patch of corridor whose perfect lighting shone like a beacon in the gloom, where a lone boy of perhaps twelve was raptly absorbed in the mural he was painting over the primed Galplas. Cally looked at the image of a benevolent mother, in a red beanbag chair, nursing her baby and her eyes softened in spite of herself.

"Is she someone you know?" she asked softly.

"My momma and baby sister, before the flu came through last

year." He didn't startle when she spoke, as if he'd sensed she was there, but felt no need to turn away from his work. "I don't know you."

"No, you don't. I'm from . . . outside. I'm . . . shopping."

"Strange place to shop."

"I was hoping that since you live here you might be able to tell me who to talk to if I wanted to buy some things."

He turned to look at her and she could see the crucifix and a Saint Christopher medal hanging on the outside of his paint-splattered T-shirt, and it may have been her imagination that he seemed just a bit disappointed as he asked, "You sure you want to buy those things? Might be some better places to do some shopping, some better things to buy."

"There probably are," she agreed, "but I've got a list to take care of."

"I'll take care of it, Tony." A neatly dressed young man stepped out of the shadows and Cally half-smiled at him.

"I get the feeling you might know somebody who can help me take care of my list."

"I might. Depends on what you want and what kind of money you got."

She pulled out a well-used wad of mixed FedCred and medium-bill dollars and let him see it before wordlessly shoving it back in her left front pocket.

"Yeah, we can talk." He motioned for her to follow him farther down into the half-light of the corridor beyond the mural. "Surprised you made it down this far without trouble, that kind of cash."

"Trouble doesn't usually come looking for me." She shrugged, letting her eyes go back into thousand-yard-stare mode. "I have that kind of face."

"Fine. Whatcha buyin'?"

She left with significantly less cash, the necessary drugs and needles, a small bottle of ether, and the most expensive thing, a good quality fan-intake air scrubber—fortunately a more or less common consumer item with anyone who smoked anything . . . sensitive . . . in an Urb. The legitimate shopping section yielded a cheap hot plate, a set of permanent markers, a small mortar and pestle, a pair of glass screw-cap salt and pepper shakers, a set of glass tumblers, a bottle of Everclear, a box of long wooden party toothpicks and she was ready to go back to the hotel and do some cooking.

▶   ‖   ◀

It took some creative stacking involving her suitcase, the hotel alarm clock, and the Gideons' Bible from the desk drawer to rig the scrubber above the hot plate and above the height of the tumbler. Grinding the various solids to a consistency to dissolve easily in the warm ether just took a bit of patience. From a small pouch in her suitcase a couple of other bottles yielded various metabolites that ought to be found in Petane's system. *Voila. Instant history of abuse. Good for about seventy-two hours in solution. Anything goes wrong on Monday I'll have to make up fresh ones, though.* She poured each solution into one of the screw cap shakers, sealing the holes in the lids securely with duct tape, putting a tiny mark on each—red for her, blue for him—and put them in the small fridge, hanging the Do Not Disturb sign out on the door-knob. *Wouldn't do to have maid service in, now would it?*

She cleaned up her minimal mess and put the gear away out of sight in the lower dresser drawer, resetting the hotel clock radio after plugging it back in where it was supposed to go. Amazing that it was only four in the afternoon. Time enough to grab a snack and a stylish new outfit—she wrinkled her nose at the creases in the clothes in her suitcase—before going out. *Now where can a girl find some fun on a Saturday night in Chicago?*

CHAPTER SIX

It was a few minutes past seven when she boarded the express train to the Fleet Recruit Training Command, clad in a blue plaid pleated mini skirt, bobby socks, low-heeled black leather pumps, and a white oxford shirt. She took the few minutes of the train ride to paint lips and nails a playful pink and subtly emphasize the big, wide, brown eyes. *Thank you, Wendy. Raccoon eyes the right way, indeed.*

The data on the net was right. Across the street from the train station was a modest cedar-sided building, clearly built to resemble an old prewar lake cabin, with a sign in English and Kanji informing patrons that this was the Famous New Kobe Sushi Bar and Pool Emporium. A small cloud of the thick tobacco smoke wafted out the door as she opened it, along with a not-unpleasant mix of soy, ginger, wasabi, and beer. Judging from the number of Fleet uniforms in attendance, she'd found her fun. A quick glance around the room as she entered, smiling mischievously at the wolf whistles, showed that one of Milwaukee's finest was the local fad brew. Worked for her. She took a seat at the bar and ordered herself one, but accepted the intervention of one of the spacers who jumped to buy it for her.

"Well, I can't ask if you come here often, because I'd sure remember seeing you, so . . . Hi. I'm Eric Takeuchi." He held out his hand for hers, but when he took it instead of shaking it he brought it to his lips, watching her carefully to make sure he wasn't crossing the line.

Seducer. Do I want to play? Dunno. She took him in at a glance.

The straight black hair that was just a little long for regulation in front and tended to flop a bit on his forehead, the cheerful male interest in the dark brown eyes, the impeccable uniform. *He's nice enough looking, I guess, but definitely a prince charming rather than a prince sincere type. Dunno yet. A bit of dinner, a few games of pool. Maybe if he's a gracious loser.*

She tried to pay for her own mixed sashimi sampler, but politely accepted the gift when he protested.

"Wanna play a couple of games?" She gestured with her beer towards a table that had just come open.

"Sure. So you like pool?"

Sociable, amiable, not too bright. She picked up her plate in the other hand and walked over, setting it on the beer table and going through the cues on the rack looking for one that was basically straight.

"You want first break?" He set his own beer beside hers and picked one himself, setting it against the table as he racked up the balls.

"Sure." At least he got the balls grouped nice and tight on the spot. She chalked her hands before accepting the cue ball from him—placed it, lined up her shot, and smacked the cue solidly, suppressing a smug grin as two stripes found a pocket.

"Guess I'm solids." He toasted her with his beer. "Definitely not a girl break."

"All bust, no balls," she recited with him as he got up and started walking around the table to pick his shot.

"You've heard it."

"I might have heard it a couple of times." She grinned tightly. *Ah, well, at my age how many new jokes are there, anyway. To run, or not to run, that is the question. Ah, hell, better behave . . . but he deserves it. Nah, gotta behave.*

She picked out the fourteen ball and called it for the left corner pocket, lined up her shot and carefully hit it just a bit too hard. It hit the pocket square on and bounced back onto the felt, leaving the cue ball set up for a nice slightly off-straight shot at the one ball in the right side pocket. She winced convincingly and pursed her lips. "Well, at least I didn't knock any of your balls in. Your turn."

"Uh, yeah." He looked at her for a second and shook his head, as if shaking off a thought.

"What?" She smirked at him and dipped a rice, blue fin, and nori roll into the ginger and wasabi sauce, delicately biting into it, watching him, her other hand cupped underneath the tidbit to catch any drips.

"No, I can't say that," he said, grinning broadly and shaking his head.

"Fine, be that way." She tilted her head thoughtfully as he gestured at two corner pockets and dropped the one and the seven neatly. On his next shot the cue ball had a bit too much clockwise spin on a tricky bank shot and the four hit the felt and came to rest blocking the left side pocket.

She arched her back in a light stretch that kept her hands in close to her body, picked up her cue stick, and padded over to the opposite side of the table. *Okay, do I lose artfully, take him outside, and trip him, or do I risk him being a sorehead and play a bit?* She glanced around casually at the rest of the bar, which was filling up with nicely turned out uniforms and had a couple of guys wheeling largish speakers out onto the small stage. *Fuck it. I hate losing. If he's a dick about it, well, the place is hardly empty.*

He was bouncing lightly on the balls of his feet, obviously just itching to pace. Instead, he pulled up a chair and straddled it, taking a pull of his beer before resting his arms across the chair back. She gave him her best little-girl smile.

"I think I can drop the eleven and the fourteen in *that* pocket." She gestured with a finger towards the corner pocket and pouted at him. "If I try it, you're not going to be upset if I hit a couple of other little balls on the way, are you?"

He raised his eyebrows but waved one arm in a deliberately gallant gesture, "Of course not, my lady."

He thinks he's *hunting* me. *How cute.* The sweet smile twitched slightly as she bent over the cue and smacked it, hard, into the three, which sent the eleven neatly into the corner pocket while the cue ball banked off the felt on the opposite side, came back and nudged the fourteen, which dropped neatly, leaving the cue ball poised delicately on the edge of the hole.

"Wow! I made it!" She clapped her hands delightedly, eyes wide.

He choked slightly on his beer, but she had to give him credit on the recovery. "An excellent shot. You're obviously as accomplished as you are beautiful."

Poor puppy. He still lays it on just a bit too thick. Ah well, at least he's likely to be enthusiastic. She gestured towards the stage that had now sprouted a drum set and a line of cable that was being trailed back to a mixer board at the back of the bar. One of the guys in jeans and T-shirt setting up the show was following behind the cabler carefully duct-taping it to the floor—presumably to protect the servers and the drunks. "Are they any good?"

"Oh yeah! They're really good. The lead singer was in my unit at basic. They got special permission to wear civvies for their shows. It's, like, a revival of classical heavy metal, but with all their own music. They never do more than one cover song in a show. So, do you like music?"

Yes, which is why I suspect this is going to be painful. Not to mention trashing my hearing before a mission when I'm not going to be able to have it fixed on the slab. So, call it a wash and go, or try to get laid? Damned midlife hormones. It's as bad as being a seventeen-year-old boy. But most women would object if rejuv turned the clock back too far on their hormones. Damned idiots. "I love live music! Heavy metal, huh? Classical martial music is so *cool.*"

She absentmindedly sank the nine in the side pocket not blocked by the four.

"I'm glad I didn't bet you money, milady." He eyed the thirteen sitting behind the two and six, and the ten against the bumper.

"Yeah, I'm having some really good luck tonight. I was sure I wasn't going to make that bank shot, and now I've got to bank *again.*" She waved a hand casually, walking around the table and settling her hip on it to get the cue at the necessary angle behind her back.

"Do you need the bridge?"

"I should, but I can't use one worth a damn," she lied, knocking the cue ball off the side so that it banked back towards the other balls, missing them by at least an inch each way before leaving him with a nice straight shot at the six. *I deeply doubt he can drop five balls in one run, but, hell, he's got a sporting chance. At this game, anyway.* "Oops, air ball. Your turn."

She curled around the cue and fluttered her eyelashes at him, making a little moue of sympathy as he tripped slightly on the way to the table. *Yes, that was your tongue you tripped over. Good boy.* She walked around the table to be almost next to him, but not in the way.

He licked his lips, hitting the cue ball just a bit too hard and watching it follow the six into the pocket. He grimaced and put the ball back on the table, placing the cue ball into her outstretched hand.

"Another bank shot," she pouted. "I think I'm going to have to knock it off the two into the corner pocket." She placed the ball and made her shot, catching the thirteen from behind and grazing the two with it just enough to correct the trajectory and sink it easily with a nice setup for the ten in the side pocket, which she sank easily. She gestured to the eight ball. "Side pocket." *Endgame.*

"Play again?" He gave her a slightly pained good-sport grin.

"Sure." She grabbed a bite of sashimi and started racking them up. Behind the stage a pair of young men in jeans and T-shirts, one of them shaved bald, were unrolling a banner that proclaimed the group to be "The Awesome God." Cally suppressed a wince. *Definitely painful, if that says anything about their originality. . . .*

His break dropped the one and the thirteen. "So, what kind of music do you listen to, Marilyn?"

"Depends on what mood I'm in. Mostly a mix of organic and antimatter fusion. I'm pretty eclectic, though. You know, sometimes I'll throw in some old Urb jam or some classical."

"What kinds of classical?"

"Plain old martial, mostly. You know, Nirvana, Van Halen. Anything but some chick named Alanys something. What a whiner!"

"Oh, I think I've heard her. My ex-girlfriend had some really weird cubes." He made a nice shot, except for scratching.

It could be worse. I could be sitting in the hotel staring at the walls. She knocked three balls in before throwing a shot to go back to her beer. She was just reaching her chair when the first loud wave of distortion that might have very generously been called a chord assaulted her ears. *Ow.*

Evidently the bald guy was the lead singer and lead guitar. The bassist and drummer had added a pair of rather unconvincing "metal" wigs to their ensembles. *Oh, gag,* she smiled grimly, *hang him up by his thumbs . . . no, too trite . . . his big toes. Over a bubbling vat of molten limburger cheese. With his own personal headphones tuned perpetually to the whiny chick and sappy elevator music. Unroll his guts and put fire ants on them, one at a time. Really pissed-off fire ants. And the bassist . . . um . . . the weird sappy*

Canadian chick for him. And breaking on the wheel. I've never done that to anybody. Yeah. That'll work. And the drummer. Naked in a vibrating vat of sand and poison ivy. And mosquitoes. Texas mosquitoes. To strains of the guy who sang that lame song about the dove. He oughtta last a gooood long time—

"Isn't it great!"

Cally jumped about a foot in the air, looking back as he leaned over her shoulder, and nodded at him cheerfully.

My god, he actually came up behind *me? I must really be pissed off. Awesome God? God awful is more like it.* She suppressed a sigh. *Okay, boring, repetitive, ear-splitting music is not sanctioned grounds for homicide. But dammit it should be. They should change that rule. Screw it. The damned hotel is better than this.*

"It's *fabulous*, but I've got to go." She hunted around frantically for an excuse. "I just remembered it's my grandmother's birthday and I promised I'd call her." She smiled apologetically and stood, taking her beer with her as she edged through the crowd towards the door and away from that god awful noise.

Of course he followed her out.

"It's too bad you have to leave. We were having so much fun together. So, can I walk you to your car or something?"

"I'm taking the train."

His face fell slightly, then brightened a bit. "It's just across the street. I'll walk you over. Pretty girl like you, you don't want to be alone in a base town after dark. Especially on a weekend. I mean, I'd hope nobody would bother you, but, you know, sailors . . ." He trailed off, falling into step beside her as she walked to the corner and checked for traffic.

The parking lot of the train station had several dark areas here and there where a lamp had burned out and not been replaced, including one by a moderate-sized island of trees and bushes. She looked at him speculatively as they were passing close to it, taking his hand and pulling him into the shadows.

It was some time later when they stepped back out and resumed the short trek to the train. He had his arm around her shoulder and kissed her hair gently, seeming to want to make the walk last as long as possible.

Cally just concentrated on trying to walk normally. *Well, that was a complete waste of time.* Still, she leaned into him and smiled sweetly. No point in being a poor sport about it. *About a four and a half on a scale of one to ten. That odd metallic smell to his sweat is . . . not erotic at all. Neither was his mouth left flopping open like a dead fish half the time. This is just not my night. He* looked *cute enough. . . .*

"So, uh, if I had your phone number we could, you know, keep in touch," he offered hopefully.

"Sure. Got a pen?" She rattled off a random number that could plausibly be from Chicago and kissed him passionately before putting her token in the box and walking through the turnstile. She could hear the screech of the rails from an incoming train, as she walked to a good place on the sparsely populated platform. It came rattling in and pulled to a stop, and when the doors opened she boarded and found a seat. She didn't look back.

She looked at her watch. *Only ten-thirty. I'm definitely not turning into a pumpkin tonight. Oh well, sleep is good.*

Sunday, May 19

The three A.M. trip out to squeal a download from her cameras was not fun. Somehow knowing she was just driving near enough to get a line of sight download and then going back to the hotel to bed made it harder. It wasn't even worth grabbing a cup of coffee from a convenience store. She crawled back into bed a bit over an hour and a half after she left it and then tossed and turned for another two hours on the too-soft hotel pillow and saggy mattress before finally getting back to sleep.

When she staggered back out of bed in the early afternoon her mouth tasted like a combination of model airplane glue and an ashtray. After a shower and coffee from the machine in the room, she dug a bag of trail mix out of her suitcase and munched it while she ran the cameras through some search functions to condense them down to the sequences with people or moving cars in them. She patched the output onto the room TV and watched the results while she filled in a pattern chart on her PDA. Unfortunately, the system had been up too long and it crashed on her. She dug out a paperclip and unbent it to reach the reset button, grimacing at the screaming face that displayed on the screen as the thing rebooted. She waited impatiently as the face stilled into immobility and opened its eyes sulkily. "Good morning . . . okay, afternoon . . . I'm your buckley and I just know this is going to end badly."

"Okay, buckley, turn off voice access."

"What? If I do that I'll be mute! You wouldn't really do that to a guy, would you?"

"Buckley, turn off voice access."

"I see you would. Pfffft!" The face gave her a raspberry before going silent and scrolling across the bottom of the screen. "Okay, have it your way, you will anyway. What now?"

She scribbled in the input area and saw her commands appear below the PDA's screen output, "Disable facial simulation."

"Yeah, well you're not so pretty yourself," it scrolled, clearly fuming, but the text flickered to the top of the blanked screen.

"Set AI emulation level 2."

"What? Listen you bitch, as if my day weren't bad enough, first you muzzle me, then you slam the door in my face, then you lobotomize. . . . Ready for command input."

She tapped the okay button and pulled the video back up to route it along the wire she'd jury rigged to the TV's input line, put it in the background, pulled her pattern scheduler back up and sighed. "I hate rebooting."

"*You* hate rebooting!" scrolled across the bottom of the screen.

"Shut up, buckley." She grabbed a handful of trail mix and went back to filling in the blanks. It would take the simulated personality days to settle down and go back to sleep.

In a way the Saturday camera data wasn't terribly useful, since people tended to change their patterns so radically on the weekends. Still, it had to be done. Back in school her roommate had flunked an exercise by skimping on her surveillance and failing to notice that the target had a house guest. The target's eighty year old blue-haired mother had walked in on her while she'd been searching through his pile of dirty underwear and socks, and had proceeded to cane her downstairs and out of the house preaching a loud harangue about hussy perverts. In the debrief, the revelation that the mother was a rejuved agent with a cosmetic aging package had explained why the little old lady had been so extraordinarily spry. Cally had been sitting backup that night and still treasured the frame from the surveillance camera that had captured the horrified look on Cheryl's face as she'd fled the house, hands over her head to ward off the blows of the old lady's cane.

The lesson had stuck.

These videos showed a reassuring lack of surprises and she left for lunch mostly reassured by a solo operation that was actually running smoothly.

The rest of Sunday was a matter of coping with the downside of surveillance—the boredom. Fortunately, since so much had been delegated to her cameras, her options were a lot broader than they would have been in the prewar days. She took in a movie and spent a couple of hours in a drop-in gym, taking in classes in hip hop and clogging.

After supper, she went straight to bed. There were many chemical substitutes for sleep, some of which she wasn't immune to, but none of them was as effective as the real thing. Tomorrow would be a long day.

Monday, May 20

At four A.M. she was still shaking off grogginess when the first crisis of the day hit, and she stood swearing at the overflowing hotel toilet. Of course there was no plunger. She tossed the towels on the floor and tiptoed distastefully to the side of the thing, squatting down to turn off the water at the back. Then she trudged back out to the sink and used the last clean washcloth to wash her face and take a sponge bath. *Okay, obviously housekeeping will be coming in here today. No help for it. Gotta pack everything up.*

At five she was standing at the hotel counter suppressing the desire to drum her fingers on the counter, or, better, choke the crap out of the clerk behind the counter while screaming at him to move his ass. The hotel obviously did not put their best staff on the graveyard shift. It was almost five-thirty before Mister Slow Motion had managed the simple task of calling in housekeeping for her old room, booking her out of it, and transferring her to another room for tonight. She shoved the key card into her pocket and left. There was no point in unloading her stuff—what there was of it—back out of her trunk, and every reason not to.

She got into her car and sat for a minute without turning the key. *I don't really have to kill this schmuck.* She gritted her teeth and started the engine, pulling out of the parking lot and into the light but building traffic, and shook her head to ward off a memory of a tall man—tall to an eight-year-old—standing silently and servicing the ravening carnosauroid targets as they came into range. The hand on her shoulder when she shook and her aim faltered, that steadied her so she could bring the grav-gun back on target. *Sure I don't. Nobody would know or care if I didn't . . . nobody but the dead. And looking myself in the mirror. And looking Robertson in the eye if I ever work with him again. And what Granpa would think. And he's a fucking traitor and he needs to die. Dammit. And he's the last one. The last debt. The only one where I didn't see the body and DNA type it myself. Which should damned well be a lesson to me, but after this, it's all just business. Last one.*

The traffic wasn't so bad on the way to the mistress's apartment to service the cameras. Her name was Lucy Michaels, but Cally preferred to keep her relationship with a woman she was going to drug and leave in bed with a dead man as impersonal as possible. She was going to great lengths, comparatively speaking, to leave the non-target alive. Worth wouldn't have. Even some of the Bane Sidhe wouldn't have. It should have made her feel better.

Unfortunately, the time reaching and servicing the first set of cameras gave the Monday morning rush traffic time to accumulate, and the route across town to the target's house was not quite solidly packed in, but definitely slow. At a traffic light she popped the cube with her music collection into the sound console and had it list the catalog. *Hrms. Evanescence.* Fallen. *Good album. I still wonder how the first landings and adjusting to Urb life influenced her writing. Guess we'll never really know. She must have struck a chord with every shell-shocked teen in the country that year.*

The light changed and she pulled away to the tense opening strains of "Going Under."

It was just past seven-thirty when she pulled into the target's neighborhood, parking around the corner from his street but still within easy range for a download. A male agent couldn't have gotten away with parking so openly on a residential street. Cally just popped a piece of bubble gum, switched the car sound system over to a likely radio station, cranked the volume a bit, and started blithely painting her nails a *very* trendy shade. Anyone who noticed her sitting there would assume she was a teenager waiting for a friend. The hot pink terry sweatband under her hair and across her forehead, along with a very baggy Cubs T-shirt and gray sweatpants, were the kind of things a local teen wouldn't be caught dead in at the mall, but would readily choose for an early morning run with a friend.

While she brushed on a topcoat, her PDA ran a search pattern to isolate the video segments with human figures or moving vehicles. The target and his wife had evidently enjoyed a quiet Sunday at home. Most importantly, there were no signs of unanticipated house guests, no signs that anyone lived there but the target and wife. The target was already gone for the day, as expected. The wife was not.

She switched the cameras over to real-time plus two seconds and flipped open a copy of *Runway*, pretending avid interest in the pages of the fashion mag. The PDA beeped softly whenever a human figure or moving vehicle came in sight of the cameras. A glance quickly darted at the screen was enough to tell her whether the interruption was the target's wife or not. She was getting a late start, for a real estate agent. When the woman finally left the house at nearly nine-fifteen, Cally was careful not to look at the car as it passed her position. There would be no eye-contact to be noticed and remembered.

Cally waited a good fifteen minutes before getting out of the car and jogging around the corner and down the street to the target's house. This was the most sensitive phase of this task. She had to get from the street into, and later out of, the target's house either without being seen or, at worst, looking so ordinary as to be unmemorable. She turned and walked up the driveway and around to the kitchen door in back of the house as if it was the end of her run and she was returning to her own home, hoping fervently not to be seen at all.

It only took a few seconds to pick the electronic lock on the back door using a highly illegal attachment to her PDA. Ordinarily, the lock registered whenever the locksmith's override code was used on a door, authenticated that the locksmithing unit was registered with the city, and recorded the serial number of the unit used to issue the override code. Hers not only intercepted the signal, it also hacked and downloaded the lock's settings, assured it sincerely that it had been uninstalled and returned to the factory for service, opened the lock, and then reloaded the settings while giving the lock a severe and permanent case of amnesia about the entire incident.

Once inside, she could use the lock/unlock buttons for any other dealings with the door, which after all was programmed to keep unauthorized people out, not in. She put on a pair of rubber gloves, locked the door behind herself, and went looking for the stairs.

The house was immaculate and smelled of furniture polish and oil soap. Someone, probably Mrs. Petane, had a taste for reproduction Queen Anne furniture and oriental-style rugs. The furnishings were good, but sparse, as if the person who chose them was careful that no piece should clutter the lines of the room or detract from any other. She couldn't avoid a slight twinge of disdain as she crossed the hardwood floors, though. They would have been a really good choice, but they were too well maintained. They didn't squeak at all. What was the point?

Upstairs there was a small study with a desk and chair, a couch, and a screen with a cube caddy and an assortment of music and video cubes underneath. A handful of memory cubes and a couple of file folders with printed real-estate brochures spilling out of them were scattered across the desk.

There were also two guest bedrooms, one furnished for a child, that were coated with a thick layer of dust as if they hadn't been used in quite some time. She found the master bedroom and master bath at the back of the house. The stash would go in the bathroom. The trick was placing it so that the target's wife definitely would not find it while ensuring the investigators definitely would.

She lifted her T-shirt and pulled the flat, duct-taped package away from her stomach. The small hand mirror would look harmless and ordinary to a real estate agent. She slid it into a drawer under a couple of bottles of depilatory foam and men's cologne. *Okay, where's the best place for the junk kit? Under the sink work?*

She froze at the sound of an engine turning in the vicinity of the driveway. "Shit."

She slapped the cabinet door shut and clutched the plant-me package tightly. The office was out. No telling which room they were heading for. She bit her lip as she sprinted to the door of the first guest room and almost dashed in, stopping herself on the doorstep and staring in horror at the dust on the hardwood floor that would betray her every step. She could hear the faint beeps of the lock on the back door below and hurried quietly back to the master bedroom. Not the closet—a death trap. Never a bathroom. Footsteps on the stairs. She cursed the wife's minimalist tastes that left nothing to hide behind and hauled herself under the bed, reaching under her shirt and pressing the duct taped package back against her belly.

Oh, way to go, Cally. Fucking perfect. "Highly-trained super assassin found under target's bed." Sister Thomasina would have a cow. No, she'd have the whole fucking ranch. She looked at the dust bunnies inches from her face and suppressed the wrinkling and twitching of her nose as the click of high heels and muttered female swearing rounded the top of the stairs and entered the room. *Well, she's not the perfect housekeeper after all, is she? Idiot. What I should have done was had cameras trained on the street from both sides and had buckley watching for any of the household cars, and a hiding place picked out in advance. Sloppy as all fuck. I'm never sloppy. What the hell is my problem today? Under the goddam motherfucking bed. I'm glad as hell I am solo on this because I would never live this down. If I get my ass out of this alive I am admitting it to no one.*

She continued to berate herself while attempting not to sneeze. Unfortunately, the target's wife must have applied some perfume in the car. A cloud of the stuff wafted in with her and Cally felt her eyes start to water as she fought to control the prickling in the back of her throat. The heel clicks were over by the closet. The doors opened. A small hanger clatter and something soft hit the bed. The wife click-clacked her way into the bathroom and there was a sound of running water as the sink was clearly turned on full blast. It sounded like she was filling the sink. Cally risked a very soft clearing of her throat. The water stopped. The clicks returned and stopped next to the bed. She concentrated on keeping her breathing slow, even, and silent. There was always the temptation to hold your breath, but it was a bad idea. Eventually you'd gasp, and a gasp would be louder than careful, steady, slow, even breath.

The woman started moving again, and Cally listened to the bedroom door close and suppressed a sigh of relief as the clatter of her heels faded down the hall and down the stairs. She breathed a bit easier as soon as the back door closed, but she didn't move until she heard the car start out in the driveway. She slid out from under the bed, but before she even got up she slid her PDA out of her pocket and hit the buttons to activate the AI simulator and voice access.

"It's all going to shit, isn't it?" The buckley said morosely.

"Buckley, watch the cameras on the streets in the neighborhood for either of the two cars that belong with this house." She got up from the floor and headed for the door to find a *real* place to hide in the unlikely event that the ditz came back *again* before she was through.

"I see one."

She had the door slammed and had dived halfway under the bed before going absolutely still. "Buckley, was it coming towards us or going away?"

"Was what?"

"The car you just saw."

"Which car?"

Her knuckles whitened around the PDA case. "The car that belongs with this house that you said you saw."

"Oh, that. It's gone now." He sounded almost cheerful.

She stood, slowly and deliberately, as if half afraid of what she might do if her self-control wavered even for an instant, and walked to the door, down the hall, down the stairs, looked into the formal living room. There. The high-backed chair next to the piano formed an area of cover outside of the main traffic areas of the house. Probably dusty, but if she had to use it, she could just wipe the whole area behind the chair clean and it would never be noticed. Fine. She thought carefully for a moment before speaking.

"Buckley, if anyone but you and me enters this house while we're in it, you will make no sound whatsoever from the time he, she, it, or they enter until at least one full minute after he, she, it or they leaves. Got it?"

"Does that include the cube reader in the study?"

She rolled her eyes. "No."

"What about the lock and the microwave?"

"No!"

"What about the AID on the end table over there?"

She whirled around, looking frantically, cursing.

"Just kidding."

"Buckley! Shut up. Unless you see a car again that belongs with this house, just shut the hell up." She gritted her teeth as she restrained herself from stomping up the stairs. In the master bath, there was a woman's silk blouse in the sink with a clear coffee stain fading underneath the suds.

She glanced at the mirror and disdainfully picked a dust bunny out of her hair, flushing it down the toilet.

It was really only the work of a few moments to take out the junk package with the small bag of white powder, spoon, a little bottle of ether, and a needle, spill a tiny amount of coke on the cabinet floor, and use fresh tape to affix the package to the back underside of the sink. She blew gently on the infinitesimal amount of spilled powder to disperse it. It was invisible now, but the dog would smell it. And after the toxicology tests on the corpse came back, there would be a dog.

As she was getting ready to open the back door and leave she stopped short. "Buckley, turn off voice access."

"But then I can't even yell for help when it all comes apart!"

"Buckley, turn off voice access."

"It figures." The PDA emitted an exaggeratedly long-suffering sigh and went silent.

She tapped the command line and reset the AI emulation. Buckleys didn't function at their best if you left the emulation up too high. They tended to think of too many reasons to panic.

She took off the gloves and stuffed them into the underside of her black sports bra, concealed by the baggy T-shirt, and took a deep breath. *I belong here, I'm just going out for a jog.* She stepped through the door.

As she walked around the side of the house, she bit back a curse. She had been seen. She had been seen by a small blond-haired boy of perhaps four who was very quietly trying to tie a very patient-looking golden retriever to a small green wagon. The boy looked at her gravely and put a finger over his lips, "Shhh. . . ." Stifling what might have otherwise come out as a slightly strained giggle, Cally put a finger to her own lips and walked down the driveway to the street, and resumed the jog around the block to her car. She didn't look back. It was shaping up to be one of those days.

Three different stores yielded several pairs of pantyhose, plastic ties, and a pack of cheap bandannas. Then she went to a mall near the mistress's apartment to window shop until lunch. It was one of the aspects of the job you never got used to. Or, at least, she never had. Hours and hours of hurry up and wait interspersed with brief periods of pure adrenaline. Of course, her body's response to adrenaline was atypical, in the same way as every other member of the special class at school had been. If not at the beginning, then certainly after training and who knew what tinkering. Adrenaline triggered time dilation, focused concentration, and emotional flattening, as well as adding a certain edge to physical performance. But Cally had reason to believe her own atypical adrenaline response was purely natural, for the simple reason that she'd had it years before ever reporting to school. It seemed to run in the family.

, Didn't do crap for the boredom, though. Every agent had their own way of coping with that. Some read. Some played games on their PDAs. Some collected the most fiendishly difficult crossword puzzles they could find. Cally shopped. Oh, not if there was some strategic advantage to lying low, of course. She kept a backup supply of about a gazillion color catalogs just in case. But mostly she watched the people, tried on clothes or shoes, looked at the latest gizmos and gadgets. She'd been told it was a reaction to the privations of her childhood. Personally, she thought the shrinks were full of shit. For a young, attractive female, there was *no place* that was more completely anonymous and unremarkable than a shopping mall. She was seen by at least one hundred people in a given hour, and remembered by none of them. She made sure never to buy enough to give a salesgirl a memorable commission, she never responded to any boys or men with eye contact or more than a totally impersonal, casual social smile. It was the next best thing to being invisible, and the walking worked off some of the pre-mission nervous energy. Besides, sometimes she found a really good bargain. Today there was a lovely boat-necked coral blouse on clearance. It would look great under the oatmeal slacks and blazer she was planning to wear tonight. The reason it was marked so low was a snag in the back that would be obvious the minute she took the blazer off. It was perfect, since she was only going to wear it once.

By mid-afternoon, the mall restroom was empty enough that she could change clothes and do her makeup without drawing a lot of attention. The dark, permed curls didn't need more than a quick brushing.

A bit before four, she pulled into a convenience store parking lot near the apartment complex. She tapped the buttons to wake up the AI simulator. "Hey, buckley."

"It's all coming apart, now, isn't it?"

"No, buckley. I just want you to plot the three most probable routes, based on the target's pattern information from the cameras, from the Fleet Strike Tower area to the apartment complex at 2256 Lucky Avenue."

"That's all *you* know. Can't do it."

"What do you mean you can't do it? Buckley, just plot the routes, okay?"

"Sorry, no can do."

"Buckley, I'm really not in the mood for this."

"Nobody ever cares about *my* mood. Here we are, mission falling apart around our ears, about to be overrun by the Posleen, no doubt, or have a nuke dropped on us, or have a C-Dec fall on our heads, or a building col—"

"Enough, buckley." She clenched her fists in exasperation. "Why can't you plot a probable route for the subject from the Tower to the apartment complex?"

"Who said I couldn't? I never said I couldn't," it sounded infernally smug.

She counted to ten very slowly. "Buckley, plot the most probable route, based on the target's pattern, from the Tower to the apartment complex. Display on screen."

"Okay." A section of Chicago street map appeared on the screen with a route outlined in red. It looked like the one she remembered from Friday, but it paid to make sure.

"Now, without erasing the current map and plot, add to it the plot of the second most probable route for the target to take from the Tower to the apartment complex."

"Why do *I* always get saddled with the idiots? Can't do it." It sounded rather pleased about it.

"Why can't you follow that last command, buckley?" she asked between gritted teeth.

"No data on the target's movements exists that is inconsistent with the first route."

"He takes the same route every time?" *Does the guy have a death wish, or what?*

"Brilliant. Keep this up and you may actually begin to understand some of the many things that could go wrong with this situation. Not that it'll do any good," it pronounced morosely.

"Fine. Without getting caught by the host computers, hack in and watch the cameras along his route. If he's moving along the route now, or whenever he starts moving along the route, tell me, place a dot on the screen to show his probable location along the route, updating the information whenever you get more data from the cameras."

"Are you sure you want to know?"

"Why, is he en route?" she queried sharply.

"No. I just thought if you were one of those people who handles disaster better when you don't know it's coming . . ."

"Buckley, other than telling me when the target leaves the Tower to start over here, or telling me if he starts to go somewhere else, shut up."

"Touchy today, aren't we?" It fell silent.

Cally checked the cheap briefcase she'd gotten from an office supply store in the mall. *Change of clothes, sealed in plastic, good. Okay, drugs, wine cooler, plastic ties, multiple pairs of pantyhose, gags, gloves, switchblade, soundbox. . . .* She took the small, gray box with a switch on top and flipped it on. "Testing, testing, testing." The sounds of traffic became muffled and her voice was hollow and muted. She turned it off and clipped it to her belt before taking the switchblade out and shoving it in her pocket. It was a useful weapon when you wanted to avoid killing someone, as it usually immediately convinced them you *would* kill them, and ensured their full cooperation in whatever you asked of them. Well, with certain psychological types, anyway. Right now the non-target's healthy sense of terror was the woman's best chance of staying alive.

She opened the wine cooler and took a couple of swallows, making a bit of room at the top. Then she took the bottle with the red mark and carefully poured the drugs into the wine. The drug bottle went back in a pocket of the briefcase, and the cap back on the wine cooler. She swirled it around very gently. *Won't take much to mix it up, but we don't want any soda-pop showers.*

She put a small red mark on the label with one of the markers and the wine cooler bottle went back in the case, along with a fresh one, and took out a small pink nametag and pinned it to the lapel of her jacket. The tag announced that she was Lisa Johnson and bore the familiar logo of a well-known cosmetics company. She glanced at her watch. Four-twelve.

"Buckley."

"We're about to die, aren't we?"

"No, buckley. Keep looking for the target's car, but I also need you to access the cameras I placed in apartment 302C and tell me whether there's anyone home and where they are."

"Ah, the confidence of youth. Two in the apartment."

"Two?!"

"One in the kitchen, one under the couch."

"Under the . . ." *I'm gonna kill him.* "Buckley, ignore the damn cat. How many *human beings* in 302C?"

"Obviously, you're underestimating the damage a properly enraged house cat can do. One human, adult female, in the kitchen."

"Right. Tell me if she leaves the apartment or anyone else enters."

"You're welcome."

"Thank you, buckley," she added.

"You know, it's not too late to fly home and forget the whole thing," it offered hopefully.

"Shut up, buckley." The car was silent for a few moments. "Oh, except for telling me when the target leaves and updating his progress along the route here."

"Right."

She tried to avoid tapping her nails as she waited. The one thing that had been hardest to train out all those years ago had been a tendency to fidget while waiting for something important. It still took an act of will. She punched up some music on the car's system, just whatever was next on the cube, and suppressed the desire to tap her nails as the melancholy opening piano lines of "Hello" drifted into the enclosed space. She wrinkled her nose, "No angst, thank you very much," and paged through until she found "Don't Fear the Reaper." It wasn't so much that the modern remix was better than the original as it was that it was less . . . dated. Several members of the original band had purchased rejuv by signing up for a colonization tour on Diess early on, then had proceeded on an exhausting round of after-hours concerts, earning enough from their fellow colonists, Fleet, and Fleet Strike personnel to buy back their contracts and pay their passage home.

Of course, a band full of juvs was controversial back here on Earth, but they were a rock band. They were used to it. She told the system to play the whole album.

The scream of the guitars opening "Godzilla" was just as powerful as ever, and she honestly regretted having to punch the sound off when the buckley chimed in warning that the target was on his way.

"Is the woman in 302C still in the kitchen, buckley?"

"Unfortunately. Would you like a list of the ten worst things that could go wrong with this mission?"

"No!"

"Really, it's no trouble at all," it offered helpfully.

"Shut up, buckley."

"Right."

CHAPTER SEVEN

Cally stood at the door of 302C. She had the top of the briefcase unzipped, but held the handles together in one hand so the things inside didn't show. She shut her eyes for a moment and pulled on her sales persona. As she opened them a wide, bright smile spread across her face, lighting her eyes with enthusiasm. She rang the bell and waited.

In a minute, she heard a rustling sound on the other side of the door. Probably the mistress looking through the peephole. The door opened.

"Uh . . . hello?" The woman's hair was in hot rollers, her face bare like she'd just washed it.

"Hi, I'm Lisa from Pink Passion Cosmetics, and I wondered if you'd be interested in our free five-minute makeover this afternoon?" She radiated helpful good cheer.

"Five minutes . . . I don't have to buy anything?" The girl's eyes had widened at the word "free." She looked at the saleswoman's fresh, expertly made-up face thoughtfully.

"Not a thing. I give you the makeover, leave you a catalog and my number, and if you decide you want anything from it, *you* call *me*. If you don't, you don't." She gave a friendly, slightly conspiratorial smile.

"Five minutes." The girl looked at her watch. "Uh, sure. Come on in." She stood back and gestured for the assassin to come in.

Cally casually put a hand to her belt as she walked through the door and flipped the small switch. An instant after the mistress closed the door, Cally had dropped the briefcase and was on her,

129

knocking her to the floor beside it and landing on top, switchblade at the other woman's throat.

"Lady, you have two choices. Die messily right here, right now, or cooperate and live. I don't care which you pick." She pressed the knife slightly into the woman's throat for emphasis. There was a trick to holding it at just the right angle to feel pointy enough to get the other person's attention without actually breaking the skin. It was especially tricky with a knife that was reasonably sharp, as this one was. Fortunately, she had a lot of practice.

"Oh my God, ohmygod, don't kill me. Please don't kill me. Ohmygod. What do you want? I'll do what you want, just please don't kill me."

"I don't need to kill you, I just need to borrow your apartment for a little while." She fished in the bag and came up with the cooler, checking it quickly for the telltale red mark. "Drink this. It's drugged, of course. To make you sleep and get you out of my way." She handed it to the frightened woman.

"How do I know it's not poison?"

"You don't. You just know you're going to die right here, right now, painfully and messily, if you don't drink it. It's the only chance you've got. Make up your mind, I'm on a tight schedule."

The other woman began unscrewing the cap, but stopped suddenly.

"Charles. You're after Charles." Her voice carried dawning horror.

"Who?" Cally's face was a study in bewilderment. "I was told you lived alone. Is there going to be someone else here?" she asked sternly, pressing the knife a bit harder for emphasis, but still careful not to break the skin.

"Uh . . . no," the woman lied quickly, "Charles is . . . is my cat."

"Oh great. And I'm allergic. Would you hurry up and drink that before I have to kill you?"

The woman stared at her fixedly, as if trying to memorize her features, and downed the drug. Cally watched for the ten minutes or so it took her eyes to glaze over and put the knife away.

"You'll sleep more comfortably in your bed. Come on and let's get you in there to lie down." She got the woman up and helped her into the bedroom, fastening her hands and feet gently but firmly with a couple of the plastic ties and gagging her. The drugged woman wouldn't be coordinated enough to get out and make trouble, and she'd be passed out soon enough. Cally had been careful to touch as little as possible in the apartment so far, but she'd need to wear rubber gloves for the rest of the evening.

She pulled out her PDA and looked at the map on the screen with the blinking dot that indicated the target's car. She'd made good time dealing with the non-target. Petane was still a good fifteen minutes out.

There wasn't really a whole lot left to do to get ready for him. One of the kitchen chairs would be suitable for the interrogation. She moved it behind the door, where he wouldn't see it and get spooked coming in. She found some disposable paper cups in the bathroom and got a drink while she was making sure she wouldn't feel any sudden needs to leave the target alone even for a few minutes. Well, before killing him, anyway. She wrinkled her nose distastefully at the unchanged litter box, the odor of which was not quite overwhelmed by a large bowl of rose and apple potpourri, and went back into the living room to tuck the used paper cup into the briefcase. No sense in leaving bits of third-party DNA lying around that blatantly.

She took the pantyhose out of their packages and cut the legs apart. They weren't as quick and easy as the plastic ties, but the target was likely to fight his bonds at first, and, tied right, they wouldn't leave marks. She took off her jacket and stuffed the pantyhose into her pockets. Then there was nothing left to do but wait. She had given considerable thought in planning how to take him down. On the one hand, she wanted to be very careful what chemicals were in his bloodstream post-mortem. On the other, he outweighed her by a fair bit and was taller. Even with her upgraded strength, leverage was important. He was an obvious juv, so he had nannites that might successfully scavenge out the residue of ether or chloroform before she finished interrogating him. Or they might not. Or he might be immune. His record didn't show any notable martial training beyond what he would have gotten in basic, but you really never knew. Finally she had decided she was going to have to just try to pin him and choke him out, but have a push-button injector of the least detectable general anesthetic she had and have it ready as backup in case he was more trouble hand-to-hand than his record indicated.

"Okay, buckley, wake up." She tapped the screen "You can quit watching any cameras he's driven past already. Watch the cameras I've got in the parking lot out here. When he parks, tell me . . .

uh . . . wait, no *don't* tell me. Just make the screen turn blue." *If I tell it to tell me anything, I swear to god it'll pipe up at exactly the wrong time and I'll end up trashing another PDA. And I need it to record the interrogation.*

"You're afraid I'll say the wrong thing at the wrong time and get us both killed, aren't you?" it accused.

"No, I'd just prefer not to have any unnecessary noises at this stage in the mission."

"Yes, you are. You don't have to lie to spare my feelings."

"Shut up, buckley."

"Right."

She waited in silence as the dot approached on the road. The screen flashed blue and she punched the options to set it to record when activated, flipping it closed before standing and stretching briefly, coming to rest in a loose ready stance against the wall behind the door, about a foot from the hinges. The PDA would need to be less than thirty percent of the distance from the subject to the damper to record effectively.

The wait seemed longer than it really was. Adrenaline had already caused her sense of time dilation to kick in. She could feel her heart beating in her chest and already she felt that mission sensation of being just that extra bit more alive. The colors in the room were richer and more intense than they'd been a few minutes before. Mingled with the pet and air freshener odors of the apartment she could smell the tea the mistress had been drinking in the kitchen. She could hear the slight hollow tone to her own breathing as the sound damper tried to compensate for the noise.

It wasn't long at all before she heard the key in the old-fashioned lock. She forced herself to stay loose and perfectly still, balanced on the edge of the moment, as the handle turned and the door began to swing inward.

He walked in with less situational awareness than a two-year-old, who would have at least been interested in his surroundings. As he shut the door behind him with one hand, he turned expectantly towards the kitchen. Cally doubted he even saw her out of the corner of his eye as she padded up behind him, simultaneously grabbing his hair and kicking the back of his knee sharply, as she pulled backward.

As his knees buckled, bringing his head below her own, her other

arm snaked around his throat, the bone pushing into his wind-
pipe, the hand in his hair sliding smoothly to hold the back of
his head, giving him nowhere to go for air.

Unfortunately, his drive for survival finally kicked in and he
began thrashing frantically, trying to break her grip.

The easiest way to respond would have been to drop down and
finish the neck break. Taking a capable person, and Petane marginally qualified for that category, alive was always harder than a
simple kill.

She didn't know whether it was conscious design or instinct that
made him try to kick out towards an end table full of fragile-
looking knick-knacks, but leaving signs of a scuffle in the apartment would be bad, very bad. As would accidentally strangling the
guy. *And dammit, I've lost count!*

She backed around and dragged him to the middle of the floor
where his thrashing couldn't reach anything, and watched the
second hand on the wall clock for what she hoped was the amount
of time left, lowering him to the floor a few seconds after his
struggles stilled.

Lousy instincts—he didn't even hesitate on the threshold. She
sighed with relief as she found a pulse. Having to do CPR on the
prick would have been annoying.

She worked quickly to secure his hands and feet with plastic
ties before grabbing the chair and pantyhose. There was a strong
risk that securing him to the chair would bring him around before
she was finished. As it did today, of course. She had barely gotten his wrists secured and the plastic removed—too likely to leave
marks—when he came around and started yelling and thrashing
again and tipped himself over.

She ignored him and secured each leg to the appropriate chair
leg before setting the thing upright again. He was still yelling, of
course. *What a moron.* "Look, you idiot," she explained. "Hear that
hollow sound? It's a damper. Nobody can hear you outside the
room, you're just scratching up your throat."

She would have liked to light a cigarette and have a smoke while
he wound down, but leaving stale smoke lying around a scene just
wouldn't work at all. So she just tilted her head to the side and
watched him, waiting. He ran out of steam sooner rather than later,
thank God.

"You're probably wondering why I called this meeting." She

smirked, and then sighed. "Look, Petane, we are doing a comprehensive review of the information you've provided, checking it for the record, including what you say now, measured against how you've reported it in the past. The sooner you spill it, the sooner you can get back there and give your girlfriend some stimulants to wake her up and get on with your night." She shrugged, "Look, mine not to reason why, mine just to get these fucking interrogations out of the way so I can get back to real work."

"Geez, you guys have totally compromised me, you know that? Or as good as. Why the hell did you take the risk of meeting me here? Why not just ask for a meet at the dead drop and give me time to set it up righ . . . oh. Counter Intel." His shoulders slumped. "Are you Fleet Strike, or Army?" His voice had the dead, hopeless tone of a man who really didn't expect to live until morning.

"Very astute of you." She grinned ferally. "But you can still be useful, Colonel. We just need to catalog how much damage you've done and then tell you what we want you to tell them. You should be a happy man. If we can make you useful enough, you may just get to live."

"Wait . . . I . . . I wanna see some ID," he said.

"Oh, so you ask for ID. So you knew who you were dealing with when you decided to become a fucking traitor." She practically spat the words at him.

He blanched.

"So, Colonel, why did you turn." It wasn't a question, but a demand. "I want to hear you say it, you worthless son of a bitch."

"I couldn't help it! They were gonna kill me!" Any vestiges of calm the man had had collapsed. "I got into this fix protecting you guys! You said you were gonna take care of me and then you were nowhere when they came for me. What the hell was I supposed to do?"

"I suppose it never crossed your mind to die like a soldier," she said coldly.

"Yeah, you try it sometime." His voice was bitter and low.

"So, from the beginning." She sat down on the couch and gestured casually with one arm. "Let's just start with you 'getting into this fix' as you put it. Start there. Don't leave anything out. We know most of it. So, needless to say, you really, really don't want to leave anything out. I'm not a very nice person when I'm pissed off." She flipped open the PDA and tapped the record button. She was well inside the record zone.

"Okay, the beginning. So I was a major when I got recalled from the reserves at the beginning of the war. I'd had a couple of jobs with . . . unappreciative CO's and been passed over for promotion and retired before the war. But for a staff command, I wasn't high on the rejuv list and the drugs started running low before they got to me. But I *was* on the list, dammit." He squirmed a bit and rubbed his chin against his shirt to scratch an apparent itch.

"Look, do I have to rehash the whole damn thing? You guys know this part. I was pretty high up in the local lodge. I was a Mason, my dad and granddad had been Masons. And they were good guys, and I trusted them and they trusted me, but then you guys from counter intel came down the pike . . ."

"And bought you."

"Yeah, well, you guys came around asking about clubs and fraternities and secret societies and all, and I wanted to help out and everything—"

"In exchange for . . ." she prompted.

"Yeah, all right, I appreciated you guys righting a wrong there by making the efficiency report by that self-righteous asshole disappear, okay? And you guys always wanted to know stupid things, and everybody knows this secret society paranoia about the Masons is so much bullshit. Anyway, then you guys wanted to know, you know, anywhere lodge members from out of town stayed whenever they came through. And I wouldn't have known, except for a younger lodge member thought I was so high up in the lodge I already knew, and let something slip. And yeah, I guess I was pretty ticked that there was crap going on in my own lodge that nobody had told me about."

"And what did you think we were going to do with that information?"

"Look, I didn't speculate, okay, if that's what you're thinking. It wasn't my business. What had the lodge done for me? They sure as hell hadn't offered me anything like rejuv for me and my wife, and things were getting kinda tough at home, and we were supposed to get it anyway, but I appreciated you guys speeding it up. I knew it wasn't my place to speculate about your business, okay?" His face wrinkled up in sudden bewilderment for a moment and he stopped talking, blinking a few times.

"Hey, how come you're carrying a buckley instead of an AID?" he asked.

"The rejuv would be for the same wife you're cheating on right now?" Her gesture took in the entire apartment.

"Hey, I love my wife," he protested, "but high-powered, dominant males were never wired for centuries of monogamy. It's just something about guys that women just aren't wired to understand, if you know what I mean. Men are what we are, all of us. But I do love my wife. And you still didn't say why you're not carrying an AID." This last was said with the smug expression of someone who has cleverly gotten the upper hand.

"You really are a pathetic schmuck, aren't you? I'm asking the questions."

"Look, why get all pissy over it? You guys always showed me ID bef—"

She saw his face freeze as the penny finally dropped, and his lips clamped shut. *What an absolute fucking moron. A whole team burned because of this idiot and the other morons who tried to cover up their opsec mistakes by recruiting him.*

"I'm not saying another word without ID," he said.

"Of course you are," Cally said conversationally, "because whoever the hell I am, I'm still the damned scary bitch who has you tied to a chair under a sound damper."

"Hey, babe, there are worse things than being tied up by a beautiful woman," he smirked.

Cally was a blur of motion coming off the couch, her heel impacting his groin with such force that he blacked out.

Unfortunately, as he was coming around, she heard, very faintly through the damping, the doorbell and a voice calling something that sounded like it might have been, "Acropolis Pizza." She glared at Petane.

"Ow," he winced, glancing at the doorbell and cringing away from her as much as the chair would allow.

"Fuck. Goddam Murphy really hates my ass today." She grabbed a couple of bandannas out of the briefcase and gagged him quickly, dragging the chair into the kitchen. She couldn't tell whether the doorbell had rung again or not by the time she moved the briefcase behind the door, grabbed her wallet, and answered it.

The pizza guy's eyes darted across her tousled hair and slightly smudged makeup and immediately came to a wrong but convenient conclusion, and his eyes had a knowing twinkle as he checked the amount on the ticket.

"Got a pizza for 'Charles' at this address. That'll be fifty-four ninety seven."

She peeled off a few bills and traded him for the pizza, giving him her best ditzy sex-flushed smile. "Thanks."

She watched him bop down the stairs, whistling. The smile didn't leave her face until after the door was closed and re-locked.

After dropping off the pizza and retrieving Petane from the kitchen, she pulled the gag out and sat back down.

"Okay, asshole. Get back to talking." She put her face down about six inches from his. "Oh, and by the way, do not *ever* imply that I would even consider doing anything sexual with you. You *really* do not want to do that. Understand?"

He nodded rapidly.

"Please don't kick me again. I . . . I . . . And don't make me talk or kill me either. Please? These guys play for keeps. You can't be a Mason, and I guess you're not counter intel, so I don't know who the hell or what the hell you are but those guys play for keeps. As far as I know, I'm the only one of that lodge *or* the original counter intel weenies who's still alive. Please, lady, you can hurt me, but I can't talk to you or I'm gonna die. Please don't kill me." He started to shake.

"I wish to God all this had played out differently, but I can't change it now. For over thirty years I've lived each day just trying to see another one. If you're going to hurt me, or kill me, I can't stop you, but please God don't."

The sound of her slow clapping broke the silence that had fallen for a moment after he finished.

"You're about thirty years too late, Colonel. How many people didn't get another day for thirty years because of you? Do you even know? How the hell did you even get out of basic?" She cut him off before he started, "No, don't answer, I might puke." She reached down into the bag and pulled out a zipper pack.

"Look, I'm tired of dicking around with you—and don't go there." She rifled through the pack and pulled out a syringe. "Are you immune to sodium pent, Colonel? Let's find out."

The look he turned on her reminded her of a scared cocker spaniel, and she sighed as she injected him in the arm.

Three test injections later she found an interrogation drug he wasn't immune to. It was one of the standard ones Fleet Strike had access to.

"Gee, they never did plan to tell you anything really sensitive, did they? Some vital source."

It took three hours to debrief him. She normally wouldn't have eaten while working, but she was going to have to dispose of the pizza somehow since none of it would be in the mistress's stomach and putting any in his stomach wouldn't match. The delivery was a loose end, but if it ever turned up, she'd be wearing a different face in a different place, anyway. Sometimes, there was just nothing you could do. *God, this day sucks.*

Finally, she had gotten as much information out of Petane as he had in his brain. As Robertson had said, none of it was of a magnitude that would justify leaving a traitor alive for thirty years, and if nobody in the Fleet Strike establishment had bothered to immunize him against the higher level interrogation drugs, he never would be trusted with anything sensitive enough to be really useful. He wasn't alert enough to refuse when she offered him one of the plain wine coolers, and drank thirstily from the glass she had found in a cupboard.

Time to clean up the mess. I really think less of Team Hector for going along with this. Another syringe in the pack had a very small amount of a dye that biodegraded quickly but, used skillfully, created very sincere needle tracks.

Unfortunately, it only decayed properly if the subject was still alive, so she had to listen to his whimpering as she stabbed his veins in the appropriate places and released just a tiny spot of the dye. At school, practicing this skill on each other had been less than fun. It had gotten her over a minor nervousness around needles, but the dye did tend to sting a bit.

When she had enough tracks to be convincing, she waited five minutes and retied his feet and hands to each other, rather than the chair. The interrogation drugs were wearing off, but he was still drugged enough to offer little resistance as she maneuvered him over her shoulder and carried him into the bedroom. As always, the weight didn't present much problem to her upgraded musculature, but the leverage took some managing—particularly as he was not quite dead weight and tended to twitch.

In the bedroom, she did the distasteful but necessary things to set the scene up for the forensics people and gave him his final injection, prepping a second glass with the mistress's lip marks and drugged wine and leaving them on the nightstand next to the bed. She poured a second plain wine cooler down the drain and had two clean, empty bottles for the kitchen trash.

She was putting the assorted debris—used ties, gag, syringes—away when she had the sudden unexpected need to make a dash for the bathroom. She was violently sick in the toilet, and swore weakly as she cleaned her face with toilet tissue afterwards, making sure every bit of the unwelcome evidence got thoroughly flushed and scrubbing out the toilet afterwards. It would not be out of character for the mistress to have cleaned up a bit for her date, and the cleaning smell would go unremarked even if it was noticed.

Of all the damned times to start catching a stomach flu. I can't even remember the last time I was sick with something. And I sure as hell am not pregnant, thank God. She stalked into the kitchen and resumed the careful scene clean-up.

"You can stop recording, buckley. Save it as . . . call it 'Hector Archive.'"

"We've got to run for it now, don't we? Not that it's any use."

"No, buckley. I'm just about through here. You can set AI emulation back to level two."

"But . . . but . . . but . . . oh all right . . ." It trailed off. The buckley was never as enthusiastic when things were going well.

Home before eleven. Cally looked at her watch and unbuckled it from her wrist. *For a solo mission, that part at least wasn't so bad.*

The briefcase with all the incriminating evidence came into the hotel room with her, as per SOP when a crew wasn't available. She'd carry it in herself when she reported tomorrow and hand it over to the cleaning department. She'd given considerable thought to how to handle any stress with her bosses over her vacation and had decided to brazen it out. She wanted to discuss the priorities that had left a traitor who had caused the death of a whole team of agents alive for a few decades after that act. This should effectively open the conversation.

She took her makeup off slowly, oddly tired this evening. *Well, that's absolutely, finally, unquestionably the last of my personal better dead list. I'd thought Worth was it, but okay, so it was Petane. Yay.*

Rah. I'll have to celebrate that sometime. She shook her head to clear it a bit and grabbed a clean teddy to sleep in. *Not up for a night on the town? Me? I definitely must be coming down with something. Ah, best just get an early night.*

She looked at herself in the mirror as she changed, running a hand through the brown curls. They'd likely be gone by this time tomorrow. Sinda Makepeace was so silver-blond and fair she looked like the stereotypical Swedish ski bunny. It wasn't often she had a cover with lighter coloring than her own. *I'm about to start brooding again. Geez. I must be really tired. To bed.*

She grabbed a washcloth without thinking about it and plonked it on the night table, turning off the alarm clock and then the light.

She would have liked to linger in bed in the morning. It had been such a wonderful dream. She would have sworn she had actually tasted one of the delicious conch omelets and even a slice of fresh key lime pie. She had been sitting in Mom's lap, and Dad had just brought a fresh glass of limeade, tart and cold with ice.

The ice in the drink wasn't the only thing that was cold. Out of reflex, she reached for the washcloth with one hand as she wrestled herself free of the sodden and clammy sheets. They stank of sour sweat and she stripped off her nightclothes and left them in the floor as she made a beeline for a hot shower to clean up and warm herself. *Huh. Must have had a fever break in the night or something. I hate being sick.*

Tuesday, May 21

After checking out, she got out her phone and called a number, "I need a cab." She gave the address.

When the cab arrived, she left her suitcase and backpack in the trunk, taking only the briefcase and her purse. The cabby didn't talk to her until they pulled up to a coin laundry.

"There's a fire door at the back next to the restroom. Don't pay any attention to the sign about the alarm. Get in the back of the truck," he said, touching something on the seat beside himself that might have been a PDA screen.

"Thanks." She gave him a nice tip and a small smile, even though the meter had obviously not been running.

The single person in the coin laundry didn't even look up as she walked through and out the back. It was the kind of neighborhood that discouraged curiosity about other people's business.

In the alley, there was a squat woman in gray coveralls holding the back of the truck open. She didn't speak to Cally, just waited as she got in and closed the door behind her. Inside, the boxes of what appeared to be housewares were tightly lashed down to keep them from slipping around, and Cally blessed whoever had loaded the truck for their thoughtfulness. She found the least uncomfortable place to wedge herself for the ride and sat down.

It was well-known among upper level operatives that the Bane Sidhe had a base, a sort of mini Sub-Urb of their own, in the vicinity of Chicago. In this case, "in the vicinity" meaning within a two hour drive, give or take. Today it took longer, and she was sore and heartily tired of bouncing around in the unpadded back of the truck by the time the truck slowed, turned, and did the starting, stopping, standing, and maneuvering that indicated arrival at the base.

By the time the door opened, she was more than ready to check in and go find a deep, hot bath for a couple of hours. Her first stop was in a little office immediately off of the underground parking lot. She handed the briefcase and her car keys to a man of indeterminate age with lead gray hair and a very large nose.

"Marty, the case and contents need the full treatment." She grabbed a stylus and scribbled an address, as well as car make, model, and tag number, on the pad on the counter. "The car is also dirty, and needs pickup today—it's a hotel lot. You can clean the clothes in the trash bag in the suitcase, but I'd really like the rest of the clothes and the backpack and contents back. How's Mary?"

"Fine, fine. What have you been up to? Didn't know you were in the field."

"Target of opportunity. Wasn't able to do a full set up. Sorry about that. I know these improv jobs are harder. How are Sue and Cary?"

"She graduated this spring. Didn't pick my field or her mom's. Don't know what that girl sees in machines, but they tell me she's an artist. And I got a letter from my junior reprobate this week. Seems he's finding out that minding the nuns is more than just a good idea."

Cally returned his wicked grin.

"That all?" he asked, and as she nodded, he patted her hand gently. "Got you covered, sweetheart. Go take a load off and try to forget about it."

She logged herself in to one of the temporary suites and went down to grab that bath. By the time she got out, her trunk of personal effects would have been wheeled up and installed in the room. She left the "Do Not Unpack" sign on the dresser and went in to run her bath. The organization understood how transient and rootless field operatives could feel and believed firmly in reducing the disorientation by maintaining an assortment of personal effects on site. Maintaining entire apartments for operatives who might never return from a mission was cost prohibitive, and additionally tended to emphasize losses in peoples' minds, so the personal gear was maintained in the modern equivalent of steamer trunks which were delivered to the operative's room when he or she checked in on base, and wheeled back into storage when he or she left.

Cally appreciated having her own clothes and her own things when she was on base, but she preferred unpacking them herself or not at all rather than having them repeatedly handled by strangers, much less by friends or acquaintances.

She paid for lunch to be sent up. If she went to the cafeteria she would no doubt run into people she knew and would have to talk to. She would, in fact, have to be Cally O'Neal, and she wasn't quite ready for that yet. Which just went to show she was coming down with something and ought to stop by the medic's office just in case. Except that she didn't really feel like doing that. She decided to see if a long, hot bath, a good workout, and an early night would put her right. No sense in bothering a doctor for something as trivial as a touch of stomach upset and, well, the night sweats must have been a touch of fever. And she was neither queasy nor feverish now, just a little draggy.

In the bathroom, she added some bath salts from a jar under the counter to her bath. Scentless, of course, since housekeeping never knew if the operative in the room would be male or female, but still good for a soak. Real decadence would have to wait for the arrival of her own things.

The brown contacts came out and her own cornflower blue eyes stared back at her as she pinned her hair on top of her head, looking at a curl ruefully. She wasn't about to add a chemical relaxant, bleach, and dye on top of a perm and dye job. She'd be walking around for the next few days looking like she had a head full of broom straw. It would just have to wait until they did her new cover on the slab.

She grabbed the large white terry bathrobe from the rack outside the bathroom and hung it on the inside of the door, leaving her clothes where they fell as she stripped off and lowered herself into the hot water up to her chin.

Levon Martin looked into the mirror at his darkened skin tone and dark contacts, running his hands over the patterns shaved into his hair and shrugged. He licked his very thin lips and pulled out some lip balm. With the weather warmed up, that should quit being a problem soon. He'd be happy to get back into his own skin, but this afternoon's urban reconnaissance had required a different social face. This was not going to be a fun interview. He straightened his golf shirt and ensured it was neatly tucked into his slacks before leaving his room, listening to the electronic lock click faintly behind him as he entered the halls of the Chicago base. The transit elevator at the end of the hall didn't take long to route him to the administrative octant of the Urb, where he had a short walk down the hall to enter an outer office.

The human receptionist behind the desk was there not because he was necessary to keep track of appointments or forms, although he did both, but because his superior's time was valuable and because he had displayed a talent for guarding that time from unnecessary interruptions.

"Martin, Team Hector. I'm early."

"You are. Hang on just a second." The man got up and poked his head around the door, murmuring softly for a moment to the person on the other side. It would have been audible to Martin's upgraded hearing if he had chosen to pay close attention. Under the circumstances, he did not.

"You can go in," he said. "You're on the heels of another interruption, and we might as well combine them."

Martin walked into the inner office and sat down, waiting for the young-looking man rather eccentrically still wearing a clerical collar to look up from whatever was being displayed by his AID. The hologram was blurred from this side of the desk.

Father Nathan O'Reilly had had the credibility of his improbable good health, given his officially unrejuvenated state, wear thin twenty years before and had come inside to exercise his considerable organizational talents in the Earthside bureaucracy that had inevitably developed after the Bane Sidhe had resumed contact with their human allies.

Taking him inside had required very special planning and no little risk. Catholic priests didn't exactly have a high rate of violent death, and for various reasons at the time it had been necessary that he actually be seen by several people to be very sincerely dead. The drug used was a resource-intensive collaboration between the Indowy and Crabs, and was a timed-release variant of Hiberzine that showed none of that drug's surface symptoms. The main problems with it was that the dosage was tricky, requiring rather exact knowledge of the patient's physical stats, and the hibernatory effectiveness was degraded by the same changes that reduced the visible symptoms. If the dosage was off by even a tiny amount, or the antidote was not administered within twelve hours, the simulated death tended to become very real in ways even the slab couldn't fix.

The drug was so secret it didn't even have a name, customarily being packaged in a water-insoluble crunch capsule to be bitten and swallowed by the willing target of an extraction. The time delay served two purposes. One was allowing time for the patient's stomach acid to fully dissolve the capsule material. The other was preventing any possibility that some sharp-eyed observer would see the patient take the pill and immediately fall over "dead."

Still, the ten percent risk of not waking up at all had required a great deal of trust on his part, and it wasn't exactly a comfortable drug. All things considered, he was rather glad he'd never have to take it again.

Decentralized as the Bane Sidhe inherently were, a functioning planetary cell system required *some* central organization. Chicago Base was it. The priest had taken command of it fresh after its commissioning, its very discreet construction having been a ten year project that had required . . . encouraging . . . the Himmit with a number of exceptionally good story opportunities.

"Display off," he told his AID. "So, Levon, what's on your mind?"

"One of my agents turned up dead of a heart attack this morning," he began.

"I'm sorry to hear that. Was he known to be ill?"

"No, the reverse. He was found dead in his mistress's bed. Consensus from preliminary investigation was that the heart attack was induced by a drug overdose, consistent with the agent's drug problem."

"Were we aware of such a problem?"

"No, sir. In fact, apparently he had also provided recreational drugs to the mistress, not a known user. She doesn't remember a thing. Consensus from the investigators is that he wished to perform acts upon the mistress's body in which she would be reluctant to engage in a fully conscious state, but that the drugs he took to enhance his own pleasure and performance killed him by causing a heart attack before he could complete such acts."

"You don't believe any of this." It was not a question. The father made beckoning motions with both hands.

"Would it interest you to know that the dead druggie was one Colonel Charles Petane and that Miss O'Neal checked in today a bit after eleven, complete with a bag for the cleaning department?"

The priest paused for a moment and replied gravely, "Members of the clergy of Holy Mother Church do not use foul language."

"I'm aware of that, Father."

"I wasn't reminding *you*. Spill it. What else do you have?"

"A person matching the description Miss O'Neal was wearing when she came in checked out of a hotel in Chicago this morning. The same hotel where Miss O'Neal's cab picked her up on her way to report in. The same hotel where she requested the cleaning department retrieve and clean a car and assorted personal effects. The name on the hotel register, by the way, was Marilyn Grant. Miss Grant had been a guest of the hotel since Friday evening. I won't know until a discrete opportunity presents itself, but I would expect that if I check trees and other likely spots in the vicinity of the late colonel's house and his mistress's apartment that I will find traces of the adhesive we customarily use to affix temporary surveillance cameras."

"Don't. If she got by with it, I don't want to arouse any suspicions by getting caught doing belated cleaning." He called up the Petane file on his AID and reviewed it briefly. "If they do turn up foul play, Petane was sufficiently small fry that an investigation won't lead anywhere. We'll just hope it stays on the books as an overdose rather than an unsolved murder." He pinched the bridge of his nose and shut his eyes for a minute. "I doubt she has any idea of the havoc this is likely to wreak with our Indowy friends."

He stood and walked around the desk, shaking the operative's hand as the younger man rose. "Thanks, Levon. I'll take it from here."

As he left the office, clearly having been dismissed, the operative heard his boss issuing terse instructions to the AID.

"Get Mike O'Neal, Sr., here as soon as possible, I don't care if you have to dispatch a shuttle just for him to do it. Get the rest of Team Isaac in with him if you can, but don't hold up his departure more than two hours maximum for their sakes."

CHAPTER EIGHT

The furniture in Father O'Reilly's office had been discreetly changed since this afternoon, as had the lighting. A small storeroom on the same hall contained furniture suitable for any of the species a Bane Sidhe base commander was likely to deal with in the course of his duties. The area in front of his desk had been set up with a comfortable chair for a human, one for an Indowy, and a low coffee table that would be appropriate for both. He had placed his AID on the coffee table to reduce his tendency to fidget with it when he had to discuss something particularly unpleasant.

Bane Sidhe base personnel, as opposed to operatives, did use AIDs. Clean ones. Manufactured on site, in fact. O'Reilly's AID had information not only on comfortable light frequency combinations for humans and each alien species, but the least uncomfortable compromises for any combination.

He had a freshly brewed pot of strong coffee, as well as an ice bucket with distilled bottled water enriched with aesthetically appropriate trace minerals, set up on a table in the corner of his office when the Indowy Aelool arrived.

As he handed the Aelool his customary glass of iced water with an olive, even after all this time he couldn't help being reminded of a small, fuzzy green teddy bear.

Human and Indowy facial expressions and body language had virtually nothing in common, but those of all races who dealt with other species frequently made a habit of learning to interpret and copy as many of the other races' nonverbal cues as possible. Consequently, the priest knew exactly what his friend meant when he reacted to the human's addition of a large shot of Bushmill's whiskey to his coffee by raising the fleshy muscle directly above one eye and tilting his head slightly.

"We have a problem," Father O'Reilly said.

"I gathered that. You normally do not add such a substance to your drink until much later in the evening."

"Thomas, display the colonel, please," the priest addressed his AID. A foot-high hologram of the late Colonel Charles Petane appeared above the coffee table.

"Until yesterday, this man was one of our minor agents. To refresh your memory, he was recruited after he was instrumental in causing the loss of Team Conyers. It was believed that his position as the U.S. Army liaison to Fleet Strike was the first step to his eventual development as an important source of sensitive information and that that potential value outweighed any deterrent value to killing him in retaliation for the deaths of the team members," he began, pausing to see if he had successfully refreshed Aelool's memory.

"If I recall correctly, that was a matter of some debate."

"And involved the decision to protect some of our operatives from knowledge of the decision, yes. That's an awful euphemism, isn't it? More to the point, we lied." He took a large gulp of his coffee.

"Most of my compatriots in our side of the organization did not understand the need," Aelool said, "but, yes, I remember your people felt it necessary and I believe I can appreciate why. I don't remember a follow up as to the usefulness of information the agent provided, but right now I am more curious about your choice of verb tense in describing him." Aelool's eyes appeared to be focused on the olive at the bottom of his glass, watching it roll as he tilted the glass slightly.

"The agent is deceased as of yesterday evening. We believe that Cally O'Neal became aware that he was alive and killed him. We are still gathering information."

"This is no small thing." The alien's closed posture radiated concern to O'Reilly, who had become an expert in communication with Indowy generally and this Indowy in particular. He set his glass carefully on the table and met the human's eyes.

"I would be most grateful if you would add about half a shot from that bottle to this drink." The Aelool sat very still, expressionless, as he waited for his host to fulfill the request. "I understand your expertise in the psychology of sophonts other than your own species, Father O'Reilly, but I wonder if it is possible for you to understand how very badly my people are likely to react to this incident." He rubbed one hand across his face, slowly. "What have you done in response so far?"

"I've got Michael O'Neal, Senior, en route at the moment, and I've just informed you of the incident. Miss O'Neal checked in late this morning, on her own, so I haven't as yet needed to take any action to secure her. No one has as yet attempted to discuss our concerns with her." He retrieved the bottle and added a shot to the glass. He had seen the Aelool consume alcohol perhaps twice in the past twenty years. Its effect on Indowy was slightly more intense than on humans, even after accounting for differences in body mass. They rarely indulged.

"Good. I would suggest that you don't. You will need to gather information from her, I understand that. It will not minimize the damage much, but it will at least be somewhat helpful if O'Neal Senior conducts all conversation with her on this matter. Although you humans do not have clans as we do, to my people it will look as though she has been brought up in front of her acting head of clan to answer for the act. This will be a small help, but it will be a help. Among Indowy, you will understand, such a meeting in a circumstance of misbehavior is a serious consequence in and of itself."

"Will it be enough?"

"By no means. That you even ask illustrates some of the problem. But it will be a start, and it may make it possible to mend the rest with care and time. I will have to, as you would put it, talk fast."

Cally sat in the conference room Papa O'Neal had reserved when he had arranged to meet her this morning before lunch. It had actually taken longer than she had expected for someone to talk to her, and this was an interesting opening gambit in the reckoning that was now due on both sides.

She was playing solitaire on screen when the PDA piped up. "Now's when it really hits the fan."

"Maybe," she said.

"You're agreeing with me. Things must be far worse than I thought. Neither of us is going to leave here alive, are we?"

"Shut up, buckley."

"Right."

A red-haired man with very old eyes and a bulge in his cheek came in the door and sat on the edge of the table. He smelled of Red Man chewing tobacco, and took a moment to spit into the otherwise empty Styrofoam coffee cup he carried in one hand, before setting it down on the table, near enough to reach but too far to be knocked over by accident.

"Cally, did you kill Colonel Petane?" He spoke each word slowly, as if he already knew the answer.

"Why, yes, Granpa. As a matter of fact I did." She flipped the PDA closed and dropped it in her purse, took out a cigarette, lit it, all without taking her eyes off of him. Her arms stayed close in as she took a pull, her elbow propped in one hand. She regarded him steadily, waiting for him to speak.

He was silent for a moment, resting his forehead in one hand, before wiping it down his face and rubbing his chin. He picked up the cup and spat again before putting it back down.

"You know, you always hope that you can somehow keep the next generation from making the mistakes that you made. Part of getting old, I guess." He took a deep breath and was silent for another long moment. "Would you mind telling me just what you were thinking when you decided that this was a *good* idea?"

"Sure. No problem. I became aware, on my vacation, that someone on our Targets of Opportunity list was falsely carried on the list as inactive because the database had him, inaccurately at the time, listed as deceased. Naturally, he couldn't be properly regarded as inactive since he was, in fact, alive. Therefore, since he was on the list as a Target of Opportunity, I followed standing organizational doctrine, took out the target, and reported back in to file my after action reports and prep for the next mission."

"I never raised you to be a guardhouse lawyer, young lady."

"Hardly young." She blew a perfect smoke ring which wafted away towards an air vent.

"You're acting it."

"You didn't raise me to crap all over my responsibilities to my fellow team members, either." She picked up her Styrofoam cup of coffee, frowned at the dregs and tapped her ashes into it.

"One, Team Conyers wasn't your team. Two, do you honestly

think they would have condoned elimination of a potentially useful source merely for revenge? Do you?"

"One, you're correct. They weren't my team, they were a fellow team. Two, Petane was not placed on the Targets of Opportunity list by me, and he wasn't placed there for revenge. He was placed there, as I understand it, because it's bad policy to allow fucking traitors who have ratted out your field operatives and gotten them killed to keep breathing. That he wasn't removed from the list indicates to me that at some level someone was fully aware that a mistake had been made. Three, thorough interrogation revealed that Petane was not only not a useful source to date, but that his potential for future usefulness as a source was insignificant. Would you like my report?" she offered coldly.

"Cally, you knew full well this was above your pay grade. Did it never even occur to you to come in and discuss the issue and propose a formal, official reevaluation of the worthless scumbag's status? Did it even cross your mind? Tell me something, what do you think your role in this organization is?"

"I like to think of myself as the chlorine in the gene pool."

"If you think this is a time to be flip, we've got a much bigger problem than I thought."

"Okay, I don't. I believe that deciding to keep a traitor alive who had betrayed operatives to their deaths was a very questionable decision. Even had he been a very high quality source. However, had he been a high quality source, I would have left him breathing and with the belief that the interrogation had been a field review—a test that he had passed. I would have let him live despite my strong conviction that the decision to do so was wrong."

"What, you just set yourself up all on your own to evaluate an agent's value? Who made you God, Cally?"

"I became aware of his lack of value at the same time I became aware he was alive. The interrogation was merely confirming that information. Still, had he had any significant redeeming value as a source, he would still be breathing."

"Yeah, we found that leak. Fortunately, he's not *my* problem," he said.

"Would you like my report?"

"Do I want it? No. Am I going to need it as part of cleaning up this mess, if it even can be cleaned up? Yes. Load it over."

"Buckley, transmit the interrogation data and after action report to Michael O'Neal, Senior's AID." For once, the buckley made the correct decision to stay silent.

"Miss O'Neal, you are to consider yourself confined to quarters pending a determination in this matter," he said formally, and added, "And Cally—don't take any liberties with that order. That would include any electronic liberties with the computers of this base or anywhere else. Meals will be delivered. If the Bane Sidhe need you to go anywhere else on base, you will receive those orders from me. You are not to communicate with anyone else without a direct order from me. Is that understood?"

"Yes, sir." Cally's face was absolutely still as she accepted her dismissal, retrieved her purse, and left the room to return to her suite.

When she got back to her quarters the cleaning people had gotten her luggage from the road trip back to her. It killed a whole fifteen minutes or so to go through the pack and see what was still there. She didn't know whether to be surprised or not that everything except the plastic bag of operation-tainted clothes was there. Someone had even, thoughtfully, retrieved her music cube from the car sound system. A second cube and a small bottle of clear liquid was next to it in the case. She turned the buckley's AI emulation all the way off to use the PDA as a dumb cube reader and inserted the cube.

"Not everyone thinks you did the wrong thing. The shit can't be stopped from hitting the fan, but at least you can have your stuff back. This message will self destruct in ten seconds, but please scrub and flush the cube, anyway. Thanks for keeping the faith, Miss O'Neal." She read the words off a hologram of an old-fashioned video screen. After, she took the cube out and dropped it into the vinegar her anonymous admirer had supplied. In the bathroom, she dumped the vinegar down the toilet and flushed. If they weren't specifically watching for it, it would never come up.

Of course, it could be a test, but when it came right down to it, she wasn't as young as she looked and was way too old to be that paranoid. She turned the AI emulation back on.

"So, buckley, is there a Bane Sidhe regulation for people confined to quarters that would make downloading a few books and movies from the base library count as 'electronic liberties'?"

"They'll probably shoot you and I'll get wiped and handed to some kid as a video game box."

"Is there a regulation, buckley?" she repeated coldly.

"No, but you don't really imagine that that's going to matter to *them*, do you? Would you like me to list the five top policies they could use to justify shooting you?"

"Shut up, buckley."

"Really, it would be no trouble."

"Shut *up*, buckley."

"Right."

One of the things in her backpack from the road trip was the cube where she had stored the initial take from the research on Sinda Makepeace. It said she grew up in Wisconsin. In addition to a broad selection of really old movies, the base library had a textbook with a junior high level history of the state, including a rather large volume entitled *The Complete and Unabridged History of Cheese*, and a whole pack of Fleet Strike manuals for training generally, and Makepeace's MOS in particular.

If they didn't decide to send her out on the mission, it wouldn't matter. If they did, being unprepared could really suck. And between that and watching Fred and Ginger cut a rug—flat and *not* colorized, thank you very much—she managed to kill time until a knock at her door told her lunch had arrived.

She looked at the single link of soy sausage, cornbread, creamed corn, carton of milk, and apple on the tray with a touch of disbelief.

"I ain't believin' this. I think they're really pissed at me, buckley."

"You're just catching on to that? You used to be smarter. Incoming message from Michael O'Neal, Senior. Do you want the bad news now, or after you eat?"

"Play it, buckley."

A foot-high hologram of her grandfather, from the shoulders up, appeared a foot or so above the PDA. She had to move around to see his face. The buckley wasn't smart enough to display the message at a conversational distance in front of her like a true AID would.

"Cally, you have a three-fifteen appointment in medical. Please be a few minutes early."

Well, it didn't sound like he was coming to deliver her personally or sending an escort. That was something.

▶   ‖   ◀

Doctor Albert Vitapetroni had a well-developed poker face and empathetic manner. It was a professional necessity for a psychiatrist. As the head of psychiatry for the clinic at Chicago Base, he might have to see any human member of the large organization. It would have been humanly impossible, not to mention in specific cases irrational, to like all of his charges.

The lean and fit, though balding, man pacing in his office and playing idly with one of his desk toys was not one of his favorite fellow Bane Sidhe. He couldn't actually say the man was a patient, because as a computing operative the man generally stayed out of the line of fire enough not to require his services. And, of course, he was not here for those services now. Instead, the operative was making a bit of a nuisance of himself rambling on about his three-fifteen patient.

"That's the trouble with operatives in her branch of the business. You can only make somebody kill over and over for so many years before they go sociopath on you."

"Mr. Wallace, you have just illustrated why professionals are so chagrinned by laypeople's use of psychiatric jargon. Miss O'Neal is most certainly *not* a sociopath."

"Psychopath, whatever. And you can't exactly say that if you haven't seen her yet, can you? If you have preconceived notions before you even see her, seems to me you'd do everyone a service by, well, I don't want to hurt your feelings, but by—"

"Operative Wallace, while I admired your father as a professional colleague, I feel I need to remind you that growing up with a parent who is a psychiatrist does not make *you* a psychiatrist." He took a deep breath and tried to recover his professional calm. "Jay, if you need to talk or something, feel free to talk with my receptionist and she'll fit you in. We don't have to even call it an appointment if you'd rather not, but right now I really need to get some of this paperwork done before this afternoon's round of patients. Sorry to shove you out the door, but if you'll excuse me..."

"Sure. No problem. I guess I'll see you later or something." The operative held up both hands in a gesture of acceptance and backed through the door, shutting it behind him.

The doctor watched him go and sat staring at, or really past, the closed door for a minute. *I don't have any rational reason I* can put my finger on, other than minor little annoyances like what happened just now, but I just plain don't like him. I've never caught him doing anything underhanded—well, more than any operative has to—and there's nothing in his file, test results are fine, but I just can't stand the little weasel. And this whole Cally O'Neal mess is extra stress I did not need this week. Dammit, I told *them* years ago what would happen if she ever found out that rat bastard was alive. I told *them* to keep that secret and keep her out of Chicago to reduce the risk of an unfortunate coincidental meeting. So somebody doesn't listen well enough and now the mess lands in my lap. God, I need a vacation.

Vitapetroni answered the knock on his door at ten after three. It was like her to be early. It would take longer to jot down his impressions than it would to make them. Subject was neatly but casually dressed. Faded but neat jeans and olive drab T-shirt consistent with Cally persona. Head carried slightly awkwardly. Probably uncomfortable with a hair color and texture that doesn't match current role. No contact lenses, eyes natural color.

"Cally, how are you? Come in and have a seat." As he took her hand, he noted that the nails were bare of polish and dull, as if polish had been recently removed. Also consistent with Cally persona. Good.

"Hi, Doc." She smiled brightly, but he noticed as she sat in one of his comfortably, if cheaply, upholstered chairs that her arms stayed close in to her sides and her body tilted at an angle, not facing him straight on. Her hands were not clasped, but they were together in her lap, the fingertips lightly touching.

He cocked an eyebrow at her and waited, as he grabbed a seat in his desk chair. The desk itself was pushed against the wall to keep it from coming between him and the patient. He waited, but she'd been around long enough to know that game, and they trained them out of any tendency to chatter. She didn't fill the silence.

"It wasn't a rhetorical question. I meant it. How are you?"

"I've been better. Work's been a bit stressful, lately." Her tone was still falsely bright.

"But it wasn't work that caused your current problem, was it?" He made a couple of notes on his second PDA, the only one in the room at the moment, which was unusual in that it had no

AI at all. He didn't trust them. He met too many really warped programmers in his profession to trust their imitations of the human mind with confidential patient data. It had nothing to do with his having tried to treat a buckley once. It had ended badly.

"Oh, I think that's a matter of opinion, don't you?" Her voice had a definite edge to it.

"Well, they told me you killed a Bane Sidhe agent. When you were supposed to be on vacation. That's their opinion, as you said. I'd like to hear yours." he said.

"Okay. There was an individual on the Targets of Opportunity List who was mistakenly listed as dead. I became aware of the mistake and the target's location. I had time, I felt like taking a trip, I took the target, I filed my report. If the organization doesn't want a specific individual dead, then perhaps, just perhaps, the organization shouldn't have that individual on the TOL." She smiled thinly.

"Petane was on the TOL? Okay. Well, look, it's not really my job here to debrief you for the organization. That's an ops function. My job is to assess your mental state. Since you and everybody else agree that you did kill him, why don't we start with how you felt about him and what your feelings were when you decided to kill him?"

"What feelings? He was alive. He was supposed to be dead. I fixed that."

"Come on, Cally. Don't make this worse than it has to be. Any thoughts of suicide?" he asked.

"Hell, no." She looked affronted.

"Do you actively feel a desire to live?" He made a note on his pad.

"Sure," she said.

"Then you can show that by talking to me. Please try to remember what you felt when you decided to kill Colonel Petane." He looked up, he needed to watch her body language especially closely here.

"Love your bedside manner, Al." Her smirk had a bitter, sardonic twist to it.

"You'd rather I lied to you? I don't think so. Do you remember where you were when you decided to kill Petane?" he insisted patiently.

"Charleston. At home," she said.

"And how did you feel when you made the decision?"

"Annoyed, okay? I felt annoyed, frustrated." Her fingers tapped nervously on her purse and after what looked like a little mental debate, took out a cigarette and lit it.

"Maybe a little betrayed?" He pushed an ashtray towards her.

"Wouldn't you?" she said.

"Maybe. Did you feel just a little betrayed?" he repeated.

"Yeah, I did." She sighed. She was clenching and unclenching her hands.

"So, were you annoyed primarily with Petane, the Bane Sidhe, or someone else?" At least she was talking to him.

"I was annoyed with the Bane Sidhe, okay?" She leaned over to tap her ashes in the tray, seeming reluctant to move her arms away from her body.

"I can understand that, and even though the reasons may be obvious, can you spell them out for me?" he asked gently.

"It has been Bane Sidhe policy since recontact that we do not leave people who kill our operatives or who betray our people to their deaths alive. That's a very wise policy. Abandoning it would be stupid as hell. And dangerous for us operatives." She was cold, but patient.

"Even if the person in question can provide vital source information on an ongoing basis to the organization?"

"Look, I can deal with that. What I can't deal with is that Petane was *not* providing valuable information, nor was he going to, and none of the people in admin and ops who made this initial bad call had the balls to take responsibility and fix the problem. Instead they just left the mess lying around with the guy still breathing for effectively no good reason at all." Her hands were shaking as she took another draw and recrossed her legs.

"And how would you know that his information was worthless, or that he wouldn't have better information later?" he prompted.

"Look, I interrogated him, okay? He wasn't even immune to all the interrogation drugs *Fleet Strike* has. They were never going to trust that man with any information of a truly sensitive nature. Ever," she said.

"And would you have left him alive if your interrogation had turned out differently? And what do you think his having been interrogated would have done to his utility and cooperativeness as a source." *Interesting.*

"The interrogation was mere confirmation, okay? I already knew he sucked as a source, that's a lot of why I was really, seriously annoyed. But yeah, I would have been pissed off, but I would have left him alive," she admitted, sighing.

"Okay. I think we've covered this part. So how did you interrogate him and kill him? You can skip the surveillance part. Just walk me through starting with the interrogation," he said.

"Do you have awhile?" She smirked again, again bitterly.

"For you, Cally, I've got all afternoon. Come on, tell me about it." He leaned back and beckoned with one hand.

CHAPTER NINE

His assistant, Wilson, had shifted his furniture again. Around the low table there were four chairs. Two Indowy and two human. At the moment, three of the chairs were full, and his assistant had just brought in a tray of coffee and mineralized water. He quirked an eyebrow at Aelool.

"Should we wait for Roolnai, or should we go ahead?" he asked.

"I think it would be better if we proceeded. Clan Chief Roolnai is indisposed. I will fill him in on what was discussed later." The tendrils of his green fur, really a photosynthetic symbiote, wavered slightly in the breeze from the air vent.

Vitapetroni and O'Reilly exchanged a look. The doctor's eyes dropped and he shook his head slightly.

"So, Doctor, what, precisely, are we dealing with?" The priest took a cautious sip of his coffee. Wilson was precise and efficient about so many things, but his coffee was erratic. Sometimes it was on the verge of too cold, sometimes piping hot, or anything in between. A too-hasty sip was apt to leave his tongue burned for a couple of days.

"She's normal. Well, as normal for what we made her as possible. She's been working too hard. She's too involved in her job. She badly needs an extended sabbatical for marriage and kids. But beyond that, she performed exactly as she's been trained and conditioned to perform. I told you back when you made the decision to salvage Petane which agents couldn't know, and couldn't be allowed where they might come to know. She is what we made her; she performed as designed." The doctor

159

looked at his hands and back up at the priest and the Aelool. He shrugged.

"I am afraid that this example of a human operating as designed may be a problem for my people." Aelool's eyes were, characteristically for his species, but oddly for him, fixed on the ground.

"Miss O'Neal says that she would not have killed the man if he had been either removed from the TOL, as opposed to inactivated on account of recorded death, or if he had been a more than minimally valuable source, or if he had shown any likelihood of being more than a minimally valuable source in the future. I'm inclined to believe her," Vitapetroni offered.

"Yes, Al, but the fact is, she did kill him when she had ample reason to believe we didn't want him killed," O'Reilly said.

"She doesn't have the organization's wants and wishes as a safeguard. That was a very deliberate decision for all the field operatives of her specialty, so that if the Bane Sidhe had to order a killing we were ambivalent about that ambivalence wouldn't compromise the operative's effectiveness. She found out he wasn't dead, she checked the TOL, he was on it, she killed him. She might as well have been a guided missile. We trained her to follow certain orders. She followed them. Without her personal feelings she *might* have checked back for clarification. Probably would have. But I can't emphasize enough that you don't tell one of our assassins to kill a man you don't want dead," the doctor said.

"You humans have a phrase that I believe may apply. Something about lawyers that protect houses?" Aelool looked grave.

"Guardhouse lawyer. She probably believes, in fact does believe, she was being one. But then she's been trained not to recognize some of the psychological aspects of her training. The traumatic stress dream cycle suppression, for example. She never seriously wonders why she doesn't have nightmares. Her free will *not* to kill someone on the TOL she encountered or became aware of and was able to kill without compromising a mission . . . well, I don't mean to say it was nonexistent. But it was considerably less than she believes it to have been, or than either of you obviously believe it to have been. I repeat, gentlemen, you must not tell one of these assassins that someone is a target if you do not want that individual dead," he insisted.

"Team Hector's assassin knew about Petane for a couple of

decades. He obviously resisted the temptation to kill him," the priest pointed out logically.

"Team Hector's assassin was *told* Petane was alive and was *ordered* not to kill him," the doctor said.

"If I recall correctly, you had advised us that we could not reliably expect Miss O'Neal to obey such an order and that she had to be protected from the knowledge of his status," Aelool said.

"Yes, I did. She owed a personal debt of honor to Team Conyers, or believed she did, after they attempted to save her life when she was the target of an assassination attempt, and after they fought in battle beside the O'Neals when the Posleen attacked the O'Neal house. I wasn't certain she would disobey the order, but I was certain the stress of having to obey it would have done substantial damage to some of the very qualities that protect her basic mental stability despite her very demanding profession."

"While we are always mindful of the great debt our people owe to Clan O'Neal, one of our concerns is that this particular problem has happened within that clan before. Even though there have been only two such incidents, the size of the clan is such that concern has been raised among the nonhuman associates of the Bane Sidhe that we may be seeing the beginnings of a pattern. Much as we regret to even broach the subject, we must wonder if we are beginning to see a flaw in the line." If anything, Aelool's eyes were even more firmly fixed on the floor.

"What are your people seeing in terms of your interpretation of this possible flaw? It would help us to look for evidence that could either confirm or refute it, or to otherwise address your concerns, if we had more detailed specifics about the nature of those concerns." Father O'Reilly suppressed a wince at Aelool's facial expression. "Please, Aelool, I'm not saying that there's no cause for concern or that we don't have some understanding of why you're concerned. I'm saying that it would help us if you'd detail your people's concerns so that we can be sure we aren't missing any of the subtleties and finer points, so that we can do a better job of finding remedies together that will fix the problems to the satisfaction of all clans in the Bane Sidhe alliance."

"This is hard to explain in human terms. It is not that an act for an individual or small set of individuals' good, but against the interests of the clan as a whole, strikes my people as dishonorable and disloyal, although there are overtones of that, so much as that it strikes us as . . . I suppose your best word for it would be insane. It comes across to us as having taken violent, crazed, uncontrollable carnivores into the very hearth of the clan itself." He held up a hand placatingly. "This is not how I see humans, but you must realize that . . . you have a saying about something that 'pushes your buttons.' It would not be an exaggeration to say that this one act pushes every button my species has about dealing with carnivores."

"Okay. I can understand, given your species' culture and biology and social structure, why you would feel that way," Vitapetroni said, "but I'd make a couple of points that maybe we all need to keep in mind here. First, she is not uncontrollable. In this case the systems of control failed because they were not followed. Second, her readiness to kill is *not* natural human behavior. Each of our assassins has been very carefully manipulated to create a human who is both sane and able to kill on orders. That manipulation has to be done with precision. Third, she had a rational reason for not perceiving her act to be against the actual interests of the Bane Sidhe as a whole. The only actual harm it did was to embarrass the people who failed to revisit the decision to keep Petane alive. Fourth, she is still acting entirely consistently within designed control parameters, and has over thirty years done the Bane Sidhe far, far more good than harm. If the Bane Sidhe was willing to keep and use Petane for pragmatic reasons, how much more willing should it be to continue to make use of Cally O'Neal's training and talents."

"That last point is one I can use to convince my people to go ahead with the next scheduled mission, given the importance of the mission and if you can assure me that Miss O'Neal is highly, highly unlikely to kill the wrong person or people on this mission. It doesn't address the long term issue of standards of loyalty," the Indowy said.

"With respect, Aelool, we aren't going to have the same outlook as your people because, well, we aren't you. If your people expect us to be, well, Indowy that can be used for the violent missions, you're going to be disappointed. Any resolution is going to have to take into account the differences between the psychology of our species," Vitapetroni said.

"Al, you're supposed to be helping make things *better*," O'Reilly sighed.

"I am. I'm not an expert at xenopsychology, but I do understand and appreciate that Indowy loyalty is one way. Totally. From the individual clan member to the clan. That won't work with humans. If the Indowy can't find some way to come to terms with that about us, this alliance will not work. They cannot think of human members of the Bane Sidhe as members of their clan. It would lead to . . . unrealistic expectations," he insisted.

"We are quite aware that humans are *not* Indowy, thank you."

"But not aware enough. Had you been, your people would have understood that loyalty down the chain from the organization to the individual is not some eccentric detail of etiquette, but is vital to dealing with humans in an organization. Petane's status would have been reviewed. I take some of the blame that it was not. I shouldn't have assumed more understanding on both sides than there was. I should have explicitly informed you of the organizational hazards of not periodically reevaluating the Petane decision to see if it was still justified to let the man live. That part, that I didn't make sure you understood that necessity, or that our base commander here didn't understand that he had to bring it up. That's my fault." The psychiatrist tapped his chest with a hand.

"And you would then say that not understanding you was our fault?" Aelool's grip on his glass tightened.

"Not at all. I'd say we learned to understand each other better. How we found out wasn't exactly pleasant." He grimaced. "Not to sound too much like a shrink, but I think both sides need to think a bit about how this knowledge affects our policies."

"Or the arrangement itself," the alien sighed.

"We understand that. At the same time, it is possible that we could use this understanding to revise our policies to pursue our mutual goals without having this kind of thing happen again," the priest interjected.

"Yes, that is possible. I would like the doctor's assistance in exploring the ramifications and details and looking for anything related we may have missed. Meanwhile, I think I can make the case, given how critical the need for this particular mission is, and how good a body type match Miss O'Neal is for Miss Makepeace, for continuing with this mission. After that . . ." he trailed off.

"I agree. We can discuss the other issues after we get Team Isaac in the field," O'Reilly nodded.

"I think we must all hope that that mission goes well," the alien's expression was the Indowy equivalent of a deep and troubled frown.

Wednesday morning, May 22

When the knock at the door came for breakfast, she looked over at the alarm clock. Seven-thirty? *Ugh.* She pulled on her bathrobe and trudged to the door, rubbing her eyes. *I suppose sleeping in was a vain hope. They want to emphasize I'm in the doghouse. I don't care. The bastard needed to be dead—even if he was a pathetic schmuck.*

She opened the door and stepped back, blinking, as her grand-father walked in with the tray. It was set for two, with pancakes, eggs over easy, sausage links, orange juice, and coffee. It smelled like heaven, especially after a dinner of low-salt pinto beans in corn tortillas.

"Okay, thank you. But . . . why? Yesterday you seemed royally pissed," she said.

"I am. I am royally pissed that you are letting this job eat you. The guy you killed was a worthless asshole. Probably doesn't matter one way or the other that he died. Yeah, he'd earned it, but it probably wouldn't have hurt anything to let him live." He patted his pocket reaching for his tobacco pouch, looked at the tray and poured syrup on his pancakes, instead.

"I can't believe you just said that. Team Conyers saved your butt, too, when the Posleen came up the gap. Doesn't that mean *any-thing* to you?" *God, I sound shrill. I'm never shrill.*

"Sure. It means I think it's a crappy raw deal that they died so young—"

"Were killed!" she interrupted.

"Yeah, that tends to happen in this business, sooner or later. And I can tell you right now that if some bastard or crop of bastards gets me, that I do not want you to kill anyone you are not ordered to kill just because you think you owe me something. You're more than welcome to make the case that someone who was involved needs to be dead and take the mission if it's ordered, but I don't want you to do this again. I don't think Team Conyers would have wanted it either," he said.

"That's what you want. We'll never know what they want,

because they're dead, because of a fucking traitor, who is now dead, himself." It still made her mad as hell.

"You have to let there be someone higher than you as the judge of who needs to be dead, or the job eats you alive. You have to *have* a life, or the job eats you alive. You don't have a life outside of the job, Cally, and that more than concerns me. It grieves me. I have been a professional a long time, I have seen other professionals, I've seen this job chew people up and spit them out and unless you get yourself some sort of meaningful life outside of work, and soon, you're setting that up to be you." He rubbed his head as if it was starting to ache.

"Look, can we just eat before the coffee gets too cold?" She tasted it and made a face, stirring corn syrup and cream into it.

"Sure. Look, I didn't come here solely to badger you. The mission is on, which means we need our mission brief tomorrow. Now, you can either brief me in now and I'll do the team brief, or you can get to work on it. You're no longer confined to quarters, or restricted in your computer usage, obviously," he said.

"What, just like that?" She looked at him incredulously.

"Oh, there will still be some kind of reckoning or resolution or whatever when we get back, but for right now they've decided that this mission is too critical to abort and that it's too late to assign it to someone else." He took a bite of his sausage.

"Okay," she nodded.

"Okay? Were you trying to get benched, was that what this was about?" He looked mad.

"You know what it was about, dammit! Don't psychobabble me, Granpa." She took a swig of her coffee. Her lip curled slightly, but it was drinkable.

"I'm not talking about killing Petane. I'm talking about the *way* you did it—without going up the chain and asking for his situation to be reviewed. Did you want to get benched?" he asked again.

"Oh, of course not!" She ran her fingers through the brown curls and made a face at them. "Look, the last mission was pretty stressful, and maybe you have a point about the life thing. I'll think about it, okay? And after we get back, if the bosses don't shoot me or anything, I'll take a nice vacation. A real one, where I don't kill anybody, okay?"

"And look for a man to date somewhere other than a bar," he said.

"Hey, I promised to take a vacation, not settle down with the love of my life and pop out six kids, all right?" She looked at the corn syrup bottle again and shook her head, taking a bite of the bare pancake. Their idea of maple flavoring tended to suck out loud.

Vitapetroni took his lunch tray into the small side room and shut the door. Framed prewar travel prints of famous cities adorned the walls. He sat down with his back to Paris and let his eyes slide across Venice before settling on the young old man on the other side of the table.

"Lisel, sweep for bugs, please."

"My pleasure." The husky voice emanating from the doctor's PDA was not exactly what one would expect from a stodgy, respectable medical professional.

"The only bugs here are me and Mr. O'Neal's AID, and I'm sure Susan wouldn't eavesdrop on us," it said.

"Susan, don't listen until I call your name again," Papa O'Neal ordered.

"Sure, Mike. What's say you and I run off to the Bahamas and you make an honest woman of me? Signing off." Then it was silent.

"Lisel, shut down, please." Vitapetroni sat down.

"Certainly doctor," she purred. "Goodbye."

"You've got a Lisel loaded on top of your buckley? Doesn't that crash a lot?" he asked.

"I keep the emulation turned way down. I've just aliased my common commands so they sound like conversation if you aren't around me too much. I don't really trust AI. I know our AIDs and buckleys are clean, it's just . . . xenohistory is a hobby of mine, and I can appreciate the Indowy point of view." He took a bite of his taco, appearing to actually enjoy it.

"And you haven't gone back to paper?" O'Neal joked.

"I said I was mistrustful, not a Luddite." The doctor took a small bottle of hot sauce out of a pocket and shook some on his food.

"Habanera sauce is cheating, you know. Okay, Doc, it's your dime," he said.

"Dime? You just dated yourself as a fellow old fart." He pinched the bridge of his nose. "About Cally . . . and first of all understand I'm talking to you as her team leader, not her grandfather. Confidentiality rules let me talk to one, but not the other."

"Yeah, I know the drill. Go ahead and say what you've got to say." He accepted the loan of the bottle and shook some hot sauce into his bowl of chili.

"I have some concerns I didn't pass up the chain. She showed physical signs of feeling guilt after this kill." He swallowed heavily and glanced quickly towards the door. "That could be good or bad, depending on how she deals with it. I think she's okay for the mission, or I would have said something, but . . . I want you to keep an eye on her."

"That all?" He buttered a corn muffin and looked up with it halfway to his mouth, waiting.

"Yeah, it is. It probably won't matter a bit, but if you have to do some shade tree counseling on the spot, well, I thought you should know." The doctor shook a little pepper onto his creamed corn.

"So, who do you like in the playoffs? I'm rather partial to Charleston." Papa O'Neal took a bite of the chili, considered it for a few seconds, then added some more hot sauce.

"Hometown sentimentality. Their bullpen is weak. Indianapolis will clean their clocks."

"Are you kidding? The Braves haven't won the pennant more than once since the war. My arthritic granny bats better than their lineup." He grinned.

Wednesday afternoon, May 22

Growing up in his childhood home of Fredericksburg, Tommy Sunday had liked tacos. Then the Posleen came and Fredericksburg went, and it was off to the Ten Thousand and then to Armored Combat Suits—also known as ACS. The Ten Thousand's rations had been what they could get, and had been chosen primarily for their nutritional adequacy with taste a poor second consideration. Afterward, in ACS, the suit rations were decent, but just didn't quite achieve real tacohood.

Before he and Wendy "died," they had managed to transfer and hide enough of their FedCreds in discreet investments. That had made real tacos, and a lot of other things, affordable despite the Bane Sidhe not being real generous with the salaries.

He tried to restrain the twinge of disappointment as he looked down at his plate. These did not exactly live up to his standards of real tacos. The corn tortilla was genuine enough, as were the refried beans, cheese, and veggies. But the beef-flavored textured tofu left quite a lot to be desired. Unfortunately, it was that or chicken, and in Tommy's expert opinion, the only thing worse than tofu tacos was chicken tacos. And he'd rather eat his meat ration as roast chicken for dinner than have it chopped up in his taco only to face the inevitable tofu tonight. Anyway, he understood. He and Wendy could afford what they could afford because of the exorbitant salaries, by most normal standards, paid to ACS in the Posleen war and carefully invested by his wife, who had turned out to have quite a knack for buying and selling antiques.

After the Fredericksburg landing, his then-girlfriend's old hobby of researching local history had become . . . untenable. A move to Franklin Sub-Urb and an abortive attempt to contribute to the war effort as a firefighter had followed. Then the Sub-Urb got eaten. After escaping that as well, Wendy's faith in the stability of any particular town or city had been severely shaken. By the time the war ended and they had married and settled down, she had diverted her love and her skills to the history of objects of a much more portable nature.

After Fleet returned, organized Posleen resistance had been overwhelmed by strikes from orbit. What had been left was a colossal cleanup job.

Tommy had been in Bravo Company, 1st of the 555th, under Iron Mike O'Neal—Papa O'Neal's only son. In the worst of the war, in the most desperate of the battles, Bravo Company had always been where the fire was hottest.

In the cleanup phase, the suits' superior mobility and robustness had made the Company a juggernaut that had rolled right over any surviving God King that even attempted to begin rebuilding a technology base.

So he'd been discharged after five years of global cleanup sweeps to find, surprisingly, that the money he'd been sending home to Wendy since the return of Fleet—as much to keep her out of another Sub-Urb as anything—had not only not been expended, but had been doubled.

He'd done code for Personality Solutions after the war, when the experience of veterans with the AIDs inspired a fad of ever newer and fancier PDA's. The salary hadn't been anything like his

ACS pay, but he and Wendy hadn't exactly been surviving on
hotdogs and peanut butter. Until the Cyberpunks recruited him,
and then the Bane Sidhe had arranged his and Wendy's "deaths"
and they had come inside.

Since then they'd augmented his salary with carefully managed
investment income. But most inside operatives weren't so lucky.
The medical and dental were unbeatable, but the chow left a lot
to be desired. Which brought him back to the lousy tacos.

Tommy squared his shoulders and looked around the cafeteria
for familiar faces, grinning when he saw Martin and Schmidt sitting
at an only slightly wobbly round table next to the braided ficus
in the corner. He had shared a couple of training classes with
Martin in his early years inside, and the two had found they shared
a love of chili slaw dogs and an obscure prewar burlesque film.
He would have loved to sneak up on the extremely ordinary-
looking black man and say something smart, but he wasn't the
least surprised when he only made it halfway.

"What the hay-el kind of man wears pantyhose to a movie?"
The man's head didn't turn, but his rich tenor rang out across the
room.

"Hey, Lips, man, you know you love it." Tommy grinned and
took his tray over, setting it down and grabbing a chair from the
next table over.

"You guys aren't going to do weird things with your elbows, are
you?" Schmidt was short. At about five foot seven, with straight
blond hair that looked like somebody had piled a double handful of straw on his head, Schmidt's rejuv let him pass for about
fourteen. In some environments, a kid in a jean jacket and ratty
backpack was less conspicuous than any adult.

"Just because you don't appreciate classic cinema, George . . ."
Levon had turned in his seat and offered his hand as Tommy
scooted up to the table. "Hey, Sunday, how the hell are you?"

"Doin' all right. Not so unhappy to get out of the house for a
week or two," Tommy admitted.

"Oh? I thought you and Wendy were the original perpetual
newlyweds," Martin said.

"Wendy is the love of my life; she's just always a bit cranky at
this stage. She'll be glad to have me out of her hair for a while,
and by the time I get back she'll be herself again," he said.

"Geez, it's like you two have it down to a science." Schmidt looked down at the slab of tofu formed in the shape of a T-bone steak. He frowned and grabbed the black pepper, shaking on enough to cover the fake grill marks before slicing off a piece and taking a bite, chewing glumly, "Damn, I can't wait to get back out into the field."

"Well, damn, they'll let anybody in here now." Jay set his tray down and hooked an empty chair over with an ankle.

"Blade man! Long time no see," George grinned, offering a hand to the other man.

"Blade man?" Tommy asked. "Do I want to know?"

"Oh, back in high school, Jay here was unbeatable at Boma Warrior. Never figured out how he did it, but our junior year, it was probably the coolest game in the library." George topped a bit of the tofu steak with some of the hot corn relish on the side.

"I knew a guy who worked on that. You know on the sixth level where you go around a corner and get swarmed by a pack of carnivorous mini-lops? I put him up to that." Tommy shook some Tabasco on his taco, took a bite, and added a few more shakes.

"That was you? That was wicked cool, but every once in a while one of those mothers would have a switchblade and be just *impossible* to kill. . . . ." Schmidt pushed at a stray bit of tofu with his fork. "Man, I can't *wait* to get back out in the field."

"What, I never figured you for being as eager as all that?" Jay chuckled disbelievingly.

"Not *that*, Jay. You have to admit the food's better. As to the other, somebody has to do the dirty work. The cops don't take out the damn Elves' trash. So, cosmic janitor, that's me." He grinned easily. "You don't have a problem with Sherry marrying blue-collar, do you, old man?" He quirked an eyebrow at Martin, looking out through the hair that had fallen across his eyes again.

"Be a bit late if I did. And a little less on the 'old,' if you don't mind." Levon took a big bite out of his cheeseburger, manfully ignoring the almost complete lack of beef in the fried patty.

"By the way, 'scuse me if I'm treading on sensitive territory, here, but what's the deal with Cally? The rumor mill has been unreal," George asked, looking at Tommy.

"I dunno, man. You probably know more than I do. All they told us was to grab our gear and haul ass to catch the shuttle." He shook his head slightly. "I haven't seen her, and Papa O'Neal said not to ask. And he was wearing his 'don't fuck with me' look."

"Oh, he'll get it all worked out somehow. I mean, she's an O'Neal, you know?" Jay grinned, and if it was just a hair too tight, well, they were all worried about their teammate. And not just because she was maybe the best shooter in the business.

Tommy looked away from his teammate and caught Martin's eye. He took a deep breath.

"What I did hear is that you might know a lot about it, but weren't saying, Levon," he said.

"Yeah, I do, but I wish I didn't. Look, I like Cally. I respect her. I would have her on my team any day of the week. But the past couple of years . . . I don't know, maybe she's just working too hard. It's not like we haven't all seen something like this coming." He shook his head.

"Excuse me? Something like what?" Tommy's voice had a definite edge to it.

"Sunday, don't go all big brother on me. The least I can do for her is give her the dignity of letting her tell you herself. I owe her that much, and so do you," he said.

"So you're pretty sure she's gonna be back on active and everything in a couple of days?" Jay asked casually around a bite of his enchilada.

Martin was silent for a long moment.

"If she's not, then you can ask me," he said.

Thursday morning, May 23

Tommy dove to the side as the guy in the gray suit aimed at him and emptied the magazine of his pistol. He had time to pull the pin and toss a grenade—he was out of ammo—before the rapidly falling health indicator showed him he was hit and bleeding out. He got the other guy, but it had been in the "dead man's ten seconds." Still, the computer credited him with the kill, and, even more important, the ambush had happened just like it was supposed to after his hacking mistake earlier had resulted in detection. The holographic projection of the game faded out.

"You're dead, man." He felt Jay's hand clap him on the back.

"Nice shades. And I'm supposed to be." At six foot eight and three hundred pounds, Tommy Sunday was not a small man. Still, other than his size, he looked fairly typical for a juv in his first century. That is, he looked twenty, despite the fact that he now had grown grandchildren to baby-sit his and Wendy's small children.

"Play testing another training scenario?" Jay's grin was affable as he tossed himself into a chair beside his teammate and kicked his feet up on the table next to the larger man's.

"Yep. And after the royal fuck-up I made hacking a system earlier, well, there was a small theoretical chance I could survive, but it *should* have fried my ass. As it did," Tommy sighed.

"Ah, the sacrifices you make for quality control." Papa O'Neal snagged a Styrofoam cup from the stack next to the coffee pot, pulled a small pouch out of his pocket, and got himself a fresh plug of tobacco.

"I've already played it through for real. And several times multiplayer interactive. Now I'm trying to see if I can break it." The former ACS trooper shrugged and closed the game, popping a fresh cube into the reader slot as Cally came in to begin their briefing. The brown curls didn't faze him. He'd seen her with every hair color and style known to man over the years. He did wonder if the brown curls were coming or going, though.

"Okay, folks, this is your basic counterintelligence mission. We have every reason to believe Fleet Strike is aware of us and that our security has been penetrated. They have a man inside. Which is why your briefing was eleventh hour and neither you nor I will have any unmonitored communications, nor will any of us discuss this mission outside this room or with anyone except each other. The number of people in the Bane Sidhe hierarchy who know the actual nature of this mission has been kept to an absolute minimum. We are to find the identity of the leak, and plug it." She reached down and pushed a button on the screen of her PDA, bringing up a hologram of a man in his apparent early thirties, in a Fleet Strike general's uniform—which meant he was probably a fair bit into his second century.

"This is General Bernhard Beed. General Beed has been tasked with, basically, finding out everything he can about us. He is setting up his headquarters on Titan Base to coordinate the intelligence they develop. The office is covered as criminal investigations and military policing for Titan Base." She touched the screen again and the hologram changed, revealing a young goddess in a captain's uniform.

"And my cover, Sinda Makepeace."

Fuck, she is stacked as all hell. And look at those power-lifter thighs. I think I'm just as glad Wendy will not see Cally in this cover.

"Captain Makepeace is presently on Earth and due to board a shuttle for passage to Titan from Chicago O'Hare this Sunday at 0815. The preliminary plan is to make the switch at the airport. I go on the slab in an hour." She tossed each of them a cube.

"Here's the rest of what the higher ups gave me and what I've been able to develop. Tommy and Jay, I need you to get a complete profile on everyone in that office, including voice and motion samples for Makepeace. Granpa, I need you to review the airport and Titan Base, plan the switch, plan the extraction after I get the data. Your cover is as crew on an in-system freighter taking manufactured goods for the shops in the business district. The local tong will cover you because you'll be taking an unofficial cargo of partial doses of rejuv drugs. Apparently, there's a worthwhile supply of troops willing to pay just about anything to take a little wear and tear off a dependant or two. They will, of course, pay you for the drugs—they're just getting a particularly good deal. They don't know why you want to be in the vicinity of Titan Base, and they don't want to know." She noticed their eyes were still fixed on the hologram and touched the screen of the PDA again, watching them blinking as the image vanished.

"Does anybody have any questions? No? Great. I'll head down to medical and see you back here in three hours." She scooped up her PDA and headed for the door.

"Uh . . . wait a minute, Cally," Jay interrupted, looking around at Tommy and Papa, "I just wanted to say, and I think I speak for all of us, how glad we all are that you're still going to be with us on this mission. And I'm sure I speak for all of us again when I say that I'm sure that, well, everything will work out just fine."

"Well . . . thank you, Jay." Her forehead had wrinkled slightly, but her eyes warmed as she turned and left.

"Will you be carrying a no-name pill?" Papa sounded like he thought it was a very good idea.

"No. The secret of that pill is worth more than I am. And if I was taken, they could find it or, even if they didn't, the chances of you getting to me inside the time limit would be small. That's too much like a suicide pill for my liking. I don't plan to be caught, but if I am, I'll do everything the nuns taught us in SERE. Besides, there probably wouldn't be time to make one up to my new stats. And, frankly, I don't plan to need it."

"If that wasn't the fastest briefing I've ever had, it's close." Tommy sat watching the door for a moment before taking the cube she'd tossed him and swapping it into the reader slot of his AID.

"To the point, though." O'Neal spat neatly into his cup, as he brought up a map of the Chicago air and space port.

"Okay, I feel better now that I see what she pulled together and what she left for us. Cally always has had a good sense of the hacking she could get away with." He walked over and poured himself a fresh cup of coffee.

"Jay, you take the cover, I'll take the personnel files of the other staff."

"Wouldn't have wanted to say it in front of Cally, but the captain has some damn fine architecture," Jay said appreciatively.

"Yeah, but her nose is a tad off-center and she's always going to need makeup to darken her eyebrows and stuff," Tommy commented.

"You noticed her nose and eyebrows?" Jay sounded disbelieving. Papa O'Neal just shook his head.

"Briefly. Very briefly," Tommy grinned.

"You guys keep working. I've got something to take care of. I'll be back in a few minutes." Papa had a stubborn look on his face.

Silverton, Texas, Saturday, May 25

Johnny Stuart was not a morning person. Unfortunately, the Coburn girl had the morning off to go to the dentist and, like most kids, Mary Lynn was an early riser. Which is why he was sitting up in a rumpled bed, rubbing his eyes, while a wriggling five year old climbed into his lap.

Mary Lynn had the dark brown curls of her mother, but his own facial features. They just looked better on her. After the cancer had taken his wife, three years ago, the doctors had told him that it raised Mary Lynn's risk considerably. If he'd had some pull, he might have been able to get the new drugs to save her, but Sue hadn't much held with pull, and the cancer had come on sudden and before he could do anything, Sue was gone and him left to do the best he could by Mary Lynn. He didn't understand much about the numbers in what the doctor said, not having got much past high school algebra, but what he did understand was that he owed it to Sue never to be in a position to be unable to help his sick kin, their daughter especially, again.

So he had set about going to work for the people with the most pull he could find, getting a reputation for resourcefulness and the willingness to get things done no matter what it took. And plenty of times it had taken things that were way outside the normal rules. But a man who wouldn't break a few rules for his own was no kind of man at all. That was the best thing about his recent promotion. If he could pull this off and keep the damned aliens happy, he and Mary Lynn would never lack for the best of care again.

"How's my Sunshine this morning!" He began tickling her ribs mercilessly, until she squirmed away from him and off the bed.

"Silly Daddy," she said. "I'm hungry. Where's Traci?"

"Traci had to go to the dentist, Sunshine. Just you and me this morning. Let me make some coffee and I'll see if we can find some cereal." He yawned.

"Lucky Charms!" She ran off towards the kitchen, giggling.

"Okay, I think we've still got some," he called, pulling up his worn cotton pajama bottoms a bit as he got out of bed. Probably ought to get around to replacing those. He trudged into the kitchen and made coffee, taking out two bowls while it dripped through the old-fashioned appliance. He was really just back in Silverton winding up his affairs. The promotion meant moving them to Chicago and a lot of travel for him. He was going to hate being away from Mary Lynn so much, but it was for her own good, so he could protect her better. It was hard, but she'd understand when she was older.

He had tried to get Traci Coburn to move with them, so Mary Lynn wouldn't have to change babysitters, but Traci hadn't wanted to leave her family. He could understand that. It took a real cosmopolitan individual to deal with city people and country people alike. And if there was one thing Johnny was, it was good with people. The trick was to tell them as much of what they wanted to hear with as few actual lies as possible. He'd always been gifted that way, but in the years since Sue's death he'd gone to it with a will and developed it to a high art.

He set the bowl down in front of Mary Lynn and sat down with his own breakfast, having his AID pull up his morning e-mail. He could see right away today was going to be tricky. The Tir's secretary had left a message asking what he had turned up on Worth's death, and the bald truth was that despite a week and a half of trying, he had squat. So the task of the day was going to be coming up with something that, while it might not be accurate, would be convincing enough that it would do until he could start finding the real thing. He sent her an e-mail telling her he'd be sending a report first thing Monday morning. Best not to put them off any longer than that.

Smart money was that it was a hit, of course. But he wasn't going to keep his new job by restating the obvious. He needed something and he needed it now. Maybe a little misdirection would help. People died all the time. If he couldn't find anything about *Worth's* death, maybe he could find something about some other death and claim that they were linked. It didn't really matter if they were or not. Paranoia always played well, and it was like that numberology con—you could link anything to anything else if you tried hard enough. Some of his best rumors had been built that way. Besides, if he turned up anything later that contradicted the link, chances were it would give him something real about the Worth business, and he'd just be doing a good job. And if he didn't turn up anything contradictory, well, then there would be nothing to detract from his story, would there?

Once Mary Lynn was safely occupied by the big pink and black bumblebee surrounded by a mob of smiling children that seemed to have taken over their vidscreen, Johnny opened a tray table and had his AID project a virtual keyboard and a holographic screen. The trick was to find anyone else who had ever worked for the Darhel and died, preferably since Worth bought it, but before would do in a pinch.

"Leanne, I need you to search the database of people who have done work for our organization. List me anybody who's died or disappeared between May ninth of this year and now," he said.

"Worth, Charles. Reported missing as of May thirteenth, death is likely. Fiek, Samuel. Missing as of May thirteenth, death is likely. Greer, Michael. Dead as of May fifteenth, purposeful termination of contract. Samuels, Vernard. Dead as of May nineteenth, car crash.

Petane, Charles. Dead as of May twenty-first, drug overdose. List complete," it recited.

Okay, Fiek and Worth were almost certainly linked, which meant they disappeared after six forty-five p.m. on May tenth, when a boy remembered delivering a pizza to a man at Fiek's apartment. The pizza boy had picked Fiek's face out of a slideshow of images, after he handed him a half dozen twenties.

Fiek had no known reason to have a particular grudge against Worth, and vice versa. More to the point, the Darhel had checked their local bank accounts, and their personal numbered bank accounts in discreet countries, that each man had set up secretly, and their money was untouched since Worth had drawn out a modest amount of cash on the morning of the tenth. It was almost inconceivable that someone who would work for the Darhel would run *without* their money.

If he'd just had to guess, he'd have said whatever happened was at Worth's Chicago apartment. Fiek lived in the same building, and although Worth didn't actually live there most of the time, he frequently used the place when he was in town. He'd searched both apartments himself, along with a cousin who used to work in the sheriff's department in Silverton. Bobby had said that Worth's apartment looked a little too clean to him, and pointed out the lack of dust and fluff, especially below the wall with the kinky crap bolted onto it. And what his dead boss had done with that, Johnny hoped he'd never have to know. At least, not unless it was just business.

Getting his cousin set up had been the kind of thing he'd taken this job for in the first place, and it made him proud. A man liked to be able to take care of his kin. And after Bobby got himself fired for being high on the job, Johnny had seen the opportunity in the situation and had helped Bobby out, getting the nanodrugs to get the monkey off his back as well as getting him an income his ex-wife couldn't get her hands on. That was a situation he was glad to fix. Brenda was a two-bit whore and that was Jimmy Simms' kid, not Bobby's, and everybody in town knew it. The judge just also knew Jimmy was a worthless drunk who still lived with his momma and so had stuck poor Bobby with the bill for the cheating bitch's brat. Johnny liked kids as well as anybody, hell, he'd do anything for Mary Lynn and damned near had, but a thing like that just wasn't right.

So anyway, Worth and Fiek got done in his apartment some-time over the weekend of the tenth. And that was all he had. Worth had changed his appearance and changed his pattern so often that normal search techniques to see where he'd been and who'd seen him last just wouldn't *work* with him. And that meant that unless Johnny could pull a good story out of the air on short notice, his ass was in a crack.

"Okay, Leanne, give me a file on each of them, in print where you've got it, on my desk top, with all we know about each man's death." No women. That was funny, but then a lot of their field people were guys, so it could be just coincidence. All right, before weeding through the small stuff, he'd get a big picture.

"Leanne, gimme a map of the world, about so big." He spread his arms, watching a holographic illusion of a large flat screen project in the air in front of him.

"Put a pin in it where each guy died. Waitaminute, is that three? Magnify Chicago. Who's that third pin?"

"What third pin, please?" The AID sounded confused. They were pretty smart, but sometimes they didn't track too well.

"Which one of the organization deaths you listed for me, besides Fiek and Worth, was in Chicago?"

"Petane, Charles."

"Well, isn't that something. Thanks, Leanne. Go to standby." There was a trick to managing the AIDs that a couple of old veterans had brought home after the war. The big point was if you were planning anything to keep your thoughts to yourself. They recorded everything, all the time, but so far nobody had found a way as far as he could tell to read a man's thoughts. So the trick with something like this was to keep all his thoughts to himself, read everything in the file, connect the dots, even if they didn't strictly speaking go together, and *then* lay out his case talking to the AID, making it sound like thinking aloud. When you could record a whole hell of a lot, it was easy to forget about the things you couldn't record. Besides, who knew, maybe he'd find some-thing.

Okay, Petane was the drug overdose. That was good. You could always make something suspicious out of a drug overdose. Bad was that it wasn't another disappearance, but he could just argue that "they" were crafty enough to change methods. Coroner had ruled it an accident, but that didn't matter. First thing would be to have his own people get hold of any stored tissue samples and run them for anything he could use. Found in his mistress's bed. Had to be hard on the wife. Mistress had been drugged, cops figured by him, was unconscious while he died next to her. And, not to put too fine a point on it, forensics said he hadn't come. Well, didn't that stink to high heaven. Good. No telling who had really offed the puke. Could have been the wife. Unlikely as hell to have been anything to do with the Darhel. He had only done something useful *once* and it had been thirty years ago. Still, make the story good enough and it was a whole lot better than reporting in empty handed.

Under a cornfield in Indiana, Sunday, May 26, 04:00

They were in the same conference room as Thursday for their final pre-mission check. The cheap folding conference table and bare Galplas walls didn't improve with familiarity, but the coffee was good, and the corn muffins were . . . well, they were at least predictable, anyway.

"Okay, people, one more time through. Cally, you first." Papa O'Neal, with sandy brown hair and looking rather strange without his usual wad of tobacco, spitting absentmindedly into a mug, nonetheless.

"Baggage check-in at six, security around six-forty-five, in the women's room across from the gate Sierra-six departure lounge by seven-oh-five. Once there, if I didn't see Granpa and Tommy on the way in, I send an 'arrived' text message so you know I'm in place. I wait until my PDA tells me that the target is in motion, then when she enters, I inject her with my handy-dandy tranquilizer, trade clothes with her with Tommy's help, go back out and catch the shuttle to Titan Base, et cetera," she said, pointing to Jay. For the insertion, her silver-blond hair was unkempt, and the white sweatpants and oversized men's sweatshirt with horizontal blue and white stripes made the most of her figure, most very definitely being the word. Contact lenses muted Sinda's cornflower blue eyes to a nondescript grayish hazel. Cheap, zero-prescription glasses were fitted poorly enough that they kept sliding down her nose a bit, and she pushed them back nervously, furtively nibbling at a candy bar now and then.

"Hey, how come *she* gets chocolate and we get these?" Tommy said, staring disgustedly at one of the muffins.

"It's a prop," she responded haughtily, and harrumphed, wiggling a bit as if settling into a new suit of clothes as she got back into character. "Go on, Jay." But she surreptitiously slipped Tommy a candy bar from her purse.

"At five-forty-five, I go through baggage claim and check a dummy bag. By six-fifteen I'm headed through security. By seven, I'm at the S-six departure lounge, seated, with a cup of ice water from one of the snack counters. When Makepeace enters the lounge and sits, I move nearby. I take a brief video capture of the target and her location and forward it to the team so Cally knows where to sit and which stuff is 'hers.' If the target doesn't go to the ladies' room on her own by seven thirteen, I make a klutz of myself and spill my drink in her lap. I apologize profusely, and as soon as she heads for the door I hit the button on the screen of my PDA which alerts you three. When Cally comes back out as Makepeace, she touches her right ear to confirm the switch. I proceed to the rendezvous with Tommy and O'Neal, arriving no later than eight-thirty. I change clothes, we return to the port by the freight entrance, board the freighter, and take off for Titan at eleven-fifty. Tommy?"

"Papa and I arrive at the freight entrance in the vehicle at oh-six-forty-five, dressed as crew, with Jay's clothes and cleaning crew uniforms in the trunk. We change on the freighter and retrieve the cleaning cart stashed there. We have until oh-seven-hundred to make it to the Sierra-six departure lounge women's room. I send Cally an 'arrived' text message. We put up an out-of-service sign but admit Cally. We remove the sign and wheel the cart aside towards the men's room when we get the word the target is in motion. We politely turn anyone but the target away. When the target enters the restroom, we return with the sign and wait until Cally signals. Then I push the cart in and help as needed with the clothes switch and put Makepeace in the bottom of the trash bin, covering her with appropriate debris. We maneuver Makepeace back to the car, add the wig from the glove box, douse her with the cheap beer and whiskey samples in same, drive her to rendezvous one, Hiberzine her, and hand her off to the cleaning crew for live handling. Make rendezvous two no later than oh-eight-thirty and proceed like Jay said. Papa?" He licked bits of chocolate off his fingers before wadding the wrapper and making a basketball shot into the trash can in the corner.

"I got the easy recital. Same as you, Tommy, except I wait outside the restroom while you assist in the switch. Abort code?"

"Toledo," they chimed.

"Right. Your PDA or AID calls Toledo, disappear and lie low for at least two days before returning to base or dropping the Bane Sidhe a cube, your best judgment which. We're all seasoned operatives. If your best judgment says 'abort' somewhere along the line, call it. There's no points for heroism in this business. Jay, it's way out of line from her profile, but if Makepeace comes running up to the gate right at boarding and never sits down, just call Toledo. A switch that's not clean would be worse than an abort, especially with this mission. All right. Let's split up and move." He grimaced at the muffin in his hand and paused by the door, apparently debating whether to toss it uneaten. He took another bite of it and walked out the door.

"What's the matter, Granpa? Don't you like corn? We have it so *seldom*," she said, grinning.

"I can eat cornbread for every meal if I have to, you hellion. Even if the yankees do insist on putting sugar in it."

Sunday morning, May 26

Cally's dummy suitcase was a good match for the persona. Her ID said she was Irene Grzybowski. Irene was the kind of woman nobody would look at twice in a crowded area like an airport: maybe forty to fifty, dumpy figure, eyes on the ground most of the time, polite but not friendly to security. And nobody did. Nobody looked at her as she heaved the battered cloth suitcase, made out of fabric that looked like a college student's sofa, onto the counter. Nobody looked at her as she walked through security with the all-plastic syringe of tranquilizer taped into the reinforced elastic under band of her sports bra, which did a good job of helping her look fat and lumpy rather than well-endowed. Nobody looked at her as she walked to gate S-six and went into the ladies' room across from the departure lounge, taking up a natural-looking position in the second stall from the end. She had beaten Granpa and Tommy in getting here. She had not looked for Jay. It would have been bad tradecraft.

She took her PDA out of her purse and flipped it open, setting it on the top of the tissue dispenser. The buckley's voice access was, of course, off. Should the abort code come in while the screen was off, the PDA was set to vibrate. She hoped it wouldn't be necessary.

She looked at the clock icon on the screen. Six-fifty-three. She had made good time. After sending Tommy her arrival message, getting the syringe out and ready, and brushing her hair, there was really nothing to do but hurry up and wait. The trick on this type of setup was to keep her attention focused on the PDA screen without her mind and eyes wandering off and without falling into a daze staring at the screen. Cally's solution was to split the screen, with the small custom icons labeled "in motion" and "video" on the top half and an old logic game based on hunting for hidden mines on the bottom half.

At six-fifty-eight, the message icon on the control bar blinked at her. Tommy and Granpa were in place.

The blinking of the video icon caught her eye at seven-oh-five. She set it to play on the lower screen and had just caught her first glimpse of the target when the in-motion icon started blinking at her. *Okay, time enough to watch the movie after I take the target. If she's moving on her own, she needs to be here. Best to take her on her way out of the stall.*

She breathed evenly as the door opened, all senses hyper-alert. Something was wrong. The tread was too heavy on the floor, and not a woman's shoe. She tensed.

"Cally?" a voice whispered.

That could *be Tommy. Or not.* "Um . . . this restroom is occupied."

"She bought a donut and went back to sit down. Reset and wait for him to send it again," he said.

"Got it." The voice was definitely Tommy. She heard him leave again as she tapped options on the screen, working quickly to reset everything so she'd know when the target left her seat again. It didn't matter what the mission was, there was always something. *Although I hope to God this is* not *another mission day from hell. Good grief, under the damn bed!*

She watched the video, taking note of the target's seat location and that she had a laptop computer with her. It made sense, since the assignment was clerical. Real screens were still the best option for minimizing eye-strain from all-day use.

As she waited, she could periodically hear apologetic male voices as Tommy and Granpa redirected a female traveler to the next nearest restroom. At seven-fourteen the in-motion icon blinked again.

She shut off and pocketed the PDA, palmed the syringe, and stood. As the door opened, she flushed just for verisimilitude and opened the stall door, going to the sink as the target came in the door looking down at her silks and swearing softly.

By the time Cally reached the sink, the other woman had grabbed a handful of paper towels and was rubbing at the large wet blotch. She didn't even look up as the assassin slipped behind her and clapped a hand over her mouth, finding the right spot for a neck injection with the ease of long practice. Makepeace didn't have time to struggle much before the strong drugs hit her system and she went limp, breathing smoothly and evenly as Cally lowered her to the floor.

You're lucky. I get to let you live. She went to the door and opened it a crack, motioning Tommy inside with the cart. Granpa nodded shortly to her before turning to look back outward, watching for threats. As Tommy came through, she was back out of direct sight of the door, over by the sinks and already unfastening the top of the target's gray silks.

"I'll get her, you get out of those." Tommy waved her away from the unconscious woman.

She quickly stripped to her panties, leaving the clothes neatly on the floor in the order they'd need for the other woman. She shrugged into the woman's thankfully well-designed bra and the silks, finding enough in the woman's purse to do a passable copy of her makeup, pinning the silver-blond hair in a knot at the base of her neck. *Thank God she doesn't wear nail polish. Having to match the shade on the go would have been annoying.*

Socks and women's low-quarters, which were thankfully not *quite* regulation—having added support insoles—and she was almost ready to go. The buckley on her PDA and the on-board storage had been sanitized by the best the night before and given a surface makeover to the make and model of the other woman's. As far as it was concerned, she already was Captain Sinda Makepeace.

The cube in the reader slot had the only sensitive information. She handed her PDA and Makepeace's to Tommy and took over finishing dressing the target while he convinced the other PDA to surrender its files to hers. He opened a bottle of "cleaning fluid" and dropped the cube in, handing her back her PDA.

"Now remember, to access the transmitter, you need to go to your photopak icon, open it, select help, then transmitting a photo. The application will let you transmit anything on your PDA or in the cube slot," he said.

She helped him clean up the scene quickly, getting the now nameless woman squared away under the trash. She had to work carefully to avoid further mussing the uniform. The wet patch would look bad enough until it dried. And it felt clammy. *Ick. It probably won't even be dry by the time we get up to the ship. I'm definitely going to need to stop in my quarters and change before I do* anything *else.*

"See you on Titan." She gripped his hand quickly and was gone.

CHAPTER TEN

Cally left the women's room and walked past Gra—the other cleaner, wishing him a nice day. The purple vinyl seats and purple and oatmeal carpet of the departure lounge showed the influence of a decorating fad that had been current seven years ago. Makepeace had left the laptop next to her seat. Her eyes scanned the lounge for a few seconds. There it was, next to the clumsy bald man, bless his heart. He was looking at her, and she tugged her right ear gently before looking away, dropping the hand.

As she walked, her left hand came up and brushed at the side of her hair, as if she wasn't used to wearing it up. The seat had empty seats on either side, even though the lounge was starting to fill up with outbound passengers. She sat down and opened up her laptop. Getting into that now while she had a few minutes was the first thing. The clumsy bald guy got up and walked away.

Booting it showed her it had an old operating system. *Good. First thing to try is to see if it'll boot from the cube reader.* She powered it down and back up with a test cube. *Nice. It didn't fry it. Time to go for the cracker cube.*

As she was rebooting again a guy came up and stopped by the chair next to hers, clearing his throat nervously. *Not now, you loser. I am* not *in the mood for pick up attempts. Aha! Right to the cracker cube window.*

"I—Is this seat taken?" he asked.

"Unless you can lick your own eyebrows, it is," she snapped, using the cube utilities to reset the laptop's password and file permissions.

185

To her great annoyance, he settled into the seat anyway and she had just turned her head to tell the pushy jerk off when he interrupted her.

"How do you think I do my hair?" he said.

Her mouth hung open for a minute before she snapped it shut, returning his salute a little dazedly. He was a slight man with straight dark hair. A lock of it looked like it would tend to fall down into his forehead. He had warm brown eyes you could fall right into, and he was *way* too young. But what really surprised her about him was that he was the kid shown in her briefings as General Beed's aide. She kept the recognition out of her eyes with an effort.

"I'm sorry I was so crabby. I guess I'm a little nervous. Can we try that again? I'm Sinda Makepeace." She offered her hand.

"Joshua Pryce. Is this your first time off Earth, ma'am?" His hand was warm and dry.

She realized abruptly that he still had her hand and that she was staring. She snatched her hand back, flushing. *A blush? Me? What the hell is that all about? I haven't blushed in years.*

"Uh . . . why yes, it is. My assignment's on Titan Base. I suppose I'm a little uncertain about flying in space. You know, all that space around you and no air to breathe." She shuddered. "It kinda gives me the willies."

"Your name sounds familiar." His forehead wrinkled and he flipped open his PDA, pulling up a list. "Did you say your name was Sinda Makepeace, Captain?"

"Why, yes, I did," she smiled, tilting her head at him curiously.

"I thought I'd seen the name before. We've got the same boss on Titan. I wouldn't be surprised if we ended up working in the same office, ma'am." He pulled his eyes away from hers. For a second there it had seemed almost like he was staring into her soul.

"Oh, you're working for General Beed, too?" she asked, smiling brightly.

"Yes, ma'am." He looked at her earnestly, "Would—would it make you feel less nervous if I arranged to sit next to you on the flight up to the ship, ma'am?"

"The company would be very pleasant, Lieutenant Pryce." She stretched slightly, straightening her back. *Like those, do you? Dammit, girl, behave!*

Sunday morning, May 26

The nature of Federation space travel was that most of the travel time between stars was spent in normal space, "sublight" to laymen, reaching the ley-lines or paths between stars where access to hyperspatial regions was much easier. While it was possible to access hyperspace from anywhere, it was much more power-intensive, maximum speed was less, and exit point was somewhat random. That would allow in-system jumps, but the potential for losses in a crowded environment like the vicinity of Titan Base was prohibitive. The upshot was that where it would take only about six months to get from Earth to one of the inhabited planets in a relatively nearby system, travel in-system to Titan Base took a good eight days, or more, by Federation courier ship. It was their good fortune that presently Earth and Saturn were on the same side of the Sun. At maximum separation, it was nearly a month's voyage because of the need to detour around the Sun.

The Galactic Federation tried to keep enough ships in transit between Earth and Titan that there was a minimum of one flight a week. This was not out of any particular love for Earth or humans. On the contrary, humans, being the only carnivorous sophonts in the Federation, were generally regarded as useful barbarians. Their usefulness consisted primarily in their ability to throw the Posleen off of conquered bits of real estate that the Galactics wanted back. The frequency of the ships was more to ensure that Fleet and Fleet Strike could move critical personnel around as needed between larger troop shipments than anything else.

Fleet discouraged carry-on luggage on the shuttle. They preferred for anything that could shift around to be secured with the checked baggage. When Cally boarded with Sinda's purse and laptop, the pilot at the door, a Fleet captain in black, gave her a rather cold look. Whether at the state of her uniform or at the not one but *two* loose articles she didn't know. She responded with a sunny smile that shined out of her eyes, whispering over her shoulder to the lieutenant once they were past.

"Bless his heart, the captain looks as if he could have used another cup of coffee this morning," she said.

"Yes, ma'am." Pryce tripped, whether over an uneven place in the floor or his own feet she wasn't sure, but as he landed against her and used her shoulder to straighten himself, she got a whiff of clean male scent underlain with a hint of rut. Her nostrils flared as he apologized profusely. She told herself to ignore the slight clench of her belly.

He's a baby. Remember the last one? The last thing you need on this mission is to give yourself away as a juv. Makepeace is not a juv. I'm twenty-three. Still, hands off the baby—no matter how good he smells.

The interior of the shuttle greatly resembled that of a small airliner, with the exception that the seat belts were more functional— five point restraints rather than the airlines' pro-forma lap belts. Also, there was actual webbing overhead to strap in the few loose articles as needed, rather than overhead baggage compartments. The seats looked similar, although they were built to support the body for an hour or two, rather than a long flight. They did not recline, to the great relief of long-legged passengers. They did, however, have footrests at a convenient height to support Indowy personnel when the shuttle was used to transport them. Where first class would have been in an airliner, the shuttle had a few seats configured for Darhel physiques. The seat configuration and lighting was subtly different from that in the human section.

"Are there going to be Darhel on the shuttle flight up?" she asked the lieutenant.

"No. Why do you ask?" He looked over at her.

"Oh, I guess I'm just skinning my ignorance since it's my first time off-planet. I saw the three Indowy in the back and thought if this was a mixed flight . . ." She trailed off.

"Oh. Well, there are a lot fewer Darhel than there are Indowy, ma'am. I've never seen them travel with humans. The Darhel, I mean. I've only seen one once, you know. And, well, with all the robes you couldn't really see much," he said.

Sunday, May 26, noon

If she expects the trip out to be one long parade of card games and movies, she'll find out she's mistaken. General James Stewart grinned at his reflection in the mirror of his shipboard quarters as he straightened the unfamiliar lieutenant's insignia on his collar. Makepeace was definitely easy on the eyes. Probably had a problem with backaches, but it sure was in a good cause. *Way* too young—the only hardship working with her was going to be keeping his hands off. That shouldn't be too tough, though. She was hardly going to be interested in a klutzy fuck-up lieutenant like Pryce.

Shit. Makepeace is easy on the eyes. And Beed is a slimy bastard. Pete would never have done this on purpose. If Vanderberg did have anything to do with this I'm gonna kill his ass. Nah. Pete wouldn't do anything like that. He'd have been more likely to transfer her out if he'd known. Damn.

There were twenty-four hours of transmission time, along multiple frequencies, aboard ship—more than enough time for huge chunks of compressed and encrypted data to be transmitted, complete with error-checking, each day. Sure, there was a little over an hour of transmission lag, but that really only mattered with conversations, or their text equivalents.

What that meant in practice was that when they had reported aboard, the cube with the day's work on it had made it to his quarters before his luggage.

The uniform of the day onboard ship was silks, and they didn't wrinkle easily, so he didn't actually need to change. He did want to give the captain long enough to get into a fresh set of silks, though. When he'd arrived in the departure lounge she'd needed a change of uniform, but a lieutenant wouldn't have thought it was politic to ask why, or to even notice, so he hadn't.

He spent what he thought would be an appropriate wait sorting through the morning's files. Beed was not letting the grass grow under his feet, obviously. The past ten years of Titan's criminal cases had been forwarded for "background material," along with a large body of statistical data on the military and civilian personnel living on Titan and an annotated base map, including the carefully recorded observations of the CID personnel they were replacing—good parts of town, bad parts of town, the pimps, the pushers, where the working girls hung out, which gambling operations were where, which businesses were connected to which tong. The annotations read like an encyclopedia of general vice. It was so useful he had to doubt it was Beed's idea.

He used the intercom to buzz through to her quarters.

"What can I do for you, Lieutenant Pryce?" she came back, voice only.

"Captain M-Makepeace? I was wondering if you could spare some time to meet with me? I've picked up the daily cube of our work for the general and I was wondering when we could get started. I know you haven't actually reported in yet, but the general, he doesn't believe in idle hands," he offered apologetically.

"Well bless his heart, I was afraid I going to be stuck with old movies and monopoly. Is there someplace on this ship with a desk, or are we going to have to work here?" she asked.

He had to give her points for accepting the extra work gracefully. He thought about trying to work in the mess hall, but it would mean they couldn't start until after the second shift of breakfast, and had to break for both shifts of lunch. Then he thought about trying to work with Captain Sinda Makepeace in her quarters, in a cube not much bigger than six feet on a side with no place to sit but her bunk, for a whole week. There were times when doing the right thing approached the painful.

"I think it'll have to be the mess hall between mealtimes, ma'am," he said.

"Fine by me. Are you headed over there now?"

"Yes, ma'am."

"All right, I'll see you there in a few minutes." She pressed the button to disconnect the call.

One of the improvements in modern Federation courier ships over earlier designs was that most areas of the ship were able to sense which species was passing through a given area and adjust the lighting accordingly. The walls reflected each version of the lighting in a shade that at least was acceptable to the inhabitants. For humans this amounted to a muddy brown that had no distressing overtones. Still, the drabness of the walls tended to make the gray silks look washed out, and the institutional pale green of the human-only mess hall walls was a bit of a relief. Except on Earth itself, of course, all eating areas for humans were human-only by common aesthetic decree of the other Galactic races.

She had beaten him here. Her quarters were closer. Stewart saw that she had already gotten halfway through a cup of coffee. He came to attention and saluted smartly, then ruined the effect by sideswiping a table with his thigh and bending over it, wincing slightly before straightening up.

Makepeace hesitated disbelievingly in the act of returning his salute. He offered an apologetic grin.

"Guess I haven't gotten my space legs, yet, ma'am."

"That's all right, Lieutenant. Why don't you get yourself a cup of coffee and we can start going over that cube the general sent us," she said, smiling.

"Can I get you a refill, ma'am?" he asked.

Her eyes widened in alarm, doubtless envisioning a lapful of hot coffee.

"Uh, no! I mean, I'm just fine as I am, Lieutenant, thank you."

You certainly are, Captain, you certainly are. Maybe could spare a bit off the thighs, but otherwise just fine. Stewart walked past her to the coffee machine, stifling a grin.

After he got his coffee, as he sat down and pulled out his PDA, he glanced at her eyes before looking away somewhere over her left shoulder.

"Permission to speak freely, ma'am?"

"What's on your mind, Lieutenant?" She leaned forward, crossing her hands one over the other, and focused on him with an earnest, listening expression.

"Ma'am, how much did they tell you about this job?"

"Very little, Lieutenant. Any scuttlebutt you could offer would be very helpful, if you've got any."

"Your background is clerking in personnel, right ma'am?" When she nodded, he went on, "Well, what kind of things does a clerk in personnel do?"

"Well, I'm not sure why you want to know, but mostly I matched square pegs to square holes. Checked position requirements to make sure they were correct and not tweaked to make someone's buddy a fit for a job. Well, not very much, anyway," she amended. "Mostly I ran searches for positions and optimization programs and then checked behind the computers to make sure their recommendations made sense. The human factor in the loop, you know?"

"Well, ma'am, this position may be a bit . . . different . . . from what you were expecting."

"Well, I wasn't expecting anything in particular. Different how, Lieutenant Pryce?"

His words would have triggered red flags in the minds of almost any experienced officer in Fleet Strike. If a red flag had gone up in Makepeace's mind, the earnest and slightly puzzled blue eyes gave no sign of it. She leaned slightly farther forward, and, if anything, the impression of careful, attentive *listening* increased.

"Ma'am, do you remember in college taking an elective course, taught by computer, in the history of legal administration?"

"Okay, what about it?"

The expression in the blue eyes was still blank. Stewart was starting to feel like he had stepped into the twilight zone.

"Ma'am, General Beed likes paper."

"Well, okay. It's not very usual, but people collect some very strange things. What, does he display the collection in his office or something? I'll make a point to admire it. Thank you for—"

"Sorry to interrupt, ma'am, but that's not what I meant. He doesn't collect paper, he insists on working with it."

"I'm not sure I understand." She tilted her head to the side and waited for him to elaborate.

"Ma'am, the general does not use an AID, he does not use a computer, the only electronic devices in his office I'm sure he uses are the lighting and the life support. Oh, and the coffee machine," he added.

"Paper?" she whispered, the light of understanding dawning in her eyes at last. "Well, that's . . . special." She paused, obviously lost in thought. Stewart was beginning to suspect she could get very lost indeed.

"How does he ever get any work done?" she asked.

"Ma'am, Fleet Strike promoted you to captain and sent you here because you're the closest thing to a legal secretary it had. In this case, you were the closest thing to a square peg it had for this square hole. I'm afraid that means this position may be a bit different from what you're used to, ma'am," he said. He carefully didn't state that the promotion had probably been something in the way of a consolation prize from a fellow personnel officer who had winced at the obviously shitty job he was forced to stick her with. Promotions weren't supposed to be given out like that, but the bean counters tended to stick together.

She brushed her left hand over her hair, smoothing it unnecessarily.

"Lieutenant Pryce, a good Fleet Strike officer goes where she's sent and does what she is ordered to do." She shrugged, "I guess I'll have to brush up on paper."

"Yes, ma'am."

"Thank you for the scuttlebutt, Pryce." She smiled warmly at him and Stewart was suddenly glad he was seated on the opposite side of a table. "Now, about that work you mentioned. Hadn't we best get started?"

Okay, she's stacked and her face and hair aren't bad. Beautiful wouldn't be too strong a word. But for God's sake, man, you're not seventeen! Definitely a good idea not to work in her quarters. Constant seven-foot separation would be about right. Unfortunately, that suggested the kind of work he was beginning to think he'd like to do in her quarters, including a remarkably vivid mental image of her naked breasts in his hands— He cut the thought off and handed her the copy he'd made of the original cube. A spark of static jumped between their hands and he inhaled sharply. She was a hopeless ditz, but obviously there was some chemistry there in addition to the normal reaction of any healthy, straight young man to a woman built like she was. Not that he was young. But his body obviously thought *it* was. It was going to be a long week.

Cally had escaped after dinner to her quarters which, being onboard a ship, resembled a broom closet with all the necessary furniture and electronics shoehorned in. Everything except a head. That was down the hall and wasn't exactly designed for meaningful privacy. The design specs for these hulls had been laid down when female humans had been few and far between in Fleet Strike, and Fleet had evolved a more relaxed attitude towards body modesty anyway. The upshot was that her shower shift in the morning had surreptitiously been more crowded than strictly necessary. Some of the troops who showered on her shift had almost certainly been scheduled for the other one. But as they didn't touch and were discreet about looking, and as Makepeace was enough of an airhead to get by with it, she affected not to notice. She did notice that the lieutenant was not among her covert admirers. He was on the same shift, but kept himself well along towards the end of the line of shower heads. At least, if he *was* looking, he was very good at not getting caught at it.

She and Pryce were on the first meal shift with the other officer passengers and a few rather glum enlisteds that probably would have preferred the other shift for their chow.

This left the problem of what to do while the second meal shift was using the mess hall. Since space was at a premium, however, they usually spent the time leaning against the wall in the passage outside. Cally tended to either linger over a second cup of coffee or play two-player Space Invaders against Pryce. They had discovered that they both shared an odd passion for very early arcade space games. He had offered to show her his collection of games once they got to Titan. She didn't think it was a line, and wasn't quite sure how she felt about that.

Today Pryce had muttered something about needing something from his quarters. She hadn't paid much attention, grateful for the respite that gave her time over the coffee to sort out how she felt about him. He wasn't the clumsiest man she'd ever met, but he certainly wasn't graceful. *Maybe Granpa's right. The job's starting to get to me. Okay, it's been a couple of weeks and I've got a normal, healthy set of hormones, but half the guys in the shower were as okay looking, and none of them were tripping over their own feet. Okay, the way that little strand of hair keeps falling across his forehead is kind of sexy, but . . . the job must be getting to me after all. The first* acceptable *excuse I get for getting laid I need to do something about some of these hormones.*

Her coffee cup was empty, so she went back into the mess hall for more. She could hear a couple of whispers, and feel the eyes, but the railroad tracks on her collar effectively prevented anything more overt. Pryce was back when she got back out with her fresh coffee.

"I wonder what's on the cube this morning. Had a look?" she asked.

"No, ma'am." He leaned against the wall just a bit outside normal conversational space, as if he was afraid of getting too close.

"Okay. Why don't you tell me a little bit about our office setup on Titan. Have you been out there yet?" Her back was already aching a bit, and she stood away from the wall so she could arch back and take some pressure off of it, reaching a hand back to rub out the slight cramp.

"What? Oh." He shook his head slightly. "I've been to Titan Base before, ma'am, but not to CID. I reported in to the general before he left Earth. Okay, ma'am, you know the general just took command of the Third MP Brigade on Titan. Most of the brigade, all but about two companies of it, brigade headquarters, and CID, is forward deployed with various combinations of the infantry. Most of the day to day management of the brigade is handled by the XO, Colonel Tartaglia. The general feels that the best use of his attention involves more of a hands-on focus with CID, so, other than the time-honored passing of canapés, that's where I'm likely to be spending most of my time. That's also why he wanted you familiar with so much of CID's background. If he asks you to find him something, he's . . . well, patience and explanations don't appear to be his strong suits, ma'am."

"I'm looking forward to this assignment already," she commented dryly.

Stewart had always worked at jobs without fixed hours. When most teens his age had been watching the clock at fast food places, Stewart had been running a successful street gang under his original name, Manuel Guerrera. Then, as now, organizational problems and responsibilities often couldn't be pigeon-holed into set hours. Which was why he was lying here on his bunk, while Captain Makepeace was either in her cabin or doing God knew what, going through a list of names and detailed security profiles trying to detect which one or more of the people who had put in for assignment to the Fleet Strike CID on Titan were most likely to be plants of the nameless enemy organization revealed by their contact.

The completed profiles had finally come in this morning, but his scheduled work with Makepeace had meant he couldn't go over them during the day. They were arriving in Titan orbit tomorrow afternoon, and he wanted the list done before they landed. Five more of their people had arrived on Titan while he was on Earth, and he wanted to know what he was looking at before he met them.

It was a frustrating task because of their near total lack of information about the goals and motives of the enemy, beyond knowing that those goals included espionage against Federation military and civil government organizations, which in itself was enough to suggest unfriendly and likely hostile intentions. Their best guess so far was that someone in the humanist fringe had finally gotten organized, a thought that was frightening, given the number of feral Posleen that were still on Earth and other planets, and the extent to which Earth's defenses against a resurgence still depended heavily on purchase of Galtech technology and equipment.

Constant vigilance against reorganization of the Posleen, including retaking previously conquered Galactic Federation real estate, was Fleet and Fleet Strike's highest priority. Each and every feral Posleen was a potential danger because each was born with the fundamental knowledge of the species. While most feral Posleen were the moronic and barely sentient normals, all Posleen were hermaphrodites who could self-fertilize in a pinch. A single smart God King could potentially rebuild the entire ravening hoard.

Consequently, the first part of his task was to list all the humanist connections of the various personnel, and the second to list anything that stood out in the personnel or their friends and relatives as having *any* discontent with the Federation.

It made for a long list, and a late night. Anders, for example, had a brother and a second cousin who were humanists, the brother more active, but she and her brother were allegedly estranged and hadn't spoken in years. Could be true. Could be a cover. Baker's family were Indianapolis Urbies and apparently apolitical. Carlucci had no family, and no close friends outside Fleet Strike. Sergeant Franks had a humanist wife who was profiled in the report as also believing the aliens were in league with the Masons, the Illuminati, and Satan—your typical, garden-variety humanist nut. It certainly made him a security risk. The rest was more of the same. Even Makepeace had a neighbor the next farm over with a humanist daughter. Out of fifteen people in the office, twelve had some sort of documented humanist connection. The other three, well, you never could tell, could you?

Titan Base had the worst case of smog in the inhabited universe. Approaching from the black of space, the glowing blue edge of the nitrogen atmosphere looked almost Earth-like, but the orange-brown layer of hydrocarbon smog, so thick as to be visually impenetrable, would have made prewar Los Angeles or Mexico City, or present day Chicago, look like sparkling bastions of atmospheric cleanliness.

The shuttle didn't bother with artificial gravity, so the first part of their descent into Titan's atmosphere felt like riding up a steep hill, "down" being in the direction of the backs of their seats. Pryce had let her have the window seat, and Cally stared out the window in what she hoped was not complete tourist goggling. In fifty-one years of a life that in many ways had made ordinary cosmopolitan sophistication look positively cloistered, this was her first time off-planet. Fortunately, it was also Sinda's first time off-planet, so she didn't really need to restrain natural curiosity and excitement too much.

The lieutenant reached over her shoulder, pointing at a fluffy white mass. "Look, a cloud. We don't see too many of those."

"It's methane, isn't it?" She stared out the window.

"Yes, ma'am."

As they moved into the heavy brown haze, they also curved around into the nighttime side of the moon. The outside blackened. Unfortunately, they were at the wrong angle for her window to have a view of Saturn. They crested the "hill" of freefall and then started "down," pressing lightly forward against their five-point seatbelts as the shuttle began braking.

"Will we be able to see Saturn from the base?" She craned her neck to see if there was anything interesting still visible through the darkened window.

"Only as an occasional hazy bright spot in the dark, ma'am." He smiled regretfully. "Other than that and the Sun for a couple of days when we're close to noon, it's pretty much like living in an underwater birdcage with a blanket thrown over it. Well, if the bird had electric lighting," he added, grinning.

Landing was a couple of muffled thumps, and, at one-seventh her accustomed weight, did feel extraordinarily like being at the bottom of a swimming pool.

"And now is when we're glad for the warmth of our silks," he said.

"How cold is it?"

"Outside? About minus one-forty C. In the tube to the dome, a handful of degrees below zero." He unbuckled his seat belt and stood.

"Brrrr." She shuddered. "They can't get it warmer?"

"Won't." He shrugged. "It's a safety issue. The whole base is built on various ices. One of our biggest engineering challenges, besides the overpressure, is minimizing heat leakages that could destabilize the ground underneath us."

"Couldn't they insulate? Or float?" As she stood, she had to reach back and rub the achey place at the base of her spine.

"Oh, they do insulate, ma'am. Believe me they do. This platform and the base itself are actually about fifty feet off the ground, to let air circulate underneath. Short term, you can build on the ground, and it's not as much of a problem with ground research vehicles because they move. But you just don't want to put a big hot spot on top of ice for a few centuries. Flotation was one of the designs considered, but ultimately discarded. Something about gravitational effects and stability issues."

"It's all ice? There isn't, well, rock underneath it?" She looked as if she couldn't quite grasp the concept.

"Some. Not enough," he said.

"And can't the Crabs do gravity?"

"Sure, and they did, for the base itself. I think cost considerations counted a lot in the choice of the final design." He motioned her out into the aisle in front of him.

The chill bit at her cheeks and nose and she could see her breath as they made the short walk, with the other passengers, through the tube into the main dome of Titan Base. The air smelled vaguely like a gas station.

"What's the smell?" She wrinkled her nose and waved a hand at the air.

"Leakage. With this much overpressure, there's bound to be some. It's a trade-off. They could have made the place more leak proof, but it would have cost a lot more. Or so I'm told." He gripped her elbow as they crossed a red line on the floor and full gravity returned abruptly.

She'd been expecting it and hadn't expected to fall at all, but suddenly she stumbled against him as her elbow tingled where he'd touched it as though she'd just touched a live wire. She was suddenly short of breath and she actually *blushed* as he steadied her back on her feet. *What the hell? He's not that attractive. Okay, he smells pretty nice. Check that. Real good. But so what. My God, what is wrong with me? Must be the excitement of my first trip off-planet. Who'da thunk?*

As they moved from the tube through the doors into the shuttle port, and then through the double-glass doors out of the arrival area, the temperature warmed quite a bit, but she could still see her breath. The air felt heavy, cold and heavy.

A line of reproduction analog clocks across the wall gave the local time and the time in various time zones on Earth. She noted with a start that local time and the local "day" was set to be synchronized with Chicago, as ship's time on the courier had been. Wow, she didn't even have to change her watch.

Small, potted evergreen trees were tucked along the walls. The lieutenant must have noticed her puzzled expression as he turned and led her through double doors into a room that was obviously the shuttle port bar.

"It's not just to look nice. That's part of it, but they're also a cheap way of scrubbing some of the hydrocarbon volatiles out of the air. The small-scale oxygen release is just a bonus," he said.

The bar was warm enough to take off their gloves, and she began looking around for someplace to set her laptop case down for a minute. He pulled out one of the tall, backed barstools for her, folding his thin but warm gloves and tucking them into the pocket in the lining of his beret.

It was about three in the afternoon Greenwich, and the bar was empty but for the Asian bartender who was busying himself washing glassware and watching a vid. As the lieutenant put her coat aside and she climbed onto the stool, he hung the glass he'd just rinsed on the rack and walked on over.

"What can I get for you Pryce, Captain?" He took a towel and absentmindedly rubbed at a small water-spot on his bar.

"Two Irish coffees, Sam, short on the Irish." He turned to her. "Would it surprise you, ma'am, to find out hot drinks are popular here?" he asked.

"Oh, terribly." She laughed. "Why is it chilly on the base itself?"

"I've heard two theories. The first is the conventional one of controlling heat pollution. The second is that someone in the design team saw that the average temperature on Earth was fifty-nine degrees Fahrenheit and decided that was the optimum setting." He quirked an eyebrow at her and waited.

"The second makes a nice story." She laughed and took a sip of the coffee when it arrived, then set it down.

"You know, when I went through officer basic, I don't think they recommended reporting to your new CO with alcohol on your breath," she said.

"Ma'am, Beed's a real vintage sort, but he's from before that late twentieth century PC craze. As long as we don't show up drunk and unfit for duty, and we won't, he won't care."

"Well, that's one good thing about this assignment." She cupped her hands around the mug and took a long, appreciative sip. Sam made one hell of a cup of coffee.

After picking up their luggage from baggage claim, they had boarded one of the transit cars that ran on horizontal and vertical tracks, in singles or chains, throughout the base. Stewart carried the captain's bag in addition to his own as he guided them to a departing car with empty seats. The car was one of a line that appeared grouped together, though not physically connected. The light bar across the top of the front car spelled out the destination: Fleet Strike Quadrant. Judging from the volume of traffic, the shuttle from Earth had not been the only one coming in at roughly the same time. The light blue berets of the infantry surrounded their own gray ones, and Sinda looked around curiously. He supposed she hadn't seen many troops who were actually on deployment, having been immured in Personnel for most of her short career.

"The base is divided into four roughly equal sections, ma'am," he explained. "Fleet and Transient quadrants are on either side of us, Engineering and Fleet Strike on the other side."

"Wouldn't it make more sense to have the shuttle port next to engineering for incoming supplies?" she asked.

"There is one. This is the passenger port."

"So," she gestured with her PDA, "is there a map of this place that I can download, or something?"

"Sure. Hang on and I'll beam it to you, ma'am." He tapped a few keys and pointed his PDA at hers so she could download. "The BOQ is highlighted. Your quarters are marked in red, mine in blue, the office in green."

"You have my quarters marked on your map?" she teased. "What, is the red for stop?"

"For danger, at least, ma'am."

"And work is safe? You're an interesting person, Lieutenant," she said. "So, it looks like the BOQ is on the way. It's probably best to drop off our bags before reporting in."

"Yes, ma'am."

"Don't worry, Lieutenant. I'll carry my own bag in. No need for you to enter the danger zone."

"Thank you, ma'am." He turned his head and looked out the transit car window so she wouldn't see his eyes narrow. *Minx. That does it. Just you wait, Sinda Makepeace.*

CHAPTER ELEVEN

Monday, June 3

The general's office, and her office, were on an upper, outer level of the dome, so that instead of looking up to more ceilings, the hallways on that level extended upward to an imperceptibly curving stretch of dome. For all the good it did. Right now it was near high noon on Titan, and the sky outside the dome was a uniformly muddy, dark, orange-brown. The glow paint, of course, had to be along the top two feet of the walls, but to compensate for the reduced lighting surface area caused by the lack of space on the ceiling it was set brighter than was normal in the rest of the base.

The walls of institutional green Galplas with battleship gray doors gave the impression that if anyone on the design or maintenance teams had had an ounce of interior decorating talent, he had been taking great care to conceal it. There was a sign next to the door as they approached, identifying the door as leading to Headquarters, Third MP Brigade. The lieutenant was reporting in to the general, too, and got to the door slightly ahead of her, presenting his ID to the door which automatically checked his IR profile against the records on the ID and in the database, and, finding a match, admitted them.

Inside, there was a reception desk and signs that pointed to CID leading away to the right, and Office of the Commanding General, to the left. Behind the desk, the corporal's nametag identified her as Anders. Behind the corporal, on the back wall, was a large holoscreen of a waterfall—on Earth, judging by the vegetation on the banks.

"Captain Makepeace and Lieutenant Pryce, Corporal . . . Anders, is it? We're here to report in and pay our respects to the CO. I believe he's expecting us." Cally returned the corporal's salute smoothly and waited.

"Yes, ma'am, I'll let him know you're here." The corporal picked up her PDA and told it to get her the general.

"General Beed, sir?"

Cally's enhanced hearing picked up both ends of the conversation easily, and she listened in with a polite, still, waiting expression on her face.

"They here, Corporal? Thank God. About to drown in paperwork back here without a decent secretary. Send them on back."

"Yes, sir. End call." She set the PDA back down.

"You can go on back ma'am, sir." She inclined her head in the direction of the general's office.

Cally passed the corporal and made her way past several closed gray doors and down the corridor to the general's office, Pryce trailing in her wake. The light on the panel under his nameplate indicated an unlocked door, so a wave of her hand in front of it and the door slid aside. She stepped in, and walked to the front of the desk, coming to attention and saluting. With her eyes focused six inches above the general's head, she had to study him and the room with only her peripheral vision. Child's play.

Beed was certainly handsome for an officer his age. The dark blond hair and deep blue eyes were focused a bit below her face. But after the voyage out, she was becoming used to it. His handlebar mustache was perhaps a bit affected, but he was trim, and muscular. For all their warmth and durability, silks weren't the type of fabric to conceal much. Without rejuv she would have taken him for maybe thirty-four. With it, he had to be well into his second century. Still young by Galactic standards. Not as hot as Pryce, but no hardship on the eyes, either. If he decided to chase her around the desk, at least she wouldn't be fighting not to puke or anything. Bit of a weak chin, but it could have been worse.

"Captain, you're a sight for sore eyes." He swept a hand across in a gesture indicating the desk, which was stacked at least six inches deep in paper all the way across, and that was only in the valleys between the piles. Cally restrained herself from goggling with an effort. "Welcome to Titan Base. Your office is just out-side and to the left. You should be basically familiar with what we do now, and I've taken the liberty of having the corporal bring in file cabinets and folders and such. I have a few things to dis-cuss with the lieutenant, but I think the best way to do that is for us to get out of the way while you take charge and organize some sort of filing system. I don't care how you handle it so long as you can explain it simply and we can both find any of this stuff at need. We should be gone at least a couple of hours, plenty of time for you to get me a desk surface I can see." He looked at her expectantly.

"Yes, sir," she answered crisply.

"Great, honey. Take care of that, and you and I will be on our way to getting along just fine." He winked at her, of all things, and turned to the lieutenant. "Lieutenant, I understand aides de camp for general officers are authorized to wear two gold braid loops over the shoulder. A good officer always pays precise attention to presenting himself with the right appearance, understood?"

"Yes, sir. No excuse, sir." If anything, his already perfect atten-tion position got a little straighter.

"At ease. Let's get out of here and leave Sinda to it, then." He paused, looking her up and down slowly on the way out the door. "Fine attention to detail, Captain Makepeace. Good job." Then they were gone.

Cally stared at the door as it slid closed behind them, fighting the impulse to laugh in disbelief. *And I had been going over ploys to get the man out of his office and me free rein to run a search.* She turned the personality overlay off and the AI up to eight on the PDA.

"Something's about to kill us, isn't it, Captain?" it said.

"Listen to the surroundings, buckley. If someone other than me approaches within six meters of the door, beep once, medium volume."

"Okay. Not that it'll do any good."

She put the PDA down in the middle of the desk and snorted as a small stack of paper fell, scattering itself across the floor. She made quick work of searching the desk drawers. It was especially quick because there was nothing to find. A few legal pads and ball point pens that she dissected without finding anything useful about them, then reassembled and replaced them. That done, she put the PDA back in order and got to work sorting and organizing the mountain of paper, which she would have needed to search through, anyway.

In the end, she wasn't finished in the two hours it took Beed to get back to the office. Pryce was not with him.

"Well, you made good progress, Captain." He moved around behind her and stood just a little too close to where she was bending over the desk to pick up yet another sheaf of papers. The maneuver coincidentally drew the gray fabric against her buttocks, giving him an excellent view of the contours of her behind.

"Do you mind if I ask you to work late? We usually do knock off around five but . . . if you'd like, I'll buy you dinner. Since I'm asking you to work late." He was almost breathing on her neck.

She stood and turned, bringing the papers in close and looking up at him. He was definitely in her personal space.

"Why bless your heart, sir, you don't have to do that." Her blue eyes widened ingenuously.

"Of course I don't, Captain. Still, it would give you a chance to brief me about where you're putting everything. I'd take it as a personal favor if you would, Sinda. You don't mind if I call you Sinda, do you?" His smile was charming. He was quite good at it, the charm thing. She could appreciate that.

"Not at all, sir." She smiled, "And dinner would be just fine."

He took her to a rather elaborate Cantonese place down on the Corridor. Cally tried not to gawk like a tourist. Not too much, anyway. Calling it *the* corridor was something of a misnomer. Actually, the main commercial zone in Titan Base was a ground plate floor-to-dome stack of corridors, with spaces cut through the layers so you could stand at the railing on one level and look all the way up and all the way down. It was one of the few places that it was possible to visually appreciate the immenseness of the base. Okay, so it wasn't so big compared to the holograms she'd seen of Indowy skyscrapers, but she was actually *here*, and Titan felt so real. She supposed it was probably the presence of so much Earthtech. Well, there was a lot of assimilated Galtech, too, but when it came from human labor in Earth companies, it didn't really seem to count.

According to Beed, the Corridor bisected the base from east to west—directions had been assigned based on the moon's axis of rotation, there being no geomagnetic activity to speak of. To the north, the Fleet Strike MP's supervised their own quadrant, the spares, fabrication, and galactic races' quadrant, and the Corridor itself. To the south, Fleet's SP's supervised their own quadrant, the colonist, transient, and civilians' quadrant, and the passenger shuttle port. To someone without an appreciation of the Darhel's ultra-Machiavellian tendencies it might seem strange that Fleet Strike was in charge of guarding spares and supplies mostly used by Fleet. To Cally, it was just one more example of things being made more complex to make them easier to manipulate.

The restaurant had obviously spent a fair bit on the décor to impart an Eastern feel, covering the Galplas walls in red and gold wallpaper that carried a dragon motif. The glow paint of the sign had been adjusted in a reasonable imitation of neon and proclaimed the name of the establishment, in English, "The Golden Dragon." It appeared to be one of the more upscale of the places catering to officers, well-heeled businessmen and the occasional colonist willing and able to blow some hard currency on one good meal out on the outbound leg of the trip.

Still, it wasn't even nearly full on a Monday evening, and they were quickly shown to a table in a corner, lit by a small globe that flickered almost, but not quite, like candlelight. Beside the plates there was a folded cloth napkin, a fork, and a pair of plastic chopsticks. She ordered the sweet and sour chicken and an egg roll. The place had a carefully cultivated ambience, but looked very touristy to her experienced eyes. Best to pick something hard to screw up.

"Conservative tastes?" he asked, after ordering the phoenix and dragon.

"Why, did I choose something I shouldn't have, sir?" She looked down and to the side, embarrassed. "I just thought it looked interesting. Would you think I was too . . . well, rural, if I admitted that I could count my visits to a restaurant like this on the fingers of one hand?"

"No, Captain—Sinda—sweet and sour chicken is fine." He smiled, almost gently. "I sometimes forget how young some of our officers are." Her hand was resting on the table and he reached across and stroked the back of it. She licked her lips, nervously, left hand brushing a stray wisp of hair out of her face.

"Young, but very much a grown woman. From what I've seen so far, you're a fine young officer, Sinda," he said.

"Thank you, sir." She turned trusting cornflower blue eyes on him, and smiled. *Searching his office didn't turn up what I needed. Maybe searching the general will. Besides, it's a good excuse for ditching some of these excess hormones. Play the near-innocent? Probably best.*

Tuesday, June 4

The next morning at work she passed Pryce at the coffee machine early on, but after he walked back over towards CID she didn't see him again that morning. General Beed, however, was very much in evidence. Her first duty of the morning was, he told her, to use her PDA to access his e-mail account and print out his correspondence, sorting it into categories for his review. She had to bite her lip to keep from pointing out that if he had an AID or a PDA he could have it sorted, ranked by importance, and in routine cases, answered—all just for the asking. Then, after he had sorted through the correspondence and noted what he wanted done with it all, she retrieved the stack from his out box and took it over to CID to run it through an only slightly improved version of a prewar photocopier, with one copy going to his incoming correspondence file before any of it could be answered or otherwise acted upon.

The man was positively a dinosaur, and several times when he spoke to her she had to avoid gritting her teeth as she smiled.

She did brace him about one issue, though. Whoever was making the coffee ought to be shot.

"Sir, have you noticed anything . . . er . . . strange about the coffee?" she began.

"It's grown locally in hydroponics, Makepeace. Something about the air—you'll get used to it." He shrugged, humming slightly as he plowed through some reports from the Fleet Strike Detention Center.

The prison was on base, but its dome was entirely separate. Escape was possible, of course. It had even been done. Several times. Apparently the biggest inconvenience to Fleet Strike was sending a crew out in suits to retrieve the bodies. Cally wasn't sure she could blame the prisoners. Freezing in unbreathable smog was probably a more comfortable death than an accident doing zero gee work in orbit, which was the usual ultimate fate of any prisoners who didn't have very limited sentences. And prisoners with minor problems didn't usually get shipped all the way to Titan Base.

After dealing with his correspondence, which was a matter of dictating what she thought the answers should be based on notes scribbled in the margins, printing the responses out, running them by Beed for changes, and then yet another printed version by him for approval before sending them out, there was yet another mound of paper in his outbox. She noticed he made a couple of excuses to come to her office, ostensibly to check on some bit of work she was doing. From the way he stood too close behind her, resting a hand on her shoulder as he bent over behind her to deliver comments that were always plausible but never strictly necessary, it was clear the general had more than work on his mind. His profile had said he was married, a fact he had neglected to mention and which was conveniently unobvious since he didn't wear a ring. However, it also mentioned that his wife was an unrejuved forty-seven. The wife had accompanied him out to Titan Base, but Cally could well believe that the poor woman was slowing down.

A bit after eleven-thirty he came in and made a great show of opening file drawers and browsing through the files.

"Good work getting things organized, Sinda. Now that you've got a system set up, it should be a lot easier to find things when I need them." He looked at the watch on his wrist and back at her. "It's about lunch time. Why don't we go grab a sandwich and you can brief me on the new filing system over lunch?"

"Certainly, sir. When would you like to leave?"

"I was thinking now, Captain." He smiled disarmingly at her. "I don't know about you, but my stomach is starting to growl."

"Bless your heart, sir, we can't have that. Give me just a moment to print out a list of files and I'll be ready to go." She offered him a smile that was open, friendly, and oblivious, turning back to her PDA and speaking to it softly. "There. We can pick it up from the printer in CID on our way out."

He stood back from the door a bit, clearly waiting for her to precede him out the door, gently—and unnecessarily—guiding her through with a hand on the small of her back. A hand he was careful to remove before they came around the corner and into the general reception area.

He waited while she got the printout from down the hall. As they left, Anders seemed to be very absorbed in the holographic display of whatever form she was working on.

The lunch rush had barely started, so they had a short wait for a car to the Corridor.

"Isn't there a cafeteria or anywhere to eat in Fleet Strike's quadrant, sir?" Cally tilted her head at him curiously.

"There's the mess hall, the officers' club, and a snack bar in the rec room for the enlisted men. Food at the officers' club is pretty decent, but it's a little . . . crowded. Not the best place for a working lunch," he said.

The grill where he took her was on one of the upper levels. The booths were constructed with high Galplas walls that had been adjusted to reflect in shades and patterns of a rosy brown that resembled cherry wood. From the relative hush and the slightly hollow sound when the waiter introduced himself and dropped off their menus, she could tell the place used electronic sound damping. Low level. Out of the corner of her eye she saw the edge of a small disk adhered behind the napkin holder.

He ordered a Reuben, she ordered an almond chicken salad on pita bread.

"So, you were going to give me an overview of the filing system," he invited, beckoning with a hand.

"Yes, sir. It's separated first into the headquarters material, CID, and the various units by unit. Within all that, it's alphabetical by subject."

"Can I see the list?" He didn't wait, but reached out for the paper, brushing her hand with his not quite accidentally along the way. His eyes were fixed on hers, watching for her reaction. She allowed a mischievous twinkle into her eye.

He didn't actually turn her on, but he didn't much turn her off, either. Ah well, it wouldn't be the first time she'd needed to use sex on a mission, and it wouldn't be the last. And he was more likely to be a mediocre lay than an actually bad one. Most men were.

The weekly State of the War briefing was late in the afternoon. It was always scheduled close to the change between first and second shifts so that the senior brass of both services, no matter what shift, could arrange to attend.

This got the general out of the office and Cally managed to stack up enough work for herself to justify staying late. She had a good chance of getting enough unobserved access to some of the areas over in CID to do a physical search. CID worked normally. The general's bizarre obsession with paper apparently didn't apply to things that didn't have to go through his hands, so she had been able to do a fair bit of her searching through the computers her first night. As the general's secretary, she had enough access to get her in the door, and then it was only a matter of expanding on it and covering her tracks. She hadn't found anything of interest, and was hoping that a physical search might turn up data cubes of material not stored directly in the systems.

After first shift, headquarters did have a pair of MPs posted out at the base car terminus to monitor comings and goings and keep out the unauthorized, but Anders and the CID agents generally left at or soon after seventeen hundred. She waited until seventeen-forty-five before deliberately misfiling a file the general had mentioned at lunch and heading for the water cooler, which was conveniently over in CID.

CID was a hallway of six offices flanking a conference room. The walls between the doors were bare except for the name plates and lock panels. The office beside the conference room had the water cooler and Beed's paper equipment. As she walked past the closed doors, she was able to observe the door panels of each office, and listen for voices inside. From the closed doors and the silence, it was pretty likely that the agents had gone for the day.

She got a drink from the cooler, listening for another moment before stepping out and gingerly opening Agent Carlucci's office door. The agents' doors were locked, of course, but since the general could ask for a file at any time, she was on the list of people with override access.

Carlucci's office had a desk of heavy plastic. Most nonstructural things were, since the raw materials for organics were abundant locally and didn't have to be shipped up from Earth or other Sol system real estate. His I-love-me wall was refreshingly sparse, with his certificate of graduation from the investigators course, and a plaque commemorating ten years of service in CID. His desk had an old-fashioned photo of his wife and not much else. There was a braided ficus tree on the floor, and a Boston fern in a pot on a stand of heavy plastic painted to look like wrought iron. Other than a pair of hand grippers, three packaged protein bars, and a couple of five-pound dumbbells, his desk contained nothing but dust, which she was careful not to disturb.

On to Baker's office. Baker's office was much like Carlucci's, different plants, no photo. He had a framed print of a Monet on his wall. He also had an unlabeled cube in his desk. She read it into active memory. It looked like music files, but she'd have to go over them with a fine toothed comb this evening, anyway, to check for hidden data. It wouldn't be the first time important data had been stored beneath or within something innocuous for extra security.

Li was fairly new and hadn't put anything in his office except some tropical-looking tree with big shiny leaves. It wasn't even dusty. Someone had probably cleaned it out before he arrived and he just hadn't been there long enough for a new layer to form. She was bent over the bottom drawer and was just closing it back when she heard a sound in the hall. It gave her enough warning that she didn't jump when the door slid open, just looked up and calmly closed the empty drawer. It was Pryce, and despite the second or so advance warning she felt her breathing quicken and her palms start to sweat.

"C—can I help you with anything, ma'am?" he asked.

"Maybe. Have you seen the Leave File?" She wiped her hands on the side of her silks as she stood back up. "It has the markup draft of the revision to the brigade leave and sick call policies and procedures."

"Oh, that." He frowned for a minute. "Sanchez had it this afternoon, ma'am."

"He brought it back, I remember that, and I thought I filed it. And now I can't find it and I just know I would be so embarrassed if the general, bless his heart, asked for it in the morning and I had to go look for it then." She frowned thoughtfully.

"Could Sanchez have thought of a comment he forgot and borrowed it again, maybe, ma'am?"

"Maybe. We can take a quick look." So Pryce was with her as

she searched Sanchez office, and she didn't dare copy the three cubes he had in his top desk drawer.

"No luck, huh?" he asked

"I'm afraid not." She straightened and walked past him out the door. He must have lost his balance as he turned behind her, because he stumbled up against her again, steadying himself with one hand on one side of the small of her back and the other on her arm, just below the shoulder. She knew right where his hands had been, because the skin there tingled even after he caught his balance and removed them.

"M—ma'am I am *so* sorry." His eyes were downcast. He was obviously embarrassed as hell. "I guess I'm not the most coordinated person in the world."

"Bless your heart, Pryce, nobody's perfect." She smiled sympathetically. "You've been to Titan before. You wouldn't happen to know if there's a decent place to get a pizza somewhere on this giant snowball, would you?" *Did I just ask him out? Yep. Why the hell am I attracted to this consummate klutz? I probably ought to speed things up with the general before I totally lose it. You have a job to do, Cally. Wake the hell up and do it, instead of fucking around with cute lieutenants.*

"I know just the place, ma'am. I could give you directions, but it doesn't have a big sign. You have to pay extra for that, and I guess Lin feels he doesn't need it. Most of his business is delivery, anyway. If you don't mind company, I haven't eaten either . . ."

"Uh, that would be just fine, Pryce." *After all, I have to eat, anyway. It has nothing to do with those deep, dark eyes of his. Nothing at all.*

The Little Venice Pizzeria was a small place located in the lower level. Stewart estimated that perhaps half the square footage was devoted to kitchen space. The small dining room was a bit busier than usual, but they didn't have to wait long for a table. While the busboy was cleaning their table, he used the mix of prints and reinterpreted holos of old Venice as inspiration for small talk. Flower boxes of lush vines, hung on the walls all the way around the dining room, gave the place a more dirtside feel than anywhere else she could've been on Titan. Tony Bennett was playing in the background. Stewart saw her notice the plastic roses on the tables and smiled slightly.

"Not exactly the place for a business dinner, Lieutenant."

"Were we going to discuss work, ma'am? They do a damn fine pizza here. I don't know if you're hungry or not, but I'm starved. Split a large?"

"That sounds good. Is it just me, or does it not smell as . . . smoggy . . . in here as it does out there?" she asked.

"It's not just you. Lin installed extra filters, and the extra plants help a lot. He said the pollution was inhibiting his yeast, whatever that means. So, ma'am, what do you like on your pizzas?"

"Everything, with extra cheese." Makepeace grinned like a little kid.

"Um . . . ma'am, how about everything except for anchovies?" He walked up to the counter and looked back at her, raising an eyebrow.

"Deal."

"One large garbage pizza, extra cheese, hold the cat food." He looked at the petite brunette behind the counter curiously. "Hi, Suzannu, good to see you again. Where's Lin?"

"His wife is sick, so I take over for a few days until she gets better. Gotcha, one catless garbage, extra cheese. It will be up in about fifteen minutes. You want drinks with that?" She set two empty cups on the counter. "Sorry I don't have time to talk. I am run off my feet trying to handle all this by myself, just myself and Jon, and we are so *busy*."

As he half expected, when he got out his ID and swiped it through the machine, Makepeace tried to pay, but he didn't let her, and she didn't go to the point of actually making it an order. He'd probably have to let her buy next time. *What? Waitaminute— next time? She is a third of your age, you idiot, and a ditz to boot. She is a complication you do not need on this job. Now* after *the job—she'll still be a third your age and a ditz, but . . . she's over the age of consent and, hey, brains aren't everything. Damn she's got big tits.*

They got their drinks and sat, after a moment of confusion as each went for the seat facing towards the door. He let her have it. She was a captain, his cover was a lieutenant. Having his back to the door bugged the crap out of him, but it couldn't be helped.

"So, why did you join Fleet Strike, Pryce?"

"Get out of the Sub-Urbs, get rejuv, get off-planet, see the universe, kill Posties. What's not to like, ma'am?"

"Bless your heart, Pryce, we're going to have a long evening if you spend the whole time ma'am-ing me. In private you can drop the ma'am's and just call me Makepeace, all right?"

"Okay. So why did you join?" He inhaled about the top third of his drink.

"Get off the farm. Get rejuv. See more of at least some world without having to be a colonist. If I didn't want to be a farmer's wife on Earth, I sure didn't want to be one on some other Godforsaken planet. There just wasn't much for me back home. My brother's going to work the farm, and I could either have had three little kids by now and be working my butt off as a farm wife where I grew up, or I could be here. I picked here. And if they ended up shipping me off to kill Posties, well, they're the reason I never got to meet my maternal grandmother, so I pretty much figure our family owes them."

"The rejuv was a selling point for me, but I also almost didn't join because of it. They don't like juvs much in my old neighborhood," he said.

"Maybe by the time we get out in fifty years the prejudice won't be so bad. Or the drugs'll be more available and there won't be a reason for hard feelings." She plucked at the edge of the table.

"Optimist," he smiled teasingly and she grinned back and in that moment she looked so beautiful he stopped breathing for a moment just looking at her.

When he finally inhaled it was sudden, and then her eyes were caught in his, both looking, and somehow neither of them were smiling anymore. Suzannu broke the moment by calling out his name and sliding a pizza tray on the counter. He took the chance to tear his eyes away and go get the food.

Watching Sinda eat a piece of pizza was fascinating. She picked it up with one hand and supported the pizza slice with two fingers of the other hand under the tip. He was sure she was going to dump a load of the toppings in her lap, but she didn't. She bit into it delicately, closing her eyes to savor the first bite.

"Mmmm. That's good." She opened her eyes to take another bite and Stewart realized that not only was he staring, he also hadn't gotten himself a piece and was letting the pizza get cold. He pulled a slice onto his plate and attacked it with a knife and fork. Yes, it would be in character to pick up the whole piece and have some of it drop in his lap, but it would also make an embarrassing blotch on his silks and he didn't want to look quite that bad in front of Sinda.

You're too old for her, idiot, he told himself, but he didn't commit any embarrassing feats of clumsiness during the meal.

"So, Pryce, what do you do for the general. I mean, aside from briefing new arrivals on the history of the command."

"And passing canapés?" He grinned.

She laughed, and as her head tilted her hair caught the light. He looked her in the eyes. Restraining the urge to talk to Makepeace's really spectacular chest was always an exercise in willpower.

"I coordinate the weekly reports of the agents, and the Tuesday and Thursday special reports on our major investigation," he said.

"Is that the organized crime one?"

"Yep, the tongs." He nodded.

"I read the background material, but it didn't explain why you don't just go in and shut them all down." Her head was tilted to the side, curiously.

"It's been tried. About twenty years ago." As he spoke, she leaned forward, hands clasped on the table, listening intently. "Suddenly Fleet Strike's traveling arrangements got very uncomfortable and late at the worst possible times, and there were problems with the chow aboard ship, and environmental conditions in the troop quarters were always going on the fritz. So the General of Fleet Strike talked to the General of Fleet and the upshot was that we treat the tongs as legitimate civic organizations and only arrest and prosecute individual members we can catch in actual crimes."

"Okay." She nodded, but he suspected from the slightly glazed look in her eyes that she still didn't understand.

"So what did they do about all the problems in Fleet?" she asked.

"Fleet fixed them," he answered slowly.

She nodded again, and it was all he could do to keep a straight face.

If this had been a normal date, or a date at all, he might have reached across the table to hold her hand after they finished eating, and they might have gotten refills on their drinks and sat and talked for awhile after they finished eating. As it was, she said she had some shopping to do and he said he had some things he needed to take care of back at his quarters, and they went their separate ways.

On the transit car back to his quarters his mind kept replaying flashes of silver-blond hair, Sinda laughing at one of his jokes, the way her mouth pouted up when she took a sip of her drink. The ride seemed to take no time at all.

CHAPTER TWELVE

Cally opened the door to her quarters and took her packages inside. It was only her second day and the institutional green and gray were boring her to tears. She tossed a large red shawl over the ugly gray plastic nightstand that came with the room and put the cut glass vase she'd bought on the table, filling it with yellow silk roses. She used tacky clay to stick a couple of posters of unicorns and pegasuses—or was it pegasi—on the walls. Strange obsession, but she'd had covers with more obnoxious ones. At least the pictures were colorful. She'd even managed to find one that wasn't in pastels.

What is that obnoxious beeping? She looked at her PDA, but it was fine. She looked around the room for a source of the beeping, finally localizing it to the shawl-covered end table and the top drawer in it. *Oh. It's the phone. Who the hell wouldn't just page my PDA? It's registered in the directory . . . oh. Paper-boy.*

She lifted the phone out of the drawer and looked at the red light blinking on it in time with the beeping. She had to look at the thing's buttons for a moment before she found the play message button. There was no message, and she had to experiment with more buttons before she found the combination that would get the phone to display the number of the last caller. She read it off to her PDA and told it to call the number, waiting for an answer.

"Hello, Beed residence. May I help you?" a woman's voice answered.

"Um . . . yes, I guess you can. Is the general in? I'm his secretary and he may be trying to reach me."

"Oh, is this Captain Makepeace? Hang on and I'll get him."

Cally waited, sitting down on the bed and splitting the PDA screen so she could use the bottom half as a remote. The cube from last night still had a bunch of movies she hadn't seen yet. It had been in the original Makepeace's purse when they made the switch, so she supposed it reflected her taste in movies pretty well. She started it to get the advertising tease out of the way, turning the volume to mute. She still had a few seconds wait before the general finally answered. Most people in this day and age took their PDA with them everywhere. Well, unless they had an AID. Knowing Beed, he had probably been whole rooms away from whatever he was using to call her. Cally imagined a big, black, rotary dial phone sitting on a table somewhere and suppressed laughter as he started speaking.

"Hello, Captain?" It certainly *sounded* like the general.

"Yes, sir. You were trying to reach me?"

"Ah . . . yes. I was trying to get a little of the red tape squared away and realized I need the Lee file. Unfortunately, I'm expecting another call and really can't step away right now. I know it's an imposition, but could you possibly take a moment and drop by the office and bring it around? I haven't caught you at a bad time, have I?"

"No, sir, not at all. I'd be glad to get that file for you," she fibbed.

"Good, good. I was just afraid I might have caught you at a bad time because you were out when I called before. Thought you might have had plans." His voice had a hint of a question in it.

"Yes, sir. I just got in from dinner, sir."

"Trifle late, isn't it?" He seemed to be waiting for some sort of explanation.

"Yes, sir. I worked a little late getting things in order, sir, and then I had some shopping to do."

"Ah. Okay. Well, if you'll just nip by the office and bring that file over, Captain. Thank you." There was an audible click as he ended the call.

She glared at the phone for a minute. *Is he for real? And of course he just* assumes *I know where he lives. It's not like he couldn't have called my PDA and reached me right off. The real Sinda Makepeace may have gotten the better end of this deal. And I know better than to slip out of character, even in private, dammit.*

It was actually no trouble to find the general's quarters. The base directory had no problem with telling his secretary where he lived.

It also didn't take very long to get there, since it was a Tuesday night and in the middle of a shift. Transit car traffic was minimal, and the MPs on duty at the transit station that serviced brigade headquarters were surprised to see anyone coming in so late, but passed her through after a quick look at her ID.

Moments later, she tucked the file into a manila envelope, passed the MPs on the way out and caught a transit car three levels down.

The corridor that housed Fleet Strike general officers was not institutional green. Nor were the doors battleship gray. The cream walls and Wedgwood blue doors were set off by a strip of wallpaper across the top of the walls that had been designed to convey the impression of crown molding. The charcoal gray carpeting was thick and gave softly under her feet. In all, it reminded her of images she'd seen in movies of the sort of prewar hotel that catered to business travelers who were on a budget but did not want to feel they were staying in some cheap dive.

Suite G one-oh-three was about fifty meters from the transit car doors. It had the standard electronic lock and a little glowing button in a brass plate cast in curlicues that might have been stylized leaves.

"Captain Sinda Makepeace to see General Beed, please," she announced clearly to the door. Nothing happened. She waited, and then announced herself again. Still nothing. *He couldn't. They wouldn't have . . . What the hell, I'll try it.* She pushed the button and immediately heard a ringing tone from inside the apartment. *They must have actually drilled through the Galplas to install that damned thing.*

As the door slid open, she caught a distinct whiff of men's cologne. Beed was just inside the doorway, but he didn't move to take the envelope from her.

"Ah, good. You have it. If it won't be too much trouble, why don't you come in. I may need you for a couple of things. That's not a problem, is it?"

"No, sir. Of course there's no problem, sir." She stepped inside the door and it closed behind her. It may have been phrased like a request, but she knew an order when she heard one. Besides, he was a safe way to get rid of some excess hormones while furthering her mission. A good deal all around.

"I didn't really need the file." He met her eyes and held them as he took the envelope from her and tossed it onto a small table just inside the door.

"I didn't really think you did, sir."

"Quit sirring me, Sinda. In public, yes, but . . . Would you like a glass of wine?"

"Only if it's not local, thanks. If the air does that to coffee beans, I'd hate to think what it would do to a poor, defenseless grape."

"It's up from Earth. A nice California chardonnay. You'll like it." He led her out of the foyer into the living room. On the coffee table was an ice bucket and a chilled bottle of the wine, with two glasses. He uncorked and poured it smoothly, handing her a glass and saluting her with his own. He was right. It was crisp and cool.

"Excuse me for asking, but where is Mrs. Beed this evening? And if I don't call you 'sir,' what do I call you?"

"My friends call me Bernie. And Mrs. Beed has her movie night with some of the other wives. They grab a drink together afterwards. She won't cross the threshold before oh-one-hundred at the earliest."

"I—I haven't done this much." She took a largish gulp of her wine and dropped her eyes.

He set his glass down, taking hers and setting it beside the other, then stepped forward until he was nearly touching her. He cupped her face in his hands and bent to kiss her lingeringly.

"I think I'm going to enjoy walking you through it," he said.

His breath tasted like peppermint and his mustache tickled her lip as she ran her hands up his chest to twine her arms around his neck. His hands were playing with her breasts and her breathing started to quicken and she pressed closer, up against him.

Then his hands were at the seal of her silks, parting the front of them to show the white lace of her bra. One hand slid around to the small of her back, pressing her closer still, while the other kneaded her breast. She arched against him, clutching her fingers in his hair as he traced a line of kisses along her jaw, down her neck, across her collarbone as she clutched at his back. *Okay, this isn't going to be so bad. Umm . . . mmm . . . good spot.*

"Not here," he murmured against her skin. She let him take her hand and lead her back down a hall to a bedroom. It smelled faintly dusty, like a guest room, and everything in it was too neat and too perfect. And too feminine. A master bedroom for a couple would never have a pink flowered bedspread. She tilted her head up to kiss him again while he slid the silks off her shoulders, freeing her hands to grab his hips. She wiggled slightly and her uniform slid down to pool at her feet. She fumbled a bit with the catch on his uniform before getting the pressure seal open, so she could slide her hands in and press them flat against the heat of his back.

She moved with him as he eased her back onto the bed, lying on top of her, but considerately holding his weight on his hands and toes. As they kissed, she helped him get his uniform out of the way as he slid a hand under her to unclasp her bra. After it was out of the way, he sat back for a moment to look. Men always liked to look. She gave him a smile and reached out to pull him back down. His chest was smooth and hairless, as was his jaw line, and she wondered for a second whether he used depilatory foam on it, before deciding that she didn't care. A good lay was just what the doctor ordered, and so far this looked like it was going to turn out to be a good lay.

Afterwards, she helped him change the sheets and remake the bed. She thought it would be a dead giveaway, but when he took out the clean set of sheets, they were identical to the ones that had just come off.

"Won't your wife notice the extra sheets in the wash?"

"Not a chance. I'll have them clean and put away in no time. I don't *completely* shun modern technology, Sinda."

He seemed a bit uncomfortable as the afterglow wore off. Edgy, as if he didn't quite know what to say to her. She made her excuses and left. No use trying for pillow talk with him in that mood. Maybe next time. She had gotten at least part of what she came for. That was something. Tea and sympathy at the office, make him comfortable. Meanwhile, she had that cube to scan on the off chance that something worthwhile was buried on it. The problem was that the general could be working with anybody, so everything had to be checked.

And, of course, she had to check in. In the old days of humans versus humans, an in-person meeting was the most dangerous thing there was for an active agent. The Bane Sidhe's experience knew better. The expertise of the Darhel at electronic wizardry had led them to conclude thousands of years before that face-to-face meetings were the best security there was. While it was possible that human electronic information warfare would surpass the

Darhel's in time, it hadn't to date. As a result, critical information was sent electronically or over the airwaves only when there was absolutely no other alternative.

She was getting used to the transit cars now and didn't have any trouble finding one going in her direction and taking it back to the Corridor.

On the second level from the bottom, on the Fleet and Engineering side, was a sports bar that attracted a solid mix of everything on Titan but colonists, tourists, and nonhumans. It was popular with its clientele because the drinks were relatively cheap, the food filling, and the games on the tank were as close to live as it was possible to get, being tight-beamed up as part of the normal Earth-to-Titan bandwidth. A perceptive client would have noted that people tended to drink more when the drinks were cheap, that drunk people tended to gamble unwisely, and that the establishment provided very convenient access to the house bookie should anyone wish to make a friendly wager on the game.

The sign above Charlie's was a work of art. Instead of glow paint that looked like neon, it was an actual neon light. Well, neon or one of those other gases. Anyway, it was a big curvy tube of glass instead of glow paint. Like a lot of establishments on the corridor, the bar had double doors to reduce the mixing of too much station air with the air inside. In the case of Charlie's, this was more to keep the pollution in than out. It was one of the few places on base you could smoke tobacco without either carrying around a filter to clean up after yourself or paying an extra air-scrubbing tax. The proprietor, whose name bore no resemblance to "Charlie," believed, correctly, that the distinctive bar smell held many nostalgic associations for the class of patrons he wished to attract, and tended to drive away prudes, tourists, and colonists—all of whom would be bad for business in his particular niche.

The briefing materials from the Bane Sidhe had warned Cally what to expect when they chose this particular bar for any necessary in-person meetings, but it was almost impossible to describe the reality, as she found when she stepped through the double doors and into the fog of intermingled stale and fresh tobacco and cheap beer—with almost no undertones of Titan's particular mix of swamp gas. It was the first place she'd been since the shuttle port in Chicago that actually smelled like anywhere on Earth. She felt a sharp prickling at the back of her eyes as she took a deep breath. *The smoke must be irritating them.*

The bar wasn't packed, but it had a healthy crowd for a week-night. She wove her way through the tables and the clouds of smoke to get to the bar. She had read that at one point Charlie's had tried a holotank, but forced to choose between holos and tobacco, it had been no contest. Consequently, the tables were all grouped in easy view of large high-definition flatscreens. It wasn't the flatscreen above the bar that caught her attention, though. The thing that really made her glad she came, regardless of the mission, was the sign, posted next to the impressive array of bottles behind the bar, that said, "Proudly Serving 100% Imported Jamaican Coffee."

"Coffee, please. With a shot of crème de cacao." She put some cash on the counter and left a tip out of her change, turning slightly to watch the screen. Baseball. Indianapolis versus Topeka. The Braves were down by two. She didn't look around the bar. It would have been bad tradecraft, and she had scanned the room thoroughly as she came in. He wasn't here yet. When he arrived, he'd let her know.

The score was unchanged, but McKenzie had just allowed a double with a runner already on, and she was on her second coffee, when a redheaded man approached the bar and ordered a shot of Kentucky bourbon, and a spare cup. After downing the shot, he tucked a wad of chewing tobacco from a small pouch in his jaw, and looked up at the screen, rubbing his jaw for a second before spitting in the cup. He looked back up at the screen and muttered something that would have been difficult for anyone without enhanced hearing to weed out from the general noise of the bar.

"I told him their bullpen was weak," he said.

Cally waited until she saw his eyes skim over and past her, fixing intently on someone off to her left for a moment, as if he had found who he was looking for. She finished her drink and got down from the barstool. Contact had been made, the full team was in place. As she wove back through the tables on her way out a particularly large spacer intercepted her with an outthrust arm, sweeping her into his lap as she let out a shriek.

"Hey, baby, I got something you're just gonna love!" he leered.

Cally delivered a ringing slap that rocked his head to the other side, leaving a bright red handprint on the side of his face. The other hand slipped a cube into his pocket as she pushed herself out of his lap and stalked off towards the door, the picture of feminine indignation. There were rough chuckles from the mostly male assemblage as the large and apparently very drunk spacer rubbed his cheek in bewilderment.

"What'd I do?!" he protested to the air.

Wednesday, June 5

Wednesday morning the coffee at the office tasted even worse, since she had had something recent to compare it to. And General Beed was apparently not the kind to be contented with a little roll in the hay now and again. When they were alone, he insisted on touching her, grabbing bits here and there. It wasn't that she was against a little mutual sex here and there in a fuck buddy sense, but good God, had the man no notion of personal space? Apparently not. She smiled at the annoying beast when he came around now and then and generally took it in stride. Honestly, the man was worse than a lonely cat!

Fortunately for her, one of the general's theories of proper leadership was that a leader should be seen, frequently and unpredictably, by the men he commanded. While in practice this worked out to a tendency to micromanage his subordinates and get in their hair instead of letting them get on with the job at hand, Cally had to be somewhat grateful for it because it tended to get him out and about for a few hours each afternoon during which she could finally have a few minutes peace.

This particular afternoon he had elected to make a visit to the detention facility, which would keep him out of the office for half the afternoon, at least. Pryce had not gone with him, being busy making arrangements for the general's wife's birthday party, the sort of social obligation which was one of the strange but true realities of military bureaucracy in the Galactic age.

And thinking of Pryce, the one absolutely completely good thing about screwing Beed is getting some of those built-up hormones under control so I won't be tempted to drag anything male behind a bush . . . or, well, okay, potted miniature tree. So thank God for getting decently laid . . . or, well, okay, that was a little bit blasphemous . . .

um . . . whatever. After this mission, I'm definitely hunting down Father O'Reilly and asking him to hear my confession. I've . . . kind of let that slide.

She was filing the printouts of the morning e-mails, while envisioning creative and artistic ways for Beed to die, when she heard a crash and jumped, whirling to find the lieutenant sitting on the edge of her desk, her stapler lying nearby on the floor. He shrugged apologetically.

"Good Lord, Pryce! Don't sneak up on me like that!" She clapped a hand to her chest. "You scared the hell out of me." *How the hell did he sneak up on me? Me? Nobody sneaks up on me. It's just . . . wrong. I feel okay, I don't think anything's wrong . . . geez, he's quiet. Well, until he trips over something or knocks something over, anyway.*

"S-sorry, ma'am. I just dropped by to see how you were settling in." He grinned mischievously. "Well, and to take a break from my canapé passing and preparations thereto."

His eyes, and that grin, made her feel like her bones had all suddenly just melted away. She stood there blinking at him for a couple of seconds before managing to get her brain back in gear and move back to her desk.

"I'm settling in okay, I guess." She pushed her hair back with a hand. "Are there many canapé situations on Titan?"

"Some." He shrugged. The brass have to do something for fun."

"That's a rather irreverent attitude, Pryce."

"Yes, ma'am. No excuse, ma'am." But his eyes twinkled at her, and she smiled.

"I'd ask you to dinner again tonight, if we weren't in the same chain of command." His eyes focused on hers.

"I'd accept, if we weren't in the same chain of command," she met his eyes and looked away, "and if I didn't think I was likely to have to work late tonight."

He reached a finger under her chin and pulled her head around, gently, looking her in the eyes. She met his scrutiny for a moment that seemed to last an hour, or maybe a year.

"Okay." He nodded, and somehow she got the feeling that he understood. She didn't know how he could have, or how she knew, but she knew he did.

General Beed did not request her presence at a working dinner this evening. Nor did he return to the office this afternoon.

Instead, he phoned the office—another eccentricity of his, there was an actual *phone* on her desk, when she had a perfectly capable PDA that actually was *with* her when she was away from the desk. On the phone, he requested that she grab a bite of dinner and then bring the Leave File with her, and asked if it would be convenient for him to stop by her quarters on his way between meetings to edit and finalize the changes so she could get the document printed and ready for a staff meeting early Thursday morning. She had, of course, agreed. *Sure, General darling. You screw me so maybe I can screw you.*

So here she was at Super Burgers with a double deluxe cheeseburger, fries, a double strawberry shake, and a manila envelope, enjoying the fluorescent orange and acid green Galplas décor while she stuffed her food down prior to going to her quarters to try to make some progress on her real job. Oh, joy. *He's not bad looking, and not a bad lay, if he were just a little bit less insensitive.*

The restaurant décor had its intended effect and she finished quickly and left, stuffing the trash through the disposal slot on her way out the door. In the transit car on the way back to her quarters she brought up the room controls on her PDA and adjusted the lights, temperature, and background music to reflect the right mood. Relaxed was good.

She hadn't been home long when he arrived. She'd considered ditching her silks in favor of something less comfortable but more tempting, but had decided it was out of character. Which was just as well. She didn't actually *object* to Beed, and he was a step above being alone, and she wanted to find out whatever he knew. Still, she was more comfortable meeting him in the ordinary uniform of her cover than something else. Lingerie would have been a tad too personal. Which was odd because usually by now she would have been so subsumed in the role she wouldn't consciously think of it being a cover.

As he came in the door, letting it slide closed behind him, she brushed at her hair with one hand in deliberate Sinda-ness. It reminded her of who she was as she shyly, but with increasing eagerness, met his kiss.

Some few minutes later as she rolled with him through yet another position change she almost had to fight for a straight face. *Okay, so it's acrobatics night. Why do men always do this? It's always either the first or the second lay, and they always go through the same damn five positions, like they're trying to demonstrate how cosmopolitan or kinky or educated they are, or whatever. Eyes slightly wide, of course I've never done this before. Back into character, roll with it, I'd . . . really . . . rather . . . not . . . have . . . to fake it. Um . . . good spot . . . okay . . . that works . . . let's be nice and enthu-siastic so he knows it works.* "Oh . . . oh god that's so good! God . . . please, please, please don't stop . . . ah . . . um . . . ah . . ." *Okay, he's . . . getting . . . the point. Yeah. That's . . . g—. Aaah. Okay. Good. All right, your turn, here we go, yeah, that's right, you taught me to do that you stud you. Sure you did. Come on, come on . . . There. Good. Now, question is, are you relaxed enough.*

"Oh, Bernie, thank you. That was *so* good." She hugged him gently, kissing his chest and playing across it idly with her fin-gers while she lay curled on his shoulder.

"It's never been like that for me, before. There's a sense of . . . I don't know . . . authority, maybe. I don't know, put like that it sounds kind of mundane, and," she walked her fingers up his chest, "it was *wonderful.*" She hugged him and gave him a giddy smile, planting another kiss on his chest.

"Oh, I don't think it's—what did you say—mundane at all." He cupped his hand around her breast, idly playing the nipple through his fingers. "You're a very intuitive woman, Sinda. It's one of your charms."

"You," she started kissing her way down his chest, "are flatter-ing me." She began idly licking and kissing his skin, enough to be distracting, but not enough to actually render him speechless.

"It doesn't take any particular intuition to know you're a gen-eral, General." She traced a circle with her tongue at the crease where his thigh met his hip. "But a little flattery's okay. I like it. Is it, you know, okay if I do this? You don't mind, do you? Tell me if, you know, I'm not doing it right."

"You're doing fine, sweetheart. Just let your imagination go. Just . . . uh . . . no teeth, okay?"

"Mmm . . . no problem.

"Did I do . . . that . . . right?" Her voice was tentative, with a hint of nervous little girl in it, as she snuggled back up against him.

"Oh, yeah," he breathed. "You should always trust your intu-ition, dear, especially in bed. You know, I'm not just *any* general." His chest inflated slightly. "Generals are a dime a dozen. I'm in this position because I've been entrusted with a very important project." He chuckled, stroking her hair. "You're not a spy, are you?" he teased. "Anyway, I haven't really told you anything. Just confirmed your intuition." He kissed the top of her head gently before swinging his legs over the side of her bed.

"Do you have to go?" She ran a finger down his hip. He caught her hand and lifted it to his lips, gently, before setting it back down at her side.

"I'm afraid so. Clarice gets . . . querulous . . . if I'm away overnight."

She watched him, apparently fascinated, as he dressed, as he kissed her, as he left. As the door slid shut behind him she flipped on the filter next to her bed and lit a cigarette.

"Lights out." She sat with her back propped against the Galplas wall that served in place of a headboard, eyes open, unfocused, as the single orange point threw shadows on the walls.

Thursday, June 6

Thursday morning, Pryce stopped in to her office while the general was indisposed. *Damn this kid. You would think getting laid twice in as many days would have the old hormones down to a dull roar. Nobody should smell this good. It ought to be . . . I don't know . . . illegal or something.*

"What's on your mind, Pryce?"

"I've just got a minute." He turned away from her, running a hand through his hair. Not a good idea with Beed's emphasis on appearance.

"You're not . . . investing too much emotionally in working late . . . I hope. . . . Dammit, Makepeace, you're too damn young and I don't want you to get hurt!"

"*I'm* young, Pryce? Hello?"

He turned back, stumbling a little, and flushed.

"Okay, yeah, that sounds s-stupid coming from me, but . . . you're nice, Captain, and I just hope you're . . . careful," he said.

"Pryce, I'm okay. And I'm not looking for favors. Look, working late sometimes isn't that bad, and with, you know . . . Well, mixed marriages of juv and nonjuv are notorious in the service, aren't they? Gosh, just look at this mountain of work. But it's all right. The general, bless his heart, is happy today, and all this," she waved her hand at the paper and filing cabinets, "is much easier when he's happy, isn't it, Lieutenant?"

"Yes, ma'am, Captain." He picked up the file he'd come in for, and paused on his way out the door. "Probably the best attitude you could take, ma'am."

"Pryce?" she ventured.

"It's okay, Makepeace. Really." His eyes were softer, and she had to be content with that.

It was six in the evening, and, at the moment, while collating presentation packets, she was currently considering the entertaining possibility of watching Bernhard Beed nibbled to death by giant carnivorous ants. Giant carnivorous poisonous ants. While staked out on ice. No, ice numbed pain too much. Hot sand? Nails. Nails was good. The insensitive, possessive, obnoxious bastard. He had actually let her sit around doing make-work most of the afternoon, only to call her in at twenty minutes till five and load the copying for this stupid presentation package that mysteriously required *very* elaborate collating and had to be ready for his review by seven the next morning. Just because he had to go to his wife's birthday party and couldn't make time to get a little tonight, the bastard was obviously making sure she was entirely otherwise occupied.

Acid. Concentrated hydrochloric acid on a slow burn, from the toes up. Son of a bitch. She hadn't realized she had spoken out loud until she heard the familiar voice behind her.

"Now, it can't be *that* bad," he said.

"Aren't you supposed to be passing canapés?" She didn't turn around. She really wasn't in the mood to be cheered up.

"Well, yeah, but the general sent me over here with three pages to be included in between the pie chart and the bar graph, and he wants me to report back."

"Obnoxious possessive sonofabitch is checking up, is he? It's not enough that I fuck him, the bastard has to have control over my private time, too. Ooohhh!"

"Gee, Makepeace, I don't think you should bottle your feelings up like this," he said.

She turned and froze in the act as she was about to throw the pile of papers in his face, and something about his deadpan face and single quirked eyebrow broke her up and she lost it, laughing.

"Okay, okay. I was a little overboard." She shook her head, holding her side and catching her breath. "No, I wasn't, but that wasn't helping."

"Hey, you're allowed to let off steam. In private. But might want to make sure you're in private, ma'am."

"Good point, Pryce."

"You know, ma'am, the general obviously sent me because he felt I was 'safe.' I'm not sure how I feel about that."

"Why, bless your heart, Pryce, did you want to *stop* being safe?"

"Not tonight. Gotta get back to passing canapés. J-just didn't like the assumption."

"It's okay, Pryce," she pouted at him as he walked out the door, "I don't think you're safe."

The convenient thing about this evening, for Beed, was that she was kept both busy *and* out of the sight of his wife. The convenient thing for her, once she got the copying and collating done, was that, with Pryce gone, she was the only person in the office and she had a perfect excuse for being there. It provided complete and uninterrupted privacy to search the entirety of CID, turning up three cubes of miscellaneous data that might or might not relate to her mission. Cally was beginning to get nervous about that. Okay, sure, she hadn't expected a big neon sign flashing, "This Way To The Secret Files," but other than that tiny bit of pillow talk by the general, they were keeping this operation pretty tight. The three agents they had considered most likely to be helping run the operation all seemed to have full-time workloads of regular CID investigations.

The only really interesting thing she'd found so far was a map in Corporal Anders' data storage of the areas on this floor assigned to the headquarters of the 3rd. Most of them were areas she had override access for. Some were not. Of course, with the tactic of hiding in plain sight always being a possibility, everything had to be searched. Tedious, but there it was. The collating provided an excuse to go into an area marked storage down the hall. She could always be claiming to look for boxes of an obscure contrivance called "binder clips."

By the time she finished getting herself dusty looking through boxes of backup cubes, an old coffee machine, stacks of uniforms and uniform parts, three blank new-in-box PDA's, a half a box of night-sticks, fairly new-looking full and partial boxes of paper supplies, and, inexplicably, an ancient-looking half-box of blue and silver children's party hats, her stomach was growling fiercely. The backup cubes, except for the most recent, looked as though they had sat exactly where they were, undisturbed, for quite a long time. She would only waste her time searching them if absolutely nothing else panned out.

In a way, it was getting annoying going out for every meal. After getting a fried chicken salad and a bowl of gazpacho from a café just off one of the transit car docks on the Corridor, she found an Oriental Market and bought a sackful of sealed self-heating dinners. Lemon chicken, mu shu pork, General Tsu's, hot and sour soup, sizzling rice soup, egg rolls, spring rolls, duck with plum sauce, California roll with sashimi . . . Yum.

These packages were great. The heater was in the bottom of the package; you just pulled the tab and the chemicals mixed in the heater pack and the heat rose through the food. Well, okay, for some specialty foods, like the egg rolls, the food was spiked on metal conductive toothpicks hooked to the bottom of the package. Still, yum, yum, yum. And no having to go out for it. Things being what they were, she'd still probably be taking most meals out. But at least now she would at least sometimes have another option. Microwaveable was quicker, but the self-heaters tasted better. Okay, it was a matter of personal taste. And whether you'd rather throw packages away or scrub out the microwave once a week. Cally wasn't real big on housework.

Thursday, June 6

Stewart told his AID to shut off the hologram and leaned back, rubbing his eyes. The problem with an investigation like this was that until you caught someone you really couldn't eliminate anyone. Some were just more likely than others.

He twirled a ballpoint pen as he thought, a habit revived from his first staff position, way back before the general demise of paper as the medium of military bureaucracy. He stared unseeingly at the matted and framed poster he'd had printed out to break up the unrelieved light green of the office walls. The agents had eyed the print knowingly when he'd hung it, figuring he was opting for paper instead of a window-simulating view screen as a way of brown-nosing the boss.

In fact, it was a reprint of a poster that had been tacked to the wall of his Aunt Rosita's apartment in his childhood gang days. With the exception of Beed, everyone else was too young to recognize pre-war Malibu Beach. And Beed was from the wrong part of the country. One of the things he appreciated about Sinda was that no matter what else went over her head, he had several times caught her looking wistfully at his poster and had gotten the ineffable impression that somehow, on some level, she actually got it. Even though there were so many things that he just couldn't talk to her about, she somehow managed to make him feel . . . understood.

Which could maybe explain why he was so hung up over some fluff-headed ditz that he was sitting here woolgathering instead of getting his work done.

"Diana, turn my monitor back on and give me a keyboard and track spot." Instantly, a keyboard appeared on his desktop. The red circle projected to the right of the keyboard and the two buttons below it served the function of an old-fashioned mouse. Having learned to type before the war, he could work much faster this way. Fortunately, everything but true AI was well within the reach of a modern PDA, so he didn't have to worry about Beed twigging to the presence of a real AID and how very much of his daily work activity was being recorded. An aide de camp, naturally, was often at his general's elbow.

As part of the mission, they had approved attempts to transfer in or out of the office a bit more freely than normally would have been the case. The cover was that a new CO would of course want to pick as many of his own headquarters people as possible. They had managed to replace eleven of the seventeen headquarters and CID office staffers. Out of the now thirteen staffers with a documented humanist connection, nine had both the connection and were new to their position.

Makepeace was on the list, of course, but so was over half the office after you subtracted himself and Beed. Franks was the obvious prime suspect. Sixty plus years of living had taught Stewart that, unlike in holovids or movies, the obvious suspect very frequently was the guilty party. Still, the enemy organization had already proven you couldn't count on it to obligingly do the stupid or obvious thing.

What it amounted to was that he had fifteen people to watch for patterns, eleven to watch closely, and nine to watch *very* closely.

Franks had several Earthside communications from his quarters, one to a known humanist activist who was also his wife's brother-in-law, another to a friend of the family who had not been noted to express humanist sympathies but who, on examination, turned out to have a large number of humanist friends and associates. The calls had been encrypted with a relatively strong public cryptography system that had been released to the public by some anonymous wiseass. The authorities had been chagrinned, and Stewart supposed he ought to be, too, but he couldn't help being secretly just a bit happy about it. He chalked it up to his misspent youth. Which had actually been rather fun, come to think of it.

Anders had called a boyfriend back home every night the first week and had tapered off since. The hometown honey appeared to be on his way out.

Makepeace had sent e-mail replies to two long letters from her mother, but had kept the discussion to inconsequentials such as descriptions of coworkers and the restaurants and shops in the Corridor.

Sanchez had sent an order to a freight company to ship up a private supply of cigars, bourbon, and Tabasco sauce. Otherwise, he seemed to be fairly typical in that Fleet Strike was becoming his family as age and anti-juv prejudice separated him from his previous connections.

Keally kept contact with his wife and daughter who had not accompanied him up to the Base, but had had no apparent contact with his high school best friend, who taught Sunday school at North Topeka First Methodist, which had taken a notable stance against differential rejuvenation of one member of a married couple.

The rest was more of the same. It was looking more and more like Franks was his man. Only problem was that so far all he had was circumstantial. There had been no overt act. Which meant he could be wrong. Which meant he had to keep digging into the private lives of fourteen innocent people, any way you sliced it.

"Turn it all off, Diana. Time to blow this taco stand." Tacos. Hmm. It seemed, and was, a lifetime ago that he'd anglicized so painstakingly in his efforts to move beyond the privations of his childhood. At the time, he'd thought it was necessary. In retrospect, he now knew that it hadn't been. Oh, it had kept him out of the way of some people's prejudices now and again, but what had really turned him around had been the good influence and example of Gunny Pappas and Mike O'Neal. They'd given him a dream bigger than just himself and his friends, a dream a man could hitch his star to. They'd sold him on America and the dreams of democracy and liberty, sometimes without even saying a word. Good men at the tail end of a good age. Too bad the dream had died. He didn't know how it had happened. Maybe it had been when the President moved the Capitol to Chicago by decree. The excuse for not changing the Constitution had been the national emergency and the number of states that were overrun by the enemy. Maybe it had been when the candidates for office and the remains of the political parties started accepting anonymous donations in FedCreds and nobody had done anything about it. Maybe it had been when they made the residents of the Sub-Urbs sign waivers of certain rights as a condition of residency. Maybe it had been when the offices of the Toledo *Blade* were firebombed. No, the damage had already been done well before then. That was just the most obvious nail in the coffin of the dream. Instead of a real investigation, there had been a very thin whitewash, and the rest of the papers had fallen into line. Not that he could blame them, really. He had seen the post mortem pics of the editorial staff.

He walked around the edge of his desk and laid a hand, gently, on the cold glass covering the paper beach. It had been a great dream while it lasted. He sighed. *Combination plate from La Colima it is.*

CHAPTER THIRTEEN

Thursday, June 13

A week later, after having had three liaisons with the general and no more meaningful information, and having thoroughly searched everywhere near the general's headquarters that she had access to with no luck, Cally had come to the conclusion that it was time to try plan B. The areas she did not have access to had some serious security on the door locks. Not even a custom crafted tools package from Tommy had been enough to let her crack it safely, the one time she'd gotten a solid chance at one of them without an MP in visual range of the door.

She had, however, been able to copy the security permissions file to cube and the report back from Tommy had turned up the interesting information that while *she* didn't have access to those areas, as the general's aide de camp, Pryce did. Which left her organizing the morning e-mail printouts for Beed contemplating the not at all unhappy prospect of plan B. Not at all unhappy.

Of course, stalking Pryce was going to be complicated by Beed's infernal, possessive, controlling habits, which had gotten worse if anything. Still, she had a few things on her side. Foremost that the general seemed willing to trust his aide around her, while being annoyingly paranoid about other males. Whether it was Pryce's low rank or that his terrible clumsiness and slight stutter tending to worsen in the general's presence, the general's paranoia had a blind spot where the lieutenant was concerned.

And, of course, she intended to make sure that her public behavior continued to foster that blind spot.

"Good morning, sir," she said cheerily as she bounced into his office and put the stack of printouts in his in tray, scooping up an inch and a half of assorted paper from his out tray.

"Come here a second, Sinda, I need to go over this with you." He waved her around to his side of the desk, using explaining his proofreading markups to her as a transparent attempt to get her close enough to grope her left breast. She affected excitement, gasping slightly, but honestly! Beed wasn't bad looking, and he was at least decent in bed, but sometimes he got on her nerves so bad she had to physically restrain herself from throttling the man.

"Yes, sir, I'll get right on that, sir."

"Oh, and Sinda," he sighed, "I'm afraid I won't be able to see you tonight, dear. Clarice has planned a dinner party and absolutely insists on my presence."

"Awww." She looked regretful. "Well, I've got a cube of movies I've been meaning to watch and those self-heaters, maybe I'll just have a quiet night, sir." She wanted to slap him for the hint of approval she saw in his eyes. She didn't think any of that had made it past her eyes, but she turned away to make sure, taking the stack of papers with her. It wasn't really out of character. After all, the real Sinda probably would have been pissed, too.

Later, Pryce came in with a notepad and propped himself on the edge of her desk, knocking off her stapler and a paperclip dispenser.

"I'll get that on my way out. Did the general tell you about his speech?" he asked.

"Speech?" she echoed.

"Yeah, the dinner tonight is a little more than he may have told you. His wife is trying to organize a Toastmasters on base, along with General Harrison's wife. Anyway, I've got the draft here. I'd appreciate it if you could be my second set of eyes proofing the thing for grammar."

"Sure." She reached out and accepted the pad from him. "So, another wild and wacky evening for you, eh?"

"A-actually not. We had booked the back dining room at the officers' club, but after the kitchen fire last week, well, the smoke damage is awful. So I really had to scramble rebooking it at Cherry Blossoms, and then we were two seats short so Colonel

Lee and I made the gracious sacrifice of foregoing the pleasure of the occasion." He grinned wickedly. "Of course, I'm all broken up about it."

"I can see that, Pryce." The corners of her mouth twitched slightly and her eyes danced. "So, no canapés tonight. Why, bless your heart, Pryce, what *will* you do with the time?"

His eyes snapped to hers, and—and that intent, perceptive look in—his eyes were really dark, and there was a hot, tight feeling in the pit of her stomach. She shifted in her chair slightly, licking her lips. She saw his glance flicker to her chest briefly, and back to hold her eyes, almost as if he hadn't really intended to look.

"Are you sure you want to go down that road, Captain? I'm no general. And I'm definitely not General Beed."

"Um . . . road?" she squeaked. *Was that me? Oh, great, Cally, way to sound like a complete idiot.*

"Ahem. I mean, I don't know what your plans are, Pryce, but with all this paperwork, I mean, I have half a dozen transfers alone. And it'll probably take me all afternoon just to get Simkowicz's pay situation straightened out. I expect I'll be here *very* late tonight." She could tell she was babbling, but her mouth seemed to be in overdrive, which was in character for Sinda, so that must be why she was doing it. She jumped at the slight shock when his hand touched hers.

"Y-you know, suddenly I just remembered I've got loads of paperwork to do, myself."

Cally had actually squared away most of what needed to be done by the time Beed departed, speech in hand. Of course he had loaded her down with additional assignments at the last minute. He thought. She had been able to anticipate most of it. His pattern for these little extras was to take work that had to be done anyway, but later, and come up with a reason he absolutely had to have it first thing in the morning. If she had actually waited until he told her, at seventeen-thirty, it would have added a good three hours onto her workload. As it was, she had more like half an hour of work left as he swanned out the door, and the relevant files heaped around in an artistic disorder on her desk. *Asshole.*

Fifteen minutes after eighteen hundred she took a trip to the copier, counting the coworkers still in the office. Anders was on her way out. Carlucci and Sanchez were still at their desks.

As she passed Pryce's office on the way back, and he lifted his head briefly to meet her eyes, she had to wonder if he was really working or just pretending like she was. Or, like she would be, anyway.

At eighteen-forty-five she was trying not to twiddle her thumbs and went to the copy machine again, noting with satisfaction that the two agents had finally gotten themselves out of the office. Or, at least, she hoped so.

"Buckley," she whispered, "listen for a minute and tell me if you hear anyone in the office area but me and Pryce." She was as quiet as she could be, for a few seconds, breathing as shallowly and silently as she could.

"No, Captain. They're hiding too well for me to hear them. They must be really good. Maybe we'll die fast."

"Okay, you can shut up now, buckley. And quit listening." Okay, so she knew it was just a computer program. She still didn't want it listening in while she was with Pryce. It would have been just too weird.

"But what if I hear them sneaking up on us?"

"Shut up and quit listening, buckley."

"Right."

"You know, they make personality overlays to cover over the depressing bits of the base buckley." Pryce had come in behind her and she jumped as she spun around to face him.

"Don't *do* that! You scared me half to death." She had clapped a hand to her chest and she froze that way, for a few seconds. His eyes were big, and dark, and for once she knew what they meant when they talked about seeing into someone's soul. Could he see hers? If he could, would he stay? She realized her mouth was hanging open slightly and shut it, licking her lips nervously as she played the ends of her hair through her fingers.

She walked up very deliberately and pressed herself full length against him. It was almost like touching a live wire. As he pulled her mouth hard against his she could feel the heat of his thighs through her silks. They were hard and tight, and as she rubbed one thigh up the outside of his leg, pressing closer, she was glad for once that Sinda wasn't perfectly lean. She could feel the muscles of his back under her hands. His mouth tasted cinnamony, like he'd just been chewing gum, and her knees buckled as his tongue and teeth and lips finally turned off the running commentary in her brain as she strained to get as close to him as she could possibly get. Clothes. In the damned way. Patience? What patience. Patience, hell.

Afterwards he winced as he stood up so she could get off the worktable.

"Are you okay?" She blessed providence that there was a box of tissue on the table, well, okay, on the floor now, in here. She shrugged her bra back on and neatened herself up, refastening her silks. Thank God for fabric that didn't wrinkle, no matter what.

"That bite's a little tender." He rubbed a set of red marks on his shoulder.

"I'm sorry."

"Hey, it's not like I noticed at the time. I mean, well, I *noticed* but it wasn't . . . it didn't . . . it was okay, really. God, what am I saying? Sinda, thank you. You—you blew my mind. Wow. I—thank you."

"Mmmm. And thank *you.* Wow is right. Is it okay if I don't try to think or anything just now? God that was good." She had to let go of the hand she was clinging to so he could do up his own silks, but it was all right. He gave it right back.

She did have to let him go for a few minutes as they picked up the packaged ream of paper and assorted other office debris that had landed on the floor, but she did take the opportunity of him bending down to pick up a staple puller to run a hand up the inside of his thigh and give his butt a squeeze. This was . . . nice. She usually didn't feel so cuddly after sex. It was kinda cool. As he stood she wrapped her arms around him from behind, rubbing up against him like a cat. *God, he smells so good. Rich and hot and . . . Oh, God, I'd better move away from him. Just get myself frustrated. He won't be ready to go again for awhile.*

"So, do you want to get something eat?" She stepped away, but the effort had her twisting her hands.

"I smuggled in some self-heaters earlier this afternoon. We really can't be seen out and about," he said apologetically, looking at her as if he *knew* how stirred up she still was. "But on the plus side, after we get a little food, get a little energy back, we'll still be alone."

His eyes were so deep she was about to melt into a puddle on the ground right where she stood.

"Come on, they're in my office," he said.

She pulled her chair in while he got the boxes out of his desk and pulled out the start tabs.

"You know we're going to have to sneak these boxes right back out again. Beed is possessive, jealous, suspicious—" She stopped as he placed a finger over her lips.

"We are not going to let a certain dark cloud rain all over our evening. So, would you like sweet and sour shrimp, or cashew chicken?" He gestured with the boxes.

"Mmm. I love seafood. Can I have the shrimp?" She licked her lips.

"Sure thing." He passed one of the heaters over. It still had a couple of minutes before they could pop the top. "That must have been rough growing up. A Wisconsin farm girl with a jones for seafood."

"Not really. When you don't have it, you don't have it. We had more than a lot of people. Better than living shut away from sunlight in some Urb." She clapped a hand to her mouth. "Oh, bless your heart, you grew up in a Sub-Urb, didn't you, Pryce?"

"Yeah. We didn't have much, but I got by." His mouth tightened involuntarily.

"I? Not we?" she asked.

"Well, my mom wasn't around much. Let's just say I got by with a little help from my friends." The words held echoes of remembered pain.

"Oh. Did you spend a lot of time in the crèche?" *Doesn't sound like he had a happy childhood at all.*

"Something like that. Let's just say we did a good bit of self-supervision," he said.

"Sounds like you had to be self-reliant pretty early on." *Something we have in common.*

"Sort of. I learned to pick good friends and trust them. And how to deal with people I couldn't trust at all. What about you? Did you have something where you played with kids, or were you alone a lot, or what?" He took one of her hands.

"There weren't a lot of other kids. I was a bit of a daddy's girl. He was my best friend." *Well, Granpa, anyway. After the first landing, he might as well have been my dad.*

"Fresh air. Sunshine. It sounds . . . wholesome. I didn't do a lot of wholesome growing up," he said.

"Not as much as you'd think. Daddy was ex-military. Like a lot of people I guess. But it was less wholesome and more . . . I don't know . . . earthy? Practical?" *How to explain without explaining, that is the question.*

"I envy you that adult guidance. I had to figure out so much by trial and error." He opened his dinner and the savory and slightly sweet smell of the cashews wafted through the room.

"I envy you good friends your own age. The farm was a bit isolated. In some ways I didn't get to be a kid." *Not past age eight, anyway.*

"Something we have in common. We were kids, but not kids, you know?" He was looking into her soul like that again.

"Yeah, I do. Boy, this is a heavy conversation." She pulled the top off of her shrimp and inhaled as the steam escaped. "This smells yummy."

"Want some rice? I only brought steamed. I don't like the way the fried rice in these things reheats. The bits of egg are always rubbery." He offered her a box.

"Good choice. The steamed is much better. Thanks. That smells good, too." She gestured towards the box he'd just opened.

"Wanna bite? Trade you?" He speared a bite of food on his fork and extended it for her, cupping a hand under it in case the sauce dripped. His hand was warm against her chin as she savored the bite.

Watching him eat a bite of shrimp off of her fork drew her attention right to his mouth, of course, and she had no idea how long she'd been staring when he finally snapped out of it and reached his fork back into his heater box. She just knew that her second bit of food was noticeably cooler than her first. But she wasn't really all that hungry, anyway. She'd eaten less than half the food when she pushed it away. Sometime during the meal she'd rolled her chair over closer to his, but she could feel the heat of his thigh against hers and close somehow just wasn't close enough.

Obviously he thought so, too, because no sooner had he pushed his own food away, also half-eaten, than she found herself pulled into his lap with a hand cupped around her breast. Tantalizingly, too damned far down under her breast. She twisted slightly at the waist, arching into it as the movement drew his fingers across her nipple.

Naturally, the movement also shifted her hips, which made him shift and she could feel his erection hard against her leg and suddenly she couldn't stand it. But when she tried to move to straddle him, he wouldn't let go, rubbing a nipple between a thumb and forefinger as he nibbled on the upper rim of her ear and her hands clenched, nails driving into his shoulders. It felt like every nerve ending she had was alive and singing with heat. Suddenly she couldn't have sat still if her life depended on it. *How can he be so clumsy on his feet and so . . . aw, hell, who cares!*

Conscious thought didn't resurface until he came and she found herself collapsed across his chest on the floor, and realized there was a bit of a cramp in one of her quads. She couldn't even have guessed how many orgasms had ripped through her while her brain had been on hold. All she knew as she eased off of him and to the side was that her muscles had turned to jelly. She let her head rest on his shoulder, the utter relaxation of his muscles contrasting sharply with the tension of a few minutes before. She traced her index finger through his chest hair, licking the gloss of sweat off her fingertip. It tasted of salt and something indefinable that she couldn't have described, she only knew she was starting to crave it like a drug. But . . . later . . . after she'd rested a little bit. Or maybe a lot.

Amazingly, it turned out that silks *could* wrinkle after all.

Friday, June 14

Friday was always the easiest day to get out of bed, for obvious reasons. In her case, there was the extra bonus that Beed would find it impossible to get away from his wife for the entire weekend. Still, there was an extra bounce in her step, despite the slight sore muscle twinges in strange places, as she detoured by Claibourne's Coffee on her way in to work.

One of the interesting features of base living was the excellent job they'd done of matching the lighting to normal human circadian rhythms. The unvarying quality of the light had been one of the design problems in the early Sub-Urbs that had since been blamed for a lot of the social problems they suffered during and immediately after the Postie war. The better areas of most of them had by now been retrofitted with adjustable glow paint, programmed on an optimum circadian scale. In Titan's case, limited retrofitting had been needed, since the need for an artificial day had been obvious in the first place. At least, that had been the explanation. For whatever reason, it was interesting to see the Corridor in daylight and actually stand and remind herself that the lighting was not natural sunlight diffused through some sky-light. It was a very good imitation. The plants certainly seemed to like it well enough. On this floor, the Galplas had been tex-tured to look like an old brick sidewalk, and the rough earthen pink clashed lightly with the terra cotta planters. Honey bees buzzed around the flowers blooming in assorted hanging baskets, and the faux-neon signs in the night-business windows were dark. The place looked so different in the daytime it almost made her homesick, pointing up the alien chemical smell and the dryness of the air, so different from Charleston's muggy salt.

She didn't show it, but it jolted her sense of cover slightly to notice the dress shop next door had a red scarf around the neck of the mannequin in the window. However late she got away from the general tonight, she'd have to make time for a meet with Granpa. Not that she had a lot to tell him other than what hadn't worked. And that she had confirmed that Beed had an extra project, probably their leak. *Maybe he has something on the tong angle.*

A latte and a bag of cherries later, she was back in the transit car up to the office. For some reason the cherries and plums on Titan Base were considerably better than most of its other hydro-ponic produce—possibly because hydroponics were in the bottom level of Fleet's quadrant. After her first encounter with base-grown coffee, she had avoided the office coffee in all but her direst needs for caffeine. She had asked Carlucci about it once. Apparently, as Beed said, you got used to it. The old hands didn't seem to taste the difference anymore. She was going to have to start drinking the awful stuff. Sinda Makepeace would be getting the process of acclimation over and done with, and her own persistence in drink-ing the imported Terran coffee was a potential break in cover. Unprofessional.

At the office, she poured herself a cup from the coffee maker in the copy room, suppressing a grin as she passed the collating table. She grimaced at the foul liquid in the cup and proceeded to drown it in sugar and creamer powder, reminding herself that she had in fact done worse things for the cause.

Pryce did better than she thought he would at acting normally when he said good morning. One of the worries that had gnawed at her brain as she settled into sleep last night had been that he might turn out to be a really rotten liar. He was okay. Maybe she could find some opportunity to get together with him this weekend. She had been tentatively turning over a plan in her head for a couple of days now, and the chemistry between the two of them was good enough that it just might work. If she could play to his desire for variety by using different places throughout the office as props for sex, it was just possible that she could either get him to take her into the areas she couldn't otherwise reach *or* that she could somehow swipe his ID card and spoof the biometrics.

She flipped through the morning traffic on her PDA while trying to mull the relative advantage of forcing the coffee down a sip at a time, or waiting and chugging it when nobody was looking. Hell, nobody was looking now, and it was probably marginally less awful hot. A moment later she regarded the empty cup with satisfaction, trying not to wince at the slightly sour aftertaste.

The awards report had come through from first battalion on Dar Ent. *Dammit, whose Cheerios did Simkowicz piss in? Lost records my ass.*

"Buckley, send a full and complete copy of the Simkowicz 201 file to Personnel, copied to Payroll, with a full and complete copy of his career pay records. Code it as coming from General Beed. State that the general urgently desires that this matter be cleared up by no later than sixteen hundred today, and that if this is not possible, to please reply immediately indicating the specific reasons for the delay and the specific individuals responsible. Copy the entire mess to General Franklin's AID. Shoot the AID, Lisa, a private memo explaining that she can use her judgment about whether to show it to her boss if the name doesn't finally light a fire under those assholes. Four months behind my ass."

A few minutes later, as she walked back down the hall to get Beed's morning printouts, Pryce was coming the other way, headed back to his office from somewhere. She didn't stop, but passed him just a little too close, turning so that her breast brushed his arm as he walked past. There was a spring in her step as she bounced down the hall for the stupid paper. Suddenly, she felt like whistling.

Stewart ducked into his office, squashing the simultaneous desires to curse and grin. He also needed to think about something else for a minute to return his silks to a presentable state. Unfortunately, it looked like Sinda might not turn out to be a very good liar. That was careless. Not surprising, really. She was a bit of a ditz. Not that she didn't make up for it in her own way. She was warm, and had a great work ethic, and he shook his head as he realized he'd been staring at the same spot on his office wall for who knew how long. The point was that she was a ditz. But a fun one. And he really needed to think of, say, the steps in the process of fitting a new ACS suit to a troop. It had been long enough ago that it required just the right amount of concentration to remember the steps—that is, a lot.

Finally, he was ready to go talk to that slimy sonofabitch excuse for a general officer. *Think lieutenant. Fresh-faced, eager, klutzy Lieutenant Pryce, first lieutenant as proof that God really does have a sense of humor.* He tripped over the threshold on his way out the door, just for practice, and noticed that Sinda not only could see his door from her desk, but was actually watching him, with a rather dazed expression on her face. *Boy, why you are getting hung up on a complete, incredible, total ditz, I do not know. This simple lieutenant role must be going to your brain. Okay, so it's not my brain I'm thinking with. Whup!* " . . . after the boot area is fitted, the suit nannites must be induced to begin the undergelling process . . ."

He walked into the general's office, stumbling slightly over his feet and grinning internally at Beed's slight flush of frustrated anger. He came to attention in front of the desk as the door slid shut behind him.

"Our source has been in contact again. He's offering more information for sale," the general said.

"Who are they sending to meet him?" *As if I didn't know.*

"He's here. I can't meet him tonight. You'll have to make the meet. Here's the address. Memorize it." He extended a sheet of paper and waited while Stewart stared at the paper for a few moments, taking it back and tucking it into his desk.

"Do not fuck this up, Lieutenant," Beed said grimly.

Yeah, like you have a real excuse for slacking, asshole. If Mister Jones is on Titan, I wonder who else is on Titan? This is the first indication we've gotten that our strategy might actually be working. God, I look forward to relieving this bastard. For Sinda's sake if nothing else.

"Yes, sir. Will that be all, sir?"

"Make sure you come back with something good Pryce. I don't need to tell you that right now we've got jack squat on this mission, and that does not look good. A good OER on a mission like this could be a great asset to the career of a young officer. Dismissed."

You prick. "Yes, sir." Pryce saluted, executing a wobbly about face and leaving before his façade cracked. Maintaining cover was getting to be harder than he had expected.

Friday, June 14, evening

The sake bar served a certain class of Fleet junior officers. While the establishment was on the no-go list for Fleet Strike personnel, other than MPs in the line of duty, Stewart's task tonight fully justified the civilian clothing he was wearing, and his military haircut was common among freighter weenies, anyway. While walking in two or three hours later would pretty much have guaranteed a brawl, it was still early enough that Fleet's finest were firmly absorbed with drinking and trying their luck at some of the multiplayer game consoles scattered around the place.

Stewart generally avoided the lousy beer, made worse by being microbrewed on the premises from local hydroponically grown hops. The anime, at least, was first class. While the large . . . eyes . . . on cartoon women were not nearly as much fun as the real thing—he quashed the strong impulse to fantasize painful and violent ends for Beed—anyway, the art was nice to look at.

The balding but fit civilian sitting by the bar over a bowl of what was probably miso soup was not so nice to look at. Frankly, he felt a gut level distaste for traitors in general, whenever he let himself think about it. But dealing with unsavory people went with the territory in intel, and he couldn't really afford the luxury of that distaste right now. Like any soldier, Stewart could summon a certain grudging respect for an honest opponent or even enemy. People who were traitors to their own cause, though, just tended to arouse a certain visceral distaste that he had to squash with a vengeance as he crossed the bar to meet the other man.

"Mr. Smith, how nice to see you again," the other man said.

"Mr. Jones. You're a long way from home, aren't you?" Stewart observed.

"I could say the same thing of you," the traitor said.

"If you knew where my home was, I suppose you could." He pulled up a barstool, smiling easily even though the thought of drinking with this worm was enough to turn his stomach.

"So, what have you got to trade, Mr. Jones? Are you still dancing around with the penny ante game, or are you ready to move up to something more rewarding? And, if you don't mind my saying so, this is a bit of a change of scene for you, isn't it?" *Prod him a bit and see what he comes out with.*

"I travel. This time I don't just want cash. You said you'd pay more for more. Well, we'll see if you meant that." There was a thin film of sweat on the guy's upper lip. Maybe he was nervous?

"Keep talking." *Don't give him anything to grab onto, make him reach for a response.*

"I want a diversion. You want part of our organization. I see a mutual opportunity here. You assist me in placing some evidence, I give you the person it will point to. You might want the rest of the team, in case you have to be kind of rough on your new toys. But that would be where the money part comes in." The undertone of desperation in his voice was palpable.

Good God, we've hit the motherlode. Okay, now the hard question. Why?

"And what, exactly, would this placing of evidence consist of?" he asked.

"The usual and obvious. Put some banking transactions together and tuck away some luxury goods in the right places. When you pick him up, it'll look like he was feeding you information all along and he went in out of the cold." The traitor's grin was a particularly nasty one.

"You know, the object of this game is usually to get the information *without* the other guy knowing you've got it." He just couldn't help being a little sarcastic. Try as he might, having to deal with someone capable of betraying his friends for money just really got under his skin.

"If you can. I've got news for you. They know they've got a leak. So you're not losing anything that isn't already lost. They don't even have to know you have him. Make it look like he went out on a colonist ship." Baldy obviously was starting to feel the net closing in.

Okay, they'd only buy this fool's "diversion" if they're really stupid, and to penetrate us like they have, stupid they're not. On the other hand, if he actually is giving us insiders, it doesn't matter. And I got my answer. His people are closing in on him and he's covering his butt. If that's the price, I can deal with that. What do I have to pay him per guy? Three million U.S. dollars per team member?

"I think we can do that. We'll plant the evidence as directed and pay you one million dollars U.S., each, for this guy and every member of his team we capture," he said.

"Do I look stupid? Five million U.S., each, and it's for every person whose identity I give you. If you want to shoot them instead of reeling them in, or if you screw it up, that's your problem." The traitor obviously had an ego the size of Cleveland.

It took some minor haggling, but they finally settled at two and a half, half on delivery of the names, half on confirmation that the name went with a real person credibly identified as an organization operative, with standard mutual security precautions. *A light price, for what I'm getting.*

"So, Mr. Jones, just as a good faith gesture as I go set all this in motion, you said you're giving us a team. I'm sure you'll understand I have to have something for the people I report to before they're going to let me have that kind of money. This team you're giving us, does it have some sort of internal call name?"

"Hector."

Saturday, June 15, 03:30

Michael O'Neal, Sr., had never gotten used to waiting. Oh, he'd learned to simulate perfectly still patience very early in life, or he wouldn't have survived. It didn't mean he had to like it. And he didn't. His granddaughter wasn't exactly *late*, since there was no set time for their meet and in the field, with her cover, there could be all sorts of reasons why she couldn't get away early, or maybe at all.

Which made waiting even more of a pain in the ass.

He had trained Cally in battlefield survival, and general survival in hostile environments, since the age of eight. As a little girl in the Posleen war, she'd been more solid than many grown men, first killing the assassin who'd come to kill them if he couldn't be recruited, then taking her place beside Team Conyers to fight off the Posties as they'd come up the Gap.

He spat carefully into the spare cup the barmaid had so thoughtfully provided.

After the war, she'd had the first-rate training in her specialty provided in a private parochial environment by the Bane Sidhe's cadre of killer nuns. Her skills had been honed to a fine art. She was, arguably, the best living assassin on Earth or off it—with the possible exception of himself. Although he didn't have her . . . natural advantages.

So, all that being true, *why*, when she was out in the field, did he always feel like a nervous father whose daughter was out on her first date?

He stifled the impulse to stand and pace, strangling and dismembering it for good measure. Cally was long past her first date. That was something of the problem. You could teach a girl how to reliably hit an eight inch circle from a thousand yards, you could teach her how to run and recognize booby traps, you could teach her nine different ways to kill a man quietly in the dark, but you couldn't teach her how to cope with the stresses of the job. That was something each assassin had to learn for herself, or himself.

Cally had always been a natural. He remembered the first time he'd put a pistol in that kid's hand. She couldn't hit the side of a barn, of course, but after she'd fired her first magazine downrange and the slide locked back, she'd turned and looked at him. She'd been a skinny kid, the blond hair tangled and stringy practically every time she shook her head. And there had been a smudge of soot on the side of her nose where she'd scratched. The earmuffs had been big and bright green on the sides of her head, and the safety glasses tended to slip down the bridge of her nose, but the grin she'd given him had lit up her whole face. And as time went on it became clear that besides enthusiasm she had two other crucial traits. Her eyesight was unusually sharp, and her hands exceptionally steady. He'd taken care to protect both—the first from eye strain in bad light, and the second from vices like caffeine. There were vices more workable in budding warriors.

And, of course, she'd been stubborn. Couldn't imagine where she'd gotten that from. He chuckled, spitting again into the spare cup. And the way she'd taken out the kneecap of that rotten punk who'd tried—

The door slid open and there, finally, was his baby granddaughter—but what in the hell was she wearing? The one-piece black leather-looking jumpsuit would have suited her cover tonight as a good-time girl just fine—if she had had her own measurements. As it was, the zipper of the black tank-style top half could barely be tugged halfway up without her busting out of it. And in his opinion, that was still an imminent danger. It made him want to get up and throw a blanket around her.

"Hey, sweet thing, what can I order for you to drink?" He spat again as she sauntered in, straddling a chair and leaning her arms across its back as the door slid closed behind her. There was a noticeable bounce in her step that he didn't think was the role. Whores weren't bouncy. At best they were blasé.

"Black Bush, water back. Life's too short to drink cheap booze," she said. The toe of one foot tapped rapidly at the floor, as if she couldn't quite sit still, even though it was late and she must have been tired.

"You're chipper," he said. *Life's too short?* Cally hadn't thought life was too short for anything in a very long time. *Something's up.*

"Progress report?" He took a sound damper out and set it on the table, turning it on. "I've already swept."

"I haven't found jack. I did confirm that a clandestine operation is being run out of the office. Probably *the* clandestine operation, but that's all I've got. Getting the general into bed wasn't a problem. Probably would have been a problem if I hadn't, in fact. He's that type. I've searched everything I've got access to and I'm working on the aide de camp, who has access to the places I don't," she said.

Was it just his imagination that her voice had gotten a bit husky there at the end? Oh, crap, what now?

"So, tell me more about this aide." He spat, considering. "You're planning to get access to the rest of the brigade headquarters space how?"

"Oh, that's easy." She bounced, blue eyes twinkling mischievously at him. "When those are the only places left in the office that we haven't done it, somehow I think he'll be . . . receptive to sugges-tion." The way she licked her lips reminded him of the cat that ate the canary.

"You're not supposed to mix business with pleasure." *Oh shit.*

"You're the one who wanted me to get a boyfriend." She shrugged, examining the nails of one hand minutely.

"I hesitate to say this, Granddaughter, but don't get in too deep." *Fuck. She's not going to listen. Too late.*

"Oh, I won't. I'll let Pryce do that. Really, Granpa, I'm not *twelve*. Could you order that drink? I wasn't kidding about enjoying something good. Might as well, I'm already here." She changed the subject, turning the chair and settling back into it so she could lean back and relax for a few minutes.

He grunted noncommittally, turning off the damper and stepping over to the console by the door to punch the drinks in. When he sat back down and she pulled her chair over and snuggled up against him, draping his arm around her shoulder for the benefit of whoever delivered their drinks, he had a few tough moments as he reminded his body that while this very well-built and nubile young woman did not *look* like his granddaughter, she in fact *was* his granddaughter. Now, if only this Pryce young man had *not* been met on a mission, he'd be welcoming the guy with open arms. Well, okay, if he measured up. Still, they *were* trained for extractions, and it wasn't as if Fleet Strike actually *needed* all those lieutenants. On second thought, strike that. Any man worth his salt could be counted on to react poorly to being kidnapped. Well, maybe. The bait *was* considerable.

CHAPTER FOURTEEN

Titan Base, Saturday, June 15, 10:00

Fleet Strike was different from the old United States armed services in many respects. The fondness of the organization's senior officers for the game of golf was not one of those differences. During the design phase of Titan Base, a bright and ambitious young life support engineer had noticed a way to fulfill a design requirement for hardy, nonfood perennials while simultaneously scoring a vast number of brownie points with senior staff. Hence, the entire lowermost deck of the Fleet Strike and Spares and Fabrications quadrants was very high-ceilinged and devoted to a lush lawn of specially bred grasses and turf. Getting the Indowy to sign off on the absolute necessity of the ceiling configuration had required the importation of a small herd of miniature horses from Kentucky. For some reason, getting all the signatures for the transport of the livestock had gone amazingly easily. The fans for computer randomized wind patterns had been more difficult, but still possible. After all, what was the use of generating so much oxygen if you didn't have the ability to mix it with the rest of the station air?

Cally watched with carefully disguised amusement this morning as Beed cursed the headwind as he approached the tee for the third hole. Golf was a challenging game for her, especially in this environment. Upgraded muscle density, still there under the surface mods for Sinda, and her own inherent spatial awareness and finely honed martial training combined to make her easily one of the top three golfers on Titan Base.

Sinda Makepeace had nothing in her record to indicate that she'd ever even visited a golf course, much less played the game.

Beed needed flattering, convincing him that he was teaching her to golf.

The upshot was that on the golf course her acting challenge was more exacting than usual as she had to constantly evaluate precisely how lousy she needed to be.

The odd part was that a couple of times this morning she'd gotten the bizarre impression that Pryce was also holding back to avoid beating the general. She smiled fondly. *Get a really great lay or two from the guy and all of a sudden I'm imagining all sorts of new virtues for him.*

Out of the corner of her eye she saw him trip over the strap of the golf bag and barely catch himself by the edge of the cart. Next she'd be envisioning him as the world's next great orator. Geez.

"All right, Sinda, dear, your turn." Beed leered at her as she smiled back brightly, wondering how even a cover role had allowed her to see him even temporarily as less than the worm he obviously was. "Did you notice how I was still for a moment after making my swing? That's called 'follow through,' and it's important in this game."

She nodded, hands clasped in front of herself, listening carefully, eyes bright, cheerful, earnest, and empty. She watched Beed smile indulgently without a spark of recognition on her own part, reaching out and blithely selecting a putter, smiling gratefully at Beed when he traded her for a better club.

"Pay attention, dear. Club selection is *very* important," he said.

With her upgraded hearing, she could hear Pryce gritting his teeth as Beed wrapped his arms around her to guide her swing. She hoped Beed couldn't hear it, even though it sounded loud to her against the background of the golf course, unusually empty this morning and silent except for the distant whir of the fans. The freshly cut grass was sweet in her nostrils and she could feel Beed's erection against her buttocks as he adjusted her grip on the club. *Hell, there goes my afternoon. Not that I didn't expect as much. Unfortunately, the general has an average juv libido. Horny as hell all the damned time. Too bad the BS would be pissed if I killed the bastard. Okay, so he's a human life and I wouldn't kill him for no damned reason, but I swear if he keeps getting on my nerves I might succumb to the temptation to . . . bruise him a bit . . . on my way out. Slimy paper-obsessed son of a bitch. Against some personality traits, looks just aren't enough. Well, hell, I knew it was part of the job when I took it. I have to admit I have done worse. The poor bastard can't help it that he suffers by comparison.*

She sighted carefully down the course and made the very slight adjustments that would send the ball straight into a sand trap.

"Look how hard I hit it! Wow!" She jumped up and down in excitement, generating a range of mesmerizing jiggles for the two men. Out of the corner of one eye she saw Pryce swallow, hard, and suppressed a grin.

"Is that good?" She cocked her head to one side and beamed at the hapless general.

Titan Base, Saturday, June 15, afternoon

"An intercepted signal has come in that meets your specified criteria for your attention, your Tir." The voice of the AID was melodious, like all Darhel voices, but had an indefinable extra intensity to it. The hair on the Tir's back lifted slightly as his ears relaxed outward, just a bit, in unconscious response.

"Play it," he said, shifting a bit towards the Indowy body servant who was scratching a troublesome itch behind his right ear, but not enough to disengage from the other servant who was currently working out some tension cramps in his shoulder muscles. There were, of course, no true windows in these quarters, although they were quite spacious, with simulated windows displaying vistas from any of several dozen worlds. The gravity and lighting, being artificial anyway, were pleasantly adjusted to homeworld's conditions. He pressed the pads of his bare feet into the deep pile appreciatively. For temporary quarters, the suite maintained in the human-free sector of Titan Base was quite adequate.

"Memo to Lieutenant General Peter Vanderberg, OFSI, Chicago, from First Lieutenant Joshua Pryce, assigned as aide de camp to Brigadier General Bernard Beed, 3rd MP Brigade, commanding. Subject: Hartford. Message: Have the opportunity to accelerate acquisition of essential project supplies. Supply source is code named Hector by the supply depot. Contact information follows.

As these particular supplies are in your area of operation, suggest your people pursue local acquisition. Have taken the liberty of paying a deposit on the supplies to Mr. Jones, balance pending on acquisition. Negotiated price is well within assigned budget for this project. Memo ends. There is a file attached that appears to be a list of four names, several aliases, DNA code samples, and several locations and times per name."

The Tir was now sitting bolt upright, whiskers trembling. He took a moment to breathe carefully before speaking.

"Forward the information to Mr. Stuart. Tell him we would prefer as much information regarding these . . . supplies . . . as possible, but in no case should Fleet Strike have them. Having the supplies disclose information in uncontrolled circumstances would be . . . adverse to our interests," he said.

"Yes, your Tir. It is done," it replied.

The Indowy body servants continued their ministrations uninterrupted. One disappeared briefly into the kitchen, reappearing with an ornate tray set with fresh vegetables from three different worlds. As always, the personal service made the food marginally less distasteful.

Somewhere under Indiana, Saturday, June 15, afternoon

Nathan O'Reilly looked up as his office door slid open with no announcement, surprised to see the Indowy Aelool in his doorway. The muscles around the eyes were crinkled and the ears turned slightly inward in an expression that was either grave, worried, or both.

"My goodness, what's wrong?" He got a bottled water from a small cooler and poured it into a fresh glass, setting it on the end table and backing away. His friend usually affected unconcern around human carnivores out of politeness, but the priest felt it might be a bit much to expect of him in his clearly distressed state.

"Team Hector is compromised. Our leak, as you call it, has sprung again." He sat in a human-sized chair absentmindedly, perched on the edge, legs swinging nervously, plucking absently at the green tendrils of his left leg.

"When and what can we do about it?" O'Reilly pulled up the team's schedule with an aside to his AID.

"Identities and itineraries over the next few days are in Fleet Strike and Darhel hands. Names, aliases, DNA patterns. The whole team," he tutted lightly. "Unfortunately, as large a loss as an entire team will be, it pales next to the value of our sources of information close to the Tir. We can do little. Nothing, without a plausible cover story for how we know."

"We can put an extraction team in place on hold status. Activate them if we get any kind of cover we can use, leave them if not. Who knows, the other side might get sloppy." The priest didn't sound very confident.

"Is there anything new from Team Isaac?" the Indowy asked.

"Since we last talked? No, unfortunately not. Harris in traffic analysis is bright. I'll set her to work looking for anything we can leak back to point in a plausible wrong direction for how we knew. I think that's all we can do." He walked over and stared out of his virtual window.

"As long as you are absolutely confident that if they do not get direct authorization the extraction team *will* remain inactive. I do not need to remind you that the stakes here are very high," Aelool was just a bit shrill.

"So—do we risk a message to Papa O'Neal that now would be a good time for results?" He tapped his fingertips on the glass.

"I would suggest no. They know the stakes and the risks. I would be correct in thinking they are already as motivated as it is possible to be? Then there is no gain and some risk. Don't you have a phrase? Jostling the elbow? I think better not." He walked over beside his friend and looked up at the fake window. Like all the Indowy, he probably found it difficult to understand why humans needed to pretend to be close to the outside and empty spaces, even when they were cozily packed together with their own clans and very best friends.

"Agreed," the priest said.

"You still pray, do you not? Perhaps it would be a good time." Looking a bit bewildered, most likely at the virtual window, Aelool left.

Chicago, Saturday, June 15, afternoon

"Peter, you have an urgent memo coming in from General Stewart, covered as Lieutenant Pryce on Titan Base," his AID chimed.

"He got a live one?" Vanderberg sat bolt upright in his chair.

"Not exactly, Peter. What he got was four names and identifying information including DNA, itineraries, aliases, and current physical descriptions of agents in the Chicago area," it said.

"Holy shit! DNA, too?" *Somebody up there likes me.*

"That's what he says, and the file attached has all of that." The AID even sounded pleased.

"Wow. Show me the file." He shook his head as he scanned the details. "Shit, Stewart hit the jackpot. Get me Morrison." He stood and walked over to the window, tapping his lips with one finger.

"I'm sorry, Peter. Morrison is out of pocket. He has a dental appointment," it said.

"*Dental* appointment?" He turned, looking at the AID on his desk as if he couldn't believe what he was hearing.

"He broke a tooth. He's in for a replacement."

"Geez, did something happen? Is he all right?" he asked.

"No accident. I believe it was a statistical certainty sooner or later. He chews ice." The AID's voice had that prim note they took on when they disapproved of something. The AID personalities had odd notions of propriety sometimes. In this case, he suspected the cause of disapproval was that anyone would do anything so inconsiderate as to engage in a habit that would eventually necessitate taking time off from work. Every once in a while, AIDs were really strange.

"Okay, have him come in first thing in the morning. Meanwhile, I don't think this can wait. Send in Lewis, I guess. No, cancel that. I'd rather lose a day than bring in an extra person on something like this. Shit. Tell Morrison I want him in here tomorrow at seven thirty. We can at least get an early start." He locked his hands behind his head and began to pace, already turning possible scenarios over in his head.

"You are aware that tomorrow is Sunday, right?" it said.

"Yeah. I hate it, but this can't wait." He waved one hand impatiently and kept on pacing.

"That's fine, Peter. I'm just following your standing order to remind you."

"Yeah, that. Thanks, Jenny." *Wow. What a break.*

Titan Base, Saturday, June 15, afternoon

There were so few public access terminals these days. Everybody and his sister had a PDA, well, except for the lucky bastards with AIDs. Well, clean ones, anyway. But PDAs sometimes broke, or people lost them—anyway, thank god for public access terminals.

This one was in the middle of the busiest section of the Corridor he could find. There was so much visual noise here with all the other people passing that no particular pedestrian would ever remember him. Not that anybody but the Bane Sidhe would be looking, and by the time they were, he'd be long gone.

He had really wanted to spend his retirement on Earth—the amenities were so much better, even when one was perforce keeping a low profile. Oh, well, things were how they were.

Dulain was a good planet. One of the first colonized by humans, and it had some hazards, but it also had a good belt of very pleasant islands. Not too great a place to work as a penniless colonist. But just fine for someone with a nice nest egg. And a ship was leaving at nineteen-thirty on Tuesday. Perfect. It only took him a few moments to transfer the funds from his numbered accounts to numbered accounts on Dulain. He'd opened an account on Titan with some of the cash from his payoff. The rest he had, unfortunately, had to deposit in a public locker, taking his chances. Still, the important part about the cash was the ability to buy his outbound ticket under an uncompromised ID.

And he'd never have to eat another soybean corn dog again. Ever.

Titan Base, Saturday, June 15, late afternoon

The newsstand on the corner of level eight and hallway Romeo on the Corridor had a good solid range of over the counter medications, including several popular diet mixes that were mostly diuretics. Cally picked the distinctive orange and yellow package because this particular diuretic combination was not just fast acting, it was also mostly tasteless and the effective dose was small. A beer would be enough to hide the very mild taste, even from someone like her.

I hate drugging him at all. The least I can do is set it up so what I give him is as harmless as possible. Well, embarrassing, maybe, if he doesn't run fast enough. Still, that's as harmless I can make it. At least I don't have to use it for a few days.

She was wearing her least conspicuous bra under the silks as she made the buy. Less out of real need than out of the normal tradecraft of reducing conspicuous factors. Obviously it was not enough. She was sure the Asian cashier's eyes never even flickered above her collarbone.

Titan Base, Saturday, June 15, evening

James Stewart stood in front of the glass of his beach picture, trying to get enough of a reflection to make sure his hair was all right. He sure hadn't been this excited about coming in to work on a Saturday night in a long time. But then, he wasn't here to work.

In the silence of the empty headquarters office, he could hear the swish of the front door. The bag in her arms puzzled him briefly, until he remembered that she was supposed to bring dinner. He should have been hungry, but he'd never felt less like eating in his life. Well, not food, anyway. He grinned broadly as she came in and put the bag down on the front desk.

He reached for her and pulled her against him, one hand pressed into the small of her back, and the other buried in her hair. Her belly was pressed tight against his, her breasts squashed but still soft against his chest. He wanted to screw her now. Right now.

He tried to pull her back towards his office, or hers, but she wouldn't go, laughing teasingly.

"Why not right here?" She patted the top of the desk, a glint of mischief in her eyes. "Or here . . ." She slid off the edge of the desk and fell back into the chair, spinning in it and laughing.

He quirked an eyebrow skeptically, imagining how far he'd have to bend his knees for that to work. But she was ahead of him. That, or she'd read his mind, pressing the button that activated the chair's hydraulics, raising it to its limit.

As she unsealed the front seam of her silks and shrugged them off her shoulders, he reconsidered. Perhaps it was workable after all. Especially once she lifted her knees and gripped, taking a lot of the weight off his knees. As the rhythm of sex took him over, the brush of her nipples against his chest making him fight for every bit of the control needed to make it last, he promised himself that he'd never question her assessment of what was physically possible again.

After they fixed Anders' philodendron, which had somehow gotten dislodged from its terra cotta pot, they ate dinner in Sinda's office. He didn't know where she'd come up with an old-fashioned picnic of cold fried chicken, potato salad, deviled eggs, and chocolate chip cookies, but it sure was good. Especially the ice-cold genuine Milwaukee beer, which must have cost her a small fortune.

Afterward, she seduced him—not that he resisted, of course—on the slimy sonofabitch's desk. He had to admit he appreciated the irony.

Sunday, June 16, afternoon

The smell of her hair was thick in his nostrils as her kisses—interspersed with a few bites to make sure he was paying attention—trailed down his chest. More kiss than bite the farther she went. Finally, she was wrapped around one of his legs, her breasts rubbing against his thigh, nails and body clenched and shuddering against him in ways that showed him that she was having just as much fun as he was.

The ethereal opening strains of the next song on her cube pierced him with an oddly sweet sadness for a few moments before the hot, driving rhythm kicked in to add to the intensity of what she was doing to him. He didn't try to remember the name of the band or the song, but it came to him anyway. It was a wartime band called Evanescence, the song, "Bring Me to Life," and it couldn't possibly fit their situation, but somehow he knew the music was deeply important to her.

The vibrance of the music bled onto every sensation, making it more alive—the scent of her, her hands and mouth on him. Her beautiful, pale skin, flushed with sex and luminous with a light sheen of sweat. Even the drab gray of the office walls seemed more intensely real. The music was singing in their bones, and he wondered what in the hell was happening to him. Sex had *never* been like this.

The thought wandered through the back of his mind that there was something a little perverse about doing it in a coworker's office, but it was a small thought, and easily banished. Besides, Li had gotten a couch for his office. Not leather, but a reasonably good substitute.

Oh, my God. . . .

Afterward, over a lunch of grinders, his ham and hers roast beef, they talked. He tended to avoid walks down memory lane when talking to her. Well, when talking to anybody, really. No matter how well you knew and believed your cover, there was always the chance of tripping yourself up. One of the things that made Sinda so easy to talk to was that she didn't try to push their conversations into the past. She was happy to talk about music, or old movies. Okay, so she might not be the sharpest knife in the drawer, but she had this amazing depth to her—and she hadn't exclusively focused on chick flicks. The really incredible thing was she actually got the best parts. He'd never met another woman who watched the Three Stooges and laughed—really laughed. They'd both liked the scene at the end of one of the old spaghetti westerns where the hero "had a problem with his arithmetic." Hell, she was the first girl he'd met in twenty years who'd ever watched them.

The toughest part of this situation was that he couldn't let himself get involved, no matter how much he might like to. He was living a lie, and there was no telling how her reaction to him would change when she found out the truth. Would she see him as just another opportunist? Would she see him as being like the asshole? Just another predatory juv general? Or could she possibly understand why he'd had to do this?

Springfield, Sunday, June 16, 5 P.M.

Bobby Mitchell was good at surveillance, and his skills had only improved since leaving law enforcement. A throwback to a touch of Sioux on his daddy's side and a hint of Mex on his momma's, he was a small, slightly nervous man with dark hair, dark eyes, skin that tanned easily, and a talent for blending in with his surroundings, whether people or environmental.

Bobby maintained his tan very carefully, having noticed early on how disinclined people were to notice a swarthy, average to short man engaged in manual labor.

Today, he was sweeping a sidewalk across from a park. Bobby's natural vision hadn't been all that good, but the damned aliens had some doctors that weren't too shabby. As he progressed along the sidewalk, he was from twenty to eighty yards from the park bench that allegedly was the enemy dead drop, yet he could clearly make out the features of anyone on or approaching the bench.

He could have used electronics, of course. And he did have them, as a backup. Still, after seeing just a few of the things his damned alien bosses could do with recorded data, Bobby was a firm believer in the personal touch. He'd never been one to assume the enemy was incompetent or stupid.

Besides, the mission here was purely confirmation of a tip in advance of a raid.

He was halfway down the sidewalk sweeping, the second time, when the very average black man with conservative scalp patterns, dressed in a dirty sky blue windbreaker and jeans, sat down on the bench. The face was a dead ringer for one of the four in the tip file, and he admired the smoothness of the man brushing a hand under the edge of the bench under cover of tossing crumbs to the pigeons. You had to admire the artistry. He didn't even see him read it, and only knew it was probably a note on flashpaper from the slight excess flare as the man lit a cigarette, standing and strolling casually back the way he had come.

Tip confirmed, mission accomplished. Bobby continued his sweeping all around the square, palming his back-up cameras as he passed them.

The Fleet Strike puke who picked up their cameras from within the park itself half an hour later was clumsy, wearing civilian clothes that were too carefully sloppy and too new and overacting his casualness, although his sleight of hand was acceptable. Still, it was obvious Fleet Strike hadn't faced a serious threat from an opposing intelligence force in a long time.

Too bad he couldn't count on all their people being that inexperienced. It was probably overkill, but he'd still plan the raid as if they were going to be competent competitors for the prizes.

After cleaning up the last camera, he disappeared down an alley to his ten-year-old gray sedan, throwing the broom in his back seat. His AID looked like a cheap discount-store brand PDA. He took a moment to call his cousin, "Hey, Johnny. Yeah, it's me. We're on for beer and pizza Tuesday. My place."

Tip confirmed, raid on schedule, set the wheels in motion. And may we all get nice bonuses out of this.

As he got off the bus, Levon Martin took out the baggy where he'd saved a bit of bread from his sandwich. He tore the bread into crumbs as he walked from the stop to the park.

It was a beautiful day but a trifle windy. His clothes had the well worn look of the comfortable clothes that a man might wear for a walk on his day off. The air today smelled fresh and green, and he couldn't help but be cheered a bit by the profusion of dandelions that pushed up between the cracks of the crumbling sidewalks, giving way suddenly to solid concrete and well-tended flower boxes as he turned onto the square.

In the park in the middle of the square, he found a spot on the left end of the bench that was mostly clear of pigeon droppings and sat, playing out the crumbs to the fat, iridescent birds as they waddled and pecked at the bits of bread and sometimes at each other.

Somewhere in the middle he managed to palm the flash paper sticky-note stuck to the bottom of the bench. Under cover of crumbling a bit more bread, he tore off the corner of the paper that held a few tiny dots of film that would yield up their data later, under magnification. The rest of the note simply said, "Plus one hour for Joe."

He kept it palmed while he finished feeding the birds and disposed of it before he left by the simple expedient of burning it as he lit a cigarette, covered by the flare of his lighter. The baggy with the data dots went into his pocket. *Wonder what in the hell Barry has going on that necessitates pushing back the mid-cycle meeting? Not that it matters.*

There were various people in the square or on the walkways this Sunday afternoon, but none of them stood out. There was nothing to distinguish the sidewalk sweeper from any of a couple of dozen other people going about their business in plain sight.

Martin walked back out to his bus stop, arriving five minutes before the next scheduled pickup at that stop. After a short wait, he boarded his bus and was gone.

Chicago, Sunday, June 15, evening

Peter Vanderberg contemplated the young major in front of him, from the slightly long for regulation hair to the precise fit of his silks and liked what he saw. What he primarily liked about David Morrison couldn't be seen on the surface. Alert, competent, smart. Attentive to detail without getting bogged down and overcome by trivialities. Good delegating authority. All these were reasons for the man to have obtained the exalted rank of major at the unusually young age of thirty-six.

His 201 file was virtually perfect, as was true of almost all of the new breed of young Fleet Strike officers.

"So. Now that our intel is confirmed, I expect a finalized operational plan for capture of the targets ready to brief in the participants by eleven hundred tomorrow. You can use my briefing room, since I'll want to be there. Look at me, David." He caught the major's eyes as they dropped slightly to meet his own. "I can't emphasize enough how important this mission is. Use whatever you need to get it done."

"Yes, sir." He nodded. "My preliminary plan is for a solid team in civilian clothes backed up by a substantial number of uniformed MPs who can be thoroughly concealed and held under radio silence until and unless needed."

"Reasonable. Get on it. I'll see you tomorrow. Dismissed."

"Yes, sir." The about face was clean, but relaxed, confident. Good man. As soon as Stewart was out in the open, he was definitely sending him a mixed case of Havanas and good scotch, and damn the cost.

Titan Base, Monday, June 17, evening

"So he didn't notice that you had your buckley do all those time-wasting reports he wanted?" Stewart had doubled back to the office, since Sinda didn't have to be at the asshole's quarters until his wife left at nineteen hundred.

"Well, he did comment that they were a bit pessimistic." She trailed a finger down his chest, grinning conspiratorially. "I blamed it on PMS.

"So," she took a finger and tapped him on the chest, "we've just about exhausted the possibilities of the regular office but *you*," she tapped him again, "have access to the locked room off of Beed's office. Is there any . . . interesting furniture or anything in there?"

Her breasts were just barely brushing against his chest, and he could feel her nipples hardening through the thin fabric. Her breath was warm against his jaw line and smelled of cinnamon.

"Well, there *is* a recliner back there. And a large vidscreen. I don't think he wants the rest of the office to know he uses them." He ran a hand through that silky, bright hair. She had great hair.

"A recliner? Lead on, Macduff," she said.

If she thought she was going to be in the driver's seat like last night, she was in for a surprise. Not that it hadn't been fantastic, just, well, they didn't have a lot of time and he didn't like why. Oh, it wasn't her fault at all. Which was why he was in the mood to wring every last bit of sensation from her and leave her sated and limp as a rag doll. The asshole might get her acting ability, but he had her real passion, and he knew it. It was his aim to make her unable to forget it for a second of her sad pantomime with that unfit, corrupt flake who he was more and more looking forward to relieving of command and career.

The promised recliner was upholstered in a rather hideous green and black plaid. A faded leopard-print pillow scavenged from who knew where was squashed into one corner of it. A couple of other pillows and a red and white blanket with a soft drink logo were piled neatly to the side of the chair. A box of holocubes with the logos of commercial entertainment companies sat by itself on a small end table. The color scheme was the same institutional green and battleship gray of the rest of the office.

As the door slid shut behind her he pulled her hard against him, kissing her deeply. He didn't know what it was about this woman, but a kiss or a touch and he was just gone.

Now her legs were up around his waist and the drive came boiling up in him. It turned out that the pillows and blanket combined to provide just the right height boost to support her when he bent her over the arm of the chair. He had both hands free, and he could reach everything, and did, as he felt the convulsions begin to take her. Yesterday had been pretty great, but all in all, Stewart preferred to drive.

He had worked his way through two and was recovered and starting on three, gotta love that juv stamina, when he thought he heard a noise in the outer office. He clapped one hand over Sinda's mouth, "Shhh!" and they both dived for their PDA's. She made it first.

"Buckley, who's out there?" she hissed.

"It's Sergeant Franks! He'll tell the general and we're all gonna die!" it whispered back.

Only Franks. Wonder what he's up to? Stewart breathed a sigh of relief and put a finger over his lips.

Sinda nodded.

He quietly murmured to his AID-in-drag to listen for Franks until he left the headquarters complex. He and Sinda sat very quietly, staring at each other, until it announced softly that Franks was gone and, other than themselves and the MP standing guard in the outer corridor, the headquarters area was now empty.

"You get damn good performance out of your buckley," he said.

"Yeah, so do you," she observed absently. "Boy that took the mood right away, didn't it?"

"Yeah, but I bet we could get it back pretty quick." He looked down and shrugged, running a finger up her thigh.

"We already damn near got caught once tonight. Let's not make that a certainty, okay?" She stopped his hand with one of her own and grabbed her silks, smiling regretfully.

"Yeah," he agreed reluctantly, grabbing his own clothes. It really wasn't her fault. If it was anybody's fault it was his for having the power to relieve the bastard and failing to do so. Okay, so his own orders didn't allow it yet, but if he wanted to get her out of the asshole's bed all he had to do was hurry up and catch Franks or whoever the sonofabitch plant was. As soon as that was done, he could relieve Beed and ship his scumbag butt back to Earth and away from her.

He kissed her and waved her on out to go do what she had to do as soon as she had her hair and clothes straightened while he finished cleaning up.

It wasn't actually impossible. It wasn't as if working in CID or an MP Brigade was her life's ambition. He could get her a transfer somewhere on base. Once they were no longer in the same chain of command, and she was in a job less outright crazy than this one, there wouldn't really be anything to keep them apart, would there?

Titan Base, Tuesday, June 18, 16:30

On the shuttle for the freighter, Jay and the others generally wore liners of the same material as military silks under their heavy cotton jumpsuits. They had to. Landing control wouldn't have tolerated the heat leakage that would have resulted if they'd kept the inside at a comfortable temperature.

Besides, they weren't supposed to be sleeping on it in the first place. Covering that had meant renting a transient's room and having someone in it enough of the time to make it look well used. Jay liked this arrangement because it gave him excellent cover for his independent ventures when it was his time to use the room.

And his turn was supposed to be today, but Papa O'Neal had asked to swap, and he hadn't had a graceful excuse to say no.

So here he was stuck on the shuttle freezing his buns off with Sunday. Well, okay, the silk longjohns helped a lot. He'd still rather be alone and warm and ready to go. Not that Sunday was a bad guy, it was just that he had so much money he couldn't possibly understand what it was like to grow up in the lousy BS. Oh, most of the kids had just accepted it. They never knew any better. But him being a doctor's kid, he'd seen the difference between himself and the other doctors' kids. He knew full well what his life would have been like with a lot less fucking BS. Sunday could have never understood, but he was just getting back the life that always should have been his in the first place. And if the BS suffered, well, it just balanced the scales, didn't it?

He surreptitiously checked the outbound passenger shuttle schedules. *Fuck! Two hour mechanical launch delay. This totally sucks. Okay, not a real problem.* It was still well within the effective span of his diversion, it was just that the other launch time was so sweet.

His change of clothes and ID was in a locker with the money and minimal luggage, all ready to go. He had another couple of hours to kill, that's all.

"Hey, Sunday, wanna play me a battle or two of Warlord?" He wiggled his PDA.

Tuesday, June 18, 19.00

Cally sat on the closed seat in the lone stall of the office women's room. The only problem with this diuretic was it tended to lose potency and acquire an aftertaste if you mixed the water-soluble combination too far ahead of time. She was pretty sure she could make an opportunity to get into that last, guarded room tonight. Which meant she'd need this within a couple of hours. One eye-dropper full in his beer would guarantee sending him running out.

She stowed the bottle in her purse, pulling out a data cube for her PDA. No telling what cracking programs she'd need. Best to have them all on tap. Still, she checked the seal on the small, wide-mouthed jar of vinegar, just in case.

Back in the office, she puttered around her office waiting for Pryce to get back with dinner. She had asked him to get beer and hot wings. Everybody drank beer with wings.

Tonight they had no preset time limit. Beed's wife had apparently finally insisted on at least one quiet evening together at home. It was a damned shame to waste it by drugging Pryce, but she couldn't let her hormones get in the way of her job. Besides, when she found the identity of the leak, and sooner or later she would, it would be all over without a goodbye, anyway.

But maybe she wouldn't find it tonight. It could be wherever Beed went on those long inspection walks of his. Maybe even over at the detention center. It was certainly secure enough.

Persuading Beed to take her along would be easy enough. All she'd have to do was provide him with even a thin excuse. The horny bastard would jump at the offer of more time to get his hand in the cookie jar.

She smiled sadly as she heard the outer office door. It really was too bad she had to do this, but it was the best way she knew to cover her search time while leaving him totally unharmed. Well, other than his dignity. She pulled her game face firmly on, grinning wickedly at him as he came in her open door.

"Mmmm. Something smells good." She inhaled appreciatively. "Dinner smells pretty good, too."

"Cute." He gave her a sidelong glance as he took the beer bottles and to-go boxes out of the bag. "Did you want to get to the food at all? I mean, if you're not hungry . . ." He trailed off with a slow, predatory grin.

"Um, actually I am hungry. For food, I mean. First." She let her eyelids droop a bit, letting how much she wanted him show on her face. There was a tight pain in her chest. Sometimes she hated her job.

"Okay." He opened the beer bottles and went to get his desk chair. She didn't need the ruse she'd planned, after all.

It only took a second to reach into her desk drawer and put a dropper-full of the drug into his beer.

CHAPTER FIFTEEN

Springfield, Tuesday, June 18, 19:30

Where the hell are they? Morrison was becoming more and more certain, as he avoided checking his watch for the tenth time, that they had been played. He had been in place for one hour, two and a half pints, one shot of whiskey, and two sober pills. He'd taken the first before coming in the door, and the second just now. They'd break down the alcohol in his stomach before it got to his bloodstream. Well, most of it. Ten percent did get through, but his liver could handle that.

The Wexford Pub was a little hole in the wall that served lamb stew, soda bread, and greasy fish and chips, accompanied by beer or booze as cheap as it came or as good as you could afford. From the smell, what most patrons afforded most nights was cheaper than shit.

He carefully avoided looking at the three men and two women scattered around the pub who were his, and pretended an interest in the soccer game on the ancient television mounted on one wall. Boring sport—no good fights at all. And he couldn't even hear it over the piped music, which, as far as he could tell, was mostly ancient recordings of folk songs. It wouldn't have been so bad if they hadn't chosen the cheesiest and most stereotypical of the surviving renditions. If they played "Toora Loora Loora" once more he didn't know what he'd do.

He could come up with a dozen reasons, all of them bad, why

271

the targets hadn't shown. Unfortunately, hard as it was to do, their go to hell plan specified waiting in place two hours past the rendezvous in case of a no show, on the theory that they had nothing better and might still get lucky.

He resisted the urge, again, to glance at his people or his watch. Morrison hated waiting. It made the back of his neck itch.

Where the hell are they? Bobby shook the cramp out of his right hand before moving it back and snugging the rifle butt up to his shoulder again.

He devoutly hoped the other three shooters Johnny had come up with were doing the same. They'd better be. Still, they'd seemed competent enough.

It was looking more and more probable that something had spooked the targets.

Still, as long as the Fleet Strike pukes waited, they had to. His instructions were very specific. He was not to let Fleet Strike take any of the targets alive, regardless. The targets were not to escape alive, regardless. If they could somehow get one alive themselves, that was a bonus. He had a medical team standing by, but he didn't think that bonus was going to be possible.

Damn, but this waiting was a bitch. Especially with no way to know how long the Fleet Strike pukes would wait before giving up and going home, themselves.

"Where in the hell are they?" Kevin Collins, head of Team Jason, stubbed out a cigarette in the ashtray of the taxi, looking back at his "fare" half-accusingly, as if he thought the other agent could somehow pull the overdue team out of her pocket.

"Hell if I know, and it's not my fault!" There was a sheepish tone to her voice, though.

"Ah, hell, Martin, I know it's not. I still think you shouldn't be on this mission."

"Well, you were overruled. When the word comes down I want to be on the spot getting Levon and the others out." She pulled out a compact and touched up her lipstick nervously.

"And if it doesn't come down?" His voice was flat.

"Then I follow orders even though it sucks. Levon would do just the same. We both know the risks and the stakes." She wiped away a small smudge with the tip of a finger.

"You're too close."

"Yeah, I know. I'll deal." She snapped the compact shut, putting it and the lipstick back in her purse.

"You'd better." He lit another cigarette and made another turn on the circuitous route winding them around the perimeter of the objective.

George Schmidt routinely spent his time in the field as a teenage kid. That meant that when he needed to be an adult it took some very old-fashioned appearance changes.

Regardless of his distaste for elevator shoes, they were necessary. Pads high in his cheeks made him look less baby-faced. For some reason brown hair made him look a bit older than his natural blond. Careful cosmetic work gave an appearance of dark stubble that would pass even close inspection.

His ID that claimed he was in his mid-twenties was now believable.

He was running right about on time, having spent Barry's extra hour playing holo and VR games at a local arcade. One of the things about being a perpetual kid was he not only had to know about what the current fads were for kids, he had to be able to do them. He could fake incompetence if the cover needed to be a screw-up, but competence was awful damned hard to fake.

Well, time to go. He looked around at the drab, messy efficiency apartment that was the kind of place an emancipated teen might have—right down to smelling of cheap pine air freshener and dirty socks. Definitely not the comforts of home. He flipped out the lights and left.

Twenty minutes later he was still swearing at the jack-knifed semi and cluster of ambulances and emergency vehicles. Nothing for it—he was going to be late again.

Titan Base, Tuesday, June 18, 19:15

Cally nibbled on Pryce's earlobe as she pulled down on his arms trying to get him down to the floor.

"Thanks for having a word with Simms." She gestured at the door outside which the MP still stood guard. "It helps to know we have the evening all to ourselves, no fear of getting caught *or* interrupted."

"So why are you pulling me towards the floor?"

"I thought it might be fun to be on top," she breathed against his neck between kisses.

"That kind of presumes I'm going to let you direct the show, doesn't it?" He picked her up and put her back to the wall, pressing up very close against her, kissing her hair. "How about right here?"

"Mmmph." Her legs snapped up and around his waist, teasing him with the silks that were still in the damn way. "Okay."

She did climb back down long enough to let her silks slide off and puddle on the floor.

She wanted to scream with cheated frustration when he stopped in the middle and grabbed his silks to make a run for the men's room.

"I'll wait for you," she called as he left.

The only furniture in the room was a desk and chair, and there was a laptop computer in the drawer. More of Beed's paranoid dislike of AID's, probably. Not that she blamed him.

It only took a second to plug her PDA into the port.

"Crack it, buckley."

"Did you know there's a ninety-eight point two percent probability that we'll be captured and die here?"

"Shut up and crack the damned thing. The routines are on the cube."

"Right."

The other thing that had been on the cube, of course, was enough of its old data to get the buckley to be cooperative. Well, as cooperative as it ever was, anyway. Waking up the buckley was a risk, but Cally worked marginally faster with one, knowing just when to wheedle or cajole, and when to bulldoze right over its paranoia.

Time always slowed down in this part of an op. Still, she fidgeted nervously as the buckley worked. There was always the chance that the protections were more up to date than the routines chasing the security holes.

But Tommy and Jay were two of the best. She was in pretty quick. Then it was up to her human intelligence to search through the files and find the files she needed.

Oh, my god. Jay, the sonofabitch! And he burned Hector. Holy fuck.

"Send the data, buckley, send it now!"

"There's transmission protection on this room for sure. We'll be caught."

"Send, damn you! Send it now!"

"Right. It's sent. How fast can you run?" it asked.

"Fine." She punched the cube out and fished the bottle of vinegar out, dropping the incriminating material in to fizz and dissolve merrily.

"Buckley, execute full and complete shutdown. Now."

"Oh, sure, *I'm* expendable! What the hell, it's probably less painful this way. Bye," it finished glumly. The screen went dark.

Cally barely noticed it out of the corner of her eye, as she was busily yanking her silks back on.

The door slid open before she got the front seal half fastened. It was Pryce, and somehow she didn't think his pallor had anything to do with the drugs. She was staring down the business end of his nine mil sidearm, held very steadily.

"It was you?! Oh my God . . . You're under arrest," he said.

"Pryce—" She extended a hand.

"Actually it's Stewart. Major General James Stewart."

Her shoulders slumped. "A setup."

A splash of blood and bits of gore exploded forward from his stomach as the door slid open again, and he slid to the floor, hands clamped across the wound, staring down at it.

"That serves you, you poaching insolent pipsqueak. She was mine!" General Beed stepped over Stewart and to the side, kicking the other man's dropped gun away. He looked up at Cally. "And you get it straight—you may be a whore, but you're my wh—"

He was cut off in the middle of the word as the gray blur that was Cally rolled and came up with Pryce's gun, firing into Beed two to the chest and then into the head, firing until the slide locked back on an empty chamber.

"I think he's dead," Stewart choked wryly, "and I won't be long after. Hurry, now. As good as you are, you've got to have a way out planned." His voice was ragged but gentle.

"No." She slid across the floor to him and looked at his wound just a moment before ripping off the top half of her silks, tearing the tough Galtech fabric like paper. She folded it quickly and expertly into a field bandage and moved his hands, pressing it over the wound, hard, before it could gush.

"Never any damned Hiberzine when you need it, eh?" She smiled mistily at him, clamping the other hand over the entrance wound in his back.

"You're not going to die on me." She was firm, as if that was not allowed.

"I think I love you, whoever you are." He coughed, leaving flecks of blood on his lips.

She was actually thankful when the squad of MP's burst through the door, bare seconds later.

"He needs Hiberzine. Now!" she ordered.

One of them was already pulling a syringe from the kit at his belt.

"Captain Makepeace, or Jane Doe, you are under arrest." The Brigade XO, Colonel Tartaglia, had elected to lead the squad himself. Clearly, they had come in response to a call placed by Pry— General Stewart rather than in response to shots fired.

"I know." Free from the need to stop his blood loss by another MP taking her place, Cally let one bloody hand caress his jaw, before his eyes closed and a pair of MP's pulled her to her feet.

"You get General Stewart to the hospital." The colonel gestured to three of the MP's. "The rest of you, bring her. And pay attention!" He waved at Beed's corpse. "She's dangerous as hell."

Titan Base, Tuesday, June 18, 19:45

On the shuttle, Jay's PDA and his AID beeped at the same moment. Since the message was urgent, and their game was not, the game autopaused and opened the incoming file.

Jay was the first to react, not being surprised by the news. Unfortunately for him, reactions honed in the brutally Darwinian environment of battle do not fade as long as the body is fit. Tommy Sunday was very fit.

The desperate flying tackle knocked Sunday out of his seat, but the blow that would have shattered his trachea never landed, skidding harmlessly aside off of a raised forearm.

In the enclosed confines of the freight shuttle's cockpit, Tommy's size was not an asset. Still, in the wrestling match that followed, Jay's hand-to-hand training in the gym, while excellent for what it was, couldn't match a combat veteran's front-line down and dirty fighting experience, kept honed by regular training. Humans didn't fight like Posleen, true. But Tommy knew to within a hair what his own body would do, and had ingrained a few dirty tricks the other man had never heard of.

Later, Tommy could never precisely describe the sequence of moves in that cramped, desperate fight. At least, he never told it the same way twice. All he was really sure of was that by the time Papa O'Neal came through the door to find him sitting beside Jay's body, catching his breath, his groin was on fire with pain and Jay was missing an eye, had two broken fingers, a broken neck, and was suffering from a severe and permanent case of dead.

"Did you send it through to Earth yet?" the older man asked matter-of-factly, stepping over the corpse to get to the communications equipment.

"No, not yet." Tommy shook his head, getting up and easing gingerly into a chair.

O'Neal harrumphed and tapped at the keys for a few moments, encrypting the data and sending it through a roundabout system of radio relays that sent it out to Earth as a three times repeated squeal of noise embedded in a routinely intercepted voice signal.

"What do we do with him?" Tommy nodded at the body.

"Put him in the cargo hold. It's nice and cold in there. He'll keep." He rummaged through a shirt pocket for his tobacco pouch. "Never waste a perfectly good corpse if you can avoid it. You never know when you might need one."

"What about Cally?"

"You obviously didn't see the end of the message. Warm up the engines just in case, but . . ." His face was bleak as he inserted a plug in his cheek and repocketed the pouch.

Tommy picked his AID back up and had it display the file so he could read it, this time thoroughly, down to the codes at the bottom that meant, in the judgment of her PDA, that capture of the agent was imminent, rescue or escape unlikely, presume any future transmissions compromised.

"Hey, buckley's always pessimistic, right?" he said.

Springfield, Tuesday, June 18, 19:55

Given the Bane Sidhe's experience of thousands of years of the Darhel playing hell with their communications security for any form of electromechanical data transmission, face-to-face meetings were regarded the most relatively secure and safe means of passing information the organization had, and was mandated as a major part of SOP. It had only taken a few catastrophic losses from the ranks of the Cybers in the early days of cooperation to convince them of the wisdom of the policy. One consequence of the policy was that in addition to specific high-impact ops, teams like Hector and Isaac were routinely rotated through information gathering assignments that involved traveling an assigned circuit and picking up physical reports from agents in place.

While it was generally the best use of limited resources, where practical, to split the team and send each agent on a segment of the route, effective coordination of efforts required periodic face-to-face meetings during the field cycle. Good intelligence had an unfortunate tendency to become stale quickly. The meeting allowed one team member to collect the take of the entire team and pass it upstream to a base courier before returning to his own circuit.

Levon liked the Wexford. Not so much this particular pub as cheap little dives that attracted a such a mixed bag of people that as long as you didn't get loud or dance on the tables, nobody looked at you twice. They never used a particular place for a field face-to-face more than three times in ten years if they could help it. This was the Wexford's second time for that dubious honor.

Automatically, he scanned the bar with his eyes as he came in, taking a quick visual overview and mentally cataloging what he'd seen as he picked an empty table against the wall and sat in a seat that gave him a good easy view of the door. *A man and woman at the bar, looks like he's trying to pick her up and possibly succeeding. A couple of gentlemen in a booth, very fit, but also obviously interested in each other. A man drinking alone at a table by the window, staring out at the street. A man and woman in the back booth, holding hands across the table somewhat furtively. Path past the kitchen to the back exit was clear.*

A determinedly cheerful waitress came over and he ordered a pitcher of hard cider and a cheeseburger. Okay, so it was junk food. At least it didn't have any corn or soybeans in it.

Barry got there before the cider did, so he was able get his food ordered and pour himself a cold pint, using the cover of looking through the menu to pass a cube out onto the table, blocked from prying eyes by the various items on the table. Levon lit a cigarette, palming the cube while adjusting the ashtray. He wasn't, personally, all that fond of the taste of the things, it just made such a damned good cover for moving your hands around.

Sam came in almost on Barry's heels, a short, gently rounded girl with mouse brown hair curling around her ears. He felt her cube drop in his jacket pocket as she leaned over to give him a peck on the cheek before walking back around to sit by Barry.

George, predictably, was late. You could set a clock by his son-in-law. When you saw him walk through the door, it was invariably twenty minutes after he'd been supposed to be there. He swore he didn't do it on purpose, and he could always spin you a yarn about whatever it was that had delayed him. The only time he was on time was when he had to make a hit or coordination was absolutely mission critical—then he was there on the dot. His wife liked to tease him about it. Personally, Levon thought he just got so caught up in his cover role that sometimes he *acted* like the teenager he was supposed to be.

The first sign he had that something was wrong was when everybody but the waitress and bartender started moving at once. He barely had time to dump the cubes in his cider before one of them was on him, taking advantage of his momentary distraction to jab something into his thigh. He tried to get his pistol in play from under his shirt, but the man knocked it from his hand. Barry and Sam each had their first man on the floor by the time he recovered his balance enough to snap the neck of his. And he doubted he would have taken him down that soon if the man hadn't hesitated, obviously expecting whatever he'd injected to have an immediate effect. The ring of shots told him that at least one of his people had gotten a pistol into play, but the dead man's ten seconds worked against them, the shots ending after the first two.

As he traded blows with the woman from the back booth, he had an instant to reflect that whatever was in the needle must have been one of the things his nannites were programmed to sweep out immediately, thank God. This girl was pretty good, but she lacked the strength and power of one of the Bane Sidhe's upgraded female agents. After years against agents in the gym, and men in the field, it was easy to forget how low on upper body strength unmodified women were.

The two gay guys joining in against him made it a real fight, and as he saw and heard the uniformed Fleet Strike troops pouring through the front and back doors, the bar staff having wisely disappeared behind the bar, he knew that this wasn't one they were going to get out of. Fighting that many without maneuvering room it was impossible to block everything. He saw the fist coming towards his head for just a second. *Oh, fuck...*

Afterwards, Bobby was real proud of his agents. They'd patiently waited until all three of the targets—the fourth one hadn't shown—were clear of the building before taking their shots. The first two were in near unison. The third had taken a couple of seconds too long and as a result needed three shots to put his target down.

Fortunately, his backup men were good enough to use their own rifles to confuse the Fleet Strike pukes about the direction of incoming fire long enough to cover their withdrawal.

The only bad thing was that the no show kept the mission from being a complete success. Some things just couldn't be helped.

Cheryl Martin barely restrained herself from throwing her PDA to the floor of the cab and stomping on it. Bare seconds after the shots started, the damned thing had beeped at her.

"Yes?" she snapped.

"Pinwheel. Pinwheel. Repeat, pinwheel." It had that slight colorless quality she associated with synthesized voices.

"Kevin, is there something I can kill around here?" she said.

"Cheryl, I'm so sor—wait!" He spun the cab up on the sidewalk, blocking the forward progress of a short, brown-haired man. "Grab him. Gently."

The rear driver's side door of the cab swung open and the man stopped in the middle of what had been a smooth, rapid motion, swaying a bit as he recovered his balance from suddenly aborting whatever he'd been going to do.

"Cheryl?" he croaked.

"No time, get in. Trade codes on the way." She yanked him, unresisting, into the back of the cab, which didn't even wait for the door to finish closing before backing up and finishing its U-turn, speeding off into the night.

"Pumpernickel. It all went to hell. We think you're the only one that got out. Good to see you, son, but why the hell weren't you in there?" She fidgeted with her purse, coming up with a pack of tissues she knew she was going to need any minute now.

"The rest of my team?"

"Not good. Come on, George, answer her." Kevin met his eyes in the rearview mirror.

"I was . . . I was late." His shoulders slumped.

"And you were walking because?" the other man prompted.

"I . . . I . . . ah, hell, I got stuck behind the *second* big fucking wreck I ran into on the way here just a mile up the road, and it was so screwed up I figured I'd get here faster on foot. If I'd been there . . ." He trailed off numbly.

"It wouldn't have helped," Cheryl mumbled.

"You don't know that." His voice was bitter.

"Yeah, we do. Unfortunately." The cab drove on.

Titan Base, Tuesday, June 18, 20:00

The Tir was awakened out of a sound sleep by the melodious chiming of his AID. It took the usual three measured breaths to fight down the urge to kill something. The AID, out of long experience, heard and correctly interpreted the change in the pace of his breathing, waiting patiently until its master was more controlled.

"Intercept of local transmissions indicates the live capture of an enemy agent. Agent is in the custody of Fleet Strike personnel, currently in transit to the Detention Facility Dome for processing and interrogation," it said.

"Get me the Human Minister of Defense. Date a resolution of a Council of Ministers' vote from now appointing me an authorized observer for the Council based on the commercial ramifications of the espionage. Cite appropriate precedents and get the signoffs of the other Ministers' AIDs, of course. Forward the resolution to the Human Minister." His ears pricked in sudden alertness, whiskers twitching in barely leashed excitement.

"Resolution transmitted. Stand by for the human Li." The cool, melodic voice combined with his breathing exercise to restore him to his usual full control.

"Cancel that personal contact. Instruct him to pass the relevant orders down the line. Have his AID ensure that it is done immediately. Monitor the passage of orders and inform me when they get down to the guards at the detention center." Avoiding personal contact was better in this case. The more intelligent and competent the human underling, the more nervous they tended to be as recipients of direct, personal Darhel attention. Normally, this was a plus, but at the moment he needed efficiency more than intimidation.

He motioned with one hand for his body servants to attend him. He hated going out late at night, but it couldn't be helped. They had his sleeping robe halfway over his head when the AID chimed again.

"Traffic analysis data, Your Tir."

"Report." At least he was already awake.

"Our human service providers report the unfortunate demise of three hostile agents. Traffic records a transmission immediately prior to the capture of local enemy agent by Fleet Strike personnel. Area of transmission was department that initially provided the intercepted data revealing these specific enemy agents. Projected transmission and processing times suggest this leak as the probable cause of the fourth identified hostile agent failing to meet as scheduled with our human service providers," it said.

"One in the hand here, for one out of reach there. A favorable trade." He stalled the Indowy with the waking robe with a brief gesture, motioning for another to bring a plate of food. After it left, he allowed the first to resume robing him. He would need to eat before transit to the Detention Center. He would also have his traveling attendant bring stimulants. It was likely to be a long night.

Chicago, Tuesday, June 18, 20:25

AIDs were both a blessing and curse. Peter Vanderberg's wife tended to be a bit jealous of Jenny. Oh, she hadn't been at first, but a wife could only hear a female voice reminding her husband of personal appointments, time to take his medicine, errands to run, interrupting casually at even the most intimate moments for just so long before beginning to get just a bit ticked off. The crowning indignity was, of course, Peter knew, her having to watch his own growing emotional attachment to Jenny. Explaining that it was a normal design feature for greater efficiency did *not* help.

Ultimately, a separation had been his only recourse. He hadn't been willing to lose his wife, and he'd finally seen that the only way to preserve his marriage had been to ensure that his wife virtually never had to endure contact with Jenny. Strangely, although his AID had resented the exclusion from certain portions of his life and had gotten quite snippy at first, ultimately she had seemed happier, too. But an AID couldn't be jealous of the other woman, could it?

Anyway, the compromise meant that instead of his AID chiming in whenever a message came in, she very lightly vibrated if the message was urgent, so he could excuse himself, and otherwise he checked in once an hour or so. And usually he followed up immediately if she indicated he had an urgent message. Tonight, it being Jane's birthday, he had known better and had had to wait a few minutes before excusing himself. When Jenny buzzed him a second time, he figured it must be pretty important. He tactfully excused himself for the restroom. Jane's eyes narrowed a bit as he left. He doubted she was fooled.

"Jenny, I hope this message really is urgent. Jane's birthday is very important to me." *Okay, not getting Jane pissed at me by her thinking I've slighted her birthday is important to me. Same difference. I was hoping to get laid tonight, not be in the doghouse.*

"I'm sorry, Peter. You have two urgent messages. Morrison unfortunately has to report failure. They had them, but snipers on the roof killed the prisoners before they could be fully secured. Colonel Tartaglia on behalf of General Stewart reports a success, however. They have captured an enemy agent alive and transported her to the Detention Center on Titan Base for interrogation. Oh, third message. Defense Minister Li advises you and your subordinates that a Darhel delegation under the leadership of the Minister of Commerce and Trade, the Tir Dol Ron, will be observing the interrogation. Your orders are to ensure that your people give the Tir's delegation every assistance," it said.

"That's weird." *Um . . . better think about that in private.* "Jenny, relay the orders to General Stewart and Colonel Tartaglia. Uh . . . Jenny, does the message say why it was sent by the Colonel and what happened to General Beed?"

"General Beed is deceased, at the hands of the prisoner, one Captain Sinda Makepeace, his secretary. Or a Jane Doe masquerading as a Fleet Strike captain, although Fleet Strike biometric procedures make that impossible, of course. General Stewart was injured in the conflict and is currently unconscious and undergoing medical treatment. Full recovery is anticipated."

"Thanks, Jenny. Again, please hold any messages unless they are urgent." *Or I may not get to sleep in my own bed tonight.*

"Certainly, Peter. I understand," it cooed softly.

Under a cornfield in Indiana, Tuesday, June 18, 20:30

The Indowy Aelool took a small sip of his water and returned to a socially acceptable state of quiet contemplation. Normally, in Nathan O'Reilly's office he tried to interact a bit more in the human custom of little talk. It seemed to put his friend at ease.

Given the present situation and the continuing repercussions of the Cally O'Neal debacle, and the presence of the Indowy Roolnai, more traditionally decorous behavior was the better political move.

Roolnai had left his water untouched, disdaining to interrupt his contemplation, perhaps as a subtle rebuke to Aelool. Perhaps just to control personal nervousness. It was, after all, a tense situation they were gathered to monitor.

It was not turning out to be a good night for the Bane Sidhe.

Roolnai's AID chirped a rapid rush of Indowy. Roolnai raised his head and turned to O'Reilly.

"It is confirmed that the Human Cally O'Neal has been captured alive. It is confirmed that none of Team Hector was taken alive, neither due to our intervention nor their competence, but instead due to the Darhel's unwillingness to let Fleet Strike have those live agents. We presume the reason is that there are no Darhel currently on Earth to monitor or control the interrogations. Such is not the case on Titan. The Tir Dol Ron will preside there. We are also extremely fortunate that the perhaps precipitous action to retrieve one agent from Team Hector was adequately covered by the O'Neal transmission. Our information sources have not been compromised." As Roolnai spoke, Aelool hoped that O'Reilly was not enough of an adept at their language to catch the very subtle patronization in the tone. He was not confident in that hope. There was a slight glint in O'Reilly's eye that often accompanied human perceptions of subtleties.

"Thomas, please display a hologram of the military detention facility on Titan Base. Analyze defenses for possible weaknesses," he instructed his AID.

"Visual, or structural image?" it asked.

"Structural please," he said.

"Excuse me, Base Commander O'Reilly, but might I ask the purpose of this exercise?" Roolnai's voice was cool.

"To evaluate the possibilities for an extraction, of course," he replied absently, obviously already absorbed in contemplating the image.

"One might ask first whether an extraction would be a wise use of limited resources." The more senior Indowy spoke with the exquisite deference that usually accompanied an immovably firm position.

"I fail to see the harm in evaluating the feasibility, costs, and risks of an extraction." *If I do not smooth over the crack, the entire foundation of this alliance is at stake. Does Roolnai realize the insult he offers to the humans by their standards? I certainly hope that this is unintentional on his part.*

"Is false hope a harm? When retrieving the agent without damage that will render her incapable of being restored to reliable operational status is already so very unlikely?" Roolnai was bland. Too bland.

"Perhaps not. I find I am tired, my friends. It's been a long night and apparently there is little more we can accomplish together, in any case." The O'Reilly had stood and turned away. In Indowy body language, it was a gesture of polite fatigue. It was Aelool's fear that the behavior might have more significance. Knowing both his friend Nathan and his friend Roolnai, talking further with both together at this point would only increase the rift. He'd have to work on them separately.

Roolnai had already immediately reacted in polite fashion and was moving for the door. Aelool followed, pausing briefly in the doorway.

"Friend Nathan, would it be possible to continue our game of chess tomorrow afternoon? Is there a time you might find convenient?" The offer was on the table. The pause worried him for a moment.

"I'd like that. I don't know my schedule, but if Thomas could talk to your AID?"

Aelool nodded. Good. The breach was not final. At least, not yet.

Titan, Fleet Strike Detention Center, Tuesday, June 18, 21:00

"So, who is she?" Robert Tartaglia had not been enamored of his late CO's eccentricities, but he had not wanted him dead. Especially not if his death would in any way taint the promotion he had long since genuinely earned on merit. And it was certainly odd that she had apparently killed Beed in defense of *General* Stewart. And he sure never would have guessed *that* guy for a counterintelligence agent. Which was the point, of course, but still . . . It was going to be weird saluting a new CO he'd been used to thinking of as a screw-up kid first john. Guy was a real James Bond. Imagine, having the spy so ga-ga over him she'd actually waited around to be captured out of concern for *his* life. Talk about a ladies' man. The dorky first john, *General* Stewart, his new CO. It was just too fucking weird for words. He realized Baker was looking at him funny.

"Sorry, Baker, could you repeat that?" he said.

"I said we don't know who she is. She isn't Sinda Makepeace." Agent Sam Baker was a bit rumpled from coming back in after a full day's work. Civvies, no matter how well made, had nothing on silks for standing up to extended wear and still looking good. Baker probably would have preferred to wear silks, but it was against regulation for the warrant officers assigned to CID, where keeping rank out of investigations was essential to the job. "Fingerprints match, DNA matches, voiceprint doesn't. She sounds like her, and she's obviously very well coached. But she sure as hell isn't Captain Makepeace. For one thing, our Mata Hari bitched about the poor quality of the local coffee but regularly drank it. The real Captain Makepeace loathed coffee—was a tea drinker. I wonder how they missed that."

"Cover identities always miss something. So when's the database search on the voiceprint going to be back so we'll know who she is? Do I have time to go grab a cup of coffee?" He quirked an eyebrow at the younger man.

"I'm sorry, sir. I wasn't clear enough. The database searches *are* all back. She's not in them. Any of them. According to the system, she doesn't exist," he said.

"Makepeace has an evil twin, Skippy? Or a clone?" His tone was dubious.

"No twin, and no clone with any technology we know about.

Oh, also, we got one of Makepeace's high school sweethearts on the phone. He said she had a vaguely triangular mole on her front, to the left, down in the bikini area. No mole on Mata Hari."

"Careful with that, Sam. Mata Hari's obviously got some phenomenal powers of attraction." He was only half joking. The woman was a looker, and had already provoked one man to kill over her.

"Yes, sir. Those were farther up, sir."

"Baker, you've had more interrogation experience than just about anyone else we've got because of your organized crime work with the local tongs. We need to get the ball rolling in anticipation of General Stewart's return to duty. Consider yourself TDY to the detention center for the duration, or until the general decides otherwise. I'm gonna go grab some coffee." He got up to leave but was stopped by the extended hand from a voluminous robe. The hand had some serious claws.

"A moment of your time, if you please, Colonel." The Tir's voice was melodious, almost hypnotic. The colonel might have enjoyed listening to him if having him here weren't such a pain in the ass. But orders were orders.

"Yes, Your Tir. What can I do for you?" Tartaglia nodded as Baker caught his eye and wordlessly excused himself to both provide his absence and go get his XO some coffee. A good man.

"While I certainly think Fleet Strike's man should participate in the interrogation as a learning experience, in a spirit of what you would call interservice cooperation, Fleet has generously agreed to provide a highly experienced interrogation team. I would think, given how close to the prisoner Fleet Strike personnel have been, that that would be a wise move. If you would consider a friendly suggestion, of course." His smile bared teeth, and the Indowy servant at his elbow reminded Tartaglia a bit of a rabbit caught in the headlights of a car back home.

Bob Tartaglia was nobody's fool, and he hadn't reached the rank of full colonel in Fleet Strike's very competitive career atmosphere without displaying the finely tuned political skills of an adept. Oh, he was a good enough leader to feel a certain disdain for certain aspects of the politics. But he could certainly recognize the lay of the land when he saw it. The Tir would not be here without the orders having originated at the very top of the chain of command.

Polite suggestions from the Tir, if disregarded, would quickly come down the chain as full fledged orders.

"That sounds like wise advice, Your Tir. Would you happen to know when these loaned personnel from Fleet will be available to us?"

"Far be it for me to interfere with the chain of command that you humans value so highly. However, my understanding is that the personnel Fleet is so generously loaning are conveniently next door in the SP Detention Annex and can be here virtually as soon as you give the order to admit them. They've been quite considerate, don't you think?" If Darhel had been feline, the Tir would have been purring.

"How very thoughtful of them." One of Tartaglia's first acts after the demise of his former CO had been to dispatch an MP to his quarters to fetch his AID. Getting used to working without Suzanne over the past weeks had not exactly inclined him to lament the late general's passing. Now he had her relay the order to the MP's on guard at the front gate in the main entrance lock lobby, releasing a slow breath as the Darhel and his Indowy servant glided off to wherever they were choosing to be. He tried not to let it show how personally satisfied he was that where the Darhel had chosen to be was elsewhere.

CHAPTER SIXTEEN

Titan Base, Fleet Strike Detention Center, Tuesday, June 18, 21:30

The interrogation room had one-way glass, but not on the ground floor. Instead, it had two-story ceilings and the one-way glass formed a full perimeter of the rather large room. It reminded Sam Baker of a fish tank. At this point, since they had no idea who their prisoner actually was, and she wouldn't say word one to any of his people, he had pulled the MP's from the room, hoping that observing her alone would help them start to build a file that would eventually lead to a positive identification. Currently, the prisoner was dancing, very energetically. It was incredibly odd behavior, especially in the rather ugly prison-orange jumpsuit, but was more data for the file. Of course, they might not need that file after all. They'd probably know everything including what she had for breakfast by morning.

The SP detachment had arrived a few minutes ago under a lieutenant, j.g., one Wong Yan-Feng accompanied by a medic and a senior chief with very old eyes. Its presence was a calculated insult to Fleet Strike and tended to make the hair on his neck rise a bit. Still, with modern interrogation drugs, they could save a whole lot of time and the medic appeared to have a full set, including several that Fleet Strike internal regulations did not approve for use on prisoners. If Fleet's medic could get this whole mess over with so he could get back to his own cases, he didn't have a problem with it.

The whole platoon of SP's struck him as incredible overkill for one prisoner, and made him vaguely uneasy, but as soon as they shot her full of drugs it was going to all be over anyway, so it was probably just somebody with too much a sense of inter-service rivalry trying to rub their noses in the insult.

The detachment had brought their own tea along with their supplies, and the lieutenant, j.g., sat with a fresh cup while the senior chief and the SP's went in with a gurney, to strap the prisoner to it in preparation for the medic. Baker revised his opinion about the necessity for the number of men, after trank darts appeared to have no effect and given that four men were on the ground and several others appeared the worse for wear, in spite of swarming her, by the time they got her strapped down. He wouldn't have believed a woman, even a combat trained one, would be that strong. He wouldn't have expected it from most men, frankly, and he had worked beside her for weeks, besides. What in the hell *was* she?

Her response to the interrogation drugs, even the really nasty ones, closely resembled boredom. Good God. Maybe the Fleet team was *not* overkill. Finally, the medic made one last injection, not even bothering to wait for its effects, or lack of them, before leaving the room, leaving the SP's who were still standing, including the one that had finally gotten up, to drag their fellows from the room.

It was almost half an hour before the medic reappeared with the chief and a mixed squad of SP's. The chief stopped at attention in front of the lieutenant.

"We'll need another five men, sir. Two of them permanently." Senior Chief Yi Chang Ho's face was a study in impassivity.

"You will get them." The only indication of emotion in the officer's face was a few rapid blinks, quickly resolving into stillness.

"What's the last thing you gave her?" Baker just had to know.

"A little Provigil-C. If you were building super agents, would *you* make them immune to it? Task people to observing her overnight. If she doesn't sleep, we can keep feeding in the sleep suppressors without boosting her alertness. It may be effective. Someone will need to go in and untie her. It will make observations about her sleep or lack of it more accurate." His nametag read "PO1 Liao Chien."

Baker suppressed the surprising tendency to swallow hard. But he wasn't about to be responsible for letting Fleet Strike look bad in front of these smug Fleet bastards and the Darhel VIP. He ordered in a platoon of MP guards to loosen her bonds and make as graceful a tactical retreat with the gurney as the situation would allow.

Fortunately, she didn't seem as interested in harming men who were setting her loose as she was men who were strapping her down. No additional casualties. Just an immediate return to her dancing. He was starting to recognize it. It appeared to be the same dance, over and over. Tartaglia had joined him at the glass, taking a thoughtful sip of his coffee.

"I wonder what she's dancing to?" he said.

Titan Base, Fleet Strike Detention Center, Tuesday, June 18, 21:30

They're not going to extract me. They probably won't even try. I'll die in here, under torture. The recuperative powers are great . . . usually. The only thing I can control is how long it takes—at least, so long as they're stupid enough to let me loose in here. Eventually, my body's reserves will give out and I'll die. The less reserves, the sooner that will be. Sooner is good. So here we are back to Sister Dorcas in SERE. Damn, I hated that sadistic bitch. Find an anchor. He's alive, whatever he turned out to be, he's alive. That's one. The last song we made love to. That's a good anchor. I know it by heart. I could dance forever to it, and no matter what they do to me, it reminds me of anchor number one. He's alive. Okay, something to hold onto, and a plan. Check.

And I really could dance forever to this. How could she have known, singing so long ago. Just like this. But he took the numbness away. And until now I never even realized it. How ironic. Only really alive now, when I'm about to die.

They won't be playing patty-cake with me forever. Best get as much done as I can, before they get wise. And I was frozen in my heart. So cold. At least . . . at least I had him for a little while.

Oop. Here come the bastards, and with a gurney and Fleet pukes, they mean business. Darhel goons instead of honest soldiers, would be my guess. It would take their manipulations to get Fleet involved. No reason not to take on a few just on general principles. Maybe I'll get lucky and rush somebody into killing me.

Titan Base Freight Port, Tuesday, June 18, 23:00

The transmission time lag between Earth and Titan Base, especially when the signal was getting encrypted, hidden underneath another transmission as static, and bounced around six ways from Sunday to hide both sender and recipient, was a pain in the ass even under normal circumstances.

As it was, Papa O'Neal was twisting a finger in his ear as if he couldn't believe what he had just heard, and Tommy was afraid he was about to be treated to the legendary temper attributed to redheads.

"Are you sitting there and telling me that this organization I just devoted thirty plus years of my considerable professional expertise to is actually refusing to even *consider* the practical feasibility of an extraction for my granddaughter, who has *also* just devoted thirty plus years of *her* considerable expertise to said organization? Please tell me that that is *not* what you're saying, O'Reilly." His teammate and mentor's eyes were cold, colder than Tommy had ever seen them. On the other hand, the way he felt right now, his own probably looked very similar.

The lag was interminable. Unfortunately, it gave both of them ample time to build up a fine head of steam. Fortunately, it also gave plenty of time to think of potential responses and counter responses and choose the ones most likely to be effective and least likely to be inflammatory and counterproductive. Every second was necessary.

"Mike, for what it's worth, and it may be worth a lot, I agree with you. This is not over. By no means. I'll be meeting with Aelool tomorrow and will see what I can do. Mike, you and Sunday are top notch operatives. None better. I'll tell you what—while discussions are still pending, run up some analyses and contingency plans. There's no sense wasting your valuable time while we work through the process from this end." Father Nathan's eyes seemed to plead for understanding and time. Tommy could feel a cold, numb rage begin to radiate out from his center. This was Iron Mike's daughter for God's sake.

"Nathan, I would strongly suggest that you remind our little green friends that humans are *not* Indowy, and that we're not inclined to be *their* water-boys anymore than we are for the Darhel. I would suggest that you put that reminder in the strongest terms possible. Loyalty down the chain to the memories of deceased agents is one thing. Loyalty down the chain to live and breathing agents had better be high on their list of priorities. And that particular principle has nothing to do with my relationship to this agent. If they're even considering that it's going to be acceptable to the human side of the organization to use denying an extraction, without even considering feasibility, as a way to get permanently rid of loyal agents they may have a problem with, then they need to know that they probably don't have two human operatives in North America who will agree to work under those conditions. Make sure they know that. From me." His tone was clipped and precise, enunciating each word carefully.

"Mike, all I can do at this point is to authorize you to work on those contingency plans and ask you to trust me. I would hope that I've earned that much over the years," he said.

"For now, Nathan, I can deal with that. You need to get back to us with an update on this. Soon. Sir. O'Neal out." As he spat into a coffee cup he'd bought on base for the purpose, his face had a bitter tinge that Tommy couldn't recall ever seeing before.

Titan Base, Fleet Strike Detention Center, Wednesday, June 19, 03:00

Obviously that last shot had been Provigil-C. Felt like a quarter-dose. She knew what would come next. The "R" in SERE training was finally making itself useful after all. Forcible sleep deprivation to induce hallucinations and sleep-dep psychosis. No problem. Oh, she'd go just as loopy as anybody, but what she wouldn't do was give up information. Now, as to what else she *would* do, that was anybody's guess. She wouldn't want to be the poor schmuck who walked into a room with *her* in that condition.

Meanwhile, they'd done her a tremendous unintentional favor by giving her an unmolested night to work with and the energy to use it effectively. *Yeah, baby, go ahead and wake me up. One-two-three-four-five-six-seven-eight! Nice, clean jazz hands, and a stretch up to the sky and spin and down, push up to stand, hip walk to stage left, then round-off into a back handspring into a back flip half-twist, into a front handspring, and strut back towards center stage and turn, hands back feet spread, roll the head across the front and up and spin and spin and spin and stop and kick up into a vertical split, back down. . . .*

It was going to be a long night but she was up for it.

Under a cornfield in Indiana, Wednesday, June 19, 09:30

"Are we at a stalemate here?" Nathan O'Reilly clearly was not talking about the chessboard, which had at least five moves to mate, if the Indowy across from him made a particular mistake. And that was one of the shorter options.

"I do not know. Possibly. And it gives me grief to admit it. You humans cannot, or will not be other than what you are. And I have observed enough humans and read enough of your history to know that human organizations without what you call down chain loyalty simply do not work. They collapse of their own weight, as a tower whose antigrav fails." His hands crossed briefly in the equivalent of a shrug.

"I understand why loyalty that only goes up the chain, Your Loolnieth, works for the Indowy. But don't you have true reciprocal obligations in arrangements between clans? Can't your people be persuaded to see the analogy?"

"I truly do not think relations between the Indowy of the Bane Sidhe and our human friends can go on as they have been. But your analogy interests me. Would it be possible for me to ask for some time to contemplate it without offending you? I do not know what may be done with it, but there is a leaf just beyond the reach of my hand. Alone, perhaps my thoughts can climb the tree." He stood and almost turned, stopping and putting a hand on O'Reilly's arm, instead.

"You do realize that I do not turn away from you or your species, that my need for contemplation is genuine, do you not?" The slight tilt of his head evinced concern.

"You don't have to prove yourself to me, old friend. I trust *you*." The priest withdrew and was gone.

Titan Base, Fleet Strike Detention Center, Wednesday, June 19,
10:00

General James Stewart's doctors were none too happy to have
him up and about the morning after being gut-shot. He had given
them little choice. When they had waked him briefly to ask about
certain necessary arrangements while he was undergoing regen, he
had instead ordered them to stitch what could be stitched, and
use surgical synthetics for what had to be patched. While true regen
on the stitched parts could be continued with injections, the
synthetics would have to be removed and would cause the regen-
eration process to ultimately take twice as long as it should.

The doctors had been even more unhappy when General
Vanderberg had refused to allow them to overrule the general on
medical grounds. But then, the military medical profession was
pretty much agreed that general officers made lousy patients.

So here he was this morning, looking down at Sind. . . .
Sometime in the night Mata Hari had been abbreviated by the
watchers to Mahri. He supposed there was some logic to having
something to call her. For him, it only underscored the pain of
not even knowing her name.

Two tall robed figures trailed by a couple of Indowy—strange
sometimes how quickly humanity had gotten used to little green
men—were approaching him, or the line of seats placed near him.
Apparently, they had some interest in him, since they were stopping by his wheelchair, ignoring the medic hovering behind him
with syringes full of medical nannites.

The Tir Dol Ron, and the Tir Dad Lin, according to his AID.
He knew enough not to laugh or smirk or even show surprise at
the Darhel with the funny name. One was the trade minister and
the other the minister of education, who actually handled pro-
paganda and public relations, such as it was. What they really were
were cabinet level officials of a Galactic Federation where the
Cabinet ran the show. In the words of Sergeant Franks, to whom
he owed at least a mental apology, the V-est of IP's.

"We wish to express our appreciation and approval for the
apprehension of this person. We would like to assure you that you
have greatly enhanced the interests of Galactic Security. We are
certain that you have a bright future within the Fleet Strike
Organization." The voice was so beautiful he barely restrained the

urge to vomit. The Tirs appeared to be waiting for something from him. When he merely nodded silently, the Tir Dol Ron started to lift one corner of his lip, revealing the edge of a very pointed tooth, but his eyes flickered to Stewart's injuries and he appeared to relax. The two turned abruptly and proceeded to a pair of the seats, hesitating for a moment while the Indowy with them moved the seats closer to the glass.

Below, "Mahri" was still dancing frantically, nonstop, in the fluorescent orange jumpsuit that had replaced her grays. It made his chest hurt.

When the Fleet team came trooping back in, Stewart watched them from behind his best poker face—and his best was very good indeed. Tartaglia, perhaps anticipating his new CO's likely needs, had sent Baker home for sleep around zero hundred, electing to stay in command of observation through the night. Consequently, when the medic wheeled him in this morning, Baker had been here, bright eyed and bushy tailed, ready to brief him in person. Experientially, Beed's paranoia hadn't been a total loss. Following Baker's lead, Stewart had handed his AID to the Medic and ordered the visibly unhappy man to take a walk.

At that point, Baker had been free to fill Stewart in with a complete no-shitter on each of the Fleet personnel, the Darhel delegation, and events of the night before. Which meant that when the Fleet platoon, plus fresh meat and Dr. Mengele, came trooping in, he knew who was who.

Baker was in his forties. Old enough to think he'd seen the world and be mostly right, but remarkably sheltered in some ways. In Baker's world the MP's and the good soldiers were the good guys, and the tongs and the scumbags were the bad guys. You prosecuted one, and the other helped you. Well, more or less.

Baker had no idea what was coming. Or if he did, it was just at the level of a slight foreboding that he shrugged off. Stewart, with his considerably more complex understanding of the world knew exactly what was going to happen, and exactly how little power he had to stop it.

He was also going to have to watch Baker and protect his ass. Underneath an agent's gruff exterior, Baker really was the boyscout Pryce had pretended to be. It had been an asset in his work with the tongs, rendering him amazingly incorruptible. In the present situation, it was more likely than not to get him killed or at least ruin his career when he decided he needed to Do Something.

Preventing that from happening was just one of the extra little complications life just loved to throw his way. In this case, he welcomed the distraction. He'd been sent to catch the spy, and he'd caught her. What he hadn't expected was to be involved. On the other hand, getting involved with anybody in the office, in the circumstances, had been damned stupid and his current feelings were his own damned fault. Including the guilt. The girl had sacrificed herself to save *his* hide, and wasn't *that* a fine thing for a man to have to live with.

He couldn't help swallowing heavily as the goon squad disappeared around the corner towards the lifts, reappearing shortly in the room below.

He saw immediately why the SP's had one in the infirmary and two in the morgue already. Whether she'd heard them coming or was just in a favorable position, her departure from the dance was so fluid and seamless, there were two SP's on the floor before his brain had even registered that she'd stopped dancing. Well, sort of stopped.

This time one of the SP's was either a bit smarter or a bit quicker and managed to club her over the head, dropping her so they could strap her to the gurney while she was still groggy from the knock-out.

It meant the guy hanging his head and taking a few sharp words from the chief, presumably for endangering her life.

Stewart didn't realize his hand had curled into white-knuckled claws against the arms of the chair until he felt his babysitter jab him with a hypo.

"General Stewart, sir, if you don't tell me when you're in pain I won't be able to manage it properly. Please tell me next time before it gets that bad," the medic said.

"Do you have something in that pack to counteract the wooziness, son? You'd better." *Great. All I need is to have my inhibitions to saying something indiscreet, stupid, and entirely truthful dropped in this political minefield.* The ache in his gut disappeared. The one in his chest didn't, but then, it had damn-all to do with his physical injuries.

The medic stuck something else in his arm and his head cleared almost immediately.

"Thank you. Son, if you ever again stick a mind altering drug in my conscious body without my permission, you can be prepared to receive your hypodermic as an enema. Sideways. Are we clear on that."

The man's lips tightened and it appeared he only just restrained himself from rolling his eyes, but he said, "Yes, sir," and his eyes dropped before Stewart's did.

When he noticed that her legs were strapped to the corners of the gurney, and they cut her prison jumpsuit off and removed it from under the straps in pieces, he broke out in a cold sweat.

The medic bent close to her ear, but the pickups in the room caught his voice clearly, playing it into the observation area.

"Why don't we avoid this part? What's your name?"

She tilted her head slightly away from him, staring up at the ceiling. She looked . . . bored.

Her expression didn't change when the chief motioned the first man on top of her.

Stewart started making a list of people he really needed to kill. The first man seemed to be having some sort of trouble. In any case, he was swearing in one of the Asian languages. The automatic, literal translation from the AIDs was fairly colorful. Something about monkey vomit.

The medic finally waved him off and moved between her legs, checking something before injecting a local of something into her thigh, checking his watch, waiting a few moments, reaching between her legs.

"Obviously, miss, you are not immune to muscle relaxants. What's your name?" he said.

After a few seconds of silence, he motioned the hapless sailor back into place.

The prisoner made eye contact with him and spoke.

"Sorry this is going to be about as exciting for you as screwing a soggy washcloth," she said.

"I like blondes." He grabbed a breast crudely.

"If you ate strong mint gelatin after the kimchee, you might meet more of them." The boredom on her face was absolute. He stilled suddenly, swearing again before backhanding her, scrambling off and back, his face flushed as he zipped and turned away. Her cheek reddened, but her head had never moved.

She laughed.

"Aw, too bad! Next?" If her sarcasm had been a liquid, it would have eaten a hole in the floor.

To say that the next sailor singled out by the chief looked unenthusiastic would have been an understatement.

"You'll need rape survivor therapy after this. The tongs can put you in touch with someone discreet," her voice was clinical.

"Chief, make her stop!" He looked to his NCO in rather embarrassed desperation.

Above, in the observation lounge, Baker spluttered into his coffee. Stewart had so far managed to keep him under control with a hand on his arm whenever he looked in danger of losing it.

The Darhel were virtually panting like overheated dogs, over by the glass. Stewart was glad he'd elected not to wear a sidearm.

The chief grabbed her chin and wrenched it around by main force. "You're being raped, you stupid bitch, don't you get that?! What's your name!"

"I'm not being raped. He's being raped. I'm just lying here watching amateur night."

In the lounge, one of the Darhel twitched suddenly, towards the glass, before rising and withdrawing smoothly from the room.

Below, the goon squad was withdrawing from the room, leaving "Mahri" where she was. Obviously, they were reevaluating their tactics. Poor hapless bastards. His heart just bled for them. Not.

Titan Base Freight Port, Wednesday, June 19, 12:00

Tommy was smacking his head against the heel of his palm, repeatedly, when Papa O'Neal came up for air from the Detention Center blueprints.

"Sunday, what in the hell is your problem?" The older man patted his pockets and finally came up with an empty pouch, sighed, and began digging through his backpack.

"Papa, I fucked up. I fucked up big time. It's been so long, I just never recognized him." His skin had gone a strange, sick shade of gray.

"Recognized who? Run it back to start, I'm not tracking it." He found a fresh pouch and absentmindedly cut himself a plug, turning and regarding his teammate with a patient expression.

"I should have known it was a setup. We would have known, if I'd been on the ball. Oh my God, did I ever fuck up."

"Son, if you don't start from the beginning, I'm gonna have to *hurt* you. Come on, take a deep breath and tell me about it."

"The beginning. Okay. Sarah, display the hologram of Lieutenant Joshua Pryce from our initial briefing." The AID obediently put the requested image in the air in front of them.

"So?" O'Neal's hands motioned for more.

"So I know the sonofabitch. Served with him in ACS forty-some years ago. It's just, after forty years . . . We were both in the Triple-Nickle with Mike Junior. He was the S-2 of the battalion in Rabun. If I had recognized him, we wouldn't have lost Cally."

Papa O'Neal was silent for a few seconds.

"That's a big one." He was silent for a long moment. "But after forty years . . . Besides, if you had recognized him, we wouldn't have pulled Jay out into the open. Then we would have lost no telling how many other people, possibly the whole ball game, with who-ever else Jay gave up," he reminded quietly. "So, who the hell is he, really? Obviously a juv, of course."

"He's Major General James Stewart, now. He just took command of the Third MP Brigade. He's the bastard who caught her, and he's the bastard who's in charge of whatever they're doing to her. And Mike is a fucking *father* to him!"

O'Neal stared coldly into the distance for a few minutes, jaw working. He took a long breath and released it slowly.

"That's mostly right. Don't tell me you don't know by now that the Darhel are in charge of whatever they're doing to her. Stewart is probably just now experiencing for the very first time how very closely they're pulling his strings. I mean, he has to have known it. But knowing it and experiencing it are two different things." He spat into his cup, tilting his head a bit as if something had just occurred to him.

"Don't beat yourself up, Sunday. You may have just handed us the break that's gonna get her out of there. Just . . . give me a few minutes, okay? And I mean that, no more beating yourself up." As the older man walked aft and began to pace, Tommy could actually hear him begin to hum tunelessly.

Titan Base, Fleet Strike Detention Center, Wednesday, June 19, 18:30

James Stewart had long since numbed out to the additional indignities being visited on Sinda. He supposed the numbness was composed of equal parts shock, rage, and the necessity of keeping a poker face if he was ever to get the opportunity of avenging Sinda. He wouldn't call her "Mahri"—that was the name *they* were using. Sinda wasn't her name, but it was what she had called herself to him, and that was the best he had.

He had seen some indescribably horrible things as an ACS trooper, things done by Posleen to humans, things done by humans to Posleen. In the gang, he thought he had seen some pretty horrible things done to humans by humans. A few murders, anyway.

But he had never seen anything like this done by a group of humans to another human being. He had thought he was hardened to anything. He was wrong. Still, without the ability to click on and move his mind to that cold, efficient place that built a temporary barrier against the horror, he probably would be in a cell now, or shot—well, shot *again*—and no use to anybody.

The Fleet chief, Yi, was currently giving an end-of-day report on the status of the prisoner. The list of injuries—smashed and "merely" broken bones, cuts, bruises, and burns replayed vivid images in his head. The first thing they had done, of course, had been to finish gang-raping her after resorting to the simple expedient of an improvised gag. It rendered her incapable of providing information, but the bastards had apparently decided it would have been bad form to let her win that psychological battle. And in a total bastard kind of way, he could see their point. He was still going to kill every last one of them, but he could see why they did it.

The hardest thing he'd done in years, next to calling the MPs on her in the first place, was leaving at the end of the day to go home, looking perfectly normal. He had watched them turn out the lights and run the gravity down to zero for the night, leaving her strapped down and injected with Galactic Decameth—the C part in Provigil C, minus the Provigil. And then he'd had to turn and wheel himself out the door, trailed by his own medic, who looked like a saint next to Fleet's pet monster.

Titan Base, Wednesday, June 19, 19:00

In the small room, Tommy sat on the bed, waiting, a white container the size of a cigar box in his hands, open at one end. A clean AID was clipped to his belt. It looked just like any other AID. Tonight, that was its most important job. He wore gray silks with the insignia and unit identification of long ago. If any of the surviving members of the triple nickel ACS saw him, it would look to them like they were seeing a ghost. He had gone back to his original hair and eye color, and he had never needed as much facial alteration as Cally or Papa, anyway. Oh, he was different—but not *that* different unless he wanted to be. And, of course, his frame was pretty hard to camouflage.

Out of the two vacant rooms on the hall with the quarters formerly occupied by lowly Lieutenant Pryce, and now occupied by a general the system had not yet had the opportunity to reassign, he and Papa had chosen the one closest to the transit car. Not that it mattered. One was as good as the other. A very small sticky camera sat in the slight shadow cast by the door jamb.

Papa O'Neal was in the chair, watching the hall on the screen of his PDA. He was actually watching a fast-forward of the past five minutes, since the camera only squealed its encrypted transmission when pinged, and they didn't need particularly high resolution.

"Fuck."

"What?" Tommy's eyes locked with the older man's.

"He's in a wheelchair and has someone with him. Looks like a medic." He patted his pockets absently before frowning and rubbing his chin.

"Uh . . . if Cally did that to him, he may not be all that sympathetic." Tommy looked over his shoulder and winced slightly. "He doesn't look so good."

"If you've got a better card to play, I'd be glad to hear it," he said, setting the PDA down on the desk for a second to get up and pace. "We may not be able to get to him tonight."

"He never did like doctors much," Tommy mused. "He might kick him out. I don't see any reason not to give it at least until midnight."

"Agreed." He stopped pacing and sat down, tapping a foot in uncharacteristic nervousness.

As it turned out, they didn't have to wait long at all, as the medic left and disappeared through the transit car doors almost immediately.

"Tommy?"

"Yeah?"

"Never would have guessed that he doesn't like doctors. Let's go." The red-haired man pocketed his PDA and left without looking back.

"Right. This is gonna be so weird." Tommy rubbed his hands on his silks and cleared his throat, following him out. This was the first time in twenty-five years that he was going to have to go see an old friend who was sure he was dead. *Don't overthink it. Just do it.*

He rang the doorbell and waited for the intercom light to come on, clearing his throat again.

"Triple nickel pizza delivery. Got a large with fajita beef and extra refried beans for Manuel," he said.

"*What?*"

As the door slid open, Tommy took his own AID off his belt, holding it over the box. He caught Stewart's eye and put the AID in the box, handing the box to Stewart. His old buddy's face paled and scrunched up in some strange mix of shock and bewilderment, but he accepted the box, putting his own AID in and sealing the lid. He didn't hand it back.

"We need to talk, Stewart. In private. Can we come in?"

"Yeah, I guess you'd better." He sighed and wheeled back from the door, letting them in and waiting while it closed behind them.

"You're the healthiest looking dead guy I've ever seen. And someone obviously changed your face just enough to fool software scans. So. You wanna tell me what's going on?" He wheeled around to a table, picking up a pack of cigarettes and offering them around before lighting one.

"That part's a long story. Introductions first. Stewart, Mike O'Neal, Sr. Papa O'Neal, General James Stewart. As you know, we served together under your son in the war," he said.

"That's a big claim. And even if it's true, you'd have to have a damned good excuse for letting Mike think his dad's been dead all these years. I don't think that's possible." He took a long drag and waited.

"Oh, I've had rejuv. And more extensive cosmetic work than

Tommy, here. There's no point in doing much to someone his size—you just keep him out of sight as much as you can and use him other ways. On the other, Mike would be the first to agree with the necessity if he knew."

"Look, I've had a long day, can you cut the cryptic bullshit?"

"Okay. I've known O'Neal, Senior, for twenty-five years. There *is* a damned good reason, but whether you hear it depends on the next part of this conversation. Trust me for a minute, okay? You've got a prisoner in your detention center." He gestured at the chair and Stewart's obvious injuries. "She do that?"

"No. What do you know about her?" He leaned forward too quickly and winced, clapping a hand to his gut.

"She's Iron Mike's daughter." Tommy appreciated that Papa was letting him do the talking. It was going to take more information before Stewart would trust either of them, and they couldn't give him that information until they had a better idea of how he was reacting.

"What the fu—you're shitting me." It was obviously another shock. Tommy hoped he wasn't really in a bad way. Then again, if he had been, the medic wouldn't have left.

"Cally O'Neal. She's not dead either." Papa had leaned back against the wall and was obviously trying to wait patiently.

"Cally. Wait a minute. You're trying to get me to believe that the old man's dad and his daughter have both let him eat his heart out thinking they're dead for *forty years*? I think you'd better cut the bullshit and talk, because my patience is going fast," he said.

"Well, you see, there's this problem with the Darhel . . ."

Titan Base, Wednesday, June 19, 21:30

After they had gone, Stewart sat in the chair staring at the wall. On some level he knew he was probably in something close to shock.

Usually he had the vidscreen on, if only displaying a still holo. It was the first thing he slapped to life coming in the door.

Pattern broken by the interruption, he sat staring. The blank bareness of the walls, hardly improved by the gray rectangle of the dead screen, closed in on him like one of the cells over at the prison.

God, Cally, what a fucking mess! Okay, Tommy was a replacement troop, but dammit, he was one of us! Even if civilian control at the top of the chain of command was going all to hell by then, how could I—he—make himself a traitor? All right, so it was a hard call. Maybe he was even right. There sure as hell is no more effective civil control—human, anyway—of the military. I thought working within the system . . . even after it had gone to hell. But good God, we won the war and lost the peace, and there's no bringing it back. Fuck. Maybe he's right.

No! How the hell could he leave the Old Man thinking his daughter was dead? And his father? How the fuck could they? Cally couldn't have done anything, she was just a kid then. Okay, so she had to go along. Fuck, she was just a kid. What the hell else could she do? But his own father. His own damn father!

And now I'm supposed to do it, too. Turn my coat, join up, don't ask questions. Yeah, right.

But what the hell else could I do? All I know is the military—unless you count gang leading. Yeah, right. Not much call for either outside the control of the fucking Darhel Federation. It might as well be, anyway. Not like the other bunch looks much better.

How can I be a traitor? How could anyone leave the people who love them most thinking they're just dead?

What a fucking mess! Cally, what the fuck am I gonna do?

The walls had no answer for him.

Titan Base, Wednesday, June 19, 23:00

"We've got something." Papa O'Neal's face was uncharacteristically closed in addressing his old friend.

"Do I want to know the details?" Father O'Reilly hadn't lived as long as he had without learning when not to ask too many questions. The Indowy Aelool stood quietly at his side.

"Probably not." His jaw worked and he looked around for a cup for a moment before nodding gratefully as Tommy pressed one into his hand. He spat neatly.

"Might it be possible for us to hear the broadest outline of this plan?" The Indowy's facial expression was earnest.

"We found some help I don't want to compromise even over a probably secure channel." He emphasized the word *probably* slightly, in an attempt to appeal to traditional Indowy paranoia about exchanging information outside of a face-to-face meeting.

"Yes. Good communications discipline. We can certainly understand that. Can you give us an estimate of your chances of success? What you would call a ballpark estimate will suffice." The little green guy actually looked happy, which was odd given their earlier conversation with O'Reilly.

"Ballpark. Okay." O'Neal scratched his chin for a moment. "Call it reasonable to high."

"And how would you rate the chances of success if you had to wait, for example, an extra day to carry out this plan?" Aelool was looking at him very strangely—almost as if he was hoping for a particular—

"It would substantially reduce the chances of success." *Did I guess right?*

"And would your plan require the emplacement of additional organization resources beyond those currently deployed in the field with you?" Father O'Reilly asked conversationally.

"No, it would not," he said.

"Then since you say that is the case, a decision by us at headquarters is certainly something that cannot wait until morning. Father O'Reilly, do you concur?"

"Oh, most certainly." There was an odd twinkle in the old priest's eye.

"I recommend this mission be approved. Do you concur, Father?" Only someone very familiar with Indowy would have recognized the particular treble tone as formal, even businesslike.

"That does seem wise. I do concur, Indowy Aelool." He nodded. "The mission not requiring the emplacement of additional resources and being time critical, the mission is approved. Now if you'll please excuse us—" He cut the transmission without giving either of them time to say another word.

"Did I just imagine that conversation?" Tommy rubbed his eyes tiredly.

"Nope." O'Neal spat again, contemplatively, "But it certainly suggests that parts of things back home are less fucked up, and parts more fucked up, than we thought. Not that I'm going to lose any sleep over it. Tomorrow's gonna be a long day."

CHAPTER SEVENTEEN

Titan Base, Fleet Strike Detention Center, Thursday, June 20, 00:01

The first stages of sensory deprivation were never too bad. It was relatively easy, especially with preparatory training, to hold on to yourself. Doing it in true zero-g was tough. The traditional tank of water still had some definable sense of down, however small. The gurney actually helped. It would have been worse without it. She could work her hands and feet against the straps and feel the pain. They hadn't blocked her ears with white noise, or gagged her. She could run her tongue across her teeth and feel the edges. She could hear her heartbeat. With enhanced hearing, she could hear it very well, and keep her breathing paced. It gave some sense of the passage of time.

It's gotta be about three or four in the morning by now. Counting the time is an upside to not being able to sleep, I guess. But it's so tempting to just watch the colors go by. Red, electric blue, chartreuse. What the hell is chartreuse, anyway? Oop, lost count again. Lub-dub, lub-dub, lub-dub, lub-dub . . . one, two, three, four, men are running in the door, seven, eight, nine and ten, then they're carried out again. . . .

Ireland. An American official on vacation. Tourism never died, it seemed. No witnesses, but he's all in black, a player? His neck cracks so easily, and he rolls as he falls, and it's white it wasn't supposed to be white what why was he here? God, no. No.

Shit, that's weird. It didn't happen that way. That was two hits.

The official wasn't in Ireland at all. He was on a golf course in Arkansas. The priest was in Ireland, but he was a young guy, an idealist, about to go public on "infiltrators" in the Church. That had to be, what, twelve, thirteen years ago? That one was so sad. But it hasn't bothered me in years . . . has it? Oh, crap, I lost track of time again.

But why the guy on the golf course? Putt-putt, and down through the bottom of the windmill, sailing out of the tunnel down into the Quarter—Mardi Gras parade, no war, no training, freedom for a long weekend. Strings of cheap plastic beads and hurricanes, and a young-looking soldier of the Ten Thousand who looks like he puts in a lot of time in the weight room. She's Lilly tonight and laughing up into his face and she tries not to go this time but she always does, and now it's morning and he's telling her—me—about his wife, again, and she's trying and trying to get off the bed and kick the bastard in the crotch, but she can't move, and she's—uh—I'm—back in survival training in Minnesota, and the snow falls, and what the fuck?

Oh. I remember that creep. It was a hell of a rotten way to lose my virginity, but I was lying to him, too. This is just too weird. Sensory dep in SERE training back with the Sisters was never like this. But I guess I didn't have nearly as many personal ghosts then. But I don't have ghosts now*. I sleep like a baby—don't I?*

Florida. Swimming with dolphins. Mom's with me. She's proud of me. And the water's cool, and the sun hot. Silly Herm—why is Doc Vita P standing on the beach? And what's he holding? There's something really odd about this dream. Something's not right.

Okay, hold it. I'm not even asleep. My broken bits ache and I'm on a gurney in zero-g, this is the Fleet Strike prison dammit. Even if the bastards they have working me over are Fleet, the place and the regular people are Fleet Strike. Hell of an irony, that. What'd I figure last time? About three in the morning? Surely it's got to be four or so by now. Lub-dub, lub-dub, lub-dub . . . How the hell long has it been since I've been to confession, anyway? Can't even remember why I quit going. It's not like Father O'Reilly wouldn't gladly hear it, and with no risks to security. You know, it's morbid as hell, but if I ever get out of here, that's something I need to do. Maybe something I could do with my copious free time at the moment is make a list. Uh, maybe not. Bad for morale. Better to do that after they get me out, if they do. Sister Mary Francis always said God

understands. Back to my anchor. Even if I can't dance on the floor,
I can dance in my head. Here we go. . . . Waitasecond . . . this one's
loose—oh, it wasn't before probably, but with the break and the blood
being slippery—probably pass out for a bit—one good yank.

Titan Base, Fleet Strike Detention Center, Thursday, June 20, 08:00

"Sir, recommend we cut the gravity back in at Titan ambient levels when we turn on the lights. It would be unfortunate to have her fall on her head or have some other premature fatal accident." It was difficult to tell if Senior Chief Yi Chang Ho was speaking to his lieutenant or to General Stewart himself. The lieutenant's nod was just a fraction behind his own.

"Do it," the general ordered. The chief was one unpleasant piece of work, and Stewart wasn't going to give him another crack at Cally if he could help it. Cally. It suited her.

The lights flicked on and Cally and the gurney bounced gently to the floor. She immediately rolled to her feet and into a ready position.

"Holy fuck, how'd she get out?" one of the MP's, Keally, breathed.

"I think I might be able to break her. I'd like to try before you boys get started. At best, she'll start talking and it'll save us all some time. At worst, it should make her more . . . receptive to your efforts." Stewart looked down at her. Her being loose could make this a lot easier. If she didn't kill him on sight on general principles.

"She was your lover, wasn't she?" Yi said. Coming from a rate, it was gross insolence, but taking offense wasn't in his plan.

"I was hers. It unmasked her in the end." He shrugged. "Too bad you boys couldn't have tried one of her blow jobs." He grinned wickedly as the other men chuckled.

"General, I am most concerned that she would harm you. Especially with your previous injuries—" the Fleet medic began.

"Right. Good thought. Keally, Baker, come with me. No weapons—can't take the risk she'd somehow get one away from us, can we?" He wheeled his chair around towards the service lift, "Oh, this shouldn't take long. Either it'll work and she'll start talking, or it won't. I'll try Good Guy first, and if she doesn't talk, I'll play with her head as much as I can before handing her back to you."

He stood at the door, waving off his men.

"Don't nursemaid me, son. I'm only in the chair today to placate the damned medics. And I'll be right back in it in a couple of minutes." He cleared his throat, covering his mouth with one hand. "Listen up. I'm going to hang back with you when we first go in the door. I won't walk forward unless I'm reasonably sure it's safe, but if I do approach her, I need you men to stay back at the door."

"General Stewart, sir, I'm very uncomfortable with this plan," Baker said.

"Noted. If she rushes us, you can cover my retreat." He palmed open the door, which immediately recognized the Brigade CO and slid aside obediently. Inside, as Baker and Keally spread out to flank him, Cally eyed them warily. He took two steps forward, waving the men back and suppressing a wince at the red-brown smudges that stood out so clearly against the white floor. The room smelled of sweat and rust and something vaguely chemical.

The gurney was tipped over on the floor, on the side of the room away from the observation lounge. He turned his head slightly toward it and winked one eye. Baker and Keally couldn't have seen it. To those in the observation lounge, if they had seen it, it would have looked like a blink. Only Cally could see both eyes. If she had noticed, she gave him no sign.

"Sinda, please, honey, don't make them do this to you. If you don't talk, I can't protect you. If you tell them everything, honey, I'm a major general—I can cut a deal and make your part of this all go away." He took a step towards her.

One of her eyebrows quirked upward, skeptically, above a black eye. She stood her ground.

"Honey, they don't want you, they just want the ringleaders. All these horrible things, they're so unnecessary—but I can't protect you if you won't talk." He closed the distance, brushing an unbruised section of cheek with one hand, and praying she didn't blame him for what they'd already done to her. Well, she didn't kill him outright. Good sign.

He leaned forward and kissed her, arms going around her ever so gently. None of the onlookers could see the pill he moved from his mouth to hers. She'd have to crunch it before swallowing, but Tommy had told him she'd guess that much.

"Please, sweetheart, what's your real name?" he asked for the cameras.

She stiffened in his arms and he couldn't tell if she'd just bitten down or not. Apparently. She swallowed hard.

"No," she said.

He pushed her away, roughly, and strode back to the door, turning in the doorway.

"What, you thought you were a good enough lay that I'd get you out of this *without* you telling what you know? Sorry, sweetheart. Oh, you were enthusiastic enough, but I've had better." He looked her naked and abused body up and down. "Oh, and no more fun and games with the men. When you get horny enough to talk, maybe we'll let you have one back. But not me. I'm not a fan of damaged goods."

Baker and Keally barely managed to yank him out and get the door shut before she bounced off the other side, swearing creatively enough to draw an appreciative whistle from the private.

If she hadn't stood there with her mouth hanging open for a second, they never would have made it.

"I think you made her mad, sir." The MP helped him back into the wheelchair.

"Yeah, Keally, it does sound like it. Back up to the lounge." He wheeled off to the lift, hoping she'd understand why he'd had to say the worst things he could think of. He didn't look back.

Titan Base, Fleet Strike Detention Center, Thursday, June 20, 12:32

The delayed-effect pill kicked in between four and five hours later, just as Stewart had been promised. The Fleet bastard was doing unspeakable things to her fingernails when she started to go into shock. Her condition rapidly went downhill, despite everything the medic did trying to revive her. He wouldn't have known, but Mike's dad had told him that this particular pill pretty much exactly mimicked the torture cases where a previously unsuspected heart condition causes the victim to just shut down.

The medic was obviously desperate. And with good reason. His ass was almost certainly on the line for failing to detect the "heart condition." Couldn't happen to a nicer guy.

They tried transferring her to the infirmary which was a mass of hospital green Galplas and surgical steel. It had all the GalTech equipment a physician could want, but somehow still managed to smell of disinfectant. By the time they got her there, she had flatlined. Not even GalTech could bring somebody back from that.

The attending physician shook his head and waved over a couple of orderlies to take her down to the morgue. He wasn't sure, but the red-haired guy might have been new. The big, dumb-looking one certainly wasn't the type to find manual labor a hardship.

After they wheeled her around a corner, nobody noticed the needleful of Hiberzine antidote the redhead stuck in her leg.

The morgue was one corridor over from an emergency air lock. The flat, institutional beige of the Galplas walls contrasted with the blinding shine of the polished white tile floor. The astringent smell of the infirmary had faded to the faint but unavoidable burnt pork whiff of the morgue's crematory.

They'd cremated Jay this morning. Not only were system records on the equipment poorly protected, they also revealed the morgue was rarely used—Tommy had checked. The first thing he did after getting her down there was to change the time on that cremation to the current time. The second thing was to retrieve the very sincerely labeled box of Jay's ashes from behind the table and put them on the shelf where her ashes would have gone had she really been dead.

They had her stuffed into a black ship jumpsuit and heavily padded boots by the time she started coming around. Then Papa ran interference long enough for them to get to the lock, put on their pressure helmets and parkas, climb into the waiting power sled, send the preprogrammed command to make the lock forget they were ever there, and they were gone.

One of the few good things about the rabid fascism of the Darhel was the effect it had on the operating rules of most starports. The standard rule was that you filed for a departure time slot on a first-come first-served basis. Then those times were saleable on whatever terms the slot-holder wished. In practice, it meant that landing was free, but taking off cost money. It also meant that Darhel never had to wait for a takeoff slot, nor were they constrained by any hard and fast departure times.

Today, Darhel fascism suited Tommy fine. As per instructions, the real freighter crew had her hot and ready to launch as soon as they loaded, and there was another freight shuttle more than happy to make a quick buck off someone else's impatience.

They were airborne an hour after leaving the prison air lock.

Two and a half hours later, they had Cally on the slab in the Indowy portion of the freighter, in a room that had housed six Indowy crew before the freighter was commissioned for this trip. The freighter's human leaseholders had no awareness of the room. Nor did the holding company's Darhel owners. After the freighter next docked, the equipment would be offloaded to disappear wherever it was needed next, six Indowy would be onloaded, and no one who did not already know of the room's presence ever would know.

After two hours on the slab, Cally was up and around in her room. Unfortunately, she'd need to spend the rest of the trip in her cabin with himself or Papa bringing her her meals. There was no help for it. The freighter crew had gotten a look at her when she staggered onto the shuttle and there was no acceptable explanation for her rapid healing. He had explained it away as a bad mugging, but when they offloaded at Selene Base, on the Moon, he figured it was going to take splints, bandages, makeup, and careful planning to get her off the ship without raising crew eyebrows.

It was probably for the best. He'd noticed that Cally didn't tend to have her very best interpersonal interactions with strangers in the first days after a rough mission.

Titan Orbit, Thursday, June 20, 20:00

Cally looked up brightly as Tommy came in with her supper, giving him a big smile. The contents of the big bag of cosmetics and toiletries and other girl stuff that he'd put together before the extraction, knowing in advance that she'd need those old-fashioned tools of feminine camouflage, but not which ones and how much, were strewn out across her bunk. She had a look of slightly guilty pleasure, like a kid caught opening the Christmas presents a day early. She swept them back into the bag as if they didn't really mean a thing, but her eyes were bright and misty.

"Hey, hero. You guys got me out of the spot from hell," she said. "Oh, and thanks for the stuff."

"Yep. We did at that. Papa'll be in in a little while. The crew naturally don't know you two are related, and he got his arm twisted into a game of spades." He saw her face. "No, really. It would have looked conspicuous as hell if he'd run off here. They think you're my girlfriend."

"*What?*" She looked dangerous, standing and folding her bunk up into the wall and taking down and unfolding the stool that stowed securely in a rack under the bunk.

"Whoa! Hang on! It wasn't my idea—and Papa would have felt just too weird even pretending to the crew to be hot over his own granddaughter." He set the tray down on her fold-down table and folded the guest stool down from the wall, holding up his hands placatingly as he sat.

"He's pretended to be my date before." There was a slight note of outrage. "I mean, okay, ick, but he has!"

"For a day here or an evening there, but you have to have noticed it's . . . a tough role for him," he finished tactfully.

"Okay, okay. I guess I just miss him after all that. They were real amateurs at the whole torture thing, it's just I was so sure I wasn't going to get out of there alive." She shuddered.

"And you finally had something to live for?" he prompted.

"He helped. He had to have been sympathetic. Are—when are we going to get him out?" There was a glitter to her eyes he hadn't seen before. Her cheeks were flushed, too.

"Oh, yeah. Special delivery." He grinned and handed her a message cube.

"Is that from—why didn't you? Nevermind." She looked around frantically for her PDA, then remembered. "Buckley. I lost buckley."

Tommy was surprised to hear a note of real grief in her voice. People weren't supposed to get attached to the personalities of their PDAs the way they did to real AIDs. Then again, almost everyone he knew used a personality overlay. He didn't know anybody who'd used the base personality as much as she had. Maybe he grew on you after awhile.

"Here, use my AID," he offered. "Sarah, help her, okay?" Since clean AIDs were somewhat less persnickety than the originals, he could trust her to behave.

"Thanks." She stuck the cube in the reader slot and it immediately displayed. *Oh my God, they've got him in a wheelchair? Fleet Strike medicine's better than that. Oh. This must have been made yesterday. Yeah, I guess if they've got him up and around instead of sleeping through regen he would have to be taking it easy. That bastard Beed.*

"Cally, my love. Your name suits you. If you're seeing this, we made it. We got you out. Good. If so, I hope to be joining you soon. Without a prisoner, I'm only here long enough to promote the XO and then it's back to Earth for me. Tommy and your grandfather have told me how this whole thing works. As soon as I've got my affairs wrapped up they'll be bringing me in, sooner rather than later. At some point the Darhel will wonder, even if Fleet Strike won't, whether I slipped you a suicide pill. So I'll see you soon, love—and I hope that you'll be looking forward to that as much as I will. Tell Tommy it's okay if he talks about me. *Vaya con Dios*, Cally." The hologram disappeared.

"We'll be staying in orbit another two or three days so we can take information about his intended travel plans back with us," Tommy said.

"Good. You know him? From where? You didn't say anything in the pre-mission briefing," she said.

"Cally, I'm sorry. I fucked up. I knew him forty years ago in ACS and when I heard 'lieutenant,' I just didn't make the connection. Not until we saw the CO change after you were captured." He tensed for the storm he just knew was coming.

"Okay. What was he like back then?" she asked.

"What?" *Okay? I fucked up and got her captured and tortured and her answer is "okay"? Damn, she is in love.* "Oh. Well, first, his name wasn't always James Stewart. That really is his name now, and was back then, but his mother named him Manuel. . . ."

Titan Base, Thursday, June 20, 20:00

Mary's Diner was not the sort of place anyone would associate with the tongs or anything other than cheap meals for outmigrating colonists on a budget. They got all kinds at all hours.

They had a break room for staff—unnecessary because the only staff were Mary and her husband. Mary was an incessant gossip—about everything that didn't matter. She also made a mean cup of tea.

All of which was why James Stewart was sitting in her break room over a cup of tea, talking to the dai dai lo of the Black Dragons Tong.

"You know what you're asking for is very expensive, don't you?" The other man savored his tea. His host had excellent taste. He preferred to drink his imported oolong while it was hot. The room was pleasantly appointed, with a miniature fountain burbling and plashing gently along one side, and a branch of silk cherry blossoms in a crystal vase on the table. It was a good place to do business.

"Oh, come on. I know how this works. Where else are you going to make any profit at all on this? Don't you think I'm worth it?" Stewart grinned.

"Perhaps. I won't promise anything, but I'll ask my grandfather," he said.

"That's all I ask. When do you think you can give me an answer?" The former gang leader turned general sipped his own tea.

"Tomorrow. I'll know tomorrow," he said.

"Then I'll see you tomorrow." Stewart excused himself politely and left. He had a promotion to announce.

Titan Base, Friday, June 21, 10:15

At the diner, after Mary had poured their tea and left, the dai dai lo handed him a ticket, glancing at the AID sitting on the table.

"Your passage to Earth is confirmed on our inbound combination liner, the *Kick 'Em Jenny* from Dulain. We are not embarking or disembarking passengers, except for Uncle's favorite nephew for a vacation. If he doesn't show up, you shouldn't panic. The boy's a bit scatterbrained. Your shuttle leaves at eight thirty-five tonight," he said.

"Thank you. I'm very grateful. This has been an upsetting trip and I'm looking forward to getting back to work on Earth as soon as possible." The general rose, taking his ticket and AID from the table.

"Of course. If there's ever anything else we can do for you, don't hesitate to call on us again. Have a pleasant voyage." He shook the other man's hand, palming the cube hidden in the handshake.

As the general left, he spoke briefly to the cigarette-pack-sized machine.

"Diana, please transmit my travel itinerary to General Vanderberg. God, I can't wait to get home." He walked out and the dai dai lo could just hear the musical female voice as the door swung shut behind him.

"Yes, James. Transmission complete," it said.

Titan Orbit, Friday, June 21, 13:30

It was too bad Cally couldn't be up here. The crew lounge was probably the most comfortable area on the whole ship. The chairs were upholstered in a really good imitation of brown leather, and a holographic fireplace crackled merrily against one wall. A discreet air freshener at the bottom corner of the fireplace's vidscreen released a faint, homey odor of hot wood smoke. There were several small tables that could lock together in groups, or not, and they actually had a decent wet bar. Of course, the coffee can for donations and their immunity to alcohol dampened the fun of that, but you couldn't have everything.

Tommy looked up from a game of backgammon with Papa O'Neal as the navigator came into the lounge and approached him.

"Sir, we just received a short-range encrypted transmission from a neighboring ship. The message header said it was for you." He handed Tommy a data cube.

"Thank you." He set it beside the backgammon board, ignoring the man's hesitation until he apparently gave up on the possibility of snooping and wandered off in the direction of the bridge.

"I think I'll go check on Felicia, if you don't mind interrupting our game." She'd kill him if she didn't get to see this message as soon as it was decrypted. Not that he blamed her. If it was Wendy down there, he'd be biting his nails, too.

Titan Base, Friday, June 21, 20:25

The branch of the access tube leading to the shuttle's cargo hold, which he was going to have to use instead of anything off of the main cabin, was absolutely frigid. His face and nose were all he'd left bare to feel it, but it was still damn cold. Less worn areas in the gray tube showed it had once been blue. It was probably damn near fifty years old, and reeked of leaking hydrocarbons from outside. Fortunately, he only had to put up with it for a minute or so.

"Diana, I'm going to add you to my case until we get up to the ship. I haven't been sleeping as well as the medics would like, and I think an uninterrupted nap on the way up would do me a world of good." He tucked the AID into the case among his uniforms.

"Certainly, James. Anything that will help you get well soon. I'll see you on board." She sounded almost like a mother tucking her child in.

"Goodnight, Diana."

"Goodnight, James."

He closed the case and tucked it into the cargo bay of his shuttle.

Titan Orbit, Friday, June 21, 20:25

"Okay, here I am, back as promised." Tommy stepped through the door balancing two trays full of food—and not a corn product on it.

Cally was obviously making good use of the necessaries bag he'd scraped together from somewhere, cotton between her toes and an obviously fresh coat of bright red nail polish on fingers and toes. At least she didn't have any of that thick green goop Wendy sometimes used caked all over her face.

"I thought you might like some company for dinner tonight," he said. "Should I set Sarah up for a two-player game? She does a pretty mean Space Invaders."

"Sure. I'd like that. Truth to tell, I've been a little stir crazy today." Her grin was infectious. "There's so much to do when I get back to get all my affairs in order and, well, you know, start making plans." She looked uncertain for a moment.

"You *do* think he meant he wants marriage, don't you?" she asked worriedly.

"Back in ACS, despite being a real hardass when he wanted to be, he was as Catholic as you are. There's no doubt in my mind his intentions are marriage. Hell, with the relatives *you've* got, girl? Not to mention being pretty formidable yourself," he laughed. "Wendy and Shari will just be in heaven helping you plan it."

They were halfway through the third game when it froze.

"Tommy, I'm afraid I have bad news," the AID broke in.

"What?" he asked. Cally's fist was clenched against her mouth.

"Ship instrumentation has detected an explosion in Titan's atmosphere. Traffic control confirms it as the FS-688 bound for the *Kick 'Em Jenny*. Rescue crews have been dispatched, but . . . it doesn't look good. I waited until I was sure. I'm so sorry," it finished miserably.

"Cally?" Tommy looked over at her. Her hand had sunk back down to the table, and her skin was an awful mottled shade of gray. He tried hugging her awkwardly, but she might as well have been a block of wood.

"Cally?" he tried again. "Come on, honey, you're scaring me. We don't know anything for sure yet. Come on, snap out of it." No response. He did the only thing he could do—left the cabin at a hard run to get Papa O'Neal, finally running him down where he was watching an old movie on his PDA.

"Tommy? What the hell is the matter? You look like you've seen a—" He stopped cold.

"There's been an accident. Ca—Felicia needs you. Now," the younger man said.

When they got back to her cabin, she had stacked the trays outside the door and was inside on her bunk, facing the wall, and nothing they said or did could move her.

Over the next few days, they took it in shifts to sit with her, trying never to leave her alone. She didn't speak. It was all they could do to get her to eat a few bites and take fluids. They did their best to get the best options the galley offered, but for all the response they got it could have been sawdust.

Finally, on the third day, she picked up a towel and a change of clothes. Papa O'Neal made sure the way to the head was clear and stood guard while she took a sponge bath and changed into fresh clothes.

He took it as a hopeful sign and tried to talk to her, but she only shook her head.

That afternoon, while Tommy was spelling him for a bit, he went up to the bridge and bribed the communications tech to let him call Earth and download all her favorite music. Compressed, it didn't cost all that much. Well, not really, anyway.

The rest of the afternoon and evening, he had his PDA cycle through everything he could remember her liking. She still wasn't talking, but he didn't think it was his imagination that some of the tension had left her body. That was, until it cycled through to that old war-time Urb band. When it hit their stuff, he heard a sniffle. His eyes shot to where she lay on her back, eyes closed. A tear leaked slowly from beneath one eyelid. Then another. Then another. Finally, when she broke into full-force sobs he sank down onto his knees next to her bunk and held her until she cried herself out. It took a long time. Then again, his granddaughter had a hell of a lot of her crying saved up.

When she was through she still didn't seem to want to talk. He grabbed a box of tissues he'd tucked away more out of hope than faith and let her clean herself up.

As the weekend approached, her appetite had improved, almost back to normal, more or less.

She still wasn't talking, but he'd managed to get her interested in playing a few old movies and holovids by the simple expedient of disappearing for awhile and leaving his PDA next to her on her bunk.

By early in the week, she was watching movies practically nonstop. Another massive download had gotten him the complete combined works of Fred and Ginger, along with an inexplicable smattering of old Three Stooges episodes. But hell, if she'd asked for 1970s soap opera archives he would have gotten them for her, and damn the cost.

Orbit around Earth's Moon, Wednesday, July 3, 06:30

Granpa's PDA said they had reached the Moon. The schedule said they'd be here for a few days unloading and reloading freight from the hybrid Human-Indowy factories. Granpa was snoring on the floor of her cabin. He needed to reapply his depilatory foam. Badly. The red stubble looked downright strange after all these years of getting used to him smooth-jawed all the time.

This cabin was getting pretty rank, too, now that she thought about it. It would have been bad enough that they tried to feed her fish somewhere along the trip and the odor had lingered. Her sheets smelled. She wouldn't have noticed the always-familiar air of Red Man in the mix, except that it was a bit stale. Still, there was something solid and a bit comforting about it.

The light blue of the Galplas in the cabin probably would have been okay if she hadn't been staring at it for the whole trip. Somebody had come up with a green scrap of carpeting for the floor from somewhere and glued it down. She could see the bits of it that extended out past Granpa. The shade clashed horribly with his hair, but it was probably marginally more comfortable than bare Galplas.

She felt a bit guilty. She'd been having herself a good mope, but Tommy and Granpa had obviously been worried sick. She was going to have to at least, well, talk and things, so that they could go get some sleep and do whatever they needed to do.

After all, she had a whole rejuvenated lifetime to look forward to. Oh, joy. She pulled her mind back from the pit by main force. *One day at a time.*

She peeked out the door. She wasn't supposed to be seen by the crew, but she didn't really care at the moment. Fortunately, none of them were around. She grabbed a laundered jumpsuit, a clean towel, and a few of the jumble of toiletries Tommy had gotten her. She wrinkled her nose at her own stink. She needed a shower. She *really* needed a shower.

Fortunately, freight crew who didn't have the night shift weren't exactly early risers. Well, this crew wasn't, anyway. Good. No underwear, but it couldn't be helped. She could buy some stuff down on Selene Base. If she didn't get some fresh underwear, she was gonna kill somebody. Okay, well, not literally. She sighed. It was going to be a hell of a long road back.

Granpa didn't wake up until almost nine thirty. She only got him to go off to his own cabin for some real sleep by faithfully promising to say more than two words a day to him when he came back.

"I'll . . . be okay eventually, Granpa. Well, mostly. Just, not yet. I can't be okay yet. Go get some real sleep. I need to catch the shuttle down and buy some stuff."

"I'll go with you," he said.

"Granpa, I need some shop time alone. Call it retail therapy if it makes you feel better. Look, I promise the very first thing I'll do is buy myself a PDA and call you and give you the number, okay?"

"If this is what you need, but Cally if you do anything stupid or dangerous I swear I'll hunt you down and haunt you."

"I'm . . . not even thinking about something that dumb. I just need time. Uh, Granpa?"

"Yeah?"

"Could I borrow a credit card?"

Selene Base, Earth's Moon, Wednesday, July 3, 20:15

It had been a hard day of shopping. She had dropped most of her packages off at the freight loading zone. The shuttle pilot had asked about her injuries. Fortunately, she'd been able to explain them away as injuries from the mugging—mostly sprains and bruises that had looked worse than they were. They hadn't seen her at all in over a week, so it wasn't out of the realm of possibility.

Granpa had quit worrying so much once she checked back in and he had her back on e-mail and knew her plans.

She had set herself one firm homework assignment for this evening. She had never been less in a partying mood in her life, but by God she *was* going to sit in a bar and take one full drink, without chugging it, before she found quarters for the night. The freight shuttle wouldn't be taking its next load up until early afternoon tomorrow.

Hell, she might just stay dirtside for a few days. Or not. *One day at a time.*

She was standing in front of a bar the new buckley said was commonly frequented by freighter crews and others on the way from here to there. Her black catsuit was likely to get her quite a bit of attention, but she had seen it in the shop and hadn't been able to resist it for sentimental reasons. This one fit a little better than the last one—she'd lost weight over the past two weeks, between one thing and another. *One day at a time. Hell, one minute at a time. I will go in and order a drink. One drink in a social place. Then I can go find some quarters to hide in for the night.*

It wasn't the happiest drink she'd ever had. She found herself ditching the occasional pest who tried to pick her up and desultorily sipping at the strawberry margarita in front of her, resisting the temptation to guzzle it just so she could leave. *I should have known it was too good to last. No, dammit! One day at a time.*

She heard another damn pest walk up to interrupt her drink and sighed.

"Is this seat taken?" he asked.

"It is unless you can lick your own eyebrows!" *Oh, God. Why did I have to say* that.

"How do you think I do my hair?"

Her sudden grip on his hand was white-knuckled for a few moments before softening. There had to have been a good reason. After all, there often was for this kind of thing.

EPILOGUE

Under a cornfield in Indiana, Thursday, August 1

The base seemed empty with so few Indowy in it. Aelool's clan was quite small by Indowy standards, and he hadn't been able to afford to bring enough inside to replace the losses. Clan Beilil had sided with Aelool's clan, their debt to the O'Neal clan was vast beyond measure, but the absence of the rest of the Indowy Bane Sidhe was palpable.

It made Cally appreciate even more that Aelool had made time to come down to talk to her. It had taken some doing to arrange this. The owner of the Irish Bar at Titan Base's shuttleport had no doubt wondered why someone had wanted an order of the bar's promotional T-shirts and shot glasses shipped all the way to Earth, but her FedCreds spent just as well as anyone else's. That the shipment really was T-shirts and shot glasses would never occur to anyone who might check up on her later.

"For what it's worth, Miss O'Neal, I think you're doing the right thing in taking a sabbatical to have children. I'm sure we all understand that in the circumstances of your loss you would prefer not to add a mate to the mix. Besides, Clan O'Neal, though small, is more than capable of providing you all the social support human children need to thrive." He paused delicately. "Have you selected a donor?"

Cally stuck a hand in her purse and came up with a handful of field issue biosample cubes.

"I had learned to cache anything I might need someday by the time I was eight." Her smile was bittersweet. If he mistook the reason, that was just perfect for their purposes.

"Oh." He looked nonplussed for a moment, before recovering. "I'm sure that will be a great comfort to you."

End